Fake Reviews

I read Unlikely Heroes by flashlight, under a blanket and turning the pages as fast as my trotters could flip them. I enjoyed the exciting adventures of the brave little band of heroes but was disappointed at the lack of creatures who looked like me. Mr. Rosche, you can do better!

  - -P. Pigg

Unlikely Heroes is, in most ways, an enjoyable read. However, its dismissive treatment of my famous sire is inexcusable! He was one of the greatest heroes ever: He was brave! He was strong! He was heroic! For the real story, seek out The Compleat and Wondrous Adventures of Donkie Otie, as narrated by his trusty thrall, Paunchy Stanza.

  --Soft Hearted

Ever since Dianne Fossey camped out in our jungle, the Mountain Gorilla has been under scrutiny. Unlikely Heroes continues the exploitation of our species, turning us into a (literal) army of supporting characters in what is admittedly an exciting, fast paced read.

  -- M.G. O'Rilla

Of course lower species exist only to satisfy the whims of the one apex creature created to rule over them all. Why then does the first book to recognize this obvious fact waste so many words on Donkeys and 'Fingered Folk' and other second raters while almost ignoring the true star: the Mighty Stallion! (Though the 'Horsey Bits' are good!)

  --Ed (Mister)

Most Unlikely Heroes

Tales of the One True Realm
Part I

W.R. Rosche

Paperback ISBN 978-1-7380093-3-6
Kindle ISBN 978-1-7380093-2-9

Cover design by: W.R. Rosche

To Pat
You gave me the words that launched me on this journey!

Introduction

Those who make the rules control history. That's how it always was; how it is; how it always will be. There is no enduring truth—there is only knowing and unknowing.

Not long ago, the events described in this book were so well known that it seemed unnecessary to formally preserve their memory. After all, the heroes were celebrated in every corner of The Realm. And the villains were rightfully scorned and vilified.

Then our leadership changed, and with that change began the great *unknowing*. Official records disappeared. Well-known events 'unhappened.' And slowly, irresistibly, a new narrative took over. Villains were transformed into 'freedom-fighting heroes.' Heroes were villainized or, worse, dismissed as 'fictional characters.'

The words that follow are my feeble attempt to push back the unknowing void. Disguised as a simple story, they speak truths that are on the verge of being erased. They do so as accurately and clearly as my aging memory and limited verbal skills allow. Read them. Share them. Remember them.

Thank you,

W.R. Rosche

Origin Story

As told by Descendants of Primum Equus

Hooved creatures are taught from very birth
that of all Gorme's creatures they have greatest worth:
To Cattle She gave strength to till the soil,
that others may be nourished by their toil;
Goats She fashioned to be cleverest and wise,
that they may their fellow creatures organize,
and wisely lead and govern from day to day
those lesser creatures who might go astray;
but best loved and gi'en dominion o'er all others,
the mighty Stallion towered o'er his brothers.

Hooved creatures soon of every size and form
came to seek great favors of Sweet Gorme.
To ope' their eyes to wisdom She them showed
an Ass who uncomplaining bore great loads.
She bade them learn from that most stalwart beast
that greatest are they who do demand the least.

Now the darkest chapter in Hooved Folk lore
does speak of Gorme's faithless helpmate Warre,
a godling old as time's first frozen state
that helped Fair Gorme this world we're in create
and o'er it watched while the Fair Goddess
did slip away to take a well-earned rest.

Warre looked upon the favored hooved beasts
and brooded on how Gorme loved e'en the least
more than She loved her faithful helpmate Warre.
The greater foul Warre's wrath did grow the more
he schemed to make Gorme's creatures suffer pain

1

and thus he labored tirelessly again
until the evil pad-paws were created
and turned against the creatures he so hated.
Thus t'was that lions and canines with delight
pursued the hooved creatures that they might
leap on their backs on any day or night
and in their hot red flesh take great delight.

After pleading with foul Warre to no avail,
the frightened hooved ones did raise up a wail
so loud and shrill their Goddess was awoke.
Upon Her waking Gorme's good heart fair broke
to see what foul evil had been wrought.
Then in the greatest wrath She rose and sought
vengeance against Her trait'rous helpmate Warre;
She cast him from Her presence evermore
and ev'ry form of comfort to him banned.
He wanders lone and friendless through the land
and to this day where'er foul Warre doth go
vile greed and greenest envy he doth sow.
Death and destruction are his only crops
for his namesake's vicious battle never stops.

Gorme saw how Her frail creatures needed aid.
For this purpose, the fingered folk were made,
but when the lowly monkey was first tried
they were weak-willed—away from work they shied.
The gorilla was made most large and strong
but 'twas discovered e'er too very long
that brute force was the thing that they most craved:
They could be hired but never be enslaved.
Last of all was the lowly bald ape made,
and all Gorme's labors were at last repaid

by a creature who was large, but not too much,
created with strength enough but only such
as might endure long labors when 'twas needed
and smart enough to know who must be heeded;
the longest of lives were they priv'leged to live,
that generations of service each might give;
strong agile fingers were placed upon their hands
that they might much better work their masters' lands;
upright on two strong legs they were made to walk
to pick up and carry much and never balk.

Gorme's final deed was to all High Creatures give
the power of speech that they might peaceful live
(even among Warre's most dreaded pad-paw packs,
for they were made their sharp claws to retract.)
Then Gorme did go to take a well-earned rest,
while waiting for the creatures She'd so blessed
this world in joyful unity to transform
into a paradise worthy of Fair Gorme.
On that joyous day She shall surely come
back to this world to reign o'er Her Kingdom!

~ 1 ~

The cloudless autumn afternoon made the booming thunderclap all the more startling. Birds took flight and squirrels froze in mid-gossip, waiting for the echoes to roll away.

The shockwave's source blinked in the sunlight. With their stubby legs, black and white fur and catlike eyes, they could be mistaken for a ludicrously large panda. They are, in fact, a more exotic beast by far. They are an Immortal Guardian: an entity who, before bursting onto an empty trail, had not walked this world for ten generations.

Wisps of frozen ether drifted off the Guardian's shoulders as they squinted at the westering sun. One shoulder supported a cloth sack: huge, lumpy and of no identifiable color.

They made a slow circle, bare feet raising puffs of dust. On one side flowed the Lone Lee River. On the other, stunted trees clung to the slopes of the Bugsplatt Mountains. Satisfied, they lowered their burden and hunkered down against a tree.

In a far-off cavern, an evil presence raises its head. Its nostrils flare; seek an elusive scent; find nothing. It slumps back against its grisly throne. But then . . . *yes!* Its dry, bloodshot eyes fly open. The creature's withered heart thuds as it senses a change in the world's equilibrium. *Oh yes!* There it is: a presence that has been absent for a long, long time. Slowly, painfully, the ancient creature shakes off its torpor. There is much to do and little time to do it.

The Guardian raised their head, listening. The clunk of a hoof on stone was joined by a voice: It had the reedy timbre of adolescence. "Our Hero is in a wild place, where feral pad-paw packs are known to prey on solitary Hooved Creatures . . ."

The new arrival stepped off the trail. It had four bandy legs, a barrel-shaped body, and a Horse-like face. Or what a Horse might have looked like, had it been spun around by its tail and tossed face first into a wall. The Guardian's shoulders sagged. *A Donkey. And a young Jack at that. Would we were dealt a more auspicious card! Yet the hand must be played."*

The Donkey continued his hushed narrative: "At the water's edge, the Hero uses his sharp, almost supernatural senses to probe his surroundings. Certain there are no nearby threats, he drinks."

The glacier-fed stream was cold, and the Donkey chuffed softly as he straightened up. He shook water from his face, then paused to admire his reflection. "What a fine specimen he is. Bold! Strong! Handsome!" He ducked his chin to adjust a short sword that hung from his neck. Satisfied at last, he swung around and came face-to-face with the giant creature who calmly watched him.

"What ho!" brayed the Donkey, drawing back in alarm.

The Guardian leaped up. "Wat Ho!" rumbled a deep bass voice. "A fine name! An excellent name! As thus shall we be known, so long as we do occupy this realm."

"As Thus?" whispered the Donkey.

"Nay, Wat," boomed the creature. "Wat Ho."

"As for me, I would as soon be known as *Thus*!" trilled the creature, suddenly speaking in a clear alto.

"Thus you must give way!" growled the bass.

"Never!" brayed the bewildered Donkey. He tore his sword from its scabbard with a force that flung it over his shoulder. His terrified, white-rimmed eyes stared helplessly at his giant adversary.

(You have alarmed the child) breathed the gentler voice. (*In silence I shall wait while you sooth the creature's anxious state.)*

The Guardian picked up the sword. Its hilt was of wood and (oddly) well chewed. They angled the blade at the Donkey who reared away, almost falling into the river. "Hold!" rumbled the Guardian as they pulled the Donkey to safety and sheathed the blade.

A thin purse hid behind the sword and behind that . . . *Yes, there it is: the Mark that binds our fate to his!"*

The Guardian pressed an index finger to their chest. "Wat Ho!"

The Donkey's face lit up. "Hoof Hearted!"

The Guardian scowled. "Rest assured, young sir, it was not I!"

"Huh?" said the Donkey, then sighed. "Yeah. That's a common mistake. My family name is 'Hearted.' In a stunningly astute move (no pun intended) my parents chose to call me 'Hoof.'"

"Greetings to you, Hoof, erm, Hearted!" intoned the Guardian.

"Just call me Hoof. Please."

Wat Ho looked down the trail; looked up the trail; looked at Hoof. *Such an unseasoned dish and yet, undeniably, the one.* They coaxed their cheeks into a smile. "I sense The Fates' work in the way our paths were bent to join today. Should you agree, we shall keep company."

Fates? Keep company? Who even talks like that? But . . . "Erm, why not?" Hoof replied. "Yikes!" He ducked under a huge sack that Wat Ho swung onto their shoulder. Muttering to himself, he trailed Wat Ho toward the westering sun.

~~~

As the day waned, so did Hoof's confidence in his decision to abandon his family farm. The trail skirted a leech-infested swamp and the footing alternated between fetlock-deep muck and hillocks of treacherous gravel. He was hungry and cold, and his hooves hurt.

The moon had risen by the time Wat Ho waddled into a clearing that lay between the trail and the river. Hoof shrugged out of his sword belt and flopped down. Wat Ho dragged their sack to the side of the clearing and loosed its ties. An impossible pile of things spilled out: a sleeping mat, blankets, pots, a kettle and more. They dug out a pawful of metal stakes, went to the edge of the campsite and pushed a feebly pulsing stake into the ground.

"Those things are neat!" Hoof exclaimed. "Can I see one?"

Wat Ho continued around the clearing as they replied. "They are with warding magic wrought. Beware for they are . . ." A bang was followed by a thud. Cutting an eye toward Hoof, who was flat on his back with a wisp of smoke spiraling above his head, they continued, ". . . with danger fraught. It's best to touch them not!" Their lips parted in their first genuine smile of the day.

~~~

A log collapsed into the flames, shooting a burst of embers skyward. Wat Ho watched them wink out, then popped a piece of fruit into their mouth. Their cat-like eyes closed as they chewed. Until a sound like a strangled goose caused one eye to open.

The Donkey had refused Wat Ho's offer of food because "real heroes live off the land, you know!" He nibbled at the dry grass and twigs he had gathered, then blew out another gusty sigh.

Wat Ho made a pot of sweet tea. They glanced at Hoof as they settled back down. "Such furrows crease your brow, as could be left there by a plow! What tale of woe weighs on you so?"

Hoof stared into the flames. "I'm okay," he said, in an 'I'm-totally-not-okay' tone of voice. "I sort of miss my family, is all."

"Have you many siblings?"

"Nah," replied Hoof. "I have a sister (I think) but she ran off with a Zebra before I was born. I never knew her, and my folks refuse to speak her name. So, there's just me and my big brother, Half."

"Half Hearted?"

"Yeah. He's okay, as far as older brothers go. But he never finishes anything! First, he tried mountaineering, but he kept falling down on the job. Moneylending appealed to him, but he quickly lost interest. The last we heard, he tried his hoof at racing but, as usual, he couldn't stay the course. There's no end to the things he didn't finish."

Hoof scootched closer to the fire. "Then there's Mother and Pops: Soft and Hard." He chuckled. "You know what they say . . ."

"That opposites attract?" ventured Wat Ho.

"What! No! Who says that? That's probably the dumbest thing I ever heard!" Hoof exclaimed.

Wat Ho's eyes closed. "In truth, my ignorance is deeper than a well," they sighed. "What is said by all, do tell!"

"Well . . . how you should never judge a creature by their name? Mother may be called 'Soft Hearted,' but she's as tough a hag as ever walked on four hooves. But my father, 'Hard Hearted,' is as gentle as a spring breeze. And don't let me get started on Uncle Stout!"

"With such a name he surely cannot fail to be as skinny as a rail!" laughed Wat Ho.

"Are you kidding?" exclaimed Hoof. "They enlarged his stall door three times because he kept getting too wide for it!" He giggled. "Skinny as a rail? Too funny!

"Seriously though, my family's something! Especially Grandsire, who started out as a travelling merchant, looking for anything he could sell for a coin or two. Then he went into an old barn and found . . . (Hoof dragged his sword closer) . . . this. The next thing any creature knew, he'd changed his name to Donkie Otie, donned a black mask and cape, and galloped off in all directions."

Hoof sighed wistfully. "What a sight he must have made, pounding down country lanes with his sword between his teeth and his cape billowing over his back. And wherever he went, his trusty thrall Paunchy Stanza puffed and blew along in his wake!

"But he stayed too long in The Northern Realm or, as the natives call it, *Aneasi Weitofrieze*. When he was crossing back to The Realm he got caught in a raging blizzard. To save his trusty thrall from freezing, the Great Hero surrendered himself to some Duke or other.

"The next thing Donkey Otie knew, he was a prisoner in the Duke's tower. Naturally, he used his famous wit, pluck and derring-do to escape. It was sheer bad luck that he ran out of the tower and straight into a pack of POTTYs."

"Potties?" said Wat Ho, raising a quizzical eyebrow.

"The Patriotic Order of Tower-torching Yeomen tried to stop King Harold from building a string of signal towers along the border. They were intended to warn the King of invasions, but the POTTYs were convinced they were sprinkling plague dust on the locals." He snorted, "They didn't know any better back then. Now every creature knows plagues come from bat poop.

"Almost every tradescreature in the Realm was forced to work on the towers. Which was the Old King's big mistake: Losing their best thralls was so bad for business that the Cows banded together and got Harold hoofed right off his throne! And that was the end of that!

"Donkie Otie was locked in one of the few towers that got finished. He escaped while some POTTYs were trying to burn it down. They couldn't, of course, what with it being solid stone and all. So they got Donkey Otie to strap on a battering ram and try to break down the tower door. He broke his head instead and ended up nuttier'n a squirrel's lunch. Paunchy led him home on a leash."

Wat Ho processed what he had heard. "The invaders the Old King feared," they asked, "did they in reality appear?"

"Of course," said Hoof dismissively. "That winter and pretty much every winter since (plagues permitting) the SnowFowl fled the snow and ice of their homeland to poop and scratch and make a mess across the southern reaches of the Realm. And every year, the heat and humidity of summer convinced them to fly back home."

Hoof's mouth stretched open in a jaw-cracking yawn. "I'm really beat!" he said. He yawned again. Wat Ho followed suit.

They lapsed into a companionable silence, broken only by the slurp of Wat Ho finishing their tea and the rumbling of Hoof's stomach. Until an invisible but hardly odorless gas drifted across the clearing.

"Hoof Hearted!" exclaimed Wat, fanning the air with a thick paw.

"Yeah, that was me," Hoof admitted. "Too much bark in my diet."

They settled down on opposite sides of the clearing. Wat Ho replayed their conversation in their mind. *How this vulgar youngster bleats and brays! Not two words did he manage to rhyme. Yet we must prepare him for the fray and do so in very little time.*

(It's been many a year since last we were here, came the reply. *Fashions change, and so must we. Not all truth is spoke as poetry.)*

You would have us be schooled by this undisciplined young fool?

(I would have you do what you must, my dearest mate.)

Wat Ho stared into the darkness until their eyes finally drifted closed. Had they glanced across the Lone Lee River, they might have noticed the fateful flicker of a campfire on the opposite bank.

~ 2 ~

The disheveled monkey plucked something out of his fur; examined it; flicked it into the fire. "I've got one!" he cried, "A three-legged dog goes into a bar looking for . . ."

". . . the villain who offed his paw!" interrupted his companion, a highly agitated Chihuahua. *"Señor,* I know all your stinking jokes! But there is nothing funny about this!" He raised his right front leg, which ended a paws-width below his elbow.

"Oh, I don't know about that," drawled the monkey. "You'd be a shoo-in for a three-legged race! Don't even need a partner!"

"¡Ai! ¡Ai! ¡Ai!" yipped the dog. I will kill you in your sleep!"

"Sure you will!" yawned the monkey. He scooped up a drooping backpack and swung into a tree. An evergreen cone ricocheted down through several branches before bouncing off the dog's nose.

When Manuel Isareali Sobad (for that was the dog's name) returned to the fire, the woods seemed alive with threats. He thrust the stump of his leg into a harness from which a dagger extended and pulled the laces snug with his teeth. Then he spun around twice and lay down. After a long while, he drifted into a fitful sleep.

The *dream* started, as always, with a moonless night. A sound disturbs his sleep. What is that? Heavy boots are pounding toward his sleeping *pueblo!* He runs toward the village barking *Danger! Warning! Danger . . .* snap! A forgotten trap is sprung. Mind-freezing pain stuns his body. But the physical pain is nothing compared to the mental anguish of hearing his villagers dragged off to a life of slavery.

What was that? Hoof's eyes flew open. A cloud drifted over the moon, plunging the campsite into darkness. He strained his ears. *Nothing.* His eyes closed, then flew open again as a snarl pierced the darkness. *That was* **so** *not nothing!* He stood up and stared into the black shadows. A bush rustled behind him and he spun, snagged a hoof in his sword belt and almost fell.

The moon emerged and a shadow under the bushes sprouted yellow eyes. The shadow grew longer as a black paw reached toward Wat Ho's wards. A flash lit the bushes and, yowling with rage, the creature leaped back. The stench of burning fur wafted across the clearing.

The eyes winked out. Hoof lay with his chin on his sword, torn between terror of the creature and irritation at Wat Ho's snores.

Manny Sobad shivered. At dawn, his journey would resume. He knew his destination by name: Coshon Aerie. The monsters of his nightmare had boasted of it while they dragged his villagers away. Where it was and what he would do when he got there were less clear.

Above him, the monkey shifted to a less uncomfortable position. His mother was a macaque, and he thought of himself as such. His father was 'other,' giving him his large size and his birth name: Peteiro Saké. But here and now, he was known as 'Pete Sake.'

He swung out of the tree, opened his drooping backpack and dug out a few bits of dried meat. "Manny?" he called. There was no response, so he tossed one at the dog's backside. The dog spun around with a snarl, then caught the next bite to come his way. He snapped up the scrap that had hit the ground, then went to sit beside Pete.

"Sorry, *Señor* Pete," he said. "Last night was not good."

They never are, thought Pete as he took another look in his backpack. "Hey! This will cheer you up!" He took out a lump of oiled cloth and spread it out on the ground.

"*¡Ay, caramba!*" Manny yipped. "*¡Un burrito!*" He downed the morsel in a few snaps of his teeth. "*¡Gracias!*" He burped. "Tell me, *Señor,* How long . . . burp . . . was that in your backpack?"

"That's a good question," said Pete as he nibbled a bit of dry fruit.

It started to rain. The Chihuahua pulled on his dagger and limped away. By the time Pete shouldered his backpack and set off after him, the dog was barely visible through the downpour.

Hoof glared up at Wat Ho. "We had a creepy visitor last night!" he brayed. "It scared me half to death. And a fat lot of help you were!"

Wat Ho shrugged. "My wards felt it best not to disturb our rest." They hid a grin by turning to add wild mushrooms to their rice.

Hoof ended his sulk when Wat Ho shared the rice. He licked his pot clean, then offered to douse the campfire. He picked the pot up by its handle and went to the river. After wading out to thigh-deep water, he rinsed and refilled the pot.

He had taken one step back toward the riverbank when the pot slipped, forgotten, from his jaws. His eyes were fixed on a torn, bloody wing that bumped against his leg. Shuddering, he jerked out of the way. When the grisly 'message' had drifted out of sight, he retrieved the pot, carried it to the campfire and doused the embers. After slipping into his sword belt, he grimly set off down the trail.

Wat Ho retied Sack O'Stuff, shrinking it down to the same huge bundle it had been the day before. As they turned to follow Hoof, rain blackened the surface of the river. The downpour swept overhead and reached Hoof. He ducked under the cover of a tree.

"Wait!" called Hoof as Wat Ho strode past him. The Guardian stopped and fixed a questioning eye on the Donkey. "So, erm . . ." Hoof looked around nervously. "It'd be safer to stick together. For you, I mean: I could protect you with my sword."

"Given an offer so fine, only a fool would decline!" said Wat Ho.

"So," Hoof brayed, "is that a yes?"

Wat Ho inclined their head and waved Hoof onward.

The clouds soon scattered. By midmorning, the silence was broken only by water dripping from leaves and the crunch of Hoof's teeth on his sword whenever a bird flew overhead.

The river was too swollen to cross; Pete and Manny hugged its bank until dense, prickly brush forced them inland. A well-traveled trail eventually took them back to the river where they filled their stomachs with water. After that, Pete stayed on the trail while Manny skulked through the underbrush, hunting for fresh food.

Manny was about to give up when he came upon a faint path. He followed it for a few steps, then caught a bewitching scent. The roar of rushing water swelled in his ears as he hurried toward the narrow gorge that now confined the Lone Lee River. Some instinct drew him onto a rickety footbridge that crossed the raging torrent.

Hoof and Wat Ho's trail ended where an ancient cataclysm had forced the river to plunge through a gap in a rust-red cliff. A natural stairway climbed halfway to the summit. Above that the trail resumed, zigzagging across the rock face. They picked their way up the cliff, then started down the other side.

A path split off, leading to the narrow river gorge. Hoof approached a decrepit wooden bridge that disappeared into the mist. He cautiously tested the first damp plank, then the second. Glancing up, he sensed movement on the far side of the gorge. The swirling mist parted briefly to reveal a dog at the end of the bridge. *Pad paw!* He jerked his sword out of its scabbard.

11

Frenzied barking broke out behind Pete. He raced back up the trail and turned onto a path that ended at a mist-cloaked gorge. He barely made out Manny, who was creeping over a narrow bridge that spanned the gorge. Then the mist parted and revealed, at the far end of the bridge, something that looked vaguely like a Horse!

Manny crept forward and resumed his barking. The Horse responded by making threatening gestures with a stubby sword. *Well, this won't end well!* Pete thought as he raced onto the bridge. He got in front of the dog and blocked his path.

"Calm down, Manny," he soothed. "We don't want to start a war."

Manny stopped barking and Pete slipped off his dagger. *Praise Gorme!* he breathed in relief.

A sharp twang rang out, and the bridge listed sharply. "Oh Snorg!" Pete scooped Manny up and, gripping the dog in one paw and the dagger in the other, raced toward the Horse-creature.

Hoof was shocked to see a large 'tree rat' charging right at him, a weapon clutched in one paw and the pad-paw in the other. He backed off the bridge—just as the far end of the bridge tore loose and fell away. Hoof's eyes flicked up to see the monkey throw the dog at his head! He ducked; the dog hit the ledge, rolled over and lay still.

Two more dull 'pops' sounded and the whole bridge tore loose. "OH, SN-O-O-O-RG!" The wail floated up from the chasm.

~~~

"Hey!" Hoof's ears twisted toward the gorge.

"Hey, Donkey!"

I must be hearing things!

"Down here!"

Hoof peered over the edge. The monkey was clinging to the dagger, which was jammed into a crack in the rock.

He stared up at Hoof. "Help me! Please!"

Hoof backed away. "There's an ugly tree-rat hanging on down there," he called to Wat Ho. "Don't know for how long, though."

Wat Ho was trying to stem the flow of blood from a gash in the dog's skull. Beside them was an open chest, containing an array of bottles, vials and waxcloth-wrapped bundles. Sack O'Stuff lay open beyond the chest, its contents bursting out over the rock. Wat Ho nodded at it. "A length of rope may give them hope."

Hoof walked over to the pile of camping equipment. "How am I supposed to find rope in this mess?" he moaned.

"If you speak the word," Wat Ho sighed, "it will be heard."

Huh, thought Hoof. *That's cool!* He brayed "rope!" and a coiled rope rose to the surface. Dropping the rope at the edge of the gorge, he bit down on the exposed end and nosed the coil over the side. It spun down to the monkey who clamped the dagger between his teeth and pulled himself paw-over-paw up the face of the gorge.

The monkey boiled over the lip of the gorge like a pirate boarding a captured ship. Hoof dropped the rope and chinned his sword as the monkey spat the dagger into his paw and swaggered toward him. "Pete Sake!" he announced, slapping his chest. "How is . . ." he trailed off when he saw the dog lying on Wat Ho's bedroll.

"Your friend can be made whole again," said Wat Ho gravely. "But not without time. And pain."

They closed the medicine chest and rose to their feet. Pete took a moment to get his mind around the creature's size. "My name is Peter Sake," he announced, " and my friend is *Señor* Manuel Isareali Sobad. But mostly he's called Manny. I go by Pete."

Manny growled softly. "You may call me *Señor* Sobad!"

"Um, okay." said Hoof. "Hoof Hearted, here!"

"It was not my fault!" growled the dog. "I got fed a bad burrito!" His eyes drifted shut. Soft snores accompanied the rapid rise and fall of his bony chest.

Pete's gaze travelled between Wat Ho and the box at his feet. The Guardian shrugged. "Only through sleep can he be made whole."

"And you are?" asked Pete.

"Wat Ho," replied the Guardian.

Pete stared at the giant creature. *What are you?* After a few beats he tore his eyes away and sighed. "Things are as they are. I'll just have to wait until he can walk."

A stirring in Wat Ho's brain turned their eyes to Manny. They started in surprise. (*Ah*) breathed the gentle voice. (*You see it too!*)

Wat Ho's head bobbed, then turned to Pete. "Going on, we'd best unite," they rumbled. "We have things to discuss tonight."

"Say what?" brayed Hoof. "Join forces with a homicidal pad paw and a tree rat? Are you . . ." He looked into Wat Ho's narrowed eyes and his rant fizzled out. ". . . serious? Of course you are!"

The Guardian slapped their paws together. "It is good to find we are of a like mind. We'll make a stretcher to bear our friend. We must travel far before the day ends."

~ *3* ~

Pete balanced the stretcher on his sloping shoulders. The front end rested on Hoof's rump. Both were tired, thirsty and hungry. Suddenly, Hoof froze beside a wall of giant boulders.

"Water!" he brayed. He dove between two boulders, dragging the protesting monkey behind him. They burst onto a flat stretch of gravel that ended at a rock wall. A sheen of water glinted on the wall, feeding a pool at its foot.

Wat Ho squeezed through after them, picked up the stretcher and carried it to a sheltered spot. Pete dug a folding cup out of his backpack, took some water to Manny. The dog lapped at it a few times. *"Muchas Gracias,"* he whispered. "Now I rest." He closed his eyes and slept.

~~~

Wat Ho sank down against a large boulder. Pete joined them, scrabbling onto a rock that put his head level with the Guardian's.

"So," Pete broke the silence, "That stuff that went on between Manny and your long-eared friend: What was that about?"

Wat Ho shrugged. "Hoof's Folk believe that pad paws were by Warre conceived: vile beasts created just for Hooved blood to lust."

Pete shrugged. "Every Folk believes in a Creator. But none of them agree on who created what or when. They all run around insisting every creature else is a 'wrong-headed demon spawn.'"

A laugh tinkled across the campsite. Pete's head snapped around, looking for its source. He found himself staring into the Guardian's gentle, violet eyes. *Huh! I was sure those eyes were green!*

15

"My friend," said a soft alto voice, "you perceive what most others may deceive. All Folk teach their young to play 'god-given' roles, from which they never stray."

Pete snorted. "And what's your role?" He bowed ironically. "Enlighten me Great . . . Mistress? Master? What are you, anyway?"

Wat Ho's eyes closed. "Master or slave; timid or brave, we are all in this the same: We are mere markers in an ancient game. The roll of a random die dictates where our futures lie. A very few break free to shape their own destiny. Such creatures are rare. Often there is only one and for ten generations there was none!" Wat Ho nodded toward Hoof. "Until our young friend. On him much shall depend."

Pete stared at Wat Ho's eyes. *They are green!* He shook his head, then chuckled. "Okay, that's a good one!" he said. "You really had me going there! So, what's the punch line?" Wat Ho remained silent. Pete studied their face. "No! You're serious, aren't you?"

At Wat Ho's nod, Pete turned to study the oblivious Donkey. "He's not exactly the keenest blade in the armory, is he?"

Wat Ho sighed. "Courage and resolve are not solely seen in the intelligent or fair of mien. Many times destiny chose the most unlikely heroes; the least of whom were called to do the greatest deeds of all."

Pete scrambled forward to come face-to-face with Wat Ho. He stared into the Guardian's eyes. "You're serious about this."

Wat Ho's eyes flickered. "As serious as we can be."

"You say 'we,'" Pete demanded. "Who's we?"

"Our minds can meld, so one may see what another beheld. If the bond grows too strong to sever, we are fated to be joined forever."

The alto voice added, "As it is for my beloved and I."

Pete took a deep breath. Let it out. "Great Mothering . . ." He stopped. "There are two of you in there?" He bit off a humorless laugh. "Well, you're as big as any two creatures I've ever met! And I guess that explains your voice. Voices?" He scratched the back of his head.

16

"This is too confusing. I'm just going to call your voice Lady Ho, if that's okay with you."

"I will gladly be called 'Lady,'" said the alto voice, "but by you alone. For all others our name must be Wat Ho's own."

"Fair enough," said Pete. He smiled wryly. "But I really don't understand why you are sharing all this with me."

"Ah," said Wat Ho. "That has to do with your friend."

"What?" said Pete. His eyes flicked to the stretcher, then returned to fix on Wat Ho's face. "Manny? What about him?"

"He too bears the Mark," Lady Ho soberly replied.

"Seriously?" scoffed Pete. "First these 'marked' creatures are so rare there might only be one in the whole world. And then you say two of them are right there! What are the chances of that?"

Wat Ho shrugged. "This morning I'd have said, 'none.' But we were called to one alone. Except for you, the other's on his own."

"Called?"

"To protect the Marked is why our Kind exists. Their beacon sends a call we can't resist."

~~~

Hoof snuggled down out of the wind and Wat Ho threw a blanket over him. The Donkey complained loudly, but not long, before yielding to exhaustion. Wat Ho sat on the ground. Pete sat on a nearby rock. The moon cast a quicksilver light over the campsite.

"We long for this wind to still," said Wat Ho. "Our bones are brittled by the chill."

"I've felt worse," said Pete

Lady Ho said, "Your ancestors were known to me: They lived at the edge of the Eastern Sea. It was an icy clime to be sure, but your people were warm and pure. I would gladly see their kind again." They studied Pete. "I see their good blood flowing in your veins."

17

Pete shuddered. "You know that's creepy, right?" He sank into his own thoughts. "This is nuts!" he burst out at last. "You say there's two of you in one body? Living forever and reciting poetry? Only a gullible fool would buy that!"

"A fool you are not," rumbled Wat Ho. "But we are what we are and speak as we were taught."

"I hate to say this, but you had one seriously inept teacher."

"Our teacher was well-skilled," insisted Wat Ho, "but from a time when creatures thrilled in discourse made to rhyme."

"But that was, what . . ." Pete counted his fingers . . . "ten generations ago? And you were there? In the flesh?"

Wat Ho's shoulders lifted in a shrug. "After a fashion, yes."

"Good Gorme!" Pete leaned closer, trying to make out the Guardian's features. "How old are you anyway?"

"Age to our kind goes unheeded," said Lady Ho. "We appear when needed, else our bodies are . . . not. Made flesh we can perish from a blow but 'old age?' That we shall never know."

"That's more freaky weird stuff!" Pete said. "Well my exceptionally old friends, we've really got to update your vocabulary. And I beg of you, please lose the poesy."

"We would be grateful for your instruction," said the Guardian.

They sat up through the night, talking, laughing and sharing.

~ *4* ~

The trail switch-backed down a steep incline to a forested valley floor. Beyond the forest, a checkerboard of walled fields lined the banks of the Lone Lee River. Further still, a town sent red-roofed tendrils out from the river's edge.

Wat Ho settled the Chihuahua on their shoulder and set off down the trail. Hoof and Pete stumbled wearily after them. At the forest's edge, they hit a wall of cold damp air. Giant conifers blocked out the sky. The forest floor was bare and, except for moss and a few thickets of coppery ferns, lifeless.

"Psst, Abuele Wat," shivered Manny. "Please to set me down. I will walk now!"

As soon as Wat Ho lowered the Chihuahua to the ground he limped up to Pete and raised the stump of his leg.

"Be careful," Pete muttered as he knotted the dagger's harness in place. He was rewarded with a scathing look.

The trail ended at a rutted dirt road. Hoof angled his nose to the left. "I smell water that way," he announced.

A hundred paces brought them to a steep gully. It was bridged by tree trunks wedged lengthwise between the gully walls and topped with dirt. The road swept across the bridge and curved westward.

A stream flowed beneath the bridge: a shining black mirror under the afternoon sun. Braying happily, Hoof skidded down the slope and splashed into the stream. The water was dark with tannin but smelled fresh. He stopped in thigh-deep water and gulped his fill.

Pete dropped his pack and dove into the stream. "Oo! That's cold!" he shrieked. He ducked his face and spit out a geyser of water.

Wat Ho retrieved a bucket and some rope from Sack O'Stuff and hauled up some water that they shared with Manny.

~~~

Pete climbed out of the stream and shook himself dry. "I'll look around," he said as he scampered up a nearby tree. Wat Ho coiled the rope as they watched Pete disappear into the canopy.

"Guys?" Hoof's voice was shrill. "I need some help, here!"

Wat Ho swung around, then froze. Water lapped at Hoof's chin. "Every time I move I get sucked down deeper!" he brayed.

"Hang on!" Wat Ho called. "We'll pull you out." They flung the bucket at Hoof. The Donkey lunged to catch the rope, then squealed when the motion sucked him deeper. Wat Ho slowly pulled the rope. Hoof's jaw and neck muscles bulged as he fought to keep his head above water. Then the rope slipped away.

"I can't!" Hoof gasped. "I just can't do it."

Pete splashed to Hoof's side. He squeezed the bucket under Hoof's sword belt and kicked back to the bank. He hooked an arm behind a sapling, then wound the rope around his forearm.

"Okay, Pete called. "Let's do this!"

Wat Ho edged onto the riverbank, easing Hoof's front legs out of the muck. Hoof got his knees onto the bank, then kicked his back legs while Wat Ho pulled on his sword belt. Suddenly, he flopped onto dry land, his muck-encrusted sides pumping like bellows.

"That was fast thinking, Pete!" said Wat Ho as they pulled the rope out from under Hoof's sword belt. They turned toward the monkey. "Pete?" they called.

Pete's right arm dangled at his side. "My arm," he panted through gritted teeth. "I think it got pulled right out of its socket."

Wat Ho laid Pete on his back. Hoof's eyes widened as Wat Ho gripped the injured arm by the wrist and pulled it up behind the monkey's head, then down toward the opposite shoulder. A loud 'pop' was followed by a thump; Hoof had passed out cold.

Pete watched Wat Ho lay their palm on a wooden chest. It fell open and they took out some cloth, then quickly and expertly made a sling for his injured arm.

"Okay," Wat Ho rumbled as they stuffed the chest back into Sack O'Stuff. "One last thing to deal with." They filled the bucket with water and poured it on the unconscious Donkey.

"HEE! HAW!" Hoof brayed as he sprang to his hooves. "What in the name of the Sweet Creator was that for!"

"If we don't clean that muck off, you'll turn into a brick of solid mud," chuckled Wat Ho. They hit him with another bucket of water.

"Jonah's jodhpurs!" Hoof shrieked. "That is really freaking cold!"

Manny laughed shrilly. "If you planned to drown *Señor burro estúpido,* you should have left him in the river."

"Hee. Haw," shivered Hoof. "V-very f-funny. *Ah-ah-ah-choo!"*

"I saw a fallen tree just upstream from here," said Pete. "It opened up enough space to make a pretty good campsite."

Wat Ho draped a blanket over Hoof's back. "Point the way," they said as they sat Pete astride the Donkey.

"Hey!" Hoof brayed indignantly.

"¡Silencio!" Manny was on his belly, creeping toward a thicket of ferns. Suddenly, he launched himself into the thicket. There was a rustle, a cut-off squeak, then silence. He trotted out of the ferns with a dead rodent dangling from the point of his dagger. *"¡Carne fresca!"*

Hoof's stomach heaved and he quickly turned his back on the disgusting sight. *Flesh-eating pad paw monster!*

"¿Qué?" Manny barked. "This is food, like all *criaturas muda.* The Goddess left them without speech, to be food for my kind."

"So that you would stop eating us!" muttered Hoof.

Pete extended his good arm and pulled the carcass off of Manny's dagger. "We've been on short rations," he explained. "A bit of fresh meat might fill the holes where our stomachs used to be."

"Do not let that . . . that *thing* even touch me!" hissed Hoof.

~~~

After tearing through the canopy, the tree hung up on a neighbor. Its root ball created a mossy cave. Wat Ho shoved Sack O'Stuff inside, then scaled the tree's sloping trunk and snapped off a few branches. They 'chopped' these into firewood with the edge of their paw, a feat that left their companions slack-jawed with amazement.

Wat Ho got a fire going. Hoof shrugged off his blanket and stood so close to the flames that, if he weren't soaking wet, he'd have caught fire. His hair hissed and steamed as it dried.

While Wat Ho set his wards, Pete strapped on a knife, picked up Manny's kill and went to the stream. His agile feet gripped the rodent while he used his good paw to skin and clean it. He impaled the dressed carcass on a stick, where it waited for the fire to burn down.

~~~

After an awkward dinner spent at opposite ends of the campsite, Wat Ho and Pete reunited over a pot of tea. Hoof laid his sword and belt out to dry near the fire. Manny chose a position across from him. He removed his dagger and started to clean the stump of his leg.

"How'd that happen, anyway?" asked Hoof.

"*¿Qué?*" Manny didn't look up. "How did what happen?"

"Your leg," said Hoof. "What happened to your leg?"

Manny looked puzzled. "Is something wrong with my leg?"

Hoof's ears reddened. "Erm . . . No? No! Of course not!"

"So!" snarled Manny. "Missing half my leg is 'nothing?'"

"Yes. No! What am I supposed to say?" moaned Hoof.

"I chewed it off," said Manny, abruptly.

"Say what?" said Hoof.

"I said I chewed off my leg," Manny repeated.

"Fine!" brayed Hoof. "I'm sorry I asked, okay? Let's just drop it!"

"It's the truth," said Pete.

Hoof's head swung around. "Say what?" he brayed.

"He's telling the truth," Pete repeated. "His leg got caught in a trap when he was all alone. He survived by chewing his own foot off."

Hoof's eyes were wide. "You . . . how . . . when . . . Oh! My! Gorme! I could never!"

Manny shrugged. "You do what you must."

"You think?" said Hoof, doubtfully. "I once got a splinter stuck in a hoof. So, I decided to chew it out."

"Not quite the same," said Manny. "Okay, is not the same at all."

"Yeah," said Hoof. "Mainly because I fainted before I got started."

~~~

Pete headed to the fallen tree and wormed through its branches until he found a suitable spot to spend the night. Wat Ho snuggled into their bed roll and started to snore. Manny mouthed his dagger and padded into a thicket of ferns. He turned in a circle before settling down with a sigh. His eyes gleamed in the firelight.

Hoof had an uneasy feeling that he was being watched. He got up, sheathed his sword and slipped the still damp belt over his head. When he lay down, he glanced at where Manny had disappeared. The dog's eyes, big and unblinking, stared out him from inside a thicket of ferns. Hoof shuddered, then turned away.

~ 5 ~

Manny emerged from his hiding place to face a cold grey dawn. He limped up to the firepit, where Hoof stared blearily into the flames. Hoof glanced down at him, then let his eyes drift over the campsite.

"Where's the tree rat?" he asked.

Wat Ho ignored him. Manny drew his lips back in a snarl.

"Sorry!" Hoof huffed sarcastically. "I meant to say, 'Where's Pete?'" Under his breath he added ". . . *the tree rat.*"

"The tree rat could use a little help!" called a strained voice.

They found Pete at the base of the fallen tree. His right arm hung out of its sling. His shoulder was a bruised, swollen mound.

"Ow?" he said plaintively.

"That does look a bit uncomfortable," Wat Ho admitted.

Their medicine chest yielded up a long metal tube that ended in a hollow needle. On the other end was a plunger.

Pete eyed the device. "What do you plan to do with that?"

"Don't worry," Said Wat Ho as they cut off Pete's sling. "This won't hurt. Hey!" they added. "Look at Hoof!" The instant Pete turned away, they plunged the needle into his shoulder.

Thud.

"Ha! Ha! the Donkey's out cold!" chortled Pete. He glanced up at Wat Ho, then at his shoulder. "Great Mother of Creation!"

"Easy, Pete," Wat Ho cautioned. "Don't move!" As the plunger drew back, the lump on Pete's shoulder shrank. "And that's that!"

24

The Guardian set the needle aside and bound the injured arm snuggly to Pete's side. "Hopefully that will hold you. But you won't be able to move on for a day or two."

"That's a problem," said Pete. "We're out of provisions."

Manny strapped on his dagger. "I will hunt!" he announced as he limped into the surrounding woods.

"Oh goody!" Hoof brayed after him. "What could be more appetizing than the smell of burning rodent?"

Pete watched Manny disappear among the trees. "That little dog sure heals fast!" he observed.

Wat Ho nodded. "The Fates are looking out for him," they said. They felt Pete's forehead. "Unlike you," they soberly added. "I'll give you something to help fight off the evil humors that are attacking you from within."

Wat Ho mixed a bitter powder with some water and urged Pete to choke down every drop. The drug soon took effect, and Pete spent the rest of the day dozing fitfully.

Hoof spent the day browsing on a narrow strip of bushes that grew at the edge of the stream. When they weren't cleaning and organizing the contents of Sack O'Stuff, Wat Ho meditated.

Manny returned, tired and empty pawed, at moonrise. They were all content to eat what Sack O'Stuff provided, then drift to their respective sleeping areas.

"I am destined to be a god!" hissed the ancient creature. "No longer will I be denied!"

"Yes Master," said the kneeling, black-robed giant. "I mean 'No Master,'" he quickly amended.

"Fool!" snapped the creature. "Why am I surrounded by fools?"

The giant cowered deeper into his cowl, saying nothing.

"Don't just kneel there, you idiot! Get my second dose."

"Yes, Master!" The giant touched his forehead to the floor then, still on his knees, backed away. He returned holding a goblet. His master choked down a thick elixir, moaning in ecstasy as its flesh filled out, taking on a glow that sickly imitated vigor and health. "Yes-s-s-s! this donor was very strong. I am ready for battle!"

The creature donned an ornate helm and popped out of existence. The black-robed giant waited until the echoing thunderclap died out, then wove some fresh, bloody bones into his Master's throne.

A sound like hammers pounding an empty metal drum brought Hoof lurching to his hooves. White-hot balls slammed into the edge of the campsite, then dripped away as if the air were melting. An orange disc formed, turned white hot, and expanded. Thick, acrid smoke drifted across the campsite as nearby ferns burst into flame.

Hoof turned away from the blinding glare and saw a glowlamp come to life inside the root ball. Muttering angrily, Wat Ho dug around in Sack O'Stuff. Then, with fists held high, they lumbered to the center of the clearing. Flames crackled around their right paw as they launched their full magical arsenal at a powerful foe.

Time seemed to stand still until, suddenly, the clouds burst. The icy deluge turned to steam as it coursed down Wat Ho's trembling body. Desperately clinging to the last dregs of their power, they roared in frustration. An answering bellow was cut short by a thunderclap. The fireballs stopped. The sudden silence was deafening.

The downpour beat out the flames that had sprung up below the disk of superheated air; the disk hissed, faded, then disappeared. A dark amulet slipped from Wat Ho's fist. They sagged slowly to their knees, then collapsed into a shaft of light that escaped the root ball.

Hoof stared at the giant. "He's not dead!" he wailed. "Is he?"

Pete laid a paw on the giant's chest. *"They're* alive," he replied. "But barely, I think."

26

Hoof stared at the water pouring down Wat Ho's face. "We can't just leave him . . ."

"Them!" Pete interrupted.

"What?" Hoof replied. "Fine! We can't leave *them* out here to drown!" He brightened. "I know! Tie a rope to them and I'll drag them into the shelter."

Pete shot him a skeptical look, then splashed into the root ball. He returned with a coil of rope, one end of which he pushed under the Guardian's neck. "Grab the end and pull," he said.

Hoof bit down on the rope. Sawing back and forth, they worked it under Wat Ho's body. With some help from his feet, Pete knotted it under the Guardian's armpits. He passed a loop over Hoof's shoulders and, calling up memories from his seafaring days, secured it with a knot he hoped would not strangle the hapless Donkey.

Hoof planted his rear hooves against a rock and pushed. Wat Ho's body edged forward; Hoof dove ahead until, a dozen earth-churning paces later, he came up against the back of the root ball.

Hoof Hearted! The voice seemed to echo in Hoof's head. *Get medicine chest. Take the scroll.*

"What?" said Hoof. "What scroll?" He swung his head back and forth. "You want me to get a scroll from the medicine chest?"

Manny and Pete had followed Hoof into the shelter. Pete flipped the rope off over Hoof's head. "What are you babbling about now?" he asked as he awkwardly tried to coil the rope.

"Well, Wat Ho just said . . . wait! You didn't hear anything?"

"No-o," said Pete and Manny at the same time.

"Well, they said to get a scroll from the medicine chest."

"The chest is next to the Sack," Pete replied as he resumed his attempt to coil the rope. "But we can't open it . . . unless . . ." He dragged the chest to Wat Ho's side and muscled the giant's paw onto the lid. The chest fell open. They all peered inside.

"Huh!" Pete exclaimed, pulling out a tightly rolled scroll. An intricate seal held it closed.

Take to village. Seek door . . . rune matches seal. Give scroll to who is there. They . . . know what to do.

"Are you serious?" wailed Hoof. "How will we find one single door in the whole town? It'll take forever!"

Scroll . . . guide you.

"Right. So, the scroll is, like, a map or something?"

Don't open it! Hurry . . . little time . . . the voice faded away.

"For what?" brayed Hoof. "Little time for what? Wat Ho!" But there was no response.

"So-o?" said Pete. "Do you maybe want to fill us in on the half of the conversation we missed?"

Hoof lowered his head. "I've got to take the scroll to the next town. There's a creature there who knows what to do."

"About what?" asked Pete.

"About Wat? Yeah," Hoof replied. "At least I hope so. I'll find them because their door is ruined. Or something; I didn't quite get that bit. But the scroll will lead me to . . . whoever."

"Yeah?" said Pete. "Well, let's take a look."

"No!" brayed Hoof. "Don't open it!"

Pete looked confused. "What use is the scroll if we can't open it?"

"No clue!" Hoof replied. "But if Wat Ho tells you not to mess with stuff, you better not mess with it! I learned that the hard way!"

"I'll go too," Pete said as he stuffed the scroll into his backpack. "With Wat Ho down and out, we need provisions." He turned to the Chihuahua. "Manny, you stay and guard Wat Ho."

Manny raised his dagger. "Nothing will get by me!" he called after Pete, who had slung his backpack over his good shoulder and hurried out of the shelter.

When they reached the road Hoof said, "Get on my back. I can move faster than you, especially with your arm tied up like that."

Pete vaulted onto Hoof's back, and they splashed down the muddy road at a spine-jolting pace. Which slowed to a walk long before they got to the town. Pete got down and shuffled along beside the Donkey.

All that day Manny patrolled the campsite, keeping a close eye on the surrounding ferns. He was alert to danger but desperately hoped to see some sign of *carne fresca*. Late in the afternoon, he went to the stream and filled his stomach with water. Night fell, and he had caught nothing to eat. His eye fell on the pot that had held their last meal. All it contained was a few waterlogged beans. He snapped them up, then went to spend the night curled up on Wat Ho's chest.

"What are we looking for?" asked Pete when they reached the town gate. He pulled the scroll out of his backpack. Its seal pulsed dimly. "Huh!" Hoof exclaimed. "That's different!"

They stepped through the gate and the scroll pulsed faster. "I guess we go that way," said Pete, pointing down a broad, dusty street.

They were studiously ignored by any creatures they met, until a pair of Brahma Bulls lumbered up to them. Their horns were sheathed in metal and ended in sharp points. Gleaming breastplates protected muscular shoulders and necks.

Pete pulled the backpack to his front and slipped the scroll inside. "Nothing to see here!" he murmured.

The Bulls shook their horns at Hoof's sword and snorted. Pete pulled it off over Hoof's head and stuffed it into his backpack.

"Apologies, officer-sirs," he simpered. "My young Ass of a master forgot to leave his toy at home. I will keep it safe."

The Brahmas inspected Pete and Hoof, shook their heads, and went on their way. Pete heaved a sigh of relief.

~~~

Darkness was closing in. Hoof traded a precious copper bit for a vegetable pie. They ate as they walked, Pete alternately taking a bite, then holding the pie out to Hoof. When the last bit of crust had been popped into Hoof's mouth, Pete wiped his paws on his thighs and checked the scroll. It guided them into an alley that was barely wide enough for them to walk side-by-side. They trod carefully to avoid an open sewer that trickled down the center.

"This isn't too gross!" said Pete.

"Seriously," Hoof replied. "Let's get out of here."

As they turned around, their eyes settled on a door that was ordinary in every way, except for the gleaming rune that pulsed in its center. It perfectly matched the rune on their scroll.

"Erm, this could be the place," said Hoof.

"You think?" scoffed Pete.

The silence lengthened. "So, what do we do now?" Hoof asked at last. "Knock and ask for the owner?"

"I don't have any better ideas," said Pete. As he raised his paw to knock, the door swung open to the sound of a crystal chime.

~ 6 ~

Hoof edged his nose over the threshold. Most of the windowless room was taken up by a counter, above which two lanterns produced a little light and a lot of smoke.

"Hello?" Hoof called. "Is any creature there?"

Behind the counter, a wall of shelves overflowed with bizarre objects. Hoof froze at the sight of a red and black spider that was the size of a small pony. Pete collided with Hoof's backside just as Hoof's teeth clacked on the spot where his sword wasn't.

"Ow!" moaned Hoof. "I bit my stupid tongue!"

"Ow!" snapped Pete. "I got your stupid tail in my eye!"

"Ow!" boomed a third voice. "You're giving me a headache!"

Hoof spun around. "Hello?" he brayed. "Who's there?"

"Hang on! I'm coming already!" said the deep, cranky-sounding voice. A black, pointy hat appeared behind the counter. This was followed by a pair of bright, bespectacled eyes that stared at Hoof and Pete. Motion resumed and the hat and eyes were joined by a bulbous nose, a wide, down-turned mouth and a pointy chin. "You better have a good reason for disturbing my nap!" said the mouth.

Pete stepped up to the counter. "We brought you this scroll."

A pair of hands plopped down on the counter. The Head tilted forward to glare at Pete. "Who sent you?" The eyes darted between Pete and Hoof, who had become tongue-tied statues. "Well?"

"Wat Ho?" whispered Hoof. The Head's cold stare continued. "Big creature?" he babbled "Really big! Black and white and . . ."

31

"Immortal," interrupted Pete.

"What?" said Hoof. "No! The creature's almost dead already!"

"Enough!" A hand stretched out and seized the scroll. "What's that old meddler done now?" muttered The Head as they opened the scroll. Their eyes darted up and down, then the scroll fell to the counter and vanished in a puff of smoke. The Head dropped out of sight.

A low door built into the counter banged open and The Head came through. Their scrawny neck emerged from a shapeless, flowered dress. The tip of their hat barely reached Hoof's shoulder. Their hands swung just above the floor, at the end of a pair of skinny arms.

"Oh! Thank! Gorme!" breathed Hoof.

"What?" snapped The Head. "Dazzled by my beauty?"

"No," said Hoof. "I mean . . . It's just . . ."

"Just what?" asked The Head.

"I thought maybe you were just a big old floating head!"

The Head snorted. "You really *are* an Ass!" She paused as if listening. "I sense nothing. The Guardian is must be very weak . . . or worse," she added, ominously.

"They were alive when we set out," Pete replied. "But unconscious. That was before sunrise. It took till now to get here. It would have taken longer but Hoof carried me most of the way."

The Head studied the Donkey closely. "So? It has a name?"

"Hoof Hearted, Ma'am!" said Hoof.

"No need to dwell on the passed," said The Head.

She trotted to the back of the room and slid open a pocket door. "Starr!" she called in an unexpectedly pleasant voice. "First thing tomorrow, we're going on an adventure!"

A delicate clip-clop announced the arrival of the most stunning Jennet Hoof had ever seen. Impudent spikes of black mane poked up between long, sensuous ears. The moist ovals of her nostrils flared in a perfect, cream-colored nose. When she smiled, her protruding teeth were like the daisies in the fields of Hoof's foal-hood. He lowered his eyes; tried not to stare at the perfect barrel of her chest where her chestnut coat faded to a rich cream that matched her nose. His eye drifted down slender legs that ended in dainty, gleaming black hooves. He glanced back up to meet her eyes—and choked.

"Gentle creatures," said The Head. "this is my protégé, Starr Nightly. Starr, these gentle creatures are . . . oh dear! I have no idea who they are!" She waved in their direction. "Introduce yourselves."

Pete bowed. "Peter Sake," he said. "I am delighted to place my inadequate and broken self at your service!"

Starr turned to the monkey with a polite curl of her upper lip. Her eyes widened. "Oh you poor creature! What happened to your arm?"

"He did," Pete replied, nodding at Hoof.

Starr angled an eye at the still-immobile Donkey. "And you are?" she asked at last.

"Heh-heh-ar-ar-arted!" Hoof stammered.

Starr shook her head. "Sorry? I didn't quite get that."

"His name is Hearted," Pete helpfully interjected.

"Hearted?" Starr turned back to Hoof. "Is that your birth name?"

"N-n-no," said Hoof.

"His birth name is Hoof" said Pete.

"Hoof?" said Starr. Her eyes widened. "Oh. My."

"Starr darling," said The Head, ending the awkwardness. "Have Pierce put a few days' provisions in the new saddlebags."

"Of course," said Starr. She turned and clopped out of the room.

"Erm, we need provisions too," said Pete.

"Do you have any coin?" snapped The Head.

"I have four copper bits!" Hoof proudly announced.

"Well, aren't you just the funniest thing!" The Head grumbled. She shuffled to the door and called, "Oh, and Starr, darling! Have Pierce toss in some of that old Donkey chow the rats wouldn't eat? And any old fruit we happen to have lying around."

"Excuse me ma'am?" said Pete. "If you could toss in a bit of mildly disgusting dog food as well, that would be appreciated."

The Head closed her eyes and squeezed her bulb of a nose. "What kind of dog?" she sighed.

"Chihuahua," Pete replied.

"And, Starr, sweetie—this is the last thing, I promise! Please bring those chimichangas we made for the fiesta!"

The Head blinked at their incredulous faces. "What? I like dogs. Small dogs," she clarified. "Big ones scare the poo out of me!"

~~~

The Head slipped back under the counter. A ladder swung up and hooked onto a rail that ran along the top of the shelves. The pointy hat appeared, an arm snaked up and something was tossed to the floor. Portions of The Head appeared and disappeared as she moved the ladder, selecting items.

The ladder disappeared and The Head backed through the portal, pulling an upholstered bag that barely squeezed through the opening.

"Hey, that looks like Sack O'Stuff!" exclaimed Pete.

"No," said The Head. "This is Bag O'Bounty." She threw a couple of blankets at Pete. "You'll sleep here. We leave in the morning."

The Emissary's eyes swept over the fresh bones that adorned the throne, then back to the creature that sprawled across them. "My Master sends his condolences," he said in a voice like distant thunder.

The dried-out husk summoned up a spark of anger, causing the three giants who stood pressed against the wall to stir nervously. "I appreciate the sentiment," it snapped, "but kindly assure your Master that I am not dead yet!"

"Hmpf," sniffed the Emissary. "Indeed. I assume my Master has communicated his requirements?"

"He has," snarled the creature. "I accept."

The Emissary inclined his head. "Very well. What you seek will be delivered . . . *after* you fulfill your end of the bargain." He squared his shoulders and faded out of existence.

After a restless night, Manny went back to circling the campsite. He was cold, hungry and exhausted. A patch of sunlight crept onto the clearing and he let his eyes close, just for a beat or two; then a little longer; then . . .

A whimper nudged Manny awake. *Was that me?* He raised his head and listened. *No, there it is again!* He peered into Wat Ho's shelter. Something moved! The dog stepped inside, then froze. *"¡Diosa Madre!"* he breathed.

Sunlight poured through an opening Manny had not noticed before. A shadow moved across Wat Ho's chest: A shadow that was deformed, vile and cast by . . . nothing! *"Es absurdo,"* Manny chuckled as he looked for a twisted root or other explanation. There was no root! He looked back in time to see a glassy claw stretch toward Wat Ho's chest. Then the giant screamed.

As Manny hurtled toward the Guardian, the shimmering outline of a skull swung toward him. Manny leaped onto Wat Ho's chest then lunged. The dagger bit into something solid and, in less than an instant, its harness turned to ice. The cold penetrated Manny's leg and shoulder before he was flung against the shelter's wall. His ribs connected with a thick root, and he landed in a breathless heap.

Wat Ho engaged in a tug of war with a barely visible foe. Slowly, their fingers opened. A scream, harsher than the first, ended abruptly and the Guardian's arms flopped to their sides. The air was stirred by invisible wings and a shadow flickered through the hole in the roof. A taunting cry reached Manny's ears. He felt his blood freeze.

Manny cautiously limped across the shelter. "¿*Está muerto?* He watched the rise and fall of Wat Ho's chest. "No," he said at last, "Not dead. But something was torn out of you." Tears of rage sprang to his eyes as he undid the ties to his dagger and flicked the weapon away. "I failed you . . . just as I failed my village. I am worthless!"

Hoof plumbed depths he didn't know he had as he raced to reach Wat Ho. But Starr Knightly, pulling a cart carrying Pete, the Head and four bags of supplies, pulled ahead. They had disappeared around a curve when he heard Pete call, "The campsite is just past this bridge."

Oh. Thank. Gorme. By the time Hoof reached the bridge, Starr was out of her harness. Not a speck of dirt had touched her flawless coat. He peeked at his reflection; he was a mass of mud and burrs.

Pete hopped off the cart. The Head threw Bag O'Bounty at him, almost knocking him into the stream. Starr shot him a sympathetic glance before swinging a pair of saddlebags onto her back.

"Hey Donkey," called The Head, "Come here." Hoof trotted over. "Closer!" snapped The Head as she grabbed Hoof's ear and pulled him right up to the cart. Before he could protest, she slung a set of saddlebags on his back and slapped his rump. "Move along, now!"

The Head climbed down and slid the cart's shafts under the cart. She tripped a lever, then pulled on one side of the cart while pushing on the other. The cart folded flat and fell on its side with a thump. "Take the cart and lead the way" she said to Pete as she relieved him of Bag O'Bounty. He wrestled the cart upright with one paw and slowly struggled up the hill.

Manny's head shot up at the clunk of a hoof on stone. "What am I doing?" he cried. "I swore to stand guard. *Que la Diosa* permits me to die trying!" He put his weapon back on and prepared to make a stand. But he was not prepared for the mechanical monstrosity that burst into the clearing. *"¿Qué clase de demonio es este?"*

"Hey, Manny," panted Pete as he stepped out from behind the flattened cart. "We're back!"

Starr emerged from the trees. *"¡Ai Caramba!"* exclaimed Manny. *"¿Más burros?"*

Manny was left speechless when the Head stepped out of the woods. Which lasted until Hoof arrived to shatter the spell.

"What's up, dawg?" he brayed.

Manny tore his eyes away from the squat, gnomish creature whose impossibly thin arms encircled a bag-shaped carpet. "You're back too?" he growled. "I hoped they'd traded you for a better model."

"Glad to see you too!" Hoof replied. "How's Wat Ho?"

Hoof's question was ignored as Manny hurried off to put himself between The Head and the fallen tree. She inspected him if he were a museum exhibit. An arm snaked out and she gripped his leg. "Well, aren't you a clever boy!" she cooed as she inspected his harness.

Manny tugged and twisted, but the creature's grip was like a vice. He nipped at her hand. "Nuh huh!" said the creature. "None of that! Here's what will happen: I let go, you behave and later, we share some chimichangas and become friends! Okay?"

"Never!" barked Manny. "Wait! Did you say chimichangas?" His eyes narrowed. *"¿De carne o de frijoles?"*

"Both," replied The Head. "Of course!"

The Head released Manny's paw and ducked into Wat Ho's cave. "This won't do," she muttered. "This won't do at all."

~~~

Pete, Starr, Hoof and The Head had dragged Wat Ho into the open. The Head stood on tiptoe, waving a metal wand over the Guardian's chest.

Several wires ran from the wand to a box that sat on the ground. More wires went from the box to a helmet that fit over her ears.

The Head's expression, or as much of it as could be seen beneath her enormous spectacles and the floppy earpieces of the helmet, was grim. She adjusted a dial on the box. A few beats later she shrugged, tore off the helmet and, in the same motion, slapped her pointy hat back on her head.

"Well?" Pete demanded.

The Head's spectacles magnified the sadness in her eyes. "I'm afraid it's gone."

"What's gone?" brayed Hoof.

"A piece of their lifeforce," replied The Head. "A Guardian's lifeforce is like what some creatures call a soul. A big part of this one was torn out. The part that's left has lost the will to go on."

Manny whimpered. "A monster came," he said. "It was like a shadow, but solid. It was made of ice, I think. The monster hurt *Abuele* Wat, then flew away." He hung his head. "I failed to stop it."

"Yes," said The Head, staring down at him. "It is good you told me this." She seized Wat Ho's right paw and turned it over. Burned into the palm was the image of a dragon. "Fire and Ice," she murmured. "Just so did the old fool open a door for the enemy."

~~~

The contents of The Head's medicine chest gleamed with metal and glass. She pulled out a flexible mask that surrounded a rigid tube. When she thrust one end of the tube into Wat Ho's mouth the mask molded to their face, fitting as if it had been glued in place. Next, she removed a glass bulb filled with swirling mist. One end of the bulb narrowed to a tube, slightly larger than the one on the mask.

"So, you're sure that stuff will work?" demanded Hoof.

"No," replied The Head.

"What? Then why are you doing it?"

"It's the only thing I *can* do!" snapped The Head. "This body is dying. And if it does, the Guardian will be unable to return. *Ever!*"

She pushed the narrow end of the bulb onto the mask's tube, breaking its seal. The mist thinned as it was drawn into Wat Ho's lungs. Wat Ho's fingers twitched. Two breaths later their eyes flew open, and a giant paw slapped at the glass bulb. The bulb, with the mask still attached, flew across the campsite. A shriek blasted from their wide-open maw. Then their eyes closed, and they lay still.

"That's it?" said Hoof. "What difference did that make?"

"It made every difference," said The Head. "Look!"

Hoof looked. Wat Ho's chest rose and fell with deep, even breaths. Then Hoof's eyes drifted up to Wat Ho's slack, expressionless face and skittered away again. "They're just sleeping, right?" he demanded.

"The body is resting, yes," replied The Head.

"And they're going to wake up? Soon?"

The Head's skinny shoulders lifted in a shrug. "The shell lives," she replied. "If and when the spirit will return to it? That I cannot say."

~ 7 ~

The Head reached for Wat Ho's ward. "Stop!" Hoof brayed, "You don't . . ." He closed his eyes; waited for the explosion; waited some more; cautiously opened them again.

"What?" The Head stared at him over her spectacles.

"But how? Why didn't?" Hoof shook his head. "Never mind."

"You really are eloquence incarnate, aren't you?"

"Am not!" Hoof retorted.

The Head collected Wat Ho's wards and Starr set new ones. Then the ladies reorganized the campsite; Pete was put to work repairing the soggy fire pit; Hoof pranced around, dreamily sweeping the campsite with a bundle of twigs; Manny scraped wet bark off the firewood. *Too much smoke makes the food bitter,* the scary lady had said.

Hoof spat out the makeshift broom and sighed. "What's it called when you feel sad and happy at the same time?"

"Sappy?" snarked Pete.

~~~

When the fire had burned down, the Head balanced a grate on the firepit and spread out the chimichangas to toast over the coals. As if by magic, they had retained their original crispness.

Hoof snapped up a bean and cheese filled roll. "Hee-uh!" he gasped as scalding beans squirted on his tongue. He sucked air through his mouth and tilted his forehead toward the ground. A mass of molten cheese dropped onto his palate. "Hee-ow!" Mooing in pain, he galloped off to thrust his face into the stream. *Oh, sweet relief!*

~~~

Unwilling to risk being laughed at, Hoof sulked by the stream. He dozed off and on, until the sound of light hoofsteps got him scrambling upright. Starr set down a bucket.

"Mr. Hearted," she said, with a prim wrinkling of her lip.

"Ms. Knightly," Hoof replied, with a formal waggle of his jaw.

"I hope this will work out better for you," she said.

Hoof eyed the bucket warily. "Donkey Chow?"

"Uh-huh," she replied.

"The stuff the rats wouldn't eat?"

Starr giggled. "Brigita wards the pantry against rodents, so the rats don't have much choice."

"Who's Brigita?" Hoof asked.

Starr wrinkled her forehead at him. "My Mistress, of course!"

"Oh!" Hoof's mouth fell open. "But she's a bald ape!" he exclaimed, "Isn't she?" He considered that. "Sort of? A Hooved Folk in thrall to bald apes is . . .is . . . *unnatural!*"

Starr's nostrils flared. "I am not 'in thrall!' Brigita is a great mage, and I am proud to be her apprentice. And I am sick to death of the prejudice and distrust among The Folk. It has to stop!"

Hoof stared at her, too stunned to speak.

"Good night, Mr. Hearted!" Starr snapped as she turned to go.

"Wait!" said Hoof, relenting. "Please!"

Starr did not turn around. "I have nothing to say to you," she said, her tone cold enough to form a skin of ice on the stream.

Hoof groaned. "My whole life I've been told that things are a certain way. When your Grandsire is the 'great' Donkie Otie . . ."

Starr gasped, then spun around to face him. "You're a descendent of Donkie Otie!"

"Guilty as charged," Hoof acknowledged.

"The Donkie Otie?" she whispered.

41

"The one and only."

"Oh, you poor dear!"

"Not the reaction I was expecting!"

A nervous look crossed Starr's face and she began to edge away. "Should I worry about being alone with you?"

"No. At least I don't think so. Why?"

"Well . . . your Grandsire had quite a reputation."

"Yeah, I know," Hoof replied. "He was a great hero!"

Starr burst out laughing.

"What's so funny," asked Hoof.

Starr's laughter died. "Wait. You were serious? Oh my!"

"Of course I was serious! Donkey Otie was probably the biggest hero to travel the Northern Realm."

"The biggest . . ." Starr hesitated. "What do you know about Donkie Otie? I mean, really."

"I know that he was Brave. And Strong. And Heroic," said Hoof.

Starr fixed Hoof with an incredulous stare. He looked away and his eyes zeroed in on the Donkey Chow. *I can't eat now! I'd look like a jerk!* His stomach begged to differ. He took a bite. *Tasty!* He glanced at Starr, then back to the bucket. *Well, just one more bite.* Any thought of his Grandsire, or anything else, fled his mind.

"Ouch!" Hoof's peeling tongue had rasped against the bottom of the pail. "Sorry," he said. "I was hungrier than I thought."

"I'm glad you could choke it down," laughed Starr.

~~~

A full moon competed with the stars that they could see above the stream. Starr sighed. "I never get to see this anymore. It's beautiful!"

"Yeah, it sure is," said Hoof, whose gaze was fixed on Starr.

Starr shot him a glance, then shyly looked away. "You're being silly!" she laughed.

Hoof broke the spell. "How do you know my Grandsire?"

The silence got awkward. "I don't," Starr said at last. "My mother encountered him when she was young. Barely older than me."

"And . . ." Hoof prompted.

"Mr. Hearted," Starr began. "Hoof . . . may I call you Hoof?"

"Please do . . . Starr." He rolled the Rs over his peeling tongue.

"Thank you. Hoof. Hearted." She giggled. Then she grew serious. "What do you really know about your grandsire?"

"Only what Mother told me," said Hoof. "I'd like to hear one of your stories about him. Please?"

Starr sighed. "I think this is a very bad idea but, since you insist, I'll tell you a story that is kind of important to me.

Donkey Otie and the Innocent Jennet

Spring had spread its delicate green fingers across the land. Rejoicing in the end of a long, cold winter, Starshine Brightly was outdoors, reveling in the fresh air. Her freshly brushed golden coat gleamed in the sunlight.

Starr glanced at Hoof. "That's my mother." She wriggled her shoulders in a very distracting manner. "I get my coloring from her." Hoof gulped but said nothing. Starr resumed . . .

Starshine was surprised (but not displeased) to spy a stranger on the lane that crossed the family estate. As he drew closer, she saw he was a tall, lean-muscled Jack. He seemed closer to middle age than youth yet was not totally lacking in appeal. Starshine shyly curled her upper lip in welcome. She could not know how this innocent act would change her life. All because of a wandering stranger and the foolish thrall that trotted behind him, choking on his dust."

"Paunchy Stanza!" Hoof blurted.

"Excuse me?" said Starr.

"Grandsire's squire was called Paunchy Stanza."

"Really?" said Starr. "I never knew that."

"Well, what did you call him?" asked Hoof.

"Dumbass, mostly," replied Starr. "Oh, I'm sorry!" she exclaimed. "It wasn't me. Really! I wasn't even born yet!"

"It's okay. Neither was I," said Hoof. He waited for Starr to go on.

The Jack got a glimpse of Starshine and pulled up so quickly that Dumb . . .

"Oh!" Starr exclaimed. "I mean . . . Fatso? No, that's not it!"

"Paunchy," supplied Hoof, helpfully.

"Yes, him," said Starr. "I'm terrible at telling stories!"

"Please go on," said Hoof "I promise to stop interrupting."

The thrall was not paying attention (or was blinded by the dust) and ran into his master's backside. The Jack slashed out a back leg and the thrall dropped like a sack of oats.

Starshine was appalled. She gathered her wits about her and trotted (as quickly as good breeding and dignity allowed) to the fence. Her groom scrambled after her; it was worth his job to leave his mistress alone with a stranger.

'Sirrah!' she politely but firmly exclaimed (because a lady is never shrill or shouty.) 'You are within the boundaries of Fair'Nuff Stuff Farm. An Estate that does not tolerate the abuse of thralls, servants, or any other Working Folk!'

The stranger angled an incredulous eye at his thrall. 'Who, him?' he exclaimed. 'But he affronted the backside of the Great Donkie Otie. It was not to be tolerated!'

'Horace!' Starshine called the groom hovering behind her.

The groom, whose name was Bruce, checked to confirm no creature else was within earshot. "Yes Mistress?" he replied.

'Please attend to that creature,' she demanded.

'A-t-t-tend to him, Mistress?' stammered the groom.

'Yes, please,' Starshine insisted. 'Surely you know what is needed. You are of the same species, are you not?'

44

The groom approached Donkie Otie—who glared at him from beneath beetled brows—with caution. He didn't know whether to watch out for Donkie Otie's back end, which had shown its ability to inflict harm, or the end that was chewing on a stubby sword.

Another groom stepped out of the stables and came to investigate. 'Horace?' said Starshine as he approached.

'Yes, Mistress?' he replied.

"If you're Horace, then who is that other one?" she sniffed. 'Oh never mind! Just go help take that fellow up to the servants' quarters and clean him up.'

Donkie Otie's eyes darted from his thrall to the grooms, then back to Starshine. He brayed with laughter.

'I see through your ruse, My Pretty!' he cried with a lecherous baring of his teeth. 'A clever trap indeed, sprung to keep me by your side. And what a shapely young side it is! Donkie Otie places himself at your service, be it for the span of a breath, a day or a season entire!'

In spite of herself, Starshine's vanity was tickled. Feeling her ears blush, she turned to nibble at some green shoots. Donkie Otie was not fooled. His eyes gleamed wickedly as he sidled up to the fence. Starshine glanced at him, looked away, then couldn't help but look back and stare.

The grooms left, carrying out Starshine's command to take the bald ape to the servants' quarters. She was left alone with the relentless Donkie Otie and was doomed . . .

"No! Please stop!" Hoof cried. "I don't want to hear any more!"

Starr stood. "I'm sorry I upset you. Yes, our families tell different stories from each other. But they're just stories: None are completely true; none are totally false." After a few beats she added, "It's been a long day, and we both have to get some sleep."

45

"Burromph!" Hoof opened a bleary eye; squinted at a bullfrog bobbing in front of his nose; closed the eye. *"BURRROMPH!"* He blew out a loud sigh that sent the frog tumbling into the stream. Struggling upright, he touched his tongue to the roof of his mouth; played with a flap of palate that had been cooked by molten cheese. He leaned over the water and stuck out his tongue.

"I guess you could look more *estúpido*. But how I do not know." Hoof cast a baleful eye in Manny's direction as the Chihuahua hobbled to the stream's edge and noisily lapped at the water.

Hoof lowered his head to drink, only to bump noses with the frog. The frog climbed onto the bank, took a few hops, then stared at Hoof. Hoof stepped forward. The frog hopped a little farther, then looked back. *Follow it?* Hoof's curiosity was aroused. *Why not?*

Masses of thorny bushes lining the edge of the stream soon caused Hoof to have second thoughts. He was about to turn back when his guide turned to stare out over the water.

Hoof tracked where its eyes were pointing and gasped. "What in Gorme's name is that?"

"Burromph!" replied the frog.

"I know, right?" exclaimed Hoof. At the stream's center, a wondrous creature hovered on gossamer wings that reflected every color of the rainbow. Then Hoof realized that it wasn't hovering; one wing was impaled on a stake! The other wing beat feebly, keeping the creature just above the water.

"Burromph?" said the frog, hopefully.

Be Brave, Strong and Heroic! Hoof was about to plunge into the stream when he flashed back to the last time he did that. He lowered a hoof. It sank into the ooze. He pulled back and, with a wet, sucking sound, the muck grudgingly released him. *But not stupid!*

"Burromph?" whined the frog.

"Yeah," Hoof agreed. "Something has to be done. But what?"

His eyes settled on a log that was stranded a few paces upstream. *If* he could free that log, and *if* it floated under his weight, and *if* he could guide it safely downstream . . . so many *ifs*. But it was the only hope the stranded creature had.

"Hoof the Headstrong to the rescue!" he chuckled, as he broke into a trot. His head banged into the log. The log was unimpressed. He backed up for a longer run, lowered his head and charged. The log rocked up, then stubbornly rolled back. Hoof stumbled away as the world began to spin around him.

"Don't just bang your head against the thing!" he chided himself as he waited for his vision to clear. "You're not Donkie Otie!"

Slow and steady, that's the way. He put his forehead against the log and churned his hooves, kicking up a spray of debris. His nose slipped into a mass of rotting leaves, but he kept going. The log rolled up out its hollow, then tumbled into the stream.

Hoof sneezed, clearing debris from his nostrils. He climbed onto the log. His legs slipped off the sides and he landed with a painful thump. Somehow, he managed to stay upright.

"Burromph!" cheered the frog. *"Burromph! Burromph! Burromph!"* The stream came alive with frogs! They surrounded the log and, kicking in unison, pushed it towards the trapped being. Hoof lowered his head then, when he felt tiny hands grab his ears, slowly lifted it up until the being was clear of the stake.

He managed to stay upright as the frogs energetically guided the log to a patch of gravel from which he scrambled up the bank. As soon as he lowered his head the winged creature slid down his nose to land on solid ground.

I will heal now, a voice whispered out of nowhere.

Hoof stared, dumbfounded, as the tear in the creature's wing sealed shut. "W-who . . . what . . . who are you?" he stammered.

The being rose up, scattering the sunlight into flights of rainbow-colored arrows. *Our name matters not, Hoof Hearted. But know that you are a true hero, and we owe you much. We will reward you with a wish. Choose well!*

Hoof was too stunned to wonder how the creature knew his name. "A-a-a wish?" he stammered. "What sort of wish?"

That's for you to decide. But you must make haste!

Hoof thought quickly. "I don't know if you can help, but I wish my friend Wat Ho would wake up. We're worried about them!"

The being rose higher into the sky. *Hoof Hearted, you ask much! But it is a noble wish, and We shall strive to honor it. For you are destined to be a true Hero who will not be forgotten. But now you must forget all that happened here.*

Hoof snorted in disbelief, "You're joking, right? No way am I going to . . ." His protest was cut short by a puff of wind that blew some grit into his eyes.

~~~

Hoof opened his eyes. He was beside a stream and, except for some bullfrogs hopping towards the water, he was alone. Panic threatened to overwhelm him until an inner voice hissed, *Breathe! If you want to be a hero, act like one!* He pushed his panic down to a manageable level, then turned in a circle.

"I must have walked in my sleep . . ." A new wave of anxiety caused him to spin around twice more. *Think! Then act.* He shook his head. "Huh! That's new!"

The wind teased the wet hair on Hoof's belly. "I'm wet! If I crossed the stream, then the camp is on the other side." As he was about to step into the water, a flurry of *burromphs* assaulted his ears. A mass of frogs formed an arrow that pointed at him, then rotated to angle downstream. "I've got to get out of here!" Hoof crashed through the brambles, heading downstream.

The Guardian floated in a void—feeling nothing, registering nothing: not even absence. There was no sound. The Guardian had no perception of having a body; had no sense of having any substance at all. That belonged to another time and place, a place of loss and loneliness. Here there was only blessed nothingness . . .

The Guardian sensed a presence. Resisted. Moments later the presence faded into the nothingness and was no more . . . Again the Guardian sensed a presence. Closer now. Too close. And there was something else. Was that sound? But it too faded away . . .

A sound came; repeated over and over. It was vaguely . . . what? Familiar? Almost, the Guardian was drawn toward it; at the last moment pulled back, rejecting it. The sound faded into the distance . . .

A voice called out. It shouted the same thing, over and over: *Guardian? Guardian? Guardian?* It stirred up a vague sense of irritation: a grain of sand to an oyster. The Guardian struggled to attach meaning to those sounds. But too soon, the voice faded and was gone . . .

Something stabbed into the Guardian's brain. It was as if a blinding light shone through their skull. The Guardian resisted; tried to block it out; tried to squeeze shut nonexistent eyes. "Do not do that, Guardian!" urged a gentle voice. "Do not try to pull away. It took an army to find you, and we are not letting you go. You have friends who care about you and a job that needs to be done. Go back to your borrowed body and get on with it."

~~~

Wat Ho woke. He blinked at a patch of blue sky surrounded by a green canopy. For the first time in a very long time, his mind was entirely his own. The loneliness cut through him like a knife. He drew a shuddering breath. Then silently, hopelessly, he began to sob.

Pete stared, then hesitantly whispered, "Wat Ho?"

The Guardian drew a breath; swiped a paw across his muzzle. His reddened eyes turned to the macaque. "Hello . . ." he hesitated, as if searching for a memory. "Hello . . . Pete." His eyes drifted shut.

"You're awake!" Pete exclaimed. "I'll get Ms. Brigita."

"No!" Wat Ho exclaimed. "No," he repeated. "This body has been healed as much as it can be. It was well done."

"I'm glad," said Pete. "And you, Lady Ho? Are you okay too?"

The Guardian's eyes closed. After several beats he whispered, "She is gone. There is a gaping wound where she was torn away."

"Oh no!" exclaimed Pete. "That's horrible! What will you do?"

"My duty." The Guardian lifted his head and ran his eyes over the campsite. He tried to sit up, gasped, and fell back. "Hoof Hearted!" A twinge of panic touched his voice as he asked, "Was he harmed?"

"No," Pete replied. "He's okay. We all are."

The Guardian gazed up at the tree canopy. "Good," he said at last. He closed his eyes. "That is good." After another lengthy silence, he added, "This body is weak. It needs nourishment."

"No surprise there," said Pete. "You've been unconscious for ages! I'll get the others and see if we can get you sitting up and fed."

~ *8* ~

Burr-covered and breathless, Hoof practically fell into the camp site. Five heads turned to stare at him, but his wide eyes were glued to the Guardian. *What? How? When?* A laugh tickled Hoof's ear. He spun around to confront—nothing. He shuddered, then turned back to the others.

"So, erm, what's for breakfast?" he brayed.

~~~

Wat Ho tired of Hoof's persistent questions. "Enough idle chitchat!" he snapped. He finished his honey-laced tea, surged to his feet, and collapsed. Brigita laid a hand on his shoulder.

"Don't get up," she said. "You must recover your strength."

Tears sprang to the giant's eyes. "It's no use! My partner . . . *she* is my strength. She breathes poetry into my life. And now she's gone! It was my fault; I made us vulnerable."

Brigita shook her head. "I saw the damage. Your partner . . ."

". . . lives!" Wat Ho shuddered. "I feel her pain, but I can do nothing." He laughed bitterly as he swiped at his cheeks. "Truthfully, I don't know what I can do about anything! It was long since last we were called, and this body is so huge . . . I can't control it on my own."

~~~

They broke camp the next morning. Wat Ho resentfully perched on the heavily laden cart. Hoof and Starr teamed up to pull it. They travelled all day, pausing only for a cold lunch. Just out of sight of the town gates, Brigita called a halt.

51

"Starr and I must go our separate way," she said.

"What?" brayed Hoof, "Why?"

"The Mage is right," said Wat Ho. He dropped Sack O'Stuff onto the road and stiffly climbed down after it. "We must not complicate things for her."

"But why?" Hoof brayed. He leaped out of his traces and turned his glare on Brigita; it bounced harmlessly off her spectacles. Starr came up to stand in front of him.

"Goodbye, Mr. Hearted," she said, delicately baring her teeth.

Hoof's ears drooped. "Will I see you again?" he asked.

"I don't know, Hoof. We may meet again." Her voice hardened as she added, "But I'm studying to be a Mage, so we can't ever be more than friends. You'd be better off forgetting all about me."

"I'll never forget you!" Hoof protested. "Never ever!"

"I won't forget you either," Starr replied.

Pete had used the time to adjust the cart's traces. Starr stepped into them and trotted briskly away. Brigita rocked in the cart behind her. Neither of them looked back.

Manny joined the others as they watched the cart round the next bend. Pete cut an eye toward the Chihuahua. "Give me your dagger. The Bulls don't like strangers carrying weapons around town."

Manny flicked off his weapon. Pete tucked it into his backpack, next to Hoof's sword.

"Okay then," said Pete. "Shall we move on?"

Wat Ho picked up Sack O'Stuff, grunted, then let the sack fall to the road. He sank down, cradling his head on his arms.

"Are you okay?" asked Pete. "Dumb question—you're not."

"I'm fine," Wat Ho unconvincingly replied. "A bit dizzy, is all. Just let me sit for a while and I'll be good to go."

Hoof stepped forward. "I can carry Sack O'Stuff."

"Do you think so?" Wat Ho sounded doubtful, "It's a big load."

"No problem!" said Hoof, with a confidence he didn't feel. "I'm stronger than I look."

"Is good you did not say smarter," mocked Manny, "because that would be a big fib!"

Wat Ho spread a folded blanket over Hoof's back and tied it in place with several passes of rope. Then he picked up Sack O'Stuff with both paws and hoisted it onto the blanket. "Hee-uh!" said Hoof as, with an effort, he locked his knees. "See," he wheezed as he stiff legged it down the road. "No problem!"

~~~

"I don't get it," panted Hoof. "Your Sack makes anything you want, right? When you want?"

"More or less," replied Wat Ho.

"So why not dump the old stuff and replace it when you need it?"

"You'd be sorry."

"Because of the trash you'd leave behind?" Hoof guessed.

"There's that," Wat Ho agreed. "But mainly, you just can't do it. What you take out is replaced by an equal magical mass. When it's put back, most of that mass goes to another dimension. If it's left behind, the Sack stays heavy. Before long you wouldn't be able to lift it."

They reached the town gate. A faded sign hung crookedly over it. "What's that say?" asked Hoof.

"Welcome! You have reached Rock Bottom." Wat Ho replied.

"Yeah," said Hoof. "That totally fits."

~~~

They carried on into the town, with the Guardian attracting more than a few startled glances. A pair of Brahman strolled up, swinging their heads from side to side. They looked the Guardian over but said nothing. One of them gave a slight nod as he lumbered by.

Pete peered down each side street they crossed. "Yes!" he sang out at last. "That's what we're looking for!" He waved at a decrepit building whose sign displayed a pawful of playing cards.

"How's that different form every other run-down shack around here," Hoof peevishly asked.

"If the sign does not deceive me," Pete replied, "that is a public house in which one might find a friendly game of chance. And games of chance (friendly or otherwise) are what I live on."

The inside of the tavern was as dingy as its outside. A surly bald ape was behind the bar, wiping a dirty mug with an even dirtier cloth. Wat Ho loomed over him and eyed the mug doubtfully.

"We'll pass on ordering drinks," he rumbled, "but we'll sit down for a while. I trust you have no objections?" The barkeep gulped, then shook his head.

As Wat Ho swung Sack O'Stuff onto a nearby table, a nearly toothless bald ape raised a chipped mug in salute. "Welcome to the backside of Rock Bottom," he cackled.

Hoof stared. "I know that uniform! You're an Imperial Guard!"

The bald ape looked down at his stained, tattered vest. "So I was," he chuckled, "in another life." He buried his nose in his mug. When he came up for air he waved at the chairs surrounding his table. "Why don't you join me?"

"Thank you, friend," said Wat Ho. He pushed a chair out of the way and dragged a bench over to replace it. "Let's make ourselves comfortable," he added as he spread Hoof's packsaddle out on the bench. Hoof gratefully flopped down on it while Wat Ho pulled up a sturdy stool for himself.

"Pleased to meet you, soldier," he said as he settled down on the stool. "I go by the name of Wat Ho. And my young companion here is Mr. Hearted. His friends and acquaintances call him Hoof."

The old guardsman chuckled. "I'm Gabriel Oldeman, but mostly I'm called Gabby. For reasons that will become obvious." He stared into his empty mug. "Could you stand an old veteran to a drink?"

"Sorry," said Wat Ho. "Money is something I can't do."

"I've got some coins!" said Hoof. A panicked look crossed his face as he felt for his purse. "Oh, yeah," he remembered. "Pete has them."

He crossed to where Pete was playing cards with three other primates. His empty sling hung down his chest as he dealt a round of cards. Regaling his fellow players with an off-color story didn't affect the speed with which the cards flew out of his paws.

"Um, Pete?" said Hoof.

"Busy!" replied Pete.

Hoof waited until Pete had finished dealing. "Pete?" he tried again.

"Still busy!" Pete replied as he peeked at his hole cards.

"I need my purse," Hoof insisted, speaking firmly.

"Purse?" said Pete vaguely, as he drummed his fingers on the table.

"Yes, my purse," said Hoof. "Which is in your backpack."

"Was," said Pete.

"What?" said Hoof.

"*Was* in my backpack," Pete clarified.

"Well, where is it now?" Hoof brayed.

"Um . . ." Pete made a show of looking around. "Over there?" he said, waving at a nearby table.

Hoof nosed through a pile of banana peels and peanut shells until he found his purse. "Um, Pete?" he said.

"Busy!" said Pete, who was dealing another round.

"Pete!" brayed Hoof, causing the other players to glare at him. The baboon muttered to the Barbary ape on his left, while the chimpanzee sullenly picked something out of her ear and ate it.

Pete slapped his palms down on the table. "What?" he snapped.

"Where's my money?" asked Hoof.

"In the pot," Pete replied, waving at the pile of coins and other objects in the center of the table.

"In the . . ." Hoof froze. "Why is my sword on the table?"

"Borrowed it," said Pete. "Donkie Otie's one hundred percent authentic sword got me into the game." He shot Hoof a glance. "Relax! You'll get it back as soon as I've won this round."

"You . . . you . . ." Hoof stammered. "Why . . . what right . . ."

"Look kid," growled the baboon. "If you're not playing, get lost!"

~~~

Hoof stormed to his bench, flung himself down and blew out a gust of air. Manny hobbled up behind him and stepped on Wat Ho's foot. Wat Ho scooped him up and set him on the table.

Gabby peered at the dog. "You look like you've been to the wars, son," he observed, with a nod toward Manny's missing paw.

Manny's bulging eyes raked the old soldier's face. "No *Señor,*" he barked. "Not yet. But soon, yes!"

"Manny, this is Mr. Gabriel Oldeman," said Wat Ho. "Mr. Oldeman, this is our companion, *Señor* Manuel Sobad."

"Buenas noches, Señor Oldeman," said Manny. "It is a great honor to meet a true warrior."

The old timer's high-pitched cackle dissolved into a wheezing cough. "That I never was, young sir. I'm just a rundown ex-guard."

"In fact," interjected Wat Ho, "Mr. Oldeman is about to tell us how his career as an Imperial Guard came to an untimely end."

"Well," Gabby said, "you know the Cows revolted, right?"

"Yeah," said Hoof. "They got fed up with Old King Harry drafting their tradescreatures to go build towers up north."

"Exactly." Gabby picked up his mug; put it down again. "They hired mercenaries to get rid of the King. Getting the daft old Horse out of the way was a piece of cake. Literally! An extra-smart ape waved a carrot cake under his nose, and he followed it right out to pasture."

Gabby met Wat Ho's eyes, then looked away. "I was guarding the Royal Stables when they led His Highness away. This silverback shot me one look and I stood down. That's what a hero I was!"

He pushed his mug from hand to hand. "The Old King's last days were his happiest! He wandered Majestic Acres, knighting farm implements and ordering the beheading of garden vegetables. He really hated brussels sprouts!" Gabby snorted. "Can't say I blame him.

"Sidelining the Old King was easy. The hard part was replacing him. Some loons wanted to pick their own leader!"

Hoof snorted, "Birds picking a leader? That's hilarious!"

Pete dropped Hoof's sword and purse on the table. "Here's your stuff. Your purse is fatter than it was. *Way* fatter!" Hoof ignored him. He threw up his paws and stormed back to his game.

Wat Ho cleared his throat. "So The Realm was leaderless?"

"Nearly. Whoever had the biggest army got to choose The Boss. Of course, they all chose themselves. But because of the plague, which army was biggest changed all the time."

Gabby eyed his empty mug. "All this talking is thirsty work!" he complained. He eyed Hoof's purse. "Did I hear you've now got a coin to spare a loyal old soldier?"

"Sure, help yourself," said Hoof. *You won't be the first!*

"If you insist," said Gabby, who was already digging in the purse. He gasped, clutched a coin in his fist and walked, with careful dignity, to the bar. "Barkeep!" he called as he slapped the coin down on the counter. "A mug of the Harvest Ale, if you please."

The bartender did a double take. He picked up the coin, held it up to the light of a smoky lantern, then bit it. Satisfied, he went to a small keg that occupied pride of place behind the bar.

"A full measure, if you please," said Gabby. "In a clean mug!"

The bartender scowled, but he got a large mug from under the bar and filled it with dark, frothy liquid he drew from the keg. He slammed the mug down, slopping suds onto the bar. Gabby swiped his fingers through the spill and licked them.

"Yep, that's the good stuff!" he crowed. "Give yourself a copper bit and put the rest on my tab."

~~~

Gabby resumed his story: "So Jumbo Wiseacre got the wannabe leaders together in what we now call the Temple of Divine Selection. He gave them each a club and told them to spent the night in 'silent contemplation' until the rooster crowed. After which they beat on each other until one was 'divinely selected' as the Supreme Leader.

"A new Leader is 'selected' every second tridecalunium. That's the thirteenth new moon between midwinter eves," he explained. "They happen every two or three winters, so the selections are usually five winters apart. The winner is called 'Regent of the Realm' and technically stands in for the next King." He snorted. "Like we'll ever have another one of those!"

"That is a novel way to select a leader," said Wat Ho.

"In theory, the creature with the best battle skills—and so best able to defend the Realm—will win." Gabby took a sip of ale. "In reality, the biggest, dumbest blockhead wins, while any candidate with the brains of a turnip ends up as a greasy spot on the arena floor."

Gabby gestured with his mug, spilling some ale on the table. He stared at the waste in horror, then quickly downed enough ale to ensure the sacrilege would not be repeated.

"But that's terrible!" Hoof exclaimed. "Leaders are supposed to be smart, and brave and . . . and . . . stuff. Not just strong."

Gabby let out a mirthless cackle. "In your dreams, youngster!" he said. "But it's okay." He lowered his voice. "By the second time around, the rules were changed so sensible citizens could pick a champion to represent them. Any creature with at least as many backers as they have fingers and toes can take part in the process."

58

"Fingers and toes?" asked Hoof. "Why not twenty?"

"If a creature can qualify by lopping off a few digits, who's going to stop them?"

"Ew!" exclaimed Hoof. "That's gross! And where does that leave hooved creatures?"

"Any hooved creature foolish enough to mount a challenge qualifies automatically. Not many do. The Herds control one of the two factions that mostly run things, so why bother." Gabby took a pull from his mug. "The other faction," he added as he waggled the fingers of his nonbeer-drinking hand, "looks out for the rest of us.

"To keep things on the up-and-up, the Gentry appoint an 'Electoral Council' to oversee the Selection. Of course, the Council is split into the same factions. Half the time they're busy trying to dope out their opponents' weaknesses. Obviously, no sentient creature is going to back a candidate that can't be bribed or blackmailed into doing their bidding! But when all is said and done, the Council installs whatever creature wins."

He shook the last drops of ale into his mouth and banged the mug down. "That hit the spot!" His face scrunched up, then brightened. "Hey! This is a Tridecalunium year. With the next moon cycle, we'll have a new Supreme Leader!" He pulled a face. "Or the same old one. Who knows?"

~ 9 ~

The barbary ape and the baboon folded. Mabel the chimpanzee's red-rimmed eyes bored into Pete as he checked his hole cards. He nodded and Mabel turned over the Savannah: a black rhino, followed by a blue rhino, then a white eight.

Pete drummed the table with his fingers, then added ten silver coins to the pot. He sat back, whistling through his teeth.

The chimp bared her teeth, called Pete's bet and turned over the Forest: a black eight. Pete sighed and counted out the minimum raise. The chimp hooted and went all in. Pete shrugged, then matched her bet. The Stream was turned over: A red eight.

The chimp flipped over a blue eight from her hole. "Four eights!" she crowed. "Read them and weep!" She lunged for the pot.

Pete clamped a paw on her wrist. "Hold on there, Mabel!" he said. "Let's see what I have." He turned over a white rhino, then a red rhino. "Well, I'll be!" he said. "It looks like my four big old rhinos beat the poo out of your eights!"

As he scraped his winnings into his backpack, Pete's neck prickled at the hot breath of a crowd gathering behind him. "Drinks on me!" he yelled, flinging a fistful of coins over his shoulder.

He used the distraction to run for it, with most of Mabel's hooting, screeching fan club in hot pursuit. The troop of chimpanzees skidded to a halt when Pete hopped up on Wat Ho's table and put the black and white giant between himself and his pursuers.

Wat Ho aimed a bemused grin at the mob. "Greetings, gentle creatures!" he rumbled. "What seems to be the problem?"

"The problem," hissed Mabel, "is that low-down, double-dealing monkey is a card cheat!"

"Yeah!" agreed a scar-faced male who was pressed up behind Mabel. "We got ways of dealing with his kind."

"That's ridiculous!" Pete protested. "Mabel dealt the last game, right? If I didn't touch the deck, how could I have cheated?"

"Listen, Bub, I know what . . ." Mabel trailed off.

"Yeah?" retorted Pete. "You know what, exactly?"

Wat Ho looked from Pete to Mabel and back. "No doubt you were both equally honest. But since my young friend was so lucky, he'll buy a round." He turned to Pete and growled, "Right?"

"Right?" said Pete doubtfully. Wat Ho's brows lowered. "Right," Pete sighed. "Barkeep," he called, "mugs of your finest for all."

As the barkeep poured mugs of Harvest Ale, Gabby somehow ended up in the chimpanzees' midst. When Pete went to settle the tab, Gabby staggered off clutching two mugs to his bony chest.

Wat Ho reattached Hoof's packsaddle, then slipped his purse and sword into Sack O'Stuff before muscling it onto the Donkey's back. He turned back to squeeze Gabby's arm. "Thank you, friend, for the companionship. We *will* meet again. Until then, keep well."

"You bet!" Gabby chirped. He drained his second mug, then said "Go to Finder's Keep. Third crossroad on the right!" He upended the empty mug on the table. "Thash the good shtuf!" he exclaimed as he slid off his stool and started to snore.

The four companions had barely reached the street when they heard an angry shout, "Hey! There's five rhinos in this deck!"

"Cool tonight," said Pete. "Makes you want to pick up the pace!"

"Where to?" gasped Hoof, struggling into a stiff-legged trot.

"I heard of a good inn," panted Wat Ho, ". . . at third crossroads."

~~~

A sign identified the inn as 'Finder's Keep.' A placard by the door stated, 'All sentient beings welcome.' To which had been added, 'except jackals!' A final addition stated in crude block letters, 'They're stinkient, not scentient!' Wat Ho read the words out loud.

"They got that right!" laughed Pete as he pushed the door open. They were met by a wall of song and laughter. Which collapsed when the Guardian ducked into the room. The thud of a tankard hitting a tabletop was the only sound to break the sudden silence.

"Greetings, gentle creatures!" called a voice like a bronze bell. "As the sign says, 'all sentient beings are welcome,' so come on in! You must qualify at least as well as this lot." A female gorilla waved at the dozen or so existing customers from behind a bar.

They crossed to the bar, where Wat Ho slid the packsaddle and Sack O'Stuff onto the gleaming floor. The gorilla pulled a lever and a platform for hooved creatures spun out. Hoof gratefully flopped down on it. He leaned his chin on the bar with an exhausted sigh.

Wat Ho sat Manny on a stool and Pete clambered up beside him. After repairing the damage to Pete's sling, Wat Ho selected a sturdy stool for himself.

The gorilla's sharp eyes took all of this in while she washed tankards and arranged them on a clean towel. Her arms stretched the length of the bar without her having to get up. When Wat Ho sat down, she put aside her cloth.

"Jawana Finder," said the gorilla.

Hoof was daydreaming about Starr Knightly "Yeah, I totally do," he sighed. "Wait, what? How'd you know that?"

"What?" asked the gorilla.

"Ho!" the Guardian cheerily replied.

The gorilla bristled with indignation. "You said what?"

"I did not," Wat Ho replied, "but you are exactly right! Wat Ho is the name I have been given. My friends here are Mister Hearted and *Señor* Sobad. The invalid is called Mr. Sake."

The gorilla relaxed. "Jawana Finder is my name. As the dirt-poor owner of this unprofitable inn, I welcome all of you!"

A baboon popped up beside Pete. "Whining about money again, Jawana?" he laughed. In a loud stage whisper he informed Pete, "She's got more gold than a Dwarfish queen. Yet she'll hold on to a copper bit like it's her first-born child." He hooted with laughter.

Jawana bared her fangs. "If a certain baboon settled their bar tab, I'd have a copper bit or two to hold! Right, Laffin?" The gorilla turned to Wat Ho. "Freeloaders!" she said. "May the gods protect us from them!" She slapped her palms on the bar and smiled. "But that's not your problem. What can I get you?"

Wat Ho rocked back, twitching with embarrassment. "I'm sorry, but I too am impecunious."

Jawana's smile slipped. "Say what?" she said.

"It means 'devoid of coin,'" the baboon clarified.

The gorilla's expression became even frostier as she growled, "I know what it means. I *don't* know what they're doing in my bar."

"Ma'am?" Pete tapped a coin on the bar. The gorilla's head pivoted toward him as he added, "I'm paying for the four of us." The baboon cleared his throat. Pete sighed. "And him."

The baboon dragged a stool next to Pete. "Y. Z. Laffin," he said, climbing up and extending a paw.

"I don't know," Pete replied. "Why?"

"Well, that's a defect we shall remedy," chortled the baboon, gripping Pete's paw. "And you are?" he added.

"Not," Pete replied.

"Not?" the baboon asked.

"Not laughing," Pete elaborated.

~~~

The companions dined well, then went to bed. Hoof was delighted to get a straw-lined stall to himself. He was snoring contentedly by the time Wat Ho finished dragging Sack O'Stuff into the stall.

Pete and Manny disappeared up the stairs that accessed the lodging provided for thralls and grooms. Wat Ho turned to follow, then shivered as a freezing draft blew in through the stable door. He pulled the door shut before heading up the stairs.

Kerosene lanterns hung at each end of a slope-ceilinged room. Two rows of four cots ran the length of the room, separated by a gap that ran under the peak of the roof. Six of the cots were occupied by strangers. Pete and Manny were snoring contentedly on the seventh cot.

The sole empty cot was next to the stairway. Wat Ho unrolled the thin mattress, then lowered himself to the edge of the cot. Ignoring the agonized squeal of the springs, he rolled onto his back. His head hit the wrought iron headboard. When he tried to scoot down, the springs emitted a loud twang and collapsed; his backside hit the floor while his toes got jammed against the sloped ceiling.

While he pondered the ways in which this was unsatisfactory, a drip hit his forehead. Squinting up at the leaking lantern, he understood why the cot was unoccupied. Jerking his head aside to avoid another drop of kerosene, he cracked his skull against the headboard.

It was not in Wat Ho's nature to curse. So, it was in steely silence that he climbed out of the cot's wreckage. He tucked his blanket under his arm and deposited the dripping lantern in an empty bucket that stood near the stairs. Then he crept down to the stable.

~ 10 ~

Where am I? Hoof looked up at a beamed ceiling that was barely visible through the gloom. *Oh yeah: Finder's Keep. With the scary yet pleasant barkeep.* He had drifted back into a pleasant dream when an arm flopped across his back.

"A-i-e-a-ie!" He rolled out from under the arm. As soon as he was upright, he kicked back hard. His hooves contacted a large body. "Hee-haw!" he bugled as he prepared to strike again.

Skittering footsteps sounded from the stairs, where Pete's legs appeared in a pool of light. He hopped down a few steps and lifted his lantern higher. "What's going on down there?"

"Yi! Yi! Yi!" Manny bounced head over tail into Pete, who rocked forward, then teetered back, smashing the lantern against a stair tread. It cracked open, sending a rivulet of flame down the stairs.

Pete grabbed Manny and leaped to a pile of fresh straw that stood next to the stairway. He gaped as the flames spread across the stairs. "Oh Gorme!" he shrieked. My backpack!" He dropped Manny and danced up the stairs, hopping from foot to paw to foot.

The burning lantern rolled to the edge of the straw. Hoof bit its handle and dragged it to the stable door. He was stopped short when the door refused to open. Three Horses, an Ox and an elderly Goat crushed against him in a mass of panicked Hooved flesh.

Wat Ho pushed through them and drove his shoulder into the door. It didn't budge. He closed his eyes. A loud *pop* startled a horse into rearing, almost crushing the Goat. Then something scraped outside the

65

door, and it flew open. The trapped creatures burst out, driving Hoof ahead of them. Manny was in their midst, dodging flailing hooves.

Wat Ho stared thoughtfully at the large tub of sand that had blocked the door. After a few deep breaths, he rocked it through the door and began flinging pawsful of sand onto the flames.

Thick smoke billowed up the stairwell, from where coughing was followed by the sound of a window banging open. Feet pounded across the attached hayshed, heading for a ladder affixed to its back wall. A few heartbeats later, two grooms burst into the stable swinging wet canvas bags. The flames were quickly beaten out.

Wat Ho's eyes shifted between the door and the tub of sand. *A trap was set; that much is clear. When next we sleep, best not be here.*

~~~

Jawana Finder entered the stable, followed by Hoof and Manny. She looked like she had been jerked out of a deep sleep and bitterly resented it. "What . . ." she stopped when the light of her lamp hit the blackened stable wall. Smoke drifted along the ceiling. "Oh. My."

Hoof cleared his throat. "A broken lantern started a fire. Wat Ho put it out." He nodded at the grooms. "Them too."

Jawana eyed the damage. "Was any creature hurt?"

Hoof, Manny and Wat Ho looked at each other. "Pete!"

Wat Ho thumped up the stairs and disappeared into the smoke. Time passed in anxious silence until he reappeared, cradling Pete in his arms. The backpack lay on the scorched remains of Pete's sling. His other paw was covered by angry red blisters. He waggled his fingers. "Gorme, that hurts!" he whimpered.

"Found . . . under his bed," Wat Ho gasped. "Blanket . . . kept out smoke." He staggered into Hoof's stall and lowered Pete to the straw. The paw that had not been protected by the sling and both feet were blistered and red. Wat Ho applied salve and loose bandages. Then he gave him something to dull the pain and help him sleep.

~~~

Holding a cloth over her face, Jawana went up to the dormitory. She came back down and collapsed onto a step. "It'll take days to clear the smoke out and clean up," she moaned.

After shaking her head a few times, she got up to join Wat Ho in gazing down at Pete. "Poor fellow! He'll have to stay put for a while, won't he?" She rested a paw on Wat Ho's forearm. "Upstairs is a mess, but feel free to use the stable as long as you need it."

"That's a very kind offer," Wat Ho replied, "but we've got to be on our way." Jawana glumly headed back to the inn.

Wat Ho turned to Manny, who was guarding Pete's backpack. "Lean it on Ye Olde Sack," he advised. "It will be safe." He trailed Hoof out to the courtyard.

Manny dragged the backpack next to Sack O'Stuff, then joined Wat Ho and Hoof. Wat Ho dropped onto a bench while Hoof went to the water trough and drank his fill.

Manny's eyes flicked from Wat Ho to the stable door. "It will be long before *Señor* Pete will be able to walk, no?"

"It will," Wat Ho agreed.

"I cannot stay," said Manny. "I must . . . I have things I must do. Things that are important. I must make haste!"

"Then we'll all move on together," said Wat Ho.

"But how?" brayed Hoof. "You can't carry that giant sack, and I can't carry it *and* Pete. We're stuck here." He suddenly thought of Starr, and the time they had spent . . . *Oh!* He cleared his throat, "Erm, maybe we could use Pete's winnings to buy a cart or something?"

Wat Ho's face split into a grin. "Now you're thinking! But use your own coin; you have a full purse."

"Oh no!" gasped Hoof. "I left my purse behind!" His eyes widened and he started to tremble. "And my sword!" he wailed.

"Relax!" said Wat Ho. "Sack O'Stuff's looking after them."

~~~

Wat Ho put Donkey Otie's sword back into Sack O'Stuff and attached Hoof's purse to the belt. "Glad to be rid of that," he said as he slipped it over Hoof's head. My kind doesn't take to money."

"Really? You seem okay with others spending money on you."

"That's the kindness of strangers: We depend on it. It's what you might call a tenet of our faith."

Hoof shook his head. "'Kindness of strangers' huh?" he snorted. "Or maybe a giant magic sack that gives you anything you want?"

"That doesn't hurt either!" grinned Wat Ho.

"Enough chitter-chattering!" barked Manny. "I need food!"

They entered Finder's Keep. Hoof nudged Wat Ho and tilted his head toward Y. Z. Laffin, who was sleeping it off in the corner. They ate at the bar, taking pains not to disturb the chatty baboon.

Manny bolted his food and went back to stand guard over Pete. Wat Ho and Hoof enjoyed a leisurely breakfast. But when Y. Z. began to stir, they decided to move along.

~~~

Wat Ho turned his back to a gust of wind that kicked up a spiral of trash and grit. After it passed, he grinned at Hoof. "I'll check on Pete. You go on and find a cart."

It took a few beats for Wat Ho's comment to register. "Wait, what?" Hoof brayed. "I'm supposed to do this on my own?"

"Got it first try!" called Wat Ho, who was striding away.

"No!" wailed Hoof. "I can't do it by myself. Hooved creatures have a hard time handling money." He stamped his hooves. "Distinct lack of fingers here, in case you hadn't noticed!"

Wat Ho turned back and raised his paws. "I'm sorry, but my kind can't do business deals." He turned and walked away.

Enraged, Hoof stormed down the alley, tore around the corner and almost ran over a jackal who was skulking near the intersection.

68

"Hey! Watch out, Ass!" hissed the jackal. Carrion-scented breath washed over Hoof as the jackal continued, "Show some respect!"

Hoof's gagged. "I'm *browlf . . .*"

"I don't care who you are! Watch yourself! Or else!"

Hoof gathered his hooves under himself and bolted. The jackal looked after him for a few beats, then slunk toward Finder's Keep.

~~~

Hoof ran until he was out of breath. He stopped and listened for pursuers. All he heard was the pounding of his heart. Until the skies opened up and everything else was drowned out by the roar of the wind-driven deluge. His ears drooped miserably.

"Hey! Mr. Donkey!" Squinting through the rain, Hoof made out a storm-battered canvas shelter. A young bald ape waved from under the canvas. "Yeah, you! Come get out of the rain."

The street disappeared under a freezing torrent. *What do I have to lose?* thought Hoof. As he got closer, he saw that the canvas covered a large wagon. A ramp banged to the ground in front of him.

"Come on up!" called the cheery voice.

Hoof clopped up the ramp. The enclosed space was wide enough for him to turn around and twice as long as he was. With the ramp up, it was cozy and dry. And smelled like wet Donkey.

"It's okay," the youngster assured him. "I like the smell of hooved creatures. It reminds me of when my Da was alive."

"Da?" said Hoof.

"That's what we call our male parent."

"Are you saying your, erm . . . 'Da' . . . is no longer with us?"

"Dead, you mean?" the youngster replied. "Yup. As a doornail!"

"I'm . . . sorry?" blurted Hoof, uncertainly.

"Really?" said the young bald ape. "Whatever for?"

Awkward! Hoof studied the creature who sat cross legged in front of him. Yellow hair hung to their shoulders. Their face was, except for patches above their bright blue eyes, hairless. A threadbare tunic draped their slender frame. Bare feet stuck out of a pair of tattered hose.

"Do you have a name?" Hoof asked at last.

"Of course!"

"Would you . . . erm . . . care to share it with me?"

"Wy . . . Wynaugh Tayka Chanse."

"On what?"

"What?"

"That's what I want to know."

They stared at each other. "What's your name?" the youth asked.

Hoof inhaled. "My name is Hearted. Hoof . . . Hearted.

The youngster's eyes widened. "That's so cool! My name is Chanse. First name Wynaugh. Middle name Tayka."

"Pleased to meet you, Master Chance," Hoof responded. "Or is it Mizz? Until you grow face hair, I can't tell your kind apart."

The youngster touched their cheek. "How about you just call me Booger? Every creature else does."

"Because," Hoof guessed, "you're pale as a ghost?"

Booger wiped their nose with a tunic sleeve. "Yeah, that's it!"

Hoof looked around. "Awesome wagon! Do you want to sell it?"

"I can't," said Booger. "It's my 'heritance'"

Hoof looked over the youngster's slight frame. "You look like you're slowly starving to death," he observed.

Booger nodded glumly. "Seems that way, sometimes."

"And yet you won't part with this wagon."

"Okay?" said Booger nervously. "And so?"

"I'll hire you and the wagon: Let's call it a package deal."

Booger's cheeks pulled back to expose two rows of small white teeth. "Are you making me your thrall?"

"Hold on!" Hoof protested. "Thralldom is for life. My life, at least; not so much yours. I'm thinking of a 'day-to-day' deal."

Booger's eyes blinked rapidly.

Are their eyes leaking? "Starting out by feeding you," said Hoof. "And getting new, um, what are those things that hide your skin?"

Booger's eyes widened "Food *and* new clothes? It's a deal!"

"Good," said Hoof. "Is there a ritual you use to seal a contract?"

"Well," Booger said, "we generally shake on it."

"Really?" Hoof was intrigued. "What do you shake?"

"Hands," said Booger.

"Hands?" said Hoof.

"A hoof will do in a pinch," said Booger. Hoof stuck out a leg and shook it back and forth. Booger spat in their palm, grabbed Hoof's fetlock and tugged it up and down. "We have a deal!"

"Glad to hear it," said Hoof. "When can you start?"

Booger looked at the sky. "It stopped raining," they announced, "So why not now?" They vaulted to the ground. "Where do you want to go, Sir?" they asked as they pushed the wagon into the street.

"Wait!" brayed Hoof, struggling to stay upright. "I want to go back down to the ground, thanks! I'd rather walk."

"You're the boss!" Booger said as they skipped around the wagon and lowered the ramp.

Hoof clattered down to ground level and heaved a sigh of relief. "First stop is Finder's Keep," he announced.

Booger's eyes lit up. "Wow! I'm going to like this job!" They picked up the tow bar and set off, chattering about what they wanted for breakfast.

~ 11 ~

Hoof and booger reached Jawana's courtyard to find her hip-deep in jackals. "Get away, you disgusting fake dogs!" she snarled as she flailed at them with a broom. Booger fled so abruptly they almost ran Hoof over. Hoof watched them disappear down the alley. *"Well, that's disappointing!"*

A large female jackal stepped out of the shadows. A 'Special Constable' badge hung from her neck. Jawana's broom quivered to a stop.

"Who are you?"

"Eora Wurest-Gnitemere. The 'G' is silent." The jackal ignored Jawana's blank stare as she continued. "If you don't want to be charged with assaulting a loyal vassal of our Supreme Leader, you'll drop the weapon. You're in enough trouble already for harboring a notorious card cheat and thief."

Jawana leaned the broom against the stable wall. "I-I-I don't know what you're talking about!" she stammered.

"Some of your 'guests' were up to no good last night. A low-life monkey, going by the name of Pete, cheated a poor, hardworking chimpanzee. When confronted by concerned citizens, he made a brazen escape, aided by his accomplices." Her eyes glinted redly as she turned them on Hoof. "They included a foolish-looking young Jack. You! Follow me," She disappeared through the stable door.

72

Two jackals herded Hoof into his stall, where Wat Ho glumly sat next to Sack O'Stuff. Pete was propped up beside him; his bandages waved like white flags at a trio of jackals that half-surrounded them.

Wurest-Gnitemere stalked up to Pete. "Name?" she barked. When Pete did not immediately respond, she growled in his ear. "I asked for your name, moron!"

"His name is Pete Sake," said Wat Ho.

The jackal's head snapped up. "Was I talking to you?" she snarled.

"My companion took pain medicine," Wat Ho said. "He's . . ."

"I asked," she growled, "if I was talking to you. Does that sound like I wanted the monkey's medical history?"

Wat Ho blinked. "No ma'am."

"Well?" barked the jackal.

"Ma'am?"

"Was I talking to you?" she snapped.

"Yes ma'am. Just now."

Wurest-Gnitemere took out her frustration on a mouthful of straw. She spat out the pulpy mass and tried again. "Before that. When I was asking this low-life criminal his name. Was I talking to you?"

"He's . . ." Wat Ho paused. "No ma'am."

"So shut up," she said. "Until I tell you different."

"Yes . . ." Wat Ho's mouth snapped shut.

The jackal turned back to Pete. "What's your name," she demanded. "I won't ask again."

"My birth name is Peteiro Saké," said Pete.

"Potato Sackey?" gloated the jackal. "Or Pete Sake? Are there any other aliases you want to tell me about?"

"No aliases," Pete protested. "It's just that no creature ever gets my name right. I stopped fighting it."

"I hear that you're quite the gambler, Mr. Sake-Sackey-whatever. Do you deny it?"

Pete waggled his bandaged paw. "Does this look like the paw of a card sharp?" he asked drily.

"Do I look like the one answering questions?" snapped the jackal.

Pete blew out a breath. "I might play a friendly game," he admitted. "For recreational purposes."

The jackal's eyes cut to Pete's backpack. "What's in there?"

Pete's eyes darted back and forth. "Just stuff," he replied.

Wurest-Gnitemere caught a lackey's eye. He grinned back at her and stepped toward the backpack.

"Wait!" said Wat Ho. "You don't want . . ."

"What I want," snarled Wurest-Gnitemere, "is for you shut it!"

Wat Ho rocked back as the jackal reached for the backpack, then flew through the air to slam headfirst into the wall. His companions spun around, snapping and barking furiously. The rest of the pack flooded in, packing the stall with smelly swarming bodies.

Booger reappeared. Finding the stall totally full of unpleasantness, they climbed onto its half-wall. "Hey Boss," they panted, "The Brahman are on the way!"

The jackals fell silent and, with bared fangs, glared up at Booger. Wurest-Gnitemere growled deep in her throat. Then she barked to her companions, "Clear out! I'll deal with those busybodies myself."

~~~

A massive Bull squeezed into Hoof's stall while his partner pulled up just outside the door. "What goes on here?" boomed the Bull.

"I am arresting a gang of criminals," came a voice out of nowhere.

"Eora," sighed the Bull. "I might have known you were involved."

The jackal stepped out of a shadow. "Rex," she growled. "Interfering with State business. Again. It will catch up with you."

Rex's laugh shook the stable walls. "Our authority is from Gorme," he said. "Your 'Supreme Leader' has no sway with us."

"That'll change," growled the jackal. "Sooner than . . ."

74

"What's the charge?" Rex cut her off.

The jackal's nostrils flared. "Theft," she snarled. "Illegal gaming. Running a confidence racket. Take your pick."

The Bull scrutinized each of the stall's occupants in turn. His eyes widened when they met Wat Ho's. "All of them?" he asked.

"That's the ringleader," she replied, pointing her muzzle at Pete. "Aided and abetted by the others."

"Proof?" Rex demanded.

"You'll find it in the backpack," she replied. "Or in that sack the giant bear is trying to hide."

Rex shrugged. "Let's start with the backpack," he said.

Wat Ho carried it to the stall door. "I'll empty it out here. Don't want to lose things in the straw."

Rex's partner watched Wat Ho empty the backpack onto the bare stable floor. Nestled among the coins was some jewelry. "Hey!" the Brahman mooed in surprise. They nosed a diamond neckband, "That was stolen from the Chubb place."

"I knew it!" Wurest-Gnitemere gloated. "I'll take over from here."

"But I didn't steal anything!" Pete protested. "That came from a nasty old chimpanzee named Mabel."

Rex rounded on the jackal. "Mabel Stickyfingers?" he scoffed. "That's your honest citizen?"

"She's never been convicted of a crime, and you know it!" the jackal replied. "Innocent until proven, right?"

Rex's snort blew a scattering of straw into the jackal's face. "When did you get to town?" he asked Pete.

"Yesterday." he replied. "Late afternoon."

"Any witnesses?"

"Yeah, sure. We were with . . ."

Wat Ho cut Pete off. "Two of your colleagues saw us come to town. They'll remember us; we're hard to miss."

"Okay," Rex nodded, "Good."

"You believe them?" snarled the jackal.

Rex peered down his nose at her. "Yes," he said. "I do."

Wurest-Gnitemere's hackles rose. "The bag contained stolen property," she growled. "You're obliged to turn it over to me."

Rex sighed. "I am," he admitted. He turned to Wat Ho, who had put everything but Manny's dagger in the backpack. Wat Ho looked a question at him. "Do it," said the bull. "All of it."

Wat Ho put the dagger into the backpack and held it out to the jackal. When she didn't take it, he dropped it on the floor.

"I'm not done, here," the jackal said, turning her glinting red eyes on Hoof. "You! Ass! Where's your share?"

Hoof discovered his purse was missing. *What? How?* "I've got nothing," he said as he turned in a circle. "Where could I hide it?"

The jackal swung her muzzle toward Sack O'Stuff. "What about that?" she asked. "Open it!"

"That's not happening," Wat Ho grimly replied.

The jackal's lips drew back in a snarl. "How dare you?"

"Eora," Rex sighed. "Just take the backpack and go! Before I have a dizzy spell and fall on you."

The jackal's eyes shot daggers at the Brahman as she closed her jaws on the backpack and backed out of the stall.

"Oh . . . and Eora?" Rex rumbled. "We will follow up with Mrs. Chubb to confirm that all her property found its way back to her!"

The jackal stiffened, then spun around and slunk away.

~~~

Rex turned to Wat Ho, "Legends speak of giant black and white bears. The stories differ, except in this: Where the bears roamed, there was trouble." He studied Wat Ho's face as he went on, "Most of my kind think the stories were made up to frighten Calves."

Wat Ho shrugged. "We're real enough."

Rex nodded. "Among those of us who believe the stories contain at least a kernel of truth, there is a debate. Were the bears drawn to strife? Or were they bringers of strife?" He watched Wat Ho closely. "So, I am asking: Are you here to cause problems?"

Wat Ho shook his head. "No. We'll be gone by sundown."

"All of you?" Rex demanded.

"Yes," said Wat Ho.

The Brahman nodded. "Very well." He clopped out of the stable, his silent sidekick following close behind.

Hoof exhaled loudly. "Phew! That's a relief!"

"Seriously?" Pete wailed. "All my coin is gone!"

Booger pulled Hoof's purse out of their tunic. "Will this help?"

"What? How? When?" Hoof was flabbergasted.

"Jackals are bad news if you have anything valuable on you. So I hung on to this for you. Just to sort of 'protect' it."

"Protect it, huh," Pete snorted. "And if we had gotten arrested?"

Booger grinned, "Then the money wouldn't have done you much good, would it?" They held the purse out to Hoof.

Hoof shook his head. "You better keep hanging on to it."

"Happy to, boss!" Booger tucked the purse out of sight.

Booger ran to the door, then looked back at their alarmed faces. "Don't panic!" they laughed. "I'm just going to move Ol' Heritance!"

Hoof followed him out of the stable. Wat Ho came out behind him, carrying Pete in one paw. Manny scrambled out from under the water trough to join them. *"¡Chacales!"* he yipped. "Not good for less-big dogs. I made myself be scarce."

Booger parked the wagon next to the stable wall and hurried up to Hoof. "Hey Boss! I believe there was talk of breakfast?"

"We could all use a bite," said Wat Ho. "Want to join us, Manny?"

Manny frowned. *"¿Qué?* Who are you biting?"

"He means we're going to eat," Hoof clarified.

They entered the inn. Jawana was grimly polishing a tankard when she heard the clack of hooves behind her.

"Hello," she said, forcing a smile to her lips as she turned around. Her grin widened. "I didn't expect to see you again, except maybe in shackles," she said. "Come sit at the bar."

They spread out and she saw Booger, who had been tucked in behind Wat Ho. She reached under the bar and pulled out a club. "Well," she growled. If it isn't 'Fingers' Chanse! What ill wind blew you into my establishment?"

All eyes turned to the young bald ape. "So," said Pete, dragging out the word. "You're called *Fingers* Chance?"

"No!" Booger protested. "Okay, yes. Sometimes. On account of some skills I have. But mostly I'm called 'Booger.'" They straightened up. "And I don't steal anymore. Well, not much. Some food now and again. If I really need to. But that's all. Well mostly all."

"Stop digging, child, " said Wat Ho. "Tell us your birth name."

"I go by Wynaugh. Wynaugh Tayka."

"Wynaugh Tayka Chanse," said Wat Ho. "A prophetic name!" He turned to his companions. "Whatever former roles were played, an honest new start has been made. Shall this one help us on our way? Speak up good friends, what do you say?"

Pete snorted. "Well, thieving card sharps and bad poets can't be too choosy about their companions, can they?"

"I hired Booger," added Hoof. "We shook body parts on the deal."

Manny stared up at Booger. "I will watch you, *Señor* skinny hairless creature. And Manuel Isareali Sobad never sleeps!"

"Well, erm, good to know?" said Booger.

Wat Ho extended a paw and rocked Booger up and down. "I'm called Wat Ho and," he raised his other paw, "this is Pete."

Pete headbutted Wat Ho's arm. "Can you put me down! Getting lugged around like a handbag is undignified!"

Jawana set aside her club and lifted an empty crate onto the bar. She lined it with towels, and Wat Ho settled Pete into it.

"Which name shall we call you?" Wat Ho asked Booger.

The youngster shrugged. "I guess I'll stick with Booger."

Manny went to a stool that stood in front of Pete. Booger scooped him onto the stool, then climbed on to the stool next to him. "Okay then! So now we eat?"

"First make sure we can pay for it," said Hoof.

Booger untied Hoof's purse and tipped it out on the bar. "Great-grandfather's Ghost!" they exclaimed. "That's more gold than I knew existed!" They sorted the coins. "That's two, four . . . seven King's sovereigns! And at least ten gold marks. Plus a lot of silver . . . and some coppers. Hey! There's even a diamond ring in here!"

Wat Ho pulled the ring out of the pile and glanced at Jawana. "Do you know a Mrs. Chubb?"

"Sort of. She's way above my social circle. Why?"

"I believe this is hers." Wat Ho slid the ring across the bar.

"Is that a fact?" said Jawana, slipping the ring onto a long black finger and holding it up to the light. She reluctantly pulled it off and put it under the bar. "I'll see she gets it back."

Pete looked like he wanted to protest but thought better of it. "So," he asked instead, "How much for us all to have lunch?"

Jawana slid three copper coins out of the pile. "That'll do it."

"And how much to repair the stable?" Hoof asked.

Jawana drew herself up. "That's no concern of yours."

"Yeah, it is," said Hoof. "It was the clumsy monkey and his sidekick who almost torched the place."

Jawana's lips quirked. "Okay." She added a silver coin to the coppers. "Now we're square."

~~~

Booger slathered butter on a third thick slice of fresh bread. Jawana laughed, "With so much butter, the bread can't soak up the honey."

"But it's so good!" Booger exclaimed. "It's the best butter I ever tasted. And the cheese: so good!"

"Isn't it though? The Cow's a friend of mine. She's a happy, jolly thing and it shows in her dairy. Too bad that most of what I had left is in that bottomless pit of yours."

Booger swallowed. "Oh! I'm sorry!"

"It's okay," she smiled. "I like a body to enjoy the food I offer. Rowena's dried up until she calves, but her sister's milking." She began stacking empty plates. When she reached Wat Ho she asked, "Are you sure you don't want to hang around a while longer?"

"We can't," he replied. "The Brahman want us gone by sundown."

Hoof bought two large wheels of cheese (not Rowena's but almost as good) and some bread. Jawana gave them a crate to carry their purchases and let them keep Pete's crate as well. Finally, she directed them to a provisioner who would supply their needs at a fair price.

Wat Ho reached across the counter and touched Jawana's arm. "It's as if you are compelled to help us."

"Yeah, funny that," she replied.

The travelers went out the back door, unaware of the pack of jackals gathering at the front entrance. Wurest-Gnitemere tore down the crudely lettered sign denying entry to jackals, then pushed into Finder's Keep. Her pack swarmed in behind her, while passersby averted their eyes and hurried on.

~ 12 ~

The sign said: *Top-Kwality Drie Goods and Provender at Rock Bottom Pryce's: Darnold Gud-Pryce, Proprietor.* It hung from a grimy two-story building that was plastered with posters describing goods sold within. A litter-strewn alley separated the building from its equally rundown neighbor on the right.

Manny and Pete volunteered to guard the wagon. Booger stayed behind and fiddled with the brakes as Hoof and Wat Ho pushed through the front door. A bell jangled cheerily.

"Howdy, folks!" called a venerable Mule who was half-hidden behind a low counter.

The bell rang again. The Mule looked up and stiffened. "Robyn!" he called. A beat later he repeated, "Robyn!" his voice breaking into something that sounded like a whinny.

A stocky gorilla appeared at the back of the store, wiping his paws on a frilly white apron. "Yes, Darnold?"

The silverback spotted Booger cowering just inside the door. Hooting with rage, he dropped his knuckles to the floor and charged.

"Wait!" Booger squeaked. "Give me a chance to . . .erk!" They were cut off by a huge paw lifting them off the floor.

"Stop!" Hoof took a shaky breath. "Please?" he added.

The gorilla held the door with one paw as he prepared to launch Booger across the street with the other. His eyes flicked back and forth between Hoof and the Mule.

"We're here to buy provisions," Hoof said. "We can pay."

81

The Mule chewed on this for a few beats, then nodded. "Put the creature down, Robyn," he said at last.

"Aw, boss!" protested the gorilla.

"Put the creature down!" the Mule repeated. "But keep an eye on both of them." He fixed Hoof with a suspicious glare.

The gorilla lowered Booger to the floor. He pointed two long claws at his own eyes and then at Booger's.

"I get it!" said Booger. "I'll wait here."

"See that you do!" growled the gorilla.

Wat Ho was engrossed in a cookware display. Hoof clopped up to him. "Are you going to buy a new pot?" he asked.

"Can't buy things," Wat Ho replied.

"Then why even come in here?" asked Hoof.

"How can I know what I need, if I never see what it is?"

Hoof turned away and almost fell over the gorilla. "Jumping Jonah's jodhpurs!" he brayed. "Don't sneak up on me like that!"

"My bad," said the gorilla. "But I *have* been ordered to keep an eye on you." He touched an index finger to his left temple "I'll use this one." He chuckled, then straightened up and tapped his chest. "I'm Robyn Banks, by the way."

"Really?" said Hoof. "Don't your fellow citizens disapprove?"

The gorilla threw back his head and hooted, exposing long canine teeth. "You are too funny, Mister . . .erm?"

"Yeah, I'm a real gas," Hoof replied. "You can call me Hoof. And while your eye is keeping track of me, your paws can carry my stuff."

~~~

Wat Ho wandered off, leaving Hoof on his own. Fortunately, Robyn Banks was happy to provide advice. He helped select food (oats, dog chow, a few days' worth of fresh vegetables and boxes of dried stuff) blankets, an axe, firestarters, lanterns, kerosene and more.

Robyn eyed Booger's thin frame. "Breeches or dresses?" he asked.

"What do you think?" snapped Booger.

Robyn shrugged, then chose an oilskin coat and cap, three long sleeved shirts, a jerkin, two pair of breeches, a pair of boots and other 'necessaries.' A duffel was added for the changes of clothing.

The creature's a he? Hoof was glad to have the question settled. "Who knew hiding all that skin was so complicated?" he said.

"I know, right?" Robyn squealed. "So much fun!"

Gud-Pryce kept track of the bill on an oversized abacus. By the time Wat Ho returned, the pile overflowed from the counter to the floor. "Hold up, Hoof!" he rumbled. "There's just one wagon!"

Booger counted out coins under Pryce's watchful eye. When the bill was settled, he snatched his clothes and ran out of the store.

Robyn set to work loading the wagon. The supplies had reached more than halfway up the wagon's canopy by the time Booger emerged from the alley wearing the more colorful of his new outfits. His boots hung by their laces around his neck.

Robyn whistled. "Hey, hey, good looking!" he called. "Hey? That's a thought!" He disappeared into the alley. A few beats later he was back with a small bale of hay. "This is on the house!" he said as he jammed the hay into the front of the wagon. "Happy trails!" Hooting with laughter, he danced back into the store.

"Odd sort of fellow," said Wat Ho as he sat Pete on the hay bale.

"Me too!" Manny barked. Wat Ho put him in the wagon.

Booger stowed his duffel and went to the tow bar. Wat Ho joined him, and they jerked the heavily laden wagon into motion. Hoof followed it down the street.

~~~

They cleared the town gate just as the sun was about to touch the horizon. "We kept our word," said Wat Ho.

"Yoo-hoo!" There was a note of panic in the distant voice. "You Folk with the wagon—please wait! It's a matter of life and death."

Manny's head popped out from the wagon. "A Cow is chasing us!" he yipped. "And she is getting closer!"

"Hold up!" said Wat Ho. "We better hear her out."

They moved around the wagon and watched a large black and white Cow close in on them. Her massive stomach sloshed from side to side with each ungainly stride.

"Oh, thank goodness!" the Cow panted as she clopped to a stop. She sucked in a shuddering gasp.

"Take your time, ma'am," said Wat Ho. "All that running can't have done you any good. Especially in your condition."

The Cow drew a ragged breath. "I was afraid you'd be long gone," she panted. "But I owed it to Jawana to try."

"Jawana?" Hoof asked sharply. "What about her?"

"O-o-h," the Cow wailed. "It was horrible! They just took her!"

"Say what?" Hoof exclaimed.

The Cow waggled her head. "Say 'what?' Why?" she asked. "Oh, never mind!" She took another breath and sobbed, "The jackals took her!" Her ribs heaved up and down in agitation.

Wat Ho laid a paw on the Cow's bony back. "You should try to calm down, ma'am. Getting so upset isn't good for either of you!"

After a few juddering breaths, the Cow continued, "They said she had a ring that was stolen from nasty old Mrs. Chubb."

A stricken look crossed Wat Ho's face. "Oh, no!"

"I'm sorry," said Hoof "But we don't know who you are. Or what any of this has to do with us."

"I'm Jawana's f-f-f-friend," the Cow stammered. "She buys my dairy, but we always make time for a nice chat over a pail of tea." She paused. "I'm not making milk right now, obviously. But I still drop in for tea and biscuits."

"You're Rowena!" Booger piped up.

"Why . . . yes," she said. "How did you know?"

"I had your butter and cheese for breakfast. It was awesome!"

Rowena's face lit up. "Thank you! Jawana buys dairy from my sister now; just until I've calved, of course. It's not as good as mine," she said out of the side of her mouth, "but she tries her best."

Then she remembered Jawana's predicament and her eyes welled up. "I was meeting Jawana for tea so I said I'd deliver my sister's dairy while I was at it. But when I got to the inn, a pack of jackals were tearing the place apart! This awful 'nightmare' creature demanded to know what I was doing there. I just told her I was delivering dairy. I didn't think Jawana and I having tea together was any of the nasty pad-paw mongrel's business!"

The Cow's eyes went even rounder. "Oh, my! You won't tell them I said that, will you?"

She rushed on, not waiting for a reply, "So I said, 'What happened here' and the nightmare said, 'None of your business, you nosy Cow, just leave your dairy. Or take it away, I don't care, as long as you move along' so I said 'Well, really!' because, well . . . she was shockingly rude . . . and then . . . and then she snarled at me and her eyes went all scary and red so I hightailed out of there, leaving my cart right there on the street." Rowena stopped for breath.

Hoof used the time to mentally process the rapid-fire monologue. *Did she answer the question? What was the question?*

The Cow tore off again: "And then I was running down the street and I ran into Brahman Rex—well I didn't actually run into him but near enough—and he tried to calm me down and asked me where I was going so fast—he's such a nice old Bull; we all love him to pieces; he's so big and strong but still just wonderful with the Calves—and I said 'Jawana's been taken by the jackals and I don't know what'll happen to her' and he looks sad and says he heard she'd been taken to the Rock Bottom jail because of a stolen ring and I said 'that's just not right, no way is Jawana a thief!' and he said he knew that, but he was powerless to do anything about it but there was a monkey and a big black-and-white bear that were mixed up in it and a lot of stolen property was recovered but you all had to leave town and you were probably long gone or at least he hoped so . . ."

The Cow took a few wheezing breaths before she went on, "But I hoped maybe you hadn't left yet so I ran to the east gate to stop you but then some creature said you came to town that way so you would likely leave town the other way so I ran and ran . . ." She finally wound down and turned her desperate eyes on Wat Ho. "You're the big black and white bear, aren't you? Please help!"

"I'm the monkey," said a disembodied voice.

Rowena moved around to peer into the wagon. "Oh you poor dear!" she exclaimed on seeing Pete. "Whatever happened to you?"

"Among other things, I got a lesson on how not to use an oil lamp," Pete replied. "But that's not important right now. What I want to say is that you're right, Jawana is not a thief. We left that ring with her so she could return it to its owner." He chuckled bitterly. "Just goes to show you what comes of trying to do the right thing."

Wat Ho shook his head. "It was me that left that ring with Jawana so it's up to me to set things straight."

"Just how do you expect to do that?" Hoof demanded. "There's no way you could wander around town and not be seen. You're not exactly easy to miss!"

Rowena cast a worried look behind her. "Well, we can't just stand here. Ooh, my hooves are killing me!" she moaned as she lifted her legs one at a time. "Listen, my farm is about two thousand paces straight ahead. At least there we can be miserable in comfort."

~ *13* ~

Rowena stopped at a gate that looked exactly like every other gate they had passed since leaving Rock Bottom. "This is me!" Her breath formed a silver cloud in the moonlight as she unlatched the side gate with her horn. "Lift the center post and the main gate will swing open."

After the wagon was through, Hoof nosed the gate shut, then trotted after the others. The land sloped toward the river; Wat Ho and Booger leaned back on their heels to keep the wagon from running them over. Lights shone through the trees that surrounded the farm buildings. One of the lights was coming toward them.

"That you, Rowena?" called a deep voice.

"I'm back, Tow," Rowena called. "And I've brought guests."

A greying bald ape emerged from the gloom, holding his lantern high. He eyed the newcomers, then raised an eyebrow at Rowena. "Just help them get their wagon into the carriage house," she sighed. "I'll explain later." She limped away toward the grange.

Wat Ho introduced himself, then pointed out his companions in turn. "This is Manny, Pete, Wynaugh and Hoof."

"Call me Booger," Wynaugh interjected.

The bald ape nodded. "Tow Morrow," he grunted.

They backed the wagon in the carriage house. Booger picked up Pete, crate and all, while Wat Ho dug out the medicine chest. Under Tow's watchful eye, they trooped into the grange.

~~~

Rowena and Hoof lay on comfortable divans. A window looked over the river; Hoof watched stars wink out as clouds rolled over them.

Wat Ho tended Pete's burns and checked his shoulder. "I'll leave the sling off. You can use that paw but don't overdo it."

A pair of young chimps bustled about, supposedly preparing the evening meal but mainly getting distracted. "They really are useless creatures," Rowena admitted, "and terrible chatterboxes," she added with a warning look. "But they're too darned cute to let go."

Rowena and her guests were eventually served a spread of grains, greens and dairy. The chimps exited the room screeching and tumbling over each other on the way out. Booger dejectedly licked his lips; he and Tow Morrow had not been served.

Tow's lips twitched. "Servants eat in the kitchen," he murmured. He led Booger to the food preparation area, where he wasted no time in filling a platter with food. Booger followed his example. They ate at opposite corners of a long table. Booger wiped his plate with a piece of bread before loading it back up with honeyed cheese.

~~~

The chimps finished cleaning up, then scampered up a narrow staircase to their nests. After locking the stairwell door, Tow led the way back to the living area. He caught Rowena's eye and nodded.

"Good," she said. "We can speak freely now."

"What do the jackals have against Miss Finder?" asked Wat Ho.

Rowena shrugged. "Who knows? After the Supreme Leader (may Gorme grant him long life and wisdom) made some of them 'special constables,' the jumped-up curs have done nothing but harass regular citizens! They even recruited mercenaries. Give gorillas some coin and they'll work for pad-paws as if they were proper Folk."

She glanced up to see Manny looking at her quizzically. "Oh, my. I'm sorry!" she exclaimed. "I really do talk too much."

"Su' Bien," said Manny. "I too can speak without prudence."

Pete snorted. "Like when he opens his mouth."

"Where are the jackals holding Ms. Finder?" asked Wat Ho.

"She's in the Rock Bottom Jail," Rowena replied. "It's really just an old warehouse the jackals had some cells added to."

"I'm going to get her out of there," Wat Ho stated.

"But how?" Hoof brayed.

Tow cleared his throat. "May I speak, Mistress?"

"Of course you may speak, darling!" Rowena replied. "Anytime!"

"The jail backs on the river," Tow said, "On a foggy night, a boat could sneak up to it. But there are lights along the river." He pointed at Wat Ho. "Those white bits will shine like a beacon."

"Oh dear!" said Rowena. "What can be done about that?"

"Well," said Tow doubtfully, "some folk hide their white hair with boot black. But we don't have a lot of boot black, and . . ." he angled his head at Wat Ho ". . . that's an awful lot of white."

"Well," said Wat Ho, getting to his feet. "If you show me what this 'boot black' looks like, I'll see what I can come up with."

Tow bobbed his head and stalked out of the room. He returned with a tin that was half-filled with black paste. Wat Ho smelled it, rubbed it between his fingers, tasted it and handed the tin back. "May I borrow a lantern, Ms. Rowena? I need to go to the wagon."

"Hang on," said Tow. "I'll get a lantern and go out with you." He came back wearing a coat. "We can't head out before middlenight," he said. "While we're waiting, I'll go fetch the milk cart. Maybe I'll be able to pick up some news while I'm in town."

Tow lit a splinter at the fireplace, used it to light the lantern, then headed out the door. He handed the lantern to Wat Ho and hurried down the lane while Wat Ho went into the carriage house. He came out with a pail of black goop that he left on the path near the grange.

~~~

Rowena kept up a polite chatter with her guests until Tow returned. "What have you learned?" she demanded.

Tow shrugged. "The townsfolk are avoiding Finder's Keep. Your cart hadn't been touched; I put it in the cold room."

"Thank you, Tow," said Rowena. She yawned broadly.

"You need to sleep, Mistress," said Tow. "The rest of us should get some too, while we can. I'll set an alarm for middlenight."

Pete and Manny decided to sleep by the fire. After showing Hoof and Wat Ho the guest stalls, Tow led Booger to a small dormitory. "Take any empty bunk," he said as he tossed him some bedding.

Tow went to a device that looked like a balance scale. One arm ended in a spoon that hung over a metal pail. The other arm held a bucket that dangled above a box of sand. Tow put three scoops of sand into the bucket and the balance tilted until the spoon was horizontal. He dug a metal ball out of the pail and set it in the spoon.

"What's that?" asked Booger.

"It's a sand alarm. The sand trickles through a hole in the bucket. When it has all run out, the ball drops into the pail and wakes us up."

"Huh! So the more sand you put in, the longer it takes?"

"That's right. Now make your bed so we can get some sleep."

~~~

Crash! Booger jumped up, got tangled in his bedding, and tumbled to the floor. His heart pounded as he tried to remember where he was. Then there was the scratch of a firestick and a craggy face loomed out of the darkness.

Tow Morrow! Booger kicked off his blanket and stood up. "The alarm works great!"

"It does so," Tow agreed. "Let's go rouse the others."

When they got outside, Booger shivered in the cold night air. "I'll meet you on the dock," he blurted and ran toward the carriage house.

Wat Ho felt around for his pail of boot black while Tow went off to fetch a lantern.

"Ah, there it is!" he said when Tow got back and lit up the path. Tow put down the lantern and helped Wat Ho black out his vast expanse of white fur.

"Gorme!" exclaimed Hoof when they were done "You look like a shadow in a tar pit." Between blinks, the whites of Wat Ho's eyes gleamed like egg-shaped lamps. "Now *that* is seriously disturbing," Hoof added.

~~~

Tow wrestled the boat's mast out of its socket. It crashed to the dock, barely missing Booger who had put on his dark hat and coat and rubbed boot black over his exposed skin. Only his teeth and eyes were visible as he helped Wat Ho carry the mast away from the edge of the dock. It looked to Hoof as if the mast was floating away by itself.

Tow reached back, pulled a ramp up from the bottom of the boat and leaned it against the dock. Hoof edged down the ramp and stretched out behind the boat's centerboard. Wat Ho settled in the stern and wrapped a paw around the tiller. Booger sat beside Tow.

"Spend much time in boats?" Tow asked Booger as he pulled the ramp back into the boat.

"Sure. I've been in boats since . . . how long ago did I sit down?"

"You'll get the hang of it soon enough!" Tow chuckled as he pushed the heavy craft away from the dock. He set Booger's oar in the lock and showed him how to grip it. "Match what I do," he said. They fell into a rhythm that, with Wat Ho at the tiller, carried them upriver in a fairly straight line.

~~~

We've been rowing forever! thought Booger. His hands had blistered and his back ached. He practically cried with relief when Tow signaled for Wat Ho to angle toward the riverbank.

"Those lights on the left are the jail," Tow whispered. "We'll go past and drift back. Less noise that way." He brought Booger's oar on board, then used his oar to scull toward the jail.

Light escaped a dirty, barred window that faced the river. Below the window, water slapped against a stone wall. Beyond that was a derelict wharf that dated from the building's warehouse days. Gas lamps burned on each side of a double door that faced the wharf.

Tow held the boat against the wharf and Wat Ho, Hoof and Booger climbed out. "I'll wait upriver," he whispered. "Signal me when you're ready to be picked up." He rubbed his stubbled chin, then added. "But if you get into trouble, I can't help. Folks know me, and they know this boat. No way am I going to let Rowena get mixed up in this."

~ 14 ~

The heavy thump on Hoof's back almost stopped his heart. "Gorme!" he hissed. "Warn a creature before you attack them!" Wat Ho's teeth gleamed under the gas lamps.

"Sorry!" he whispered. "But one of us has to go check the front."

"Hoof swallowed hard. "Right. So that would be me, then?"

"Right," said Wat Ho. "Just go to the front of the jail, scope out any guards, and come right back."

What does 'scope out' even mean, Hoof wondered as he hurried along the waterfront, then turned up the first alley that led away from the river. He had gone about fifty paces when a door crashed open, trapping him in a blast of light and bad music.

"Well Hel-lo sailor!" sang a cheery voice. "Hey, I know you!"

Hoof's stomach lurched. *Robyn Banks!* The door slammed, cutting off the noise and light. Hoof managed one step before Robyn called, "Stop right there, Sugarplum! I want a little word with you." Hoof grudgingly turned back.

"Word around town is that you've been a very naughty Jack!" cooed the gorilla. "The other word around town is that you and your buddies are no longer 'around town.' And yet here you are. So spill, darling! This fat old gorilla is fit to die of curiosity."

The door banged open and a Stallion stepped out, trailed by his groom. Robyn shuffled sideways, hiding Hoof from the Horse's view. "G'night, gorgeous!" he cooed. The Horse snorted in disgust as he edged by. "I was talking to your groom!" Robyn called after him.

"Miserable old Cow," Robin muttered. "Now, where were we? Oh, yes . . . you were about to tell me everything!"

Hoof exhaled. "Do you know Jawana Finder?" he asked.

"Of course I know Jawana! I know every creature, darling!"

"Do you know what happened to her?"

Robyn hesitated. "Surprisingly, no. The jackals wrecked her place and she has not been heard from since. Some are saying . . ."

"She's in the jail," Hoof blurted, "I'm breaking her out."

"What?" Robyn exclaimed. "No way!"

"Way," said Hoof.

"Oooh!" said Robyn. "That is so exciting! Can I help?"

"Yeah. By letting me get on with it!" brayed Hoof.

"Oh, don't be an . . . erm . . . Donkey," said Robyn. "So the jackals have her? Hmm, my nephew Runnon's contracted to them. My word but that boy's dumb! His head's so empty a bird once built a nest in it. Oops!" Robyn put his fingers to his lips. "I'm running on again. About Runnon. Ha! Ha! The point—and I do have one—is that Runnon's a guard at the jail. You should see his uniform: It's too funny! No wait, you will see it: He's working tonight. Oooh, that's good!"

"Seriously? How is that good?" asked Hoof.

Robyn poked Hoof's shoulder. "Because, Duck Lips," he crowed, "I'm due to catch up on the family gossip. And if the young fool is distracted while you do your thing, well . . . it can't hurt, can it?"

Hoof shook his head. "I'm just, erm, 'scoping' things out."

"Well giddy up, Buttercup!" said Robyn. "Scopes away!"

They staggered past the jail, acting as if they had downed too many jugs of fermented juice. Hoof made out a lanky shape slouching in the building's recessed entrance. The guard's head lolled, then snapped up, banging his helm against the wall. The helm bounced to the ground and rolled away. The guard booted it twice before catching up to it.

"That's my nephew," Robyn whispered. "We're so proud!" He hid his face behind a paw. "Can't let him see me out here or we'll blow the caper . . . sneak, sneak, sneak." He exploded with laughter.

The guard stared after a portly, hysterically giggling gorilla who was being propped up by a skittish young Donkey. "Runnon old stick," he said, "You missed one fine party!" He slapped his helm on and returned to his hidey hole.

~~~

Upon being assured that no nephews would be harmed during the rescue, Robyn Banks offered to create a diversion while Booger and Wat Ho broke into the jail. Hoof and Tow were to wait in the shadow of an upstream boat house.

Wat Ho and Booger stood across from the jail. They made themselves as inconspicuous as a giant ball of sticky black fur and blackface-wearing sidekick could manage. Booger's boots hung around his neck; he had taken them off so he could move silently.

Long before they saw him, they heard Robyn belting out a bawdy showtune. Eventually he staggered into view; staggered back; stumbled forward several paces; pinwheeled back.

The guard leaned forward, pushing back his ill-fitting helm. A khaki jacket hung from his shoulders. The rest of his 'uniform' consisted of a frayed belt wrapped twice around his waist. "Uncle Robyn?" he called "Is that you?"

Robyn lurched to a stop. "Well, blesh my furry shoal," he slurred. "If it ishn't little . . ." He rocked forward, straightened up too quickly and landed on his backside.

"Uncle Robyn!" the young ape cried as he ran to his uncle's aid. A keyring clipped to his belt jangled at each step. "You're drunk!"

Robyn squinted up at his nephew. "I reshemble that remark," he giggled. He tugged on a fistful of the young gorilla's jacket just as an oilskin-clad shadow flitted by. A heartbeat later the shadow unlocked the door to the jail and slipped inside. A large black blob squeezed in behind him.

~~~

Wat Ho and Booger stood, panting, with their backs to the door. A half-dozen steps led down to a dimly lit room. Wat Ho squatted down, spotted a uniformed gorilla sprawled behind a desk. He jerked back. Several breaths later, he looked again. The gorilla hadn't moved. A heavy truncheon dangled from his paw, threatening to slip to the floor.

"The idiot's asleep!" The voice came from a dark shape that lay propped up against the back of a cell.

"Jawana?" Wat Ho took a few steps into the room, shadowed by Booger. The shape weakly raised a paw in greeting. "Booger, you're on!" Wat Ho hissed as he pushed him toward the cell.

Booger stumbled forward to kneel at the cell door. Boot black ran down his face as he tried each of Runnon's keys. None fit. He turned to Wat Ho and shrugged. They both turned to the sleeping guard.

Booger crept up to the gorilla. Squinting into the gap between his backside and his chair revealed no key ring. He eased his fingers into a jacket pocket. A paw latched on to his wrist in a vice-like grip.

"Got you, you dirty thief!" crowed a guttural voice.

There was a dull crack and the grip on Booger's wrist relaxed. Booger looked up to see Wat Ho standing over the unconscious guard with the truncheon clutched in a hairy paw. "Thank you," Booger said. "That ape could have broken every bone in my body!"

As Booger dug through the guard's pockets, Wat Ho approached Jawana's cell. She lay against the wall like a pile of discarded black rags. Only her eyes moved; she swiveled them up to stare at Wat Ho.

"Why are you doing this?" she asked.

"I left that ring with you," he replied, "It's up to me to fix this."

"That's just dumb!" said Jawana. "If it wasn't the ring, they would have found something else. Your little guilt trip is going to get you and your friend into a shedload of trouble. For nothing!"

Booger found the right key and pulled open the door. "Mizz Jawana," he said, "I've been in trouble my whole life, so you don't have worry about me. But you've got some other friends outside and if we keep them waiting much longer, trouble is going to find them. So please, Mistress, let's go!"

Jawana pulled herself to her feet, took two steps and collapsed against Wat Ho. He grabbed her arm and pulled her upright. Booger stepped forward to prop her up from the other side. They had half-carried, half-dragged her to the steps when they heard a voice berating the guard on the other side of the door.

"That's Wurest-Gnitemere!" Jawana gasped. "We're dead!"

"Is there another way out?" asked Wat Ho.

"There are doors at the back," Jawana replied. "But they've been chained shut for ages."

"So we'll unchain them," said Wat Ho. "Booger, I'm counting on you to get us out of here."

Booger snatched up a lamp and raced away. Wat Ho hooked his paws under Jawana's arms and awkwardly backed out of the room, pulling her after him. He was halfway down a dusty corridor when shouting erupted from inside the jail.

"Hurry, Booger!" he panted. "The guard's awake!"

"Almost got it!" A chain rattled to the floor and Booger threw his weight against the heavy door. Its rusted hinges protested as he forced his way onto the wharf, waving the lamp over his head.

"There!" Hoof brayed. "That's Booger!"

Tow angled past the wharf—too quickly. Booger dropped the lamp and dove forward to get a grip on the boat's gunwale. The boat's momentum almost pulled him into the river but he hooked his other elbow behind a bollard and managed to hold on.

The jackals' yapping got louder as Wat Ho backed across the wharf. He had made it to the edge when a rotting plank gave way. He and Jawana fell into the boat. It rocked wildly and was torn out of Booger's grasp. When he lunged forward to grab at it, his coat caught on a nail, holding him fast. *Snorg!* He struggled futilely as the boat drifted out of reach. *"Just go!"* he hissed. "Get out of here!"

By the time Booger freed his coat, the jackals were pouring onto the wharf. He bellowed to draw their attention away from the water, then sprinted away. The pack ran after him.

Tow pushed Jawana off of him and pulled for the middle of the stream. A solitary jackal, larger than the others, watched their pack disappear into the fog. Suddenly their muzzle lifted high, sniffing the air. The jackal's head swung toward the river, eyes glinting red as they stared into the darkness.

A ripple spread from the portal's center and resolved into a grey, emaciated face. Their eyes narrowed. "This better be good news!"

"It is, My Lord," Eora Wurest-Gnitemere replied. "The seed you planted was not detected. The fools actually believe they escaped!"

The creature's laughter changed to a wheezing cough and the image blinked out of existence. The jackal stared into the empty portal for a moment, then stood up and padded away.

~ 15 ~

Tow's eyes were fixed on the jackal as he pulled to the middle of the river. He said nothing until the jackal disappeared, then he lifted his oars out of the water and cursed softly.

"I'd gladly throw the lot of you overboard," he said, "but Rowena will have my guts for garters if I don't deliver the gorilla safe and sound. But I beg of you, please be gone by dawn!" He started a steady stroke that carried them swiftly downstream.

When Wurest-Gnitemere padded back into the jail, Robin and Runnon Banks were tied to straight-backed chairs. The inside guard stood over them, the truncheon clutched in his fist.

"Can I hit 'em, Boss?" the Guard pleaded.

"Not just yet, Gus," she replied, her voice piercing the stale air like an icepick. "Have patience. Your chance will come."

Gus's face split into an evil grin. "Okay, Boss. I can wait."

Wurest-Gnitemere sat back on her haunches and licked her lips. "Which of you apes attacked Gus?" she demanded.

"W-what?" stuttered Robyn. "We didn't attack anybody! I've never even been in here before. So listen here, Dearie . . ."

In less than a heartbeat, the jackal's teeth were pressed to the gorilla's throat. "Call me 'Dearie' again and I'll reach into your mouth with my teeth and rip out your tongue."

Robyn's eyes were like saucers. "Y-y-yes, ma'am. I mean no ma'am! I mean . . ." He took a breath. "Okay. I'll just shut up now."

"Do that." The jackal dropped to the floor and turned her attention to Runnon Banks. "Who paid you?" she demanded.

"Erm . . . you?" Runnon replied.

The jackal took a bite out of his chair. "Idiot!" she said as she spat out a mouthful of splinters. "Who paid you to let the prisoner escape?"

Runnon whipped his head around. "Wait, what now? The prisoner escaped! When? How?"

Wurest-Gnitemere spun around in a blind rage until her jaws snapped shut on her tail. "You're going to pay for that!" she snarled. Then her ears pricked up and she whirled to face the entrance.

Booger couldn't shake the jackals. He was thoroughly lost by the time he plunged into a dark alley and ran headfirst into a brick wall. The next thing he knew, he was flat on his back in a filthy puddle.

Dozens of unblinking eyes gleamed in the light bleeding from a nearby window. Fighting waves of dizziness, Booger got up. He backed away from the advancing eyes until his shoulder hit something round and hard. A downspout? *Yes!* He spun around and climbed.

The jackals piled on each other's backs, leaping and snapping at their prey. Claws raked Booger's calf. He roared with pain and rage; kicked downwards with all his might. A satisfying crack reached his ears and the turmoil below him paused.

When he reached the roof's overhang he arched back and got both hands on the gutter. It groaned but held as he pulled his chin over to squint at the steep mansard roof. To his relief, a ladder was attached to it, right above the downspout. Except for a bad moment when his boots snagged on the gutter, he had no problem wrestling himself up far enough to grasp the bottom rung. A few beats later he flopped onto the building's flat central roof.

He lay on his back and took stock: His legs were long strips of pain; there was a deep, bleeding tear in his calf; his heel hurt where it had hit a jackal's bony skull; he was trapped on a roof with no idea where he was. But he also had a full purse! *Could be worse!*

He laced on his boots and limped to the end of the roof. The gap between it and the neighboring building was about two paces wide. *Well, it's not like I've got options.* He backed up, got his legs pumping, and launched himself into space.

When Runnon Banks heard the slow clopping of heavy hooves on the steps, he opened his eyes and dared to hope.

Rex Brahman lowered his bulk down from the bottom step. "I really loath stairs," he rumbled as he took in the tableau in front of him.

"Then do better at avoiding them," snarled Wurest-Gnitemere.

The Brahman peered down at her for several long, slow blinks. "You're up late, Eora," he said. "Or is it early?"

"I could say the same for you. What are you doing here at, what is it, about three-quarter night?"

"Just a routine patrol. When I saw the door was wide open, I got concerned about your prisoner." His massive head swung toward the cells, then back to face the jackal. "Where is Ms. Finder?"

Wurest-Gnitemere met the Brahman's eye. "Flown the coop," she spat. "Thanks to those two," she added, tilting her head at Robyn and Runnon. "You're interrupting my investigation into the matter."

Rex's eyes passed over Robyn to focus on Runnon. "Isn't that one of your pet monkeys?" he asked.

"He was an, erm, 'employee,'" the jackal replied. "Mercenaries! You can't trust them as far as you can spread their guts."

"Who was guarding Ms. Finder?" Rex asked.

"It was Gus," Runnon hurriedly volunteered.

Rex turned to the inside guard, who tried to hide the truncheon behind his back. "That would be you?" he rumbled. Gus's head jerked once and Rex swung back to Runnon. "And you were doing what?"

"I was guarding the front entrance," Runnon replied.

Rex cut an eye toward Robyn, who hastily explained, "I'm his uncle. I was on my way home from the Lymp Lyzard, so I stopped to keep Runnon company. Catch up on family news and whatnot."

The Brahman studied Robyn's face, then turned back to Gus. "You saw the prisoner escape?"

Gus's eyes flicked between Rex and the jackal. "No," he mumbled. "A half-grown bald ape tried to pick my pocket. Then I got clopped on the head and that's the last I knew."

Wurest-Gnitemere's ears pricked up. "A young bald ape?" she crowed. She turned to Rex and added, "Like the one who led you to the pack of thieves I was going to arrest earlier? Be assured I will report your blatant interference to the appropriate ears!"

"Noted," said Rex. "When did you learn of the escape?"

"Just now. I came back to resume my interrogation of the prisoner. This moron," she said, indicating Runnon with her snout, "was about to let me in when Gus staggered out and . . ." She paused. "It was Gus that opened the door!"

Rex nodded head towards Robyn and Runnon. "And these two were both outside at the time?"

"I was outside all night!" Runnon insisted. "I never left my post."

The jackal glared at him, then looked away. "He was outside when I got here," she grudgingly admitted.

"How did Ms. Finder escape?"

"Through a cargo door in the back. It had been closed and secured with chains. Some creature opened it from the inside."

"But we know of no creatures who were inside, except for the prisoner and this gorilla, Gus?"

The jackal curled her lip. "Aren't you forgetting the bald ape?"

"Ah yes," rumbled Rex. "The bald ape. Who may resemble a creature seen leaving Rock Bottom. And had no known link to these gentlecreatures." He sighed. "Far be it from me to suggest they file a complaint for wrongful arrest but if they did, I'd have to hear it."

Wurest-Gnitemere glared up at the Bull as if she would like nothing better than to rip his throat out. She lowered her eyes. "Fine!" she growled. "Untie them, Gus."

"Huh? What, Boss?" said Gus.

The jackal bared her teeth and he hurried to comply. A few beats later, Robyn and Runnon were halfway to the door.

"Wait!" Wurest-Gnitemere growled and the gorillas froze in mid-stride. "Leave your uniform. And your keys."

A panicked look spread across Runnon's face as he reached for his belt, then slapped at his pockets. Wurest-Gnitemere's ears twisted forward. "Where are your keys?" she demanded.

"I-I-I don't know!" Runnon wailed.

"You're not leaving until I have those keys!" the jackal snarled. "Because if you don't have them, you're not leaving. Ever!"

The Brahman had gone to inspect Jawana's cell. Recoiling from the stench of feces and decay, he sneezed, raising a cloud of chaff and filthy straw. He stared at the floor, then looked up to ensure no creature was watching. His lips twitched into a grin as his hoof sent something skittering across the floor. It stopped under Runnon's chair.

Rex loudly cleared his throat. "What's that?" he innocently asked. "Under that chair?"

Trembling with relief, Runnon scooped up the keys that Booger had tossed aside after they failed to open the cell door. "They must have fallen when Gus pushed me onto the chair."

"You should leave," Rex said. "Both of you." Runnon dropped the keys, tore off his belt and jacket and raced Robyn to the exit.

"Always a pleasure, Eora," boomed Rex. "I'll let myself out the back way. Never been a fan of stairs."

103

Tow snugged the boat up to the dock and wearily clunked the oars down on the wooden planks.

"Hello?" a sleepy voice called out of the darkness. "Who's there?"

"Mistress?" said Tow. "What are you doing out here?"

A large black and white shape clopped onto the dock. "Oh thank goodness!" she mooed. "I've been so worried. I've been watching for you for ages. Well," she admitted, "until I fell asleep."

"Rowena, you silly Cow!" said Jawana. "It's cold enough out here to freeze the lips off a penguin! What were you thinking?"

"Jawana!" the Cow let out a joyful bellow. "All I could think about was you! My best friend in the 'joint,' the 'jug,' the 'hoosegow.' But these gentle creatures sprung you and here you are!"

Jawana tried to get up, stumbled, and fell back into the boat. "I can't," she whimpered. "I can't do it!"

Tow threw a line over a cleat and pulled it taut. "We'll look after you, Miss," he said, "just as soon as I've tied up."

When the boat was secured, he took Jawana's arm. "Hey, Ho!" he called. "A little help here!"

Wat Ho climbed onto the dock and helped lift Jawana out of the boat. Her paw brushed his side. "What the . . ." she said as she jerked her fingers away. "What is that?"

"It's called boot black," said Wat Ho, "but it's used to color fur."

"Well that's not too disgusting," said Jawana.

~ 16 ~

Jawana eased into a warm, cow-sized tub and began to soak off layers of grime and filthy straw. Wat Ho backed out of the bathing chamber and rubbed at the mess stuck to his own body.

"And this?" he asked. "How do you remove this substance?"

"Wait here," said Tow. "I'll see what I can find." He went into an outbuilding; returned juggling a lantern, a can of kerosene and a brick of soap. He handed the kerosene and soap to Wat Ho, then led him to a tiled room containing a pool-sized horse bath.

"It's not heated," he said, "but there's lots of water. Scrub with the kerosene, then soap and water." He chuckled as he hung the lantern from a peg. "I'd stay away from open flames for a while!"

Hoof followed Rowena into the grange, where Pete and Manny anxiously waited. Pete's eyes bounced between Hoof and the door. "So where's the bald ape?" he demanded.

"I don't know," Hoof replied. "Last I saw of Booger, he was leading a pack of jackals away from us."

"Yeah," said Pete, "and running off with my money!"

"No," sighed Hoof. "Running off with my money."

~~~

Wat Ho lumbered into the grange and held up a warning paw. "Don't even start!" The others burst out laughing; reducing a brick of soap to a tiny nub had turned him into a giant, streaky grey powderpuff.

A whimper from Jawana silenced the laughter. "My legs ache!" She flung her blanket aside. "And I'm burning up!"

105

Wat Ho knelt next to the gorilla and gently probed her wounds. She shrieked, then fell back and lay still.

"For the love of Gorme," cried Rowena, "What are you doing?"

Wat Ho ignored her outburst as he went to get his medicine chest. "We'll need hot water!" he said.

"I'll get it," said Tow. He hurried from the room.

Soiled cloths piled up as Wat Ho cleaned Jawana's wounds. Then he ground pinches of herbs and powders in a mortar. The hot water arrived and he stirred it into the mixture, making a thick, dark tea.

Wat Ho lifted Jawana's eyelid and inspected her pupil. "Sorry, but I have to wake you up." He waved a vial under her nostrils.

"Great beetling toadspawn!" Jawana shrieked as she batted at Wat Ho's paw. "Will you leave me alone!"

"Sorry Miss Jawana, but you need to be awake."

"Really? And this had to involve you driving a spike through my brain?" Jawana swiped at her nose. "Okay, I'm awake. Now what?"

Wat Ho grinned. "You'll drink something to make you sleep!"

Jawana's eyes narrowed. "Say what?" she growled.

Wat Ho held out the mortar. "Your wounds are festering. This should clear the poison out of your body. And help you sleep."

The gorilla sniffed at the thick, dark liquid and gagged. "You can't be serious!"

"As serious as a slow painful death," Wat Ho replied.

Keeping her eyes on Wat Ho, Jawana took a breath and poured the sludgy tea down her throat. "That. Was. Unpleasant." Her head lolled to the side and she started to snore.

Wat Ho closed the medicine chest. "She needs rest."

"She can't stay here!" Tow said. "The jackals will track her down."

"Well, we're not throwing her out on the road!" mooed Rowena.

Tow stared out the window. "There's an old, abandoned farm just across the river. Your friends should be okay there, for a few days at least. But we can't get the wagon over there, and it sure can't stay here." He rubbed the back of his neck, thinking. "My cousin lives not far from here," he said at last. "He's enthralled to an old Horse who's too senile even to notice when they're out of food. I'm sure that, for a few copper bits, my cousin will hide the wagon."

Rowena spoke up. "Take your cousin whatever amount is needed. It's the least I can do for Jawana's rescuers!"

Booger huddled at the end of the block. Below him, a faded canvas awning hung over the street. *That might slow me down enough to not break any major bones.* He swung his legs off the roof, slipped, and fell. He hit the awning and bounced twice before a seam in the canvas parted. He fell through . . . and came to a quick, jarring stop.

"Hokay den, Tom," a thickly accented voice called from below him. "I vill be seeing ya next quarter-moon, yaw?"

"For sure," a voice replied. "Give my best to the Missus."

Booger felt a cart rock under him, then lurch into motion as a merchant continued on their rounds. He stared at the sky until he dozed off. He snapped awake as they crossed the river. A gull landed at his feet. It tilted its head as if deciding whether Booger would be tasty.

"Go on! Git!" hissed Booger; he aimed a feeble kick at it.

"Too slow, skinbag!" the bird croaked as it took off on slow, flapping wings. It gained altitude, then banked toward Booger's head.

"No! Don't you dare!" He whipped his head to the side. Too late.

~~~

The cart stopped and a hairy back disappeared into a nearby building. Booger counted twenty slow breaths; when the creature didn't return, he swung to the ground and peered into the cart.

A cloth-covered pail held some leftover bread and cheese. He tied the cloth around his calf, picked up the pail and limped away, counting on 'downhill' to lead to the river. He would head downstream; his

Master and Ol' Heritage lay that way. But first he needed to find somewhere safe to hole up and rest.

~~~

Booger's hopes rose at the sight of a rusty gate that dangled from one broken hinge. The lane beyond it was covered with hip-high weeds and bushes. *No creature's been here for a long time,* he thought.

The lane ended at a cluster of buildings. Most had fallen in, but the grange had fared better. A corner of the roof had collapsed and a window was broken. Other than that, it was in good shape.

Booger reached through the broken window and dropped his lunch pail onto the floor. He almost snagged his arm on a shard of glass that stuck up from the frame. He spread his coat over the sill, then climbed into a large room containing only a potbellied stove and a stool.

A door on the far side opened onto the kitchen. A handpump stood in front of a grimy window. He gave it a half-hearted stroke. Then his disappointment and frustration took over and he jerked the pump handle up and down. To his surprise, a brown trickle flowed from the spout, quickly thickening to a clear stream. He rinsed his hands, then held his head under the spout and washed off layers of mud and gull guano. Finally, he drank his fill of cold, sweet water.

He peered into a kitchen annex that was mostly filled with firewood, then explored the remaining rooms. He did not see much of interest, until he spied a ladder attached to a wall. It led to the former living quarters of fingered servants. The low-ceilinged room was lit by four small windows set into one wall. *This will do!* Booger hoisted his lunch into the attic and climbed up after it.

~ 17 ~

Wat Ho piled blankets and enough supplies for a few days along the wall, then sat Sack O'Stuff on the blankets. He and Tow pulled the wagon out of the carriage house; Hoof nosed the door shut and trotted after them.

The eastern sky was pink and gold by the time Tow nodded at a rutted lane that was partly blocked by a broken gate. "We go through there," he said. "Watch out for the ruts."

A few rundown buildings stood at the end of the lane. A hunched-over bald ape dug potatoes in what was once a garden.

"Stop here," said Tow. "Listen, Master Hearted," he murmured, "this is an old-style Equine household. So, you're in charge."

Hoof looked startled. "Me? In charge of what?" he brayed.

The stranger's head jerked up. He squinted at them for a few beats, then plunged his fork into the ground and started toward them.

"Wait here," said Tow. He met his cousin halfway and held out the purse. After a brief but animated conversation, it disappeared into a potato sack that hung around the stranger's neck. Then they wordlessly marched up to the wagon.

"Master Hearted," Tow said. "This is Knowl Morrow, enthralled to the Venerable Stallion Tread Lightly. On behalf of his Illustrious Master (who is regrettably indisposed today) he will safeguard your goods until you can return to claim them."

Hoof took in the worn state of the stranger's clothes. Bony knees showed through gaps in his breeches. His grey tunic was shapeless and threadbare. *It's like some creature crafted a scarecrow out of Tow!* He thrust that thought aside and tried to act 'masterful.'

"I am most decidedly regretful of your illustrious master's lack of disposedness," he babbled. "Please permit me to offer my most solicitous, erm, solicitations."

Knowl gave Hoof a sharp look, then dropped his eyes. "Sirrah!" he replied. He side-eyed Wat Ho, then glanced at Tow. "Odd sort of thrall," he muttered out of the corner of the mouth.

"You've no idea," Tow murmured in reply. He raised his voice and asked, "Where do we go from here?"

Knowl led them to the only outbuilding with an intact roof and four walls. He dragged some broken equipment out of the building while Tow set the crate of fresh food on the ground. The wagon was backed inside and the broken equipment piled in front of it.

Hoof looked on in alarm. "Are you sure this will be safe?"

"Don't worry, young Sir," replied Knowl. "No reasoning creature would look for anything of value on this estate." His eyes drifted to the foodstuffs. His throat bobbed as he pointedly looked away.

Tow poked Hoof hard, making him jump. "Oh . . . erm . . . yeah," said Hoof, haltingly. "I hope your Master will not think it disrespectful of me to present these unworthy gifts."

Knowl bowed. "My Master will be honored," he intoned gravely. "Be assured you will always be welcome here."

Tow cast an eye at the sun. "Time's passing," he observed. "We've got to get back before the traffic picks up."

Knowl aimed a dirty finger at the far side of an overgrown field. "Cut through those woods. It'll save you many steps."

"Thank you, Cousin." Tow clasped Knowl's hand. "Be well." Knowl nodded curtly, turned, and marched toward his garden. Tow spun around and strode briskly away in the opposite direction.

"We better go," said Wat Ho. "Our guide's leaving without us."

Tow and Wat Ho put Jawana on a stretcher and, with Rowena mooing anxiously behind them, carried her to a decrepit broad-beamed boat that was tied up to her dock. They laid the gorilla on one side the centerboard; Hoof stretched out on the other. Blankets and supplies were piled up to hide them from view. Sack O'Stuff and Pete's crate sat in the stern. Manny huddled in the bow.

"I don't know what to do about you," Tow sighed, squinting up at the bear-like creature who towered over him.

"No need to worry!" Wat Ho replied. He snapped off a reed, blew through it, and stuck it in his mouth. "I learned this from your ancestors," he lisped, then dove into the frigid water. A furry black paw gripped the boat's tiller. That, and the reed sticking up from the water, were all that betrayed Wat Ho's presence.

"You'll freeze to death before we get there," said Tow.

Wat Ho stuck a thumb up in the air, then regripped the tiller.

"It's your funeral!" Tow tacked upstream as if heading for Rock Bottom. But every other tack took them closer to the far bank. He waited until no boats were in sight, then swung about and ran downstream with the wind.

~~~

The abandoned farm had no usable dock, so Tow raised the centerboard and ran the boat onto a gravel beach. Wat Ho emerged from the river. "L-l-like I s-s-said," he shivered. "N-no p-problem."

Tow and Wat Ho piled the blankets and supplies above the waterline. As soon as he was freed, Hoof leaped over the side and stumbled up the beach. Manny scrambled after him.

Tow put Pete at Jawana's feet and muscled one end of the stretcher onto the gunwale. Wat Ho took hold of it while Tow grabbed the other end and led the way to the grange. He kicked open the door to what had been the main living area.

As soon as they had put the stretcher down, Tow headed for the door. "I've got to go before the boat gets noticed," he said. "I'll be back at middlenight, the third night from now."

Booger's eyes flew open. *Intruders!* A pair of heavy boots stomped across the floor beneath him. *And at least one of them is fingered.*

A deep voice spoke and another voice rumbled a reply. The boots retreated. Booger sat up, mentally cursing his bad luck. *Some villain could come nosing around up here and that would be that!* He stood up, hissing when he put weight on his wounded leg.

Hooves clopped across the floor below him A shrill voice spoke. *There's a bunch them down there!* He eased a window open and prepared to make a break for it.

Wat Ho laid a blanket over Hoof's back, then balanced a bag of oats and a bag of dogfood on the blanket. "Drop that in the room where we left Jawana," he said. "I'll be right behind you."

When Hoof got to the open door, Manny scooted past him. Hoof followed him in, bent his front legs, and tipped his load onto the floor. He saw a large piece of cloth hanging from the window.

"Manny!" he whispered, loud enough to spook a flock of starlings that was outside the window. "Some creature else has been here!"

Manny trotted over. "This stinks of your pet ape," he growled.

"Say what?" he brayed, "Hey Booger, where are you?"

A mass of flailing arms and legs fell past the window.

~ *18* ~

Booger closed his eyes; opened them again. The blurry Horse was still there: A Horse that had been spun around by their tail, chucked face first into a wall and was not happy about it.

"Booger? Booger!" brayed the creature. "Can you hear me?"

Not a horse. "Boss?" Booger croaked. "Hoof Hearted?" He giggled. *Bad idea!* "Ow! Ow! Ow!" he gasped. "That really hurt!"

Hoof looked away. "I think he's broken," he said.

"Probablemente, Señor. Always bald apes get their brains scrambled. Their big heads have too much room for them to slop around."

~~~

Pete sat up straight when Booger limped into the grange. "Hey!" he shouted. "Where's my money?"

"Maybe you should ask the jackals?" Booger replied. "All I have is my Boss's money." He pulled his coat from the window sill, then went to the pile of supplies. "Has anyone seen my duffel?"

Wat Ho had walked in with a load of blankets. He blinked at Booger, then shook his head. "It's back in your wagon," he said.

"Swell," Booger grumped. He snatched a blanket off the pile and stomped into the kitchen. After blocking the door with an old bench, he stripped and washed his clothes under the pump. He hung them to dry, then shivered through an icy rinse.

Wat Ho hung a blanket over the broken window, plunging the room into darkness. He stroked a glowlamp to life and checked Pete's burns. "We'll let your paws get some air."

"Thank the gods!" Pete dug in his crate and fished out a deck of cards. "It's about time!" Slowly, stiffly, he shuffled the deck.

Booger returned, wrapped in a blanket. Wat Ho glanced up and exclaimed, "You're bleeding!"

"I got scratched up pretty good," Booger admitted.

"Take care," said Wat Ho as he peeled off Booger's makeshift bandage. "You can catch nasty things from jackals."

After Wat Ho had bandaged his leg, Booger went to sit on the floor beside Pete. Pete eyed Hoof's purse, which dangled from a cord that held Booger's blanket in place. "Maybe I can win some of my coin back," he said, holding up the deck of cards.

"It's not mine to lose," Booger replied.

"I've never let minor details like that stop me," Pete grumbled.

Booger touched the purse. "This is a lot of money," he said. "I don't get why you gave it to Master Hearted in the first place."

"I can't hang on to the stuff! If I don't get robbed (or mugged by jackals) I lose it in my next card game. Putting the gold in Hoof's purse seemed like a way to make some of it stick around."

Wat Ho dragged a bench from the kitchen and pushed it up to a wall. Booger scrambled up and they each grabbed one side of Jawana's blanket and hoisted her onto it. "Hopefully that will be a bit more comfortable for you," rumbled Wat Ho.

~~~

Flickering light and heat spilled into the room from the open stove. Booger went out and shivered into his damp clothes. He stood at the stove tending a vegetable stew as his clothes dried.

114

Wat Ho cleaned and dressed Jawana's wounds and coaxed her into eating a few vegetables. He finished off with a batch of the bitter 'tea,' which she choked down with a minimum of complaint.

"Are you okay?" he asked. "It's not like you to be so quiet."

Jawana curled a lip at him and went back to staring at the fire.

~~~

Hoof couldn't sleep. He watched a sliver of window transform from charcoal through grey. When it reached silver, he clopped across the room and swiped his nose at a log that propped the door shut. "Ouch! Snerd buckets and blast!"

Booger was at his side in a flash. "What's wrong, Boss?"

"Splinter!" muttered Hoof. Tears streamed from his eyes as he added, "Right in the nostril!"

Hoof spent the day pacing around the grange. Jawana sat against the wall, watching the Donkey through slitted eyes as he clopped in and out of the shadows. Manny sniffed at her legs, then turned away in disgust. "I will hunt," he announced as he hurried out the door.

Booger and Pete huddled under the glowlamp. Much to Pete's chagrin, Booger displayed a talent for gambling. When he wasn't checking on Jawana, Wat Ho slept.

~~~

When night finally arrived, Hoof collapsed to the floor beside Jawana. He plunged into a dreamless sleep, only to be dragged awake by Jawana's bench banging against his ribs. He lifted his head and a wave of heat hit his face. Then the back of a hand connected with his nose.

"Ow! Double Snerd buckets!" he brayed, blinking back tears. "Hey!" he shouted. "Something's wrong with Jawana!"

Wat Ho loomed over them, clutching a glowlamp. He held a paw over the gorilla. "We've got to cool her down," he said, thinking quickly. "The river will do it! We'll use her blanket to carry her." He gave Booger a gentle shove. "Go take the other side!"

115

Booger stumbled around and gripped the blanket. "Ready!" he said. A fist connected with his cheek. "Snails' whiskers," he muttered, "gorillas are built with way too much arm!"

"Go to her feet," said Wat Ho, "but watch out for her claws."

Booger gripped the very end of the blanket. Wat Ho grabbed the other end and they lifted Jawana clear of the bench. Hoof kicked away the log propped against the door, then hooked the door open with his nose. Wat Ho backed through. Booger stumbled after him.

They set Jawana down at the water's edge. Wat Ho grabbed her wrists and, chanting grimly, backed into the river. Cursing and shrieking, Jawana tried to bite her tormentor. When that failed, she aimed a kick at his head. Finally, she let out a wheezing exhale and went limp. A cloud oozed out of her mouth and condensed into the shape of a bat. With a flap of its wings it was airborne, raking its claws across Wat Ho's cheek before fading into the darkness.

Wat swung around and pulled Jawana up the gravel beach. When her feet were clear of the water, he let go and slumped down.

"Is she dead?" Booger asked anxiously.

Wat Ho looked at the gorilla. "No," he replied.

There was a long pause. "Is she dying?"

"I don't know. I hope not."

Wat Ho's face felt as if it had been sprayed with acid. He touched it, then wiped his fingers on some grass. Booger stepped closer. "Aren't you going to wash that stuff off your face?" he asked.

Wat Ho shook his head, then struggled to his feet. "Help me carry her back to the grange."

~~~

Jawana remained unconscious throughout the next day. Wat Ho sat up with her, placing wet cloths on her forehead. When he judged it was middlenight, he picked up an unlit glowlamp and crept out into a cold drizzle. After waiting for his pupils to reach their widest, he crept

116

through almost total darkness to the river. The gravel beach crunched underfoot; he sat down to wait.

His ears pricked up. *Yes!* There it was again: the creak of an oar. He picked up the glow light and, with two quick touches, flashed it on and off. He counted ten breaths and did it again. After the third flash, he heard the crunch of a boat hitting the gravel beach.

He crept to the water's edge, holding his paws in front of him. A paw contacted the hull of a boat. "I'm here," he called.

"Glad to hear it," Tow Morrow replied. Tow splashed into the water opposite Wat Ho and they pulled the boat up the rocky beach.

Tow kept his fingers on Wat Ho's back as the giant led the way into the grange. Wat Ho propped the door shut and lit the glowlamp. Tow swiped at his face, glanced at Wat Ho and did a double take.

Wat Ho shook his head. "Don't ask."

Tow nodded. He shifted his eyes to Jawana, who lay with her arms dangling on either side of her. "The gorilla's not well?"

"She's unconscious," said Wat Ho. "We'll use the stretcher."

Manny slipped out from behind the stove. Booger and Hoof had started to stir as well.

"We have to cross the river before dawn," Tow said. He looked in Jawana's direction. "Are you all up to it?"

"We'll do what we must," Wat Ho replied.

The rain had stopped by the time the boat was loaded and ready to sail. Wat Ho pushed them out to deeper water and flopped in over the bow. Tow headed across the river, angling upstream to counter the current. Wat Ho noticed where the boat was heading.

"I hoped we'd be let off closer to the wagon," he said.

"My mistress wants to see you," Tow replied.

"Really?" said Hoof. "What for?"

"Not for me to say," Tow replied.

~ 19 ~

Rowena was walking a rut into her floor when Booger threw open her door. He stepped aside to let Wat Ho and Tow bring in Jawana's stretcher.

"Oh Jawana!" Rowena gasped. "Put her on my divan." Wat Ho and Tow had barely settled the gorilla down when Rowena pushed in and ran a rough tongue over her cheek.

"Get off me, you daft Cow!" Jawana opened an eye. "Rowena?" she croaked. "What are you doing here?"

"It's you who's 'here,' my dear," the Cow replied.

"Okay. That's . . . nice." Jawana began to snore softly.

"Sleep is what she needs," said Wat Ho. "We should go somewhere we won't disturb her."

Rowena led them into the kitchen, where the table was weighed down by a half-dozen picnic baskets. "Granny's knock-kneed knickers!" Hoof exclaimed.

Rowena blinked. "It is rather a lot, isn't it," she admitted. "I wanted the chimps to sleep, so I kept them hard at work." She cut an eye toward Wat Ho and gasped, "Oh my! Mr. Ho, you're wounded!"

Wat Ho touched his cheek, but all he said was, "Tow said you wanted to see me?"

"Oh, yes. We had a visitor: a short little thing: all arms, eyes and nose. She left . . ." She swung around. "Tow? Where are you?"

"Here." Tow came in with a glass jar that he thrust at Wat Ho.

"The creature left that . . . thing . . . for you, Mr. Ho," said Rowena.

Wat Ho peered at a slender grey worm that writhed in the jar. "Did Mage Brigita explain this?" he asked.

"All she said was it would draw out poison," Tow replied. He held up a cloth bag. "Her companion left this."

Booger set Pete on the table and took the bag. He pulled out an ornate box. "Hey! There are words on this!" His face fell. "I never learned reading." He held the box out to Wat Ho.

Wat Ho set the worm down and took the box. His expression grew serious as he read,

"My Dearest Hoof:
Someday the gift you find in here
Will light the way when all seems lost
So you may win free but at the cost
Of something that your heart holds dear"

Wat Ho ran his fingers over the box. "I sense a summoning spell," he said. He fixed Hoof with a stern gaze. "Such magic is not free. The stronger the magic the higher the price to be paid."

Hoof swallowed, then said, "I don't care. Open it. Please."

Wat Ho pushed on the lid. A gleaming star fluttered out of the box. It circled the room to settle on Hoof's shoulder, brightened briefly, then faded away. It left a star-shaped patch of white hair.

Hoof shuddered. "Well!" he said. "That was unexpected!"

Manny limped in and sniffed at the air. "The young lady Donkey, she is here?"

"She left Hoof a mysterious gift," said Pete.

"Wait!" said Booger. "There's something else." He pulled out a slender package, to which a note was affixed by a star-shaped seal. He tossed the bag on the table and handed the note to Wat Ho.

"For Manuel," Wat Ho read. "A good friend, loyal and true."

Booger unwrapped a beautifully-crafted blade. Its guard protected a fur lined metal cup. Booger held it down to Manny; it snapped into place over his stump. Manny whipped the weapon back and forth. It had no laces yet stayed firmly attached. He stopped, and a sheath unrolled from the hilt, closing up around the blade in a perfect seal.

"*¡Increíble!*" Manny yipped. "*¡Es mágico!*"

Pete pulled the gift bag over and peered inside. It held what looked like an oversized deck of cards. He knotted the ends of the drawstrings together and slung the bag over his shoulder.

Wat Ho touched his scarred cheek. "Please excuse me," he murmured. He picked up the glass jar and slipped out of the grange.

~~~

A lantern burned on Rowena's dock. Wat Ho slumped beside it. From time to time he picked up the jar and studied the 'thing' that was inside. Until, in one motion, he twisted off the lid and raised the jar to his cheek. The worm struck and he hissed in pain.

The moments stretched out in agony until, at last, the worm dropped away. He lowered his paw. A fat, sluggish coil half-filled the bottle. He flipped the hood off the lantern and tipped the worm into it. It squealed, then disappeared in a puff of flame. He pushed the lantern into the river and got to his feet.

He staggered through the near darkness until he bumped into the kitchen's back door. He fell into the room, turning to land on his back. Rowena let out a terrified bleat. Her eyes were fixed on Wat Ho's cheek, which was laid bare to the skull. Teeth gleamed through the gaping hole in a sick mockery of a grin.

Hoof and Booger rushed forward, then both took a horrified step back. Booger awkwardly rubbed Hoof's neck as the Donkey soaked his chest with racking sobs. He couldn't tear his eyes away from Wat Ho's face. So he saw the transformation begin. "What the . . ."

The flesh around Wat Ho's wound twisted and writhed. Strands of muscle stretched across the gap. Blood vessels formed and pulsed redly. Flesh grew and was covered by skin. Then the new flesh quivered and collapsed like a bursting bubble. The wound was covered by patchy fur. It looked ragged and unfinished.

Wat Ho's eyes opened. They swung back and forth, taking in the anxious faces. He raised a paw to his cheek; probed at it with an insistent finger. "Thath naw righ'," he slurred.

~~~

The eastern sky was tinged with pink when Tow Morrow rejoined the group that huddled in the kitchen. "Jackals are searching the neighbor's farm!" he announced. "There's no time to lose. I can get you away from here by boat but, for most of the way, we'll have to cut through the woods. You have to leave everything behind."

"Not Sack O'Stuff," said Wat Ho. "It comes with me!"

Tow shook his head. "How is that going to work?" he demanded. He jabbed a finger at Pete. "That one can't even walk! Miss Jawana can barely move! You're not exactly in top form yourself. There is no way any of you can carry any extra weight."

Wat Ho shrugged. "None of that matters. I can't leave . . ."

"You two are being foolish!" bellowed Rowena. "I've got all those picnic baskets to deal with. The least I could do is deliver much-needed provisions to dear old Tread Lightly. There'll be room in the cart for other 'things' too. Tow, get my cart ready and loaded."

When Tow looked like he was about to protest, Rowena glared right back at him. With an ironic tug of his forelock, he turned and stalked out of the grange.

~ 20 ~

Tow morrow pulled hard on the oars and aimed for the tree-lined shore. At the last instant he ducked down and swung the oars into the boat. They scraped into a shallow stream that had been invisible from the river. Green branches slapped at its passengers.

"*Pfft!*" Hoof started to spit out a mouthful of leaves, then chewed thoughtfully. He stretched up for another bite.

"It's too shallow take the boat any farther," Tow said as he tied up to a branch. He pointed to the left. "We go that way. Quietly!"

"I will make a reconnaissance," yipped Manny as he flopped into the stream. He scrambled up the bank and disappeared into the foliage.

Tow and Booger splashed into thigh-deep water. Wat Ho settled Jawana into their arms. Gripping each other's wrists in a chair lift, they angled toward a break in the tangled brush.

Wat Ho steadied the boat as Hoof leaped to the bank. Then he gingerly lowered himself into the water. Pete squeezed a cloth bag to his chest as Wat Ho lifted him out of the boat.

Hoof waited on a footpath that hugged the foot of a low ridge. Wat Ho set Pete on his back; the macaque's bandaged feet stuck out as he leaned forward to grab the Donkey's mane.

~~~

After about two thousand paces the stream, except for a small tributary, bent to the right, disappearing into a ravine. The trail carried on straight ahead, bounded by the ridge on one side and the tributary on the other. Both ended at a spring-fed pool that stood at the foot of an

122

embankment. Tow and Booger were on their way around the pool when Manny sprinted down to join them.

"*Señora* Rowena, she is in trouble!" he yipped. He took a panting breath before going on, "It is the *chacales!*"

The tendons in Tow's neck stood out. "Where?" he demanded.

Manny pointed with his nose. "That way. On the road."

"We've got to put you down, Miss," said Tow to Jawana. After she was settled under a tree, he squared his shoulders and took a breath. "Wait here. But if I'm not back by dusk, you'll have to find your own way to the Lightly farm." He hurried away as fast as his aging legs could carry him.

Rowena longed to gore the vile creature blocking her path. But the two jackals behind her would have been delighted at the excuse to hobble the slow-moving Cow.

"Mistress! Mistress!" The voice sounded desperate. And distant. "I'm sorry I was late, Mistress! But you should have waited!"

"Tow?" Rowena gasped, scarcely able to believe her ears.

The jackals spread out to confront the gangly two-legger who quickly closed in on them. "Thank you!" Tow gasped. "Your concern for my Mistress's welfare is appreciated. But I am here now and will keep her safe. You may be assured of that."

The jackals took Tow's measure as he stood over them, clenching and unclenching his hands. The leader's attention shifted to the cart. "What's in there?" she demanded.

"We are delivering cheese and milk to a Venerable Stallion who lives down this road," Tow replied. "Would that we had something to reward your kindness but, alas, times are hard."

"Mind what you say, thrall!" snarled the jackal. "Instead of complaining, you should be singing the praises of our Supreme Leader.

Thanks to his tireless efforts, you are living in the greatest time that this Realm has ever known!"

Tow ducked his head. "You are right, of course. How very foolish of me not to have noticed!"

The jackal turned and bounded over a stone wall. As her companions turned to follow, one of them growled, "Take care, thrall. There may be a gang of dangerous criminals on this road."

"I'm sure they too are enjoying the best of times," Tow muttered. When the jackals were out of sight, he groaned, "Mistress, what *will* I do with you?"

"You'll let me get this cart to where it has to go. After which I'm going home, putting my hooves up and having the chimps crack open a crock of VodCow!" A concerned look crossed Rowena's broad face. "Where did you leave our friends?"

"They're at the end of Dead Snake Ravine."

"Well, hadn't you better get back to them?"

"No, Mistress. I'm not leaving your side. Cousin Knowl can see to your, erm, 'friends,' while I escort you back home."

Wat Ho slid down across from Jawana. He stared at his fingers as if they were the most interesting things in the world. "I was careless," he said at last, "and it almost cost all of us our lives." He looked up and searched Jawana's eyes. "Can you forgive me?"

Jawana snorted. "For what? How was any of this your fault?"

"It was all my fault," Wat Ho insisted, "starting with the ring. But for that, none of this would have happened. And then I was too wrapped up in myself to see what was happening to you. That . . ."

". . . is nonsense," Jawana interrupted. "Crumpt's pet jackals and I have a long history. If it wasn't the ring, it would have been something else. None of it had to do with you."

She settled back and took a few calming breaths. "I've been wounded before and I will be wounded again. Mind you," she added, waving at her legs, "this is a special kind of misery." She raised her eyes to Wat Ho's face. "And what happened to you? That's really something else again."

Wat Ho he exhaled heavily and leaned back. "Evil things are rising up around us." He tapped his cheek. "And this is the price for taking them too lightly."

~~~

Hoof was trying to work the tension out of his neck when he heard a distant cackle. His ears twisted nervously. "What was that?"

Jawana opened an eye. "What was what?"

The sound came again, louder now. "That!" said Hoof.

Manny moved to Pete's side as other shrill voices joined in. *"¡Los chacales!"* he yipped.

Wat Ho lumbered to his feet as the racket drew closer. He rested a paw on Hoof's back. "Now would be the ideal time," he muttered.

Just then, a bush on the far side of the stream started to shake. Hoof jerked his sword out of its scabbard, barely managing to keep its hilt between his teeth. A grizzled two-legger pushed through the bush. "Ga'ey?" Hoof exclaimed, "ott are u ooing ere?"

"No time to chat, young fellow," Gabby Oldeman replied as he splashed across the stream, clutching a canvas sack in each fist. "Half the town's jackals are closin' in on you. You gotta move on."

Wat Ho felt a sharp pang for his absent partner. *This is not enough! I have not done enough!* He shook his head. "There's no way we can outrun them," he said. "Not in the shape we're in."

"Leave me here," said Jawana. "The rest of you will be all right. There's no point in all of us being captured."

"That's not happening!" said Booger.

"Not after going to the trouble of rescuing you!" added Hoof.

125

"You're wasting time!" complained Gabby, who had hobbled about rubbing each of them with his cloth sacks. "I'll lay a false trail to lead the jackals away. And I brought a friend to help. Fair warning: she can make folk nervous; please don't go all crazy on her."

He whistled sharply. "Okay, Shelah. Show yourself."

A clump of bushes parted and Hoof reared in panic. Manny's hackles rose as he crouched in front of Pete, who tried to climb a bush.

"Now I just asked you all not to do that!" Gabby complained. "This is Shelah Down. Unlike me, she don't talk much. But she's a good friend in a fight." Gabby chuckled. "As long as she remembers which side she's on!"

A massive black panther turned emerald-green eyes on Gabby. He raised his hands. "Joke!" he said. "You always know what side you're on!" A beat later he murmured, "I just wish we did." The panther's lips pulled back and Gabby gulped. He glanced at Wat Ho and whispered, "Nice kid but zero sense of humor."

The panther stretched out at Jawana's side. The terrified gorilla tried to shrink away. "What are you doing? Get away!"

"Relax, Jawana," Gabby said. "She's inviting you to get on her back! You're dead lucky! Shelah never takes to strangers."

"I guess dead lucky beats just dead," Jawana muttered. She slung a leg over the panther's back, then wrapped both arms around her neck. The big cat rose effortlessly and padded into the shallow stream. Her gait was so smooth that Jawana hardly felt she was moving at all.

Gabby put Pete on Hoof's back. "Pick it up, folks! You're just about out of time." Hoof followed the panther, stepping gingerly on the rocky stream bed. Booger picked up Manny and followed.

Wat Ho clasped Gabby's hand. The shadows that had clouded the old veteran's eyes were gone. "Don't give me a thought," Gabby said. "I've waited on this for a long time. Now go!" Wat Ho squeezed the old veteran's shoulder and set off after the others. Gabby went in the opposite direction, slapping his scented sacks against every tree and bush he passed.

The jackals were getting closer, and Shelay was heading straight at them! Hoof was about to go into full panic mode when the panther turned up the main channel of the stream. They were out of sight by the time the jackal pack surged past the end of the ravine. The yapping faded as Gabby led them away.

After about five hundred paces, Shelay left the stream and cut through a strip of woods that ran between two fields. The distant yipping and barking took on a mad, frenzied tone. Then there was silence. A single tear rolled down Shelah's cheek as she smoothly carried on. She moved like a shadow, mesmerizing Hoof with her twitching tail. Until she froze and he almost stumbled into her.

Shelah growled. Hoof skipped back in alarm and planted a hoof on Booger's foot. The young two-legger grunted in pain. "Get off!" he hissed, giving Hoof's backside a two-handed shove as Shelah swung around to face them. She stared up at Wat Ho, swinging her head from side to side.

"What is it, Shelah?" asked Wat Ho. "Do you sense danger?"

Shelah shrugged.

Manny moved forward. "I will see," he whispered. He crept under the dense bushes. Pete wobbled from side to side, almost falling off Hoof in his effort to see what was happening. Manny returned, backing through the undergrowth until he could turn to face them.

"La herencia de Booger! It is at the edge of the woods. And there is a two-legger. The thrall of the old Horse, maybe."

"Well, let's get going!" said Hoof.

Shelah shook her head from side to side.

"You don't want to be seen." Wat Ho said. "I understand."

"So what happens now?" asked Pete.

"I'll go make sure it isn't a trap," said Hoof. "Tow Morrow's cousin thinks I'm the boss of you, so I have to lead the way.

"Wait!" Booger hissed.

"I said I'll go alone!" Hoof snapped.

"Well then," said Booger, "I better get the monkey off your back." He transferred Pete to his own shoulders.

Hoof's ears glowed pink. "Right," he mumbled. "Okay then."

He emerged on a field that boasted a bumper crop of tall weeds and short bushes. Ol'Heritance was hidden behind a rock outcrop. Next to it, like a Calf nuzzling its mother, was Rowena's cart. Leaning on the cart was Knowl Morrow.

Hoof kicked at a stone to announce his presence. The old two-legger spun around with a pitchfork clutched in his gnarled hands. "Greetings, Master Hearted," he said as he lowered his weapon. "My Master will be pleased to learn you are well."

"I trust your Venerable Master is fine in fettle," Hoof replied. "I can hardly express my gratitude for the kindness he has shown my unworthy household." He chinned his sword and made a slow circle. "You are unaccompanied?" he asked.

Knowl let out a wheezing chuckle. "Aye, I do prefer *'a Capela.'*"

Hoof nodded wisely. "Indeed," he said, "They protect against both rain *and* sun." He raised his voice and brayed, "Okay! Get your useless selves out here!"

"Ahem," said Booger, who was standing right behind him. "One useless 'non-thrall' at your service, kind and generous master."

Knowl Morrow's eyes widened when he saw Wat Ho struggle out of the bushes with Jawana in his arms. Booger put Pete down and helped the Guardian lift her onto the wagon's bench seat.

Wat Ho crossed to Rowena's cart and heaved a sigh of relief at the sight of Sack O'Stuff. Knowl Morrow leaned on the cart beside him. "Most of what Mizz Batteau sent is in your wagon," he said.

Wat Ho's eyebrows went up. "Mizz Batteau?"

Knowl Morrow's lips quirked. "Rowena Batteau," he said. "One of the finest creatures to draw breath." He shook his head. "She insisted on leaving this cart full of food. It was far too much for a couple of old wrecks like us." He waved at Ol'Heritance, "Most of it's in there. I also strapped a barrel of water to the back."

"Thank you for that. I am sure the food and water will be very useful," said Wat Ho.

"Orders were not to touch that," said Knowl, pointing at Sack O'Stuff. "Left you a spot for it though, right near the front."

"That was well done," Wat Ho said. He picked up Sack O'Stuff and, grunting, he rammed it into the space that had been left for it. After catching his breath, he turned to the venerable two-legger. "The Honorable Donkey Hoof Hearted feels a great gratitude to your, erm, Right Venerable Master for his assistance. And to you."

Knowl Morrow waved it off. "So he said, in his own peculiar way. We were paid in good coin and we honor our deals." He ran a hand over his face. "Though it may yet cost us dear."

Hoof overheard the exchange. "Booger," he murmured. "Put a suitable piece of silver in the old two-legger's hand when we leave."

"Yes, Boss." Booger tipped a few coins into his palm and picked through them in the fading light. "This will do," he said, selecting one and returning the rest to the purse.

Knowl Morrow pulled Rowena's cart out of the way. He pointed into the gloom. "Tow helped me move your wagon here, so that you wouldn't have to come up all the way up to the grange. If you skirt the edge of the woods, you will reach the road. There's a break in the wall you can get through. That way, they won't be able to track your scent straight to us."

"That is wise," said Wat Ho. He squinted at the cloud-covered sky. "There will be no moon," he added. "We will have to find our way through the darkness."

"That means no creature else is likely to find you," said Knowl Morrow. He stepped toward Hoof and bobbed his head respectfully. "Goodbye, young Master Hearted. May you and yours fare well."

"And you and yours," Hoof soberly replied.

Wat Ho sat Pete down beside Jawana and tucked a blanket around them. While they were all occupied, Booger gripped Knowl Morrow's hand, pressing the coin into it. "From my Master."

Booger took up his position beside Wat Ho. They picked up the tow bar and the wagon jerked into motion. Knowl Morrow held up the coin to the fading light. Then he stared after the wagon until it disappeared into the darkness.

They plodded on through the night. When the eastern sky became a purple bruise, they pulled into a copse of trees and parked behind a stone wall. They ate a cold meal then, hoping they were hidden well enough to elude their pursuers for one more day, they slept.

~ *21* ~

Their sleep was shattered by the braying, bleating and squawking of hundreds of creatures. Hoof leaped up and stared across a field that sloped down beyond the trees. On it, a wooden platform towered over a raving mob. And on the platform stood . . .

"Aunt Gertie's gumdrops!" Hoof brayed, "What is that monster?"

"*¡Es muy grande!*" said Manny, awestruck.

"And orange!" added Pete, who had crawled out from under the wagon to kneel beside the others.

"And scary!" Hoof rejoined the conversation.

"And orange!" repeated Pete.

Jawana used a wagon wheel to pull herself upright. "It's an orangutan," she shouted over the noise of the crowd.

The imposing orange creature quieted the crowd with an oddly tiny paw. "No! No! Seriously, you're much too kind!" said his mouth as his paws urged the crowd on to an even greater effort.

Finally, the noise settled down. "My friends! I stand before you as your Divinely Selected Supreme Leader!" His head swung back and forth as he made eye contact with as many adoring creatures as he could. "No creature has ever been as Supreme as me! Or if it comes to that," he chuckled, "as divine. I wrote the book on how to be the Supremist Leader ever!" He paused, then added. "Well, I didn't *write* the book. I don't know how to write. Or read. I'm smarter than that!"

Smarter! Smarter! Smarter! roared the crowd.

"Exactly!" grinned the ape. "I'm too smart to waste time learning things I can hire other, dumber creatures to do. Because I have a very, very big brain. My brain is so big I have to keep most of it in other creatures' heads. That's the way to manage a big brain."

(Big brain! Big brain! Big brain!)

"None of you would know this, but when you have a big brain, you only want to use it for big ideas. You don't waste it on details. Like facts. Big brains don't need facts. When you have a big brain like mine, you make your own facts, whenever you need them!"

(Fake facts! Fake facts? Fake. . .) the chant petered out when the orangutan directed a disapproving glare at his audience.

He waggled a finger. "Not fake," he corrected them. "Alternative! That's what they are! Alternative facts. The Fake News crowd spout their dumb, annoying facts. But for every fact they have, I have my own, better, smarter alternative fact!

"My friends, a Supreme Leader will be selected in less than a quarter moon. Now you and I know that if things are done fairly, that will be me." The speaker leaned forward and lowered his voice. "But the fact is . . . and it wounds me to say this . . . evil creatures are conspiring to steal the Supreme Leadership from me."

You could have heard a pinfeather drop in the shocked silence that followed. Then an outraged roar swelled through the crowd.

The orangutan called for silence. "It's true: My lying, thieving opponents are conspiring to steal the Supreme Leadership."

He ran his eyes over the sea of angry faces. Suddenly he raised his tiny fists in the air and roared, "Are we going to let that happen?"

"No!" shouted a small scattering of voices.

The orangutan cupped a paw to his ear. "What?"

"No!" shouted a few more voices.

"What did you say? I can't hear you!"

"NO! NO! NO!" shouted the crowd, in full voice now.

The orangutan raised a paw to his head (careful not to disturb the tuft of thinning orange hair) as if deep in thought. "Well," he said at last. "We know what to do, don't we?"

The crowd's puzzled silence irritated the orangutan. "The next new moon will see the Installation of a Supreme Leader," he roared. "Go to The Capital, all of you, to celebrate that wonderful event. And go make sure that the true, *Divinely Selected* Leader is Installed!"

"What in the name of Nora's knobby knees is going on here?" breathed Hoof. Then jumped at an answer from behind him.

"That is one of your typical MORON rallies."

Hoof spun around and came nose to nose with a wizened old Billy Goat. A beat-up straw boater slid around the top of his head. Half the brim had unraveled and hung down alongside the Goat's face. He tilted his head, caught the dangling straw between his teeth and chewed. A contented expression crossed his face.

Hoof stared at the odd newcomer. "How do you do, Sir," he said at last, remembering his manners.

The Goat swallowed noisily. "About as well as can be expected, I suppose," he replied.

"I don't get what you meant," said Hoof. "About morons."

But the Goat was distracted by Manny sniffing at his fetlocks.

"I'm sorry about my friend's behavior," Pete apologized. "I'm sure he means no offense, Mr. . . . um . . . Mr. . . . ." faltered Pete.

"Sol Goode," replied the Goat.

"Thanks for understanding," said Pete.

~~~

The crowd broke up, leaving behind mounds of greasy wrappers and empty beer pots. Gulls dropped from the sky to gorge on discarded food. The Goat shook his head, then took a bite of his hat. "Let me see what you eat," he said, "and I'll know what you are made of."

133

He turned back to his audience. "M-O-R-O-N," he spelled. "It's an acronym for 'Make Our Realm Outstanding Now!'"

"Catchy slogan," said Wat Ho as he lifted Pete onto the wagon seat and peeled off his bandages. "Those look good!"

Sol stretched under Wat Ho's arm to chew on a used bandage. "Not bad at all!" he said. A bit tangy, though."

Wat Ho blinked down at the old Goat a few times, then turned back to Pete. "I'll just wrap your feet lightly," he said, as he applied fresh ointment. "You can stand on them. Even walk around a bit, as long as you take it easy."

He closed his medicine chest and eyed Sol Goode. "So that was the Realm's Supreme Leader," he mused.

Sol swallowed noisily. "Alddon Crumpt? Yes. Yes, indeed. Many of his staunchest supporters are total morons."

"So it would seem," said Wat Ho. "But tell me, what happens, exactly, when your Supreme Leader is selected?"

"Last time, the cock had barely finished crowing when Crumpt flopped down in a corner of the arena. He didn't move a muscle while all the other candidates whaled away at each other.

"Finally, only one beat up, exhausted candidate was still standing. Crumpt snuck up behind her and bopped her on the head. Then he walked out and announced he was the winner.

"The Electoral Council debated for days but couldn't find a way to disqualify him. His first act after being installed was to disband the Council. He felt disrespected that they took so long.

"This time, he's scared half to death because he knows he can't pull that trick again. There's a rumor that he's trying to stack the new Electoral Council in his favor."

The Goat swallowed the last of his straw boater. A few beats later a confused look crossed his face. "Say!" he said, waggling his ears "Any of you have a spare hat? The top of my head gets sunburned."

~~~

Manny wandered away from the others and stretched out in a patch of sunshine. Sol Goode ambled up to stand over him. His alert, inquisitive eyes studied the dog. "You look troubled," he observed.

Manny studied Sol Goode's face for some time. Finally, he whispered, *"Perdóname, Señor* Goode," so quietly the Goat had to lean in to hear. "Do you know of a place called 'Coshon Aerie?'"

The old Billy Goat let out a startled bleat. He looked around, as if concerned about being overheard. "Young sir, that is not a name to be spoken lightly—or at all, if it can be avoided!"

"I meant no harm, *Señor*," Manny replied. "But my villagers were taken by traders in slaves. I heard voices, of which one spoke of a 'Coshon Aerie.' I believe that is where my villagers were taken . . . to be worked to death!"

Sol Goode's face softened. "That is a terrible thing, *Señor* Sobad. But the time comes when a creature must—not forget, certainly—but at least try to move on."

"No *Señor,*" Manny bluntly replied. "I cannot . . . as you say . . . move on. I will rescue my villagers. Or die trying."

"You choose a difficult path," sighed Sol Goode. "First, you must cross the seas to the Island of Dark Shadows."

"¡Si!, ¡Si!" barked Manny. *"¡La isla de sombras oscuras!* Of this they spoke!"

"That alone is a treacherous journey. Especially in winter, when gales are constant. Then there is the cliff on which 'Coshon Aerie' is perched; it can be reached only by sea and it can't be scaled. By reputation, it is a place from which no creature returns alive. Deservedly or not I cannot say—no sane creature would try to go there!"

Manny tapped his forehead. "As you can see, *Señor,* my brain is too small to clutter up by vague fears. So I beg of you, please tell me how to find this 'Island of Shadows?'"

Sol Goode sighed. "I know of a creature," he grudgingly admitted, "who may choose to help you. Or not. If they choose not, it could be very dangerous for you. If they do choose to help you, it will be even more dangerous. Please young sir, won't you reconsider?"

"No, *Señor,*" Manny replied. "I cannot."

The Goat sighed. "Very well; let it be on your own head." He looked around as if to make sure he would not be overheard. "In the Realm's Capital, there is sometimes found a ship's captain who goes by the name of 'Kloue van Wraak.' I was told that in her language, her name means 'Claws of Vengeance.' You will never find her. But if you let it be known in certain bars and taverns on the Old Waterfront that you want to meet with her, she may choose to find you. And may Gorme preserve you if she does!"

"The Capital is large!" exclaimed Manny. "What bars? What taverns? Can you not be more clear? I have no time to lose!"

Sol Goode's mouth snapped shut. "I have taken up too much of your time," he said. "Goodbye and good luck!"

He spun around and, with surprising agility, picked his way across the refuse-littered field. He barely slowed down long enough to snap up a greasy delicacy or two before fading into the trees.

Wat Ho watched the old Goat disappear into the woods. "Where's he off to in such a hurry?"

Manny tried to look indifferent. "He did not say," he barked.

~ 22 ~

Jawana crafted a lunch of cheese, refried beans and tortillas. Booger swiped the last tortilla around the bean pot, then slumped to the ground. "That was so good!" he groaned.

Jawana beamed. "Wat Ho's not the only one who can work a bit of magic in the food department!"

A steady stream of creatures passed the wagon, none of whom showed any interest in them. "You know," said Wat Ho, "when we're surrounded by MORONs, we don't stand out at all."

"Say what, now?" said Hoof.

"A lot of dubious characters came to hear the Supreme Leader. The jackals ignored them. If we act like we belong, they may not bother us either. Let's move out while the road is full of MORONs."

"I'm willing to give it a try," said Jawana. A puzzled look crossed her face and she added, "Where are we going, anyway?"

Booger shrugged. "I go where Mr. Hearted goes," he said.

Hoof blinked at that but, before he could say anything, Manny spoke up. "Me, I go to The Capitol," he said.

"Which way is that?" Hoof asked.

"West," Jawana replied. "West and some ways south."

"You know The Capital?" asked Manny excitedly.

"Let's just say I knew it," Jawana replied.

"The Capital is that way?" Hoof asked, aiming his nose at the far side of the field.

"Yes," said Jawana. "Though the road doesn't go straight there."

"Good," said Hoof. "I feel I have to go that way too."

"Well," said Wat Ho, "Since we all agree, let's get on our way."

"Hey!" Pete protested. "Don't I get a vote?"

"No!" the others replied.

The sun was low in the sky when they reached a village that stood where the River Road was met by a trail that ran inland. An inn stood on one side of the junction, across from a dry goods store and bar.

"This may be as good a place to stop as any," said Wat Ho.

When Hoof and Booger entered the inn, they were greeted by a stressed-out baboon. "I'm sorry," he said, "but I've never had so many creatures show up on the same day! And, to top it off, a certain party insisted on taking my biggest room all for themself. All I have left is one stall and two bunks."

"I'll take them," said Hoof. "But what about our wagon?"

"You can park it in the courtyard," the chimpanzee replied. "The gate's barred after dark, and a guard dog is on duty all night."

After paying for their lodging and meals, Booger planted himself in front of Hoof. "So, erm, Boss?" he said, scuffing at the floor with his toe. "The jackals wrecked my best breeches. Can I go across the way and buy another pair?"

"Erm, sure," Hoof said. "We do have an image to maintain."

Booger snorted at that but didn't hesitate to dash out the door. "Happy to do my part!" he laughed.

It took Booger a while to select one pair of breeches from among so many. Then a second garment caught his eye—it was as soft as down and covered in a bright floral print. He stared at it for a long time before slipping it inside his jerkin.

When he went to pay, he decided to buy a second purse as well. At the last moment, he groaned, pulled the flowery garment out of his jerkin, and laid it on the counter. "This too," he sighed.

The chimpanzee minding the store drew her lips back in a humorless grin. "Wise decision!" she said, tilting her head.

Booger followed her gaze and locked onto the cold eyes of a security gorilla. His mouth suddenly felt very dry.

The chimpanzee's grin widened. "That's three duclats."

The security gorilla curled a lip at Booger, who abandoned any thought of disputing the price. "Of course," he said through clenched teeth as he handed over the coins.

He hurried back to his wagon and stashed the new clothing in his duffel. Then he slipped all of the Sovereigns and all but two gold marks into the new purse and bound it around his waist. The old, now much lighter purse he hung around his neck.

A heavy bar slammed into place, then footsteps crossed the courtyard and entered the inn. Booger waited several beats, then jumped down from the back of the wagon. An ornate coach gleaming in the lantern light drew him like a magnet; he took a step forward.

"I'd go inside now, if I was youse," growled a deep voice. It came from a huge, brownish dog who outweighed Booger by a lot. Heavy cheeks drooped down on either side of a serious set of teeth. The dog's snout wrinkled disapprovingly.

"Hello Sir. Yes, Sir," said Booger as he edged away. "I was just admiring that fine carriage. Do you know who's it is?"

The bull mastiff stepped forward. "No creatures allowed in the courtyard once da gate closes," he growled. "If you're after needing some 'at, whistle me up and I'll escort youse to your rig."

"Right," said Booger as he sidled toward the side door to the inn. "Gotcha!" He glanced back at the coach before going inside.

He found the others in a dark corner of the common room, with Wat Ho hiding his cheek behind a paw. "Yeah," he said as he sat down. "Your scar is *totally* the most noticeable thing about you."

~~~

For the days that followed, the travelers got up with the sun and walked until sundown, stopping only to eat a cold roadside lunch. On the fifth day they slogged through driving rain and fetlock-deep mud. They reached an inn at nightfall, wet, miserable and too tired to do more than shovel in whatever food was placed in front of them.

Hoof sensed a brooding menace seeping through the inn. He studied the other patrons: red-garbed fingered folk to one side; blue-bandanaed Hooved creatures and their grooms on the other. Both groups glared at each other. The slightest nudge could tip them towards violence. He turned to catch Wat Ho watching him. The Guardian had an odd expression on his face; it almost looked . . . approving?

Hoof shivered, then shook his head to clear it. "How much further is the Capital?" he whined. "I feel like I've been walking forever!"

Wat Ho snorted and turned away. Jawana's eyes flicked back and forth between the two. "It's at least six more days," she said at last.

"Seriously? How is that even possible?"

"What do you mean?"

The Supreme Leadership thingy is in The Capital, right?"

"That's right. In a special arena just outside of the city."

"Well, if Crumpt was around Rock Bottom the same time as us, how could he even get there in time?"

"The Supreme Leader has a coach pulled by teams of Stallions," Jawana explained. "Fresh Horses take over two or three times a day. They can cross the whole Realm in three or four days."

~~~

The storm broke and the land dried out under a warm sun. Even Wat Ho's spirits had risen by the time they stopped for the night.

When they woke, clean and refreshed, their fellow guests were in turmoil. The red-garbed set sulked. The blue-bandanaed crowd laughed and sang. The two factions shouted insults at each other. A waiter broke up a fight between a troop of chimpanzees and a brown bear.

As usual, Wat Ho selected a table in a dark corner of the common room, where he was joined by Hoof and Booger. A peevish waiter came to take their order.

"What's going on?" asked Hoof.

"The Blues claim our Supreme Leader lost the Selection." The waiter scowled. "They're lying! No way did our Leader lose!"

Hoof looked up to see Pete and Jawana at the door, scanning the crowd. She spotted Wat Ho's towering bulk, tucked Manny under one arm and started towards them. A black bear lurched into her and her paw flashed out. The bear flipped over and landed on their back. Jawana carried on as if nothing had happened.

"Wow!" exclaimed Hoof. "Did you see that?"

Then the waiter banged a pail of mash down in front of Hoof and everything else was forgotten. But before he could take a bite, something plopped into it. He looked up, did a double take, and froze.

"What the Charlie D is that?"

An exceptionally hairy creature dangled from a web of rope that covered the ceiling. A long arm stretched out and with almost infinite slowness, it snagged its claws over the next rope in the web. Their back leg moved just as slowly, then their body rocked forward.

"I've seen their kind before," said Pete, "back when I sailed the high seas. But never this far north; sloths like it warm."

The creature reached the wall and climbed, headfirst, down a rope ladder. He stopped at Wat Ho's ear. "Hell . . . oh . . .Guardian." His eyes took in Wat Ho's damaged cheek, slowly closed, then opened again. "Well . . . come to my . . . humble inn."

Disturbed by his low, rumbling voice, a horde of brown moths crawled out of the hair on his back. They flew around him twice, then burrowed back into his hair.

"Hello, old friend," said Wat Ho. "What's happening?"

"Too much," droned the sloth.

"So what's the fuss about?" asked Pete.

"Alddon Crumpt's . . . trick," breathed the sloth.

"But that was five winters ago!" said Hoof. "Wasn't it?"

"This time they all fell down." Hoof ate several swallows of mash as he waited for the sloth to continue. "Except one skinny old Giraffe. His knees were too bad to get down."

Booger signaled to the waiter and ordered juice. "When he saw he was all alone," continued the sloth, "he hobbled out and declared himself to be 'Selected.' The other candidates are . . . displeased."

There was a pause as his audience ensured that the sloth had finished. Pete broke the silence. "So what's going to happen?"

"Given a choice between the orangutan and the Giraffe—who may not live out his mandate—the Council will back the Giraffe. But as you can see . . ." The Sloth side-eyed a scuffle that had broken out nearby, ". . . the Red Necks won't let that happen without a fight."

"But how do you even know what happened?" asked Hoof. "The Capital is days of travel away from here!"

The sloth ruminated on this. "As soon as the rain stopped, the messengers took wing. They're mostly Eagles and can cover the Realm in three days. "It's scary how fast news spreads through the air."

～～～

Pete and Wat Ho left the inn together. "That sloth back there?" said Pete. "It's nuts, but it looked like you two knew each other!"

"We do," said Wat Ho.

"How is that even possible?"

"Sloths live in slow motion. By the time they're a year older, a generation has passed by for the rest of the world."

~ 23 ~

The muddy expanse of the Mighty Mojo River spread out before them. On the hillside below them, a flock of school-lambs formed a woolly semicircle around an elderly ewe. Beyond them, a fist of bald apes idled on a stone wharf.

Jawana saw the bald apes scramble to their feet. She turned her eyes upriver, where a flat-bottomed barge sailed ponderously downstream. "That's what I hoped to see!" she murmured.

The vessel's square sail flapped as it angled toward the wharf. A troop of monkeys pulled the sail up and tied it to its spar. The foresail was struck and weighted lines flung to the bald apes.

The lambs saw the barge and, bleating excitedly, gamboled towards the wharf. Booger and Pete burst out laughing as their frantic teacher ran after them. Evan Wat Ho managed a lopsided grin.

"Listen up," Jawana said. "Booking passage on that barge would spare us days of slogging. But we have to get down there before any creature else takes the space!"

Jawana ran on ahead, reaching the barge as it was being tied up. "Ahoy, Captain!" she bellowed. "Get your butt out here!"

A brown bear, wearing a captain's cap and wristbands, leaned over the ship's rail. He glowered at Jawana. "Some creature's aimin' to get their arms fed to 'em." he growled. "Would that be you?"

"No," Jawana replied as she leaped for the boat's rail and swung aboard. "I aim to offer you some easy money. All you have to do is take a few passengers and a wagon to the Capital."

The wagon jounced to a stop next to the barge. Pete leaned out to check it out. A bear in a captain's cap ran his eyes over the wagon, then the creatures gathered around it. They reached Wat Ho and his head shook hard enough to knock his cap off. He stalked away. Jawana called out to him. He froze, then growled a reply. He did not look back as he pushed into a small cabin at the back of the barge.

Jawana came down the gangway. "It's all good!" she said. "Captain Waite will be pleased to take us to the capital!"

Pete snorted. "I saw how 'pleased' he was," he muttered. "If I sleep on that boat, it'll be with one eye open."

Jawana went to Booger with an outstretched paw. "Okay, moneybags. The cruise will cost one-and-a-quarter gold marks."

Booger gaped. "Did you book passage or buy the boat? Fine," he added with sigh. "Step into my counting house." He went to the back of the wagon and, after checking for prying eyes, teased a gold mark out of Hoof's old purse. He dropped it into Jawana's palm and dug around some more.

"Come on Booger!" she snapped. "We sail today, you know?"

He stuck out his tongue, then handed her four more coins.

~~~

Jawana came out of the Captain's cabin. "Okay," she said, "They'll put the wagon on board now. But we won't sail until the sun lines up with the purple line on the sunclock."

"Why are we stuck here half the afternoon?" asked Pete.

"The Captain has to sleep; he'll be up all night," Jawana replied.

Booger watched his wagon get picked up by a hoist. Three burly bald apes swung it around and set it behind the mast. A ship monkey bolted its wheels to the deck to secure it in place.

Pete dug out a deck of cards and raised his eyebrows at Booger. "Are you sure? " said Booger. "You already owe me eight sovereigns!"

"Beginner's luck," Pete retorted. "Any other takers?"

"No thanks," Wat Ho replied. "I need a nap." He laid his head on a coil of rope and closed his eyes.

"And, erm, I've got some business to take care of," Jawana hastened to say. "See you later!"

Hoof said, "I'm going ashore, too." When Booger started to get up, he added, "By myself."

"Okay," Booger said as his thin fingers deftly shuffled the cards. "If you're sure. Have a good time!"

Hoof almost had second thoughts as he eyed the seedy waterfront. But he chinned his sword, then clattered down the gangway.

~~~

Hoof was getting bored of his aimless wandering when his eyes suddenly locked on a beautiful Jenny attached to a milk cart. "Starr!" he brayed. "Starr! It's me!"

The Jenny's eyes widened in alarm. She turned and galloped back the way she had come with the cart careening behind her. Hoof galloped after her. The Jenny pulled up at a stable, slipped her traces and dodged through a swinging red door.

Hoof butted the door. It didn't budge. "Starr," he called. "You said we could be friends. Won't you please talk to me, at least?" He gave up and headed back towards the wharf.

He spun around at the sudden clatter of hooves, but it was just a young Mule. He turned and plodded on.

"Hey mister!" called a childish voice. "Wait up, will ya!"

Why must these youngsters bray their heads off? It's so annoying!

"Wait up, you Donkey! Mother wants to talk to you."

Mother? Hoof swung around as the young Mule clopped up to him. "Who's your mother?" he asked.

The tall, gangly youngster stared down at him. "What do you mean 'who's my mother?' You just chased her home!"

"That was your mother?" Hoof blurted. "But you're a Mule!"

"I'm a Hinny, actually. Lotta dummies don't know the difference."
There's a difference? "Why would she want to talk to me?"

"How would I know? She just said to find you and bring you back." The Hinny swung around and trotted back up the street.

"Do you have a name?" Hoof called after him.

"Yes," the Hinny replied.

~~~

Hoof followed the Hinny through the red door. The interior of the stable was plain, but larger than he had expected. The whitewashed walls gleamed in the light from a window set into the back wall. The furnishings were simple but shone from frequent scrubbing.

The Hinny retreated to the far corner, from where he glared at the new arrival. The only other occupant was a wizened chimpanzee who squatted on a stool, massaging their gnarled paws.

"Mother!" brayed the Hinny "He's here!"

A side door swung open, and she entered. Hoof stared: It was Starr, as Starr might look after a few more winters went by. Still beautiful, but a bit careworn and softer around the edges. Her upper lip curled nervously, revealing strong, straight teeth.

"Greetings," she said. Her voice quavered. She took a breath. When she started over her voice was steady. "Welcome to our humble abode. May I offer you some refreshment?"

Hoof ducked his head in the manner appropriate for meeting one's elders. "It is an honor to meet you, Ma'am. I thank you for your hospitality, but I want for nothing."

"Surely you must be thirsty after all that running." Her laughter tinkled dryly. "I know I am. Greta!" She turned her gaze toward the chimpanzee. "Please fetch some fresh water."

The chimpanzee got up and shuffled through a side door.

"I am Starshine Brightly," said the Jenny, curling her lip politely.

Hoof's mind raced. "Hoof Hearted," he distractedly replied.

The young Hinny puffed with laugher. Starshine struggled to suppress the twitching of her own lips as she snapped, "Jetsome Brightly! That was rude. I think you had best leave the room!"

"Aw, come on, Ma" Jetsome brayed. "I didn't mean nothing!"

"I meant nothing," Starshine corrected her son.

"Yeah, that's what I said. Me neither," he replied.

Hoof's eyes were glued to his hostess as the chimpanzee returned, dropped a low table in front of him, then shuffled out again. "Why did you run away?" he asked at last.

Jetsome's behavior and bad grammar were forgotten as Starshine considered his question. "I mistook you for a creature I couldn't bear to face . . . ever again. I'm afraid I panicked."

"But you sent your son after me," Hoof said.

"Yes." she replied. "I realized you are much too young to be who I first thought you were. But that sword . . ." She shuddered.

Hoof touched his chin to the hilt. "It was my grandsire's," he said.

"Oh! My! Gorme!" Jetsome brayed happily. "You're Dummy Otie's grandson!"

Hoof attention remained fixed on Starshine. "You knew my grandsire," he said.

"Yes," she admitted. " A long time ago."

"Can you tell me about him?" Hoof asked.

Greta returned with a bucket of water that she banged on the table in front of Hoof. She glared at him for several beats before she forced herself upright and shuffled away.

Starshine waited until the chimpanzee had left the room. "I would rather not," she said at last. "As I said, it was long ago. He was charming, in a crude sort of way. But he wasn't very nice: He was vain and selfish and often . . . cruel." Her gaze flicked toward a painting that hung on the opposite wall and she smiled. "But he gave me the greatest gift I could ever have wished for."

Hoof followed her gaze and gasped. "That's Starr Brightly!" His eyes shifted to the Jenny. "You are Starr's mother?" Starshine nodded. Hoof gulped. "So, is Donkie Otie Starr's father?" She nodded again. But . . ." Hoof brayed hopelessly, ". . . that makes Starr my *aunt?*"

"Half-aunt, yes," Starshine whispered.

Jetsome whinnied in delight. "And I'm your half-Ass uncle!"

~~~

Starshine glossed over the hard times brought on by Starr's untimely arrival, preferring to dwell on the good things that happened after she met a Stallion who was strong, kind and true. They became life mates and Jetsome was the high-spirited result of their union.

Slightly exaggerated tales of Hoof's adventures were lapped up by the young Hinny. When Hoof realized how much time had passed, he gasped. "Oh my!" he brayed. "If I don't get back right now, the boat will leave without me!"

"Jetsome will guide you," Starshine said. "He knows the quickest route to everywhere in this town."

"Thank you," Hoof said. "It has been a real pleasure to meet you."

"And you as well," said Starshine. "I'm glad I sent Jetsome after you." As Hoof turned to go, she added, "You look like your grandsire, but you are not at all like him. I hope you know that."

~~~

"I know this town like the back of my hoof," Jetsome stated proudly. "I'm gonna take over Mother's milk run soon, so she can retire. We go that way," he added, pointing with his nose.

Hoof tried to gather his thoughts, which wasn't easy with the excited youngster chattering in his ear. "I like your sword. It was Donkie Otie's, huh? I bet you want to be just like him, huh?"

"No!" snapped Hoof. "He was a vain, selfish creature who cared only about himself. I want to be *nothing* like him!"

"Oh!" Jetsome replied, briefly taken aback. "Okay, then." A few beats later he said, "So What's your boat called, anyway?

"I don't know," Hoof admitted.

Jetsome snorted. "I hope you know it when you see it." He turned down an alley. "C'mon. This is a shortcut to the wharf."

Hoof turned to follow but was stopped in his tracks. After a few paces Jetsome looked back. "You comin' or what?"

The white star on Hoof's shoulder started to burn. "No." he said. "We're not going that way."

"Suit yerself," Jetsome groused, "but it'll take a lot longer to get to yer boat."

They reached the wharf as two bald apes bent over the barge's gangway. They had just time enough to jump out of the way before Hoof thundered between them.

Jetsome trotted alongside the barge. "Bye!" he shouted. "It was nice to meetcha. Oh, and the boat's called *The Dancing Sea Cow.*" His hooves beat a tattoo on the stone.

The kid can read? "I enjoyed meeting you too," Hoof brayed. The barge had cast off and was being pushed clear of the wharf when he added, "When you see Starr again, give her my love, okay? And tell her I understand."

~ 24 ~

A troop of boat-monkeys screeched and whooped overhead, adjusting the sails in response to the Captain's bellowed commands. Below them, Jawana stared at the muddy water passing under the bow. Hoof dodged through a maze of crates to stand beside her. She eyed him quizzically but said nothing.

Hoof sighed deeply.

"If you think this is slow," said Jawana, "try going upstream."

"Huh?" Hoof climbed out of his mental fog. "I'm sorry, Jawana. I was sort of daydreaming."

"I said it's faster going downstream than up," Jawana said.

"Yeah? I guess that makes sense." He drifted off again. *Starr's my aunt! Her mother's nice—I see where Starr got it from. And Jetsome's okay once you get to know him. A bit rambunctious, but still . . . They're a great family. A family I never even knew I had!*

Hoof began to take an interest in his surroundings. A triangular sail snapped above his head, billowing between the main mast and the bowsprit. Behind the mast, a huge square of canvas angled toward the stern, barely clearing the top of Ol'Heritance.

The Captain rested his paws on the spokes of a gigantic wheel. His eyes shifted between the river and the sails. Suddenly, he barked a command and spun the wheel while the monkeys skittered about, tightening or loosening ropes to adjust the sails. The vessel changed course to pass between two buoys bobbing on the river.

150

Hoof let out a whoop of excited laughter. Jawana shot him an amused glance. "Back among us, are you?" she chuckled.

They fell into a companionable silence. Darkness fell and a mist began to rise off the river. Monkeys set colored lanterns fore and aft.

Hoof shivered. "I'm getting cold. And hungry."

"Me too," Jawana agreed. "It's time we scared up some supper."

~~~

They found the others gathered around Wat Ho, apparently hanging on his every word. Jawana squeezed down between Wat Ho and Pete. Hoof moved around to look over her shoulder.

"The Supreme Stallion (they weren't 'Kings' back then) accidently trod on a map. Which left a smudge where the Mighty Mojo meets the Big'nwett Sea. A half-moon later he noticed the mess and bellowed, 'The Goddess has spoken! The magical hoofmark shows where to build my new Capital!'

"The Master Mariner was ordered to build a dozen giant barges. Then the Honorable Holder of the Adze had to fill them with granite from the Royal quarry. Wheels turned and saws sawed and whips cracked on the backs of half the realm's creatures. Two summers later the barges set sail. The celebration lasted for days!

"But blocks of stone do not turn themselves into palaces. The Exalted Goat Governor of the Eastern Province was ordered to assemble an army of stonemasons, joiners, glaziers and weavers. This task rolled down many bureaucratic layers to land on the backs of the farmers, foresters, and builders who make up the bedrock of The Realm. They rounded up an army of drunks and troublemakers and sent them off, happy to be rid of a bad lot.

"There were two key things the Supreme Stallion overlooked. One: The mouth of the Mighty Mojo River was known as 'The Bay of Biting Bugs.' There was a reason for this. Two: The delta was home to a very warlike tribe of 'blue-skinned' apes. (It was actually just blue paint, but they scared the Charlie D out any creature foolish enough to wander into their territory.)

"When the unfortunate workers reached their destination, they were swarmed by millions of biting bugs. Half of them were driven mad. Most of those who kept their sanity went native. 'You'll never rue going Blue,' became a catchphrase up and down the river.

"Three summers later, a party of dignitaries sailed downstream on a barge filled with vintage barleywine and rich preserves. Their job was to start provisioning the Royal larder. But instead of fine palaces, they found only a few empty huts and an unfinished log wall.

"The dignitaries left the barge and battled their way through Blueskin territory to get back home. After bathing and perfuming themselves, the survivors prostrated themselves before His Supremeness. Their agreed-upon script was that 'the work had progressed but not quite as quickly as had been hoped.'

"The Supreme Stallion set off to personally oversee the completion of his new Capital. When he saw the state of things, he had a heart attack and collapsed. But to every creature's surprise, the tough old Horse recovered. It was a fly that did him in; it got through the mesh surrounding the Royal Stall and bit him on the nose. A few days later he succumbed to a rare Equine fever.

"The Supreme Stallion left no direct heir and there was little desire to come up with a replacement. The Goat Governors, who had always run everything anyway, created a Leadership Council. Their first act was to declare that, since there was no Supreme Stallion, there was no need for a new capital. Their second act was to grant amnesty to the so-called deserters who had abandoned the futile attempt build one in a bug-infested swamp.

"Most of the deserters crept back out of the swamp. They cleared a couple of islands at the middle of the delta, where they avoided the worst of the bugs. They made peace with the Blueskins and used the vast amount of available granite and luxury merchandise to build what became an unassailable, highly profitable port city."

Wat Ho paused for a few beats, then lifted his shoulders in a shrug. "And that was that," he declared. "It was clear that, for several generations to come, the Realm would pose little threat to itself or to its neighbors. So, we left. Nor had we any reason to return . . . until now."

There followed a period of silence as all eyes stared at Wat Ho, whose own cat-like eyes seemed to twinkle in the lantern light.

"That's, erm, quite a tale," said Jawana at last.

"Yeah!" exclaimed Booger. "What I want to know is how that bug get through all that mesh to bite the Supreme Whasis?"

"Well, now," said Wat Ho. "That's an interesting story . . ."

"For another time," Jawana cut in. "Right now, it's time to do something about feeding ourselves."

~~~

Booger tore off a mouthful of stale bread. He moistened it with a sip of water, chewed vigorously for several beats, and swallowed. "If things were so great under the Goats," he asked, "why did The Realm go back to Horse Kings?"

"No idea," Wat Ho replied. "That was after my time."

"Well," said Jawana, "I don't claim to have 'firsthand' knowledge, but legend has it that, about five generations ago, a prophet came out of the northern wilds. He stood taller at the shoulder than a Giraffe's head and had antlers as deep as ploughshares and wide as a stable door. The creature staggered into an outpost of the Church of the Most Absolutely Divine Goddess starving, swarming with ticks and babbling about 'being spoken to by Gorme Herself.'

"After being nursed back to health the creature wandered The Realm, preaching to huge crowds. Most creatures just wanted to get a look at the 'huge great beastie' but they stayed to hear his message: The

Goddess had granted the Horse dominion over all others and it was a sacrilege that Her Chosen Ones had ended up as vassals to a wretched flock of bleating Goats.

"In reality, the Goats had treated the Horses well, letting them keep their hereditary lands and chattels after the Supreme Stallion died. Horses were rich and as usual, wealth fed greed. They decided to overthrow the Regime. To win support, they promised to share the 'greedy Goats untold riches' with the citizens of The Realm."

"That didn't happen!" brayed Hoof. "Did it?"

"No," Jawana replied. "First of all, the Goats weren't nearly as rich as the Horses made out. Plus the Horses owed a fortune to the mercenaries they hired. In the end, they were too greedy to share even what was left. They claimed that, as a 'tithe to The Church of the MAD Goddess,' its value to the souls of the masses outweighed any worldly enjoyment they would have received."

"But seriously," Pete interjected. "The Goats were still in charge, right? What difference did all that fuss make?"

"The Goats suffered, at first," said Jawana, "but it didn't take Horsekind long to realize that they were hopeless at running a vast Realm. They begged the Goats to return to their old roles. Things went back to the way they were before, except a Horse was named 'Supreme Monarch' and, finally, The Capital was moved to the mouth of the Mighty Mojo River.

"The Central Government occupies many palaces, spread over three islands. The center island was the 'Royal Seat.' Now it's called Regency Island and is where the Supreme Leader lives.

"The Royal Seat used to be surrounded by a high stone wall. With its drawbridges raised, it was an invincible fortress. But after generations of peace, most of the wall was torn down. The stone was used to extend the piers and warehouses that cover half the island. The channels were dredged to accommodate the largest ships. The drawbridges are still raised, but only to let ships pass under them.

"Travel to the surrounding islands, where most citizens live and work, is mainly by boat." She closed her eyes. "It was so beautiful," she said dreamily. Then she snapped out of it and briskly added, "I suppose it still is."

Manny, who had pretended to be dozing, piped up, *"Señorita* Jawana, it is clear you love your Capital. But you left to run an inn deep in the, what do you call them, the boondoggles. But why?"

Jawana laughed. "I think you mean 'boondocks.' But frankly, 'boondoggle' probably applies equally well."

Wat Ho cleared his throat, "You didn't answer the question."

"Didn't I?" she replied. When all eyes remained fixed on her she relented. "I loved The Capital and enjoyed the role I was given to play. But after the last change in leadership, things changed. I left under somewhat of a . . . well, let's call it a 'cloud.' And on that note," she added as she got to her feet, "I'm going to get some sleep."

They spread out across the deck, making themselves as comfortable as they could. Except Booger, who propped himself up against a crate and prepared to keep watch for the night.

~ 25 ~

Booger slid sideways and slammed an elbow into the deck. *Ouch!* He rolled onto his back and squinted up at tightly furled sails. A dozen ship-monkeys' eyes gleamed down from where they squatted, ghostlike, on the spar. *What the hey?*

Coarse laughter echoed across the deck. The gangway crashed into place and two bald apes stomped across it. Booger scooted backwards across the deck, barely avoiding an open hatch.

Manny's eyes flew open to the sound of marching boots. *The evil ones! They have returned!* A growl tore from his throat as he scrambled out from under a blanket, only to grabbed from behind. He twisted around and sank his teeth into a fleshy paw.

"Ouch! Stop it, Manny! Settle down; it's me, Pete!" Manny stopped struggling. Pete let go of him and rolled to his knees.

The bald apes carried a crate suspended between two poles. They reached the hatch and lowered the crate into the hold. Then they picked up the poles and marched off the ship.

Jawana and Hoof had gotten up to see what the commotion was about. As Booger crossed the deck to join them, he heard the guttural snarl of a large cat, quickly silenced. His heart was in his throat as he sprinted the last few steps to get behind Jawana. He watched uneasily as two more crates were lowered into the hold. Then the bald apes stomped off the ship for the last time and the ship cast off.

Jawana yawned. "Well, it's back to sleep for me!"

Booger grabbed her arm. His voice quavered as he asked, "Do they carry creatures in the hold? Like giant pad paws?"

Jawana burst out laughing. "I'm sorry," she said, "I shouldn't laugh, but I'm afraid your imagination is running away with you." She was still chuckling to herself as she crawled into her makeshift nest.

~~~

The third evening brought cold, soaking rain. A shipmonkey appeared at the small forward hatch and waved for Pete to join him belowdecks. Manny scampered in behind him and the hatch slammed shut. Manny made himself useful by disposing of pesky rodents. Pete lured his hosts into an all-night card game.

The rest of the travelers dealt with the rain as best they could; Jawana rebuilt her nest in the front end of Ol'Heritance; Booger settled for a lumpy bed in the back; Wat Ho and Hoof squeezed under an old sail that had been stretched between two stacks of crates.

~~~

Booger woke to sunlight glancing into his eyes. *The Dancing Sea Cow* was so quiet he could hear Jawana breathing. He rolled to his knees, backed out of the wagon and stared in amazement.

The ship was tied up at a flagstone wharf. Neat stacks of crates lined a stone wall that ran along the back of the wharf. Beyond the wall, a very old town clung to the face of a steep hill. A cobbled street climbed the hill in wide terraced switchbacks.

Residences graced the ends of each curve, growing larger and more pretentious as they neared the summit, where a stone wall enclosed a castle. The castle's central roof soared to a majestic, four-sided peak. A flag flapped at the pinnacle, displaying a rampant red dragon on a green background.

"Holy Cow!" Booger exclaimed. "Where the Charlie D am I?"

"It is impressive, isn't it?" The voice was as silky-smooth as a pat of Rowena's butter. It emerged from a portly silverback. The parts of the gorilla that were not hidden under a red waistcoat were perfectly groomed. A monocle squeezed between the gorilla's right eyebrow and cheek magnified the eye that twinkled behind it. His left arm cradled a red satchel that almost disappeared against his waistcoat.

Booger was distracted by a thump and startled yelp. He leaned around the gorilla and caught a glimpse of Jawana pelting across the wharf to duck between two stacks of crates. He raised his eyes, acting as if his only interest was in the view. "Is that a real castle?" he asked. "I never saw one of those before."

The silverback's lips formed an indulgent smile. "That is the Palace of the Eleventh Illustrious Stallion Waterstrider," he announced. "It is my honor to serve as his Grace's, ahem . . . *Chamberlain.*"

Booger stared mutely. *Am I supposed to applaud or something?*

Thankfully, the awkward silence yielded to the sound of marching feet. A stream of bald apes, all in green tights and vests, strode in single file along the wharf. "Ah yes," murmured the Chamberlain. "It's about time the porters got here."

As the porters walked across the deck, parcels flew out of the open aft hatch. The porters lurched about, catching them before they fell to the deck. The Chamberlain and the Captain pored over a clay tablet, on which they marked off items as the porters marched by. When the last porter departed, the gorilla scratched a signature into the tablet, handed it to a ship-monkey and strode off the ship. Booger stared after him; something looked different, but what?

~~~

Booger had kept one eye on the activities going on around him and the other on the gap through which Jawana had disappeared. She did not come out. After the Chamberlain left, he went ashore to investigate. On both sides of the narrow passageway, stacks of crates rose above his head; at the end was a stone wall. He backed out, scratching his head, and bumped right into Captain Waite.

The startled bear roared and swung around, poised to deliver a crushing blow. "Ah," he said, after a brief internal struggle. He lowered his paw. "Where be you goin' in such a hurry?"

"I-I'm looking for Jawana!" Booger stammered. He glanced at a satchel that hung from the bear's shoulder, then quickly looked away. "I thought maybe we could see the town." A puzzled look crossed his face. "While you slept?"

"Yeah, well. First, I gotta go . . ." Waite paused. "How'd you like to earn a few copper bits?"

"I'd like it fine, I guess."

Waite glared at a clutch of laborers who crowded past them. "We can't talk here. Meet me in my cabin."

He lumbered back to the vessel, leaving a mystified Booger to stare after him. The gangway creaked under the bear's weight as he stomped aboard. Booger took a deep breath, trotted as far as the cabin door, then hung back, chewing on a fingernail.

"Get in here!" The throaty growl made the door vibrate.

"Yessir!" Booger yelped. He squeezed into the cabin, half of which was taken up by bear. A nest spread across the remaining floor, piling up against a narrow table that stood in the corner. A scritching sound at Booger's ear made him jump. He spun around and came face to snout with a grinning spider monkey. The monkey, decked out in a red pillbox hat and vest, squatted on a shelf.

"Hallo?" said Booger. The monkey raised a paw in greeting.

Waite shrugged the shoulder from which the satchel was suspended. "Killer, get this off me."

Killer? thought Booger as the monkey leaped onto the bear's back. Gripping the satchel's strap, he backed over the bear's head, knocking the Captain's cap off as he jumped to the floor.

"Sorry Master!" his squeaked. He picked the cap up and balanced it between the bear's ears.

159

Waite rolled his eyes at Booger. "That bag needs deliverin' to a certain party and no creature else. Don't even think about losin' it!"

"Don't' worry, Sir," Booger replied as he picked up the satchel by its strap. "I'll guard it with my life!"

The Captain snorted. "And exactly what's that worth?"

"To me, a lot!" Booger replied.

"Good!" The bear's lips stretched into a scowl. "Because if you mess this up, I'm gonna rip out your lungs and feed 'em to you!"

"Understood, Sir!" said Booger. "Where do you want me to go?"

The Captain's beady red eyes glared into Booger's wide-open blues. Then he choked out a ragged laugh. "You got guts, kid," he allowed. "I'll give you that. I just hope you've got brains too."

"I'm not book smart," said Booger, "but I've kept my skin in one piece for," he counted on his fingers, "four winters since Da died."

"D'you read?" snapped The Captain, who was not one for expressing false sympathy.

"Not as such, no," Booger admitted. "But I know my numbers. I learned them playing cards with Pete Sake."

The Captain snorted. "Why does that not make me feel better?" He scratched his head, knocking off his cap. The monkey scampered down to recover it. "Oh, just leave the dirt-blasted thing!" The Captain glared at Booger. "Oh well," he growled at last, "I've gone this far, so I may as well go through with it. So listen up."

Booger pointed at the sides of his head. "I'm all ears, sir."

"That's good. Because I was beginnin' to think you're mostly mouth. Now shut it and listen!"

Booger squeezed his lips shut and looked attentive while the bear went on, "Just inside the gate is a road that follows the city wall around the town. Halfway around is a square surrounded by shops and stalls. A 'colleague' of mine has a shop there: number twenty-seven. That's a two and a seven, wrote side-by-side. Got that?"

Booger nodded and The Captain continued, "The shop is at the far end of the square. It sells fabrics from across the Big'nwett Sea. Tell the owner you got fabric samples from Captain Waite. The owner will say they're overstocked and aren't interested. You say, 'these are special and you'll be sorry if you don't at least look at 'em.' He'll ask if they're 'duty-paid.' To which you say, 'all requirements have been met.' Got all that?"

Booger repeated the instructions. Waite grunted approvingly. "Okay. That'll do."

Booger grinned. "So this is like spy stuff, huh? If the owner doesn't give all the right answers, then I'll know they're an imposter!"

"Exactly," said Waite. "Or if he's not a pygmy hippopotamus."

Booger blinked at him. "You couldn't have led with that?"

Waite shrugged. "The hippo's gotta give you an envelope. Don't let him have the satchel until you get it, then you bring it here. Right away, with no dawdlin' in the town. Is that clear?"

"As glass," Booger replied. He picked up the satchel and slung it over his shoulder. It banged against his knee.

"Come. I fix," squeaked the monkey. Booger stepped over to the shelf and the monkey tugged the satchel's strap through its buckle until the satchel hung at Booger's hip. He bit through the strap with his needle-sharp incisors, pushed the buckle's prong through the new hole, and patted Booger's shoulder. "Good?" he asked.

"Good," Booger agreed.

161

~ 26 ~

Hoof was at loose ends. Both Booger and Jawana had vanished and Wat Ho and Pete were off swapping stories about some Gorme-forsaken island. His hopes rose when Booger came back, to be dashed again when he scurried into Waite's cabin. When Booger and Waite finally emerged, he hurried to cut them off.

"Hey Booger!" he brayed, "Where are you off to?"

Booger slid his eyes to Waite, then Hoof, back to Waite, then to the deck. "I'm, erm, running an errand for the Captain?"

"Great! I'll help you."

"I ain't layin' out for two visas!" growled The Captain

"Laying what now?" said Hoof, wrinkling his forehead.

"He means 'pay for,'" said Booger.

"Well why didn't he say so?" grumped Hoof. "It's not like . . ."

"Yeah, I owe you some coins," Booger interrupted. "I didn't forget!" He shot a warning look at Hoof, then turned to the Captain. "Could you subtract his visa from what you are paying me?"

Waite shrugged. "If that's what you want," he said.

~~~

The Harbor Master was a grey-whiskered Donkey who seemed to know Captain Waite well. His eye traveled from Booger's straight blond hair to his bare feet and back up again. "This is new, innit?"

Waite shrugged. "Aye," he rumbled. "He's workin' his passage. First time I had a baldie on board."

162

The Harbor Master nodded at a pinch-faced scribe who stood hunched over a desk. "They can be useful at times," he allowed. "Picky eaters though. Sticks and leaves are not for the likes of them!"

"Too true!" laughed Waite. "But they follow orders well. This un's after makin' a delivery. Charge his visa to my shore account."

The scribe picked up a blank form. "Name?" he croaked.

"Boog . . : erm . . . I mean Wynaugh Tayka Chanse.

"Spelled?"

"Erm . . . just like it sounds?"

The scribe moved his lips as he wrote. He stamped the visa and handed it to Booger.

The Harbor Master eyed Hoof. "And this handsome rascal?"

The bear sighed, then growled, "Put his visa on my account too."

The scribe glanced at Hoof. "Your name?" he asked.

"Hoof Hearted," he replied. "Esquire."

"Also spelled like it sounds?"

"Yes. No! I don't know!" Hoof raised a front leg. "It's Hoof, like this . . . and Hearted, like this." He touched the hoof to his chest.

The scribe smirked. "Like I said." He filled out and stamped the visa, then rolled it up and tucked it into a tube to which a ribbon was attached. He tied the ribbon around Hoof's neck.

The Harbormaster coughed. "It's an extra copper for the case."

"Of course," growled the bear. He turned to Booger. "Get a move on, Chanse. I'm goin' back to get some sleep."

"Aye, aye, Captain!" said Booger. He saluted Waite's back, then looked at the Harbormaster. "How do we get into town?"

The Harbormaster pointed with his lips as he replied, "Go to the end of the wharf and turn left. The gate's right there."

~~~

A double gate towered over the harbor. A door was set into one panel. It was flanked by armed guards. Booger held out his visa. A guard

163

examined it, looked Booger up and down, then handed it back. "Welcome to Waterstrider City, Master Chanse."

The second guard plucked Hoof's visa from its tube. "Welcome to Waterstrider City, Mister . . . " His lips twitched. "Sir!" he said as he showed the visa to his companion. The guards' laughter followed Hoof and Booger through the thick stone wall.

They turned left onto a narrow road. After a few hundred paces the wall angled inland and climbed steeply. Two more turns took them to the edge of a broad market square, where their progress was blocked by a crowd of agitated creatures.

"What's happening?" brayed Hoof.

A toothy young Jenny turned an appraising eye in Hoof's direction. "It's the Supreme Leader!" she lisped excitedly. "He's about to speak!"

"Really?" said Hoof. "What's their name?"

The Jenny looked shocked. "Alddon Crumpt, of course!"

"The orangutan?" exclaimed Hoof. "Didn't he lose?"

The young Jenny's eye narrowed. "That's fake tidings!" she said. "Shame on you!" she added as she edged away.

"Come on," said Booger, nudging Hoof with his elbow. "We have to get to the far side of the square."

"Follow me," said Hoof. He jammed his head between a baboon's backside and a shop wall and scraped forward. Booger tucked in behind him as they headbutted their way around the square.

When they reached a storefront that stood higher than its neighbors, Hoof looked out over the crowd. A stage had been set up at the far side of the square. The throng was pressed up against three sides of it; the space behind it was kept clear by City Guards.

A quartet of bald apes struggled onstage, lugging a podium. Hoof froze, causing Booger to bump into him. "Hey!" Booger cried.

"Look out there!" brayed Hoof.

"You look out!" Booger retorted.

"No, look out *there!* Something's happening."

A red-vested gorilla walked onstage. He raised a monocle to his eye and inspected the crowd. "That's the Chamberlain!" said Booger. "He was on our ship earlier."

The gorilla inflated his chest and roared, "Prepare to hear His Munificence, the Eleventh Illustrious Stallion Waterstrider!"

A flourish of trumpets blared as a black Stallion clopped up a ramp behind the stage. A few half-hearted huzzahs drifted over the square as the trumpeters scuttled away.

The Stallion's lips stretched into what may have been a smile. "Thank you!" he said in a high, nasal voice. "To quote my late nemesis Johana Seekhehr, 'When you cut things to the quick, the proof is in the pudding.' On that note I must introduce the current Regent. . ."

He was interrupted by the Chamberlain pulling his head down and whispering urgently in his ear. "Seriously?" The Stallion sounded as if something was stuck in his throat. "I meant to say that I am, erm, proud to introduce a . . .a . . . ."

The Chamberlain spoke again, and the Horse went on in a flat monotone, "a great creature, citizen, leader and, dare I say it: semi-divine being. I give you your Supreme Leader and, erm, mine too, apparently: the one, the only, the never-to be-believed Alddon Crumpt."

The crowd erupted as the heavyset orangutan danced onstage. He capered about, drinking in the crowd's adulation before stopping next to Waterstrider. He gave the stallion's shoulder a seemingly friendly pat, followed by a hard shove. "Shift it, chum!"

The podium was draped in a tapestry portraying the new emblem of the One True Realm: an orange fist on a 'field' of bananas. Arching above the fist, raised red letters spelled out 'One True Realm.' Across the bottom was the new motto, crafted by the Supreme Leader himself: *The Oneliest! The Trueliest! The Realmliest! Ever!*

Crumpt quieted the crowd. "Nice, isn't it?" he said, waving at the tapestry. He quoted the motto from memory. "Isn't that great! Because if a realm wants to be great, it's gotta have a great motto. And that is a great motto. One of my many wonderful gifts to the Realm."

He stepped behind the podium. "Can I be serious here? You'll bear with me for a few beats, won't you?" His head swung from side to side as he made eye contact with the crowd.

"You know what makes a Realm great? I mean, besides its motto? And our Realm has a great motto—I made sure of that. I did that. Me. But even more than a great motto, it needs great leadership. Like I gave you for five winters. And . . ." he brought a fist crashing down on the podium, "will give you for many years to come!"

Alddon! Alddon! Alddon! The chant rang through the square.

Crumpt seemed to swell even larger as the noise washed over him. But then his shoulders slumped. "But you know what?" he said, shaking his head dejectedly. "You know what? My enemies are spreading lies. Terrible, evil lies," he continued, so quietly that the crowd had to strain to hear him. "They are saying . . . and this is so ridiculous I can't believe any creature would take it seriously . . . they are saying that I lost the leadership selection!"

After a few beats of shocked silence, cries of distress swept through the crowd: *No! No way! Fake tidings!*

Crumpt called for quiet. "It gets even dumber. Those lying traitors are saying I lost . . ." he shook his head in disbelief, " . . . to a Giraffe!"

Gasps and forced laughter gave way to shouts of outrage.

"And not just any Giraffe," Crumpt continued. "I mean a young healthy Giraffe could, I don't know, slow me down for a few beats. I mean they do have those long freaky necks." He snorted. "Naw, who am I kidding? I'd destroy the freak in a heartbeat!

"But this imposter that supposedly beat me," he said as he thumped his chest. "This is no young, healthy Giraffe. No!" He raised his paws and shrugged. "This is an old Giraffe. And I mean really old!"

"How old is he?" some creature helpfully bellowed.

"This Giraffe is so old he was around when Waterspitter's alleged ancestor was the Horsey King! *Laughter.* He's so old a baboon walks under him to hold him up. *More laughter.* He's so old," Crumpt paused dramatically, "He's so old his grandchildren have grandchildren!"

Riotous sustained jeers and laughter.

"Fake tidings," Crumpt said, shaking his head sadly. "Fake tidings are everywhere! You know why? I'll tell you why. Because the spreaders of fake tidings are everywhere. They call themselves Town Criers. Ha! Town Liars is what I call them!"

He singled out some creatures who cowered in a roped-off area near the stage. "There are some right there! They'll go back to their communities and cry about me like little babies. Because, (he made a sour face) because they think crying about things that don't concern them is a Gorme-given right."

He raised his paws and shrugged. "And maybe it is; I wouldn't know about that." He raked his eyes over the nervous Town Criers. "But I do know who you are. And my loyal supporters know where you live . . . and where your families live."

He raised his palms. "Now I'm not advocating violence or anything like that. Gorme forbid! But if good creatures are pushed too far and take matters into their own paws? Well, maybe that's not the best. Maybe it's even wrong. A little bit. But who can blame them? Not me. In fact, I've pardoned more than a few 'honest' mistakes."

His eyes speared a young mountain lioness who was hiding near the back of the group. "Hello!" he exclaimed. "There's a kitten down there I don't know. Who are you? Yes, you—the lovely young lioness at the back."

The lioness, seeing she had no way to escape, raised her head high. "Anita Mitten, Great Frozen Daily!" she announced.

"Indeed? From the Great Frozen North, *eh?*" He addressed the crowd. "That's the way Northerners end every sentence. "Eh. Eh. Eh. Isn't that annoying? It is, isn't it? So annoying. Eh?"

The lioness wiped a snarl off her face as Crumpt's beady eyes swung back. "I hope you never lose your mittens, you naughty kitten," he leered. "It'd be a shame to freeze those pretty little paws off!

"But now," he continued, "what's this I hear about your Realm choosing a Great Northern Goose as your leader. Now I really hope *that's* fake tidings!"

The lioness shook her head. "No, Sir," she said. "It's true. The new government is in fact led by a goose."

"Aw," said Crumpt. "That's a shame." He turned to the crowd. "Vile, disgusting creatures, geese! Very unpleasant. They show up everywhere. And everywhere they show up, there's poop. A goose is the only creature in Gorme's Green Garden that poops more than it eats. That's an actual fact I plucked out of my big, big brain!

"I'm sure there are some fine, upstanding geese out there, raising nice little goosy families." He snorted. "I'm just kidding! Geese are nothing but walking poop-shoots. Unsanitary things, messing up our ponds and parks. Somebody should have put a stop to it! But did the Horsey Kings put a stop to it?"

No! bellowed the crowd.

"Did the previous so-called Supreme Leaders put a stop to it?"

No! bellowed the crowd.

"So who's going to put a stop to it?"

You! called a voice from the crowd. *You'll put a stop to it!*

Crumpt cupped a paw to his ear. "What? I didn't quite catch that."

Many more voices joined in: *You'll put a stop to it!"*

He touched his chest. "You want me to put a stop to it?"

The crowd now was in full voice, shouting: *Yes! Stop it! Stop it! Lock up the geese! Lock 'em up! Lock 'em up!*

Crumpt looked thoughtful. "But what about the geriatric Giraffe? Don't you think he'll put a stop to the goose invasion?"

No! No way! Junk the Giraffe! We want Crumpt! We want Crumpt!

"Thank you, my friends! *You* know the Realm needs me. *I* know the Realm needs me! But there's some know-nothing, do-nothings in The Capital who think they get to decide who the next Supreme Leader will be. And I need . . . no . . . the *Realm* needs good, patriotic creatures like you to show up in The Capital in a few days to convince those losers to Install the rightful leader—which is me—and not some decrepit old Giraffe."

He raised his paws imploringly, "So what are you going to do?"

A dozen rough voices shouted, "Storm The Capital!"

Crumpt made an impatient 'get on with it' motion and the chant gained momentum as it ran through the crowd.

A grin split the orangutan's face. "And when I'm reinstalled . . ." Crumpt waited out a thunderous roar from the crowd. "And when I'm reinstalled," he repeated. "Do you know what I'm going to do?"

Kill the Giraffe! Kill the Giraffe! Kill the Giraffe!

"No, no." Crumpt raised his paws in an unconvincing protest. "There's no need for that! No, he'll die soon enough on his own." Crumpt turned his attention back to the young lioness.

"Miss Mitten, I have a message for your so-called leader. After I'm reinstalled, I'm going to build a big old wall along our northern border. And your leader and his loosy-goosey cronies are going to pay for it!"

There was stunned silence in the crowd, until a lone voice shouted, *"They're birds, you moron!"*

Crumpt froze. Only his eyes moved as they raked over the crowd. "What?" he bellowed. "What's that?"

"Geese can fly, you idiot! A wall would be as useless as you are!"

Booger and Hoof exchanged glances. "Does that voice sound kind of familiar do you?" asked Hoof.

At a nod from Waterstrider, the Guards sprang into action, pushing through the increasingly edgy crowd. Creatures lucky enough to be near the exits began to melt away.

"Crumpt won the last selection by pretending to be an opossum," shouted the voice, slipping through the crowd to evade the Guards. *"And Waterstrider wants to help him cheat again!"*

Waterstrider's wild, white-rimmed eyes raked the crowd. "Johana Seekhehr?" he bugled. "Guards! Bring that gorilla to me now!"

There was a mad stampede for the exits as more of Waterstrider's Guards pushed into the crowd. Crumpt gripped the edge of the podium so hard it broke apart in his fists. He threw the pieces away, then spun around and loped off the back of the stage. He ducked into a shop where he was joined by a jackal.

"Waterspider!" spat Crumpt. "That miserable stick insect is going to pay for this!"

"Yes, Supreme Leader," agreed Eora Wurest-Gnitemere as they ran to a secret tunnel that led under the city walls.

~ 27 ~

Hoof and Booger pressed themselves against the wall, staying out of the way of the stampeding mob.

"That was her, right?" Hoof brayed.

"Johana Seekhehr is Jawana Finder? You figure?"

The square was soon empty of everything but Guards and garbage.

"I hope she got away!" said Hoof.

"Well," said Booger, "I know for a fact she's good at disappearing. Come on, we've got a parcel to deliver."

Booger read out shop numbers. "Two-three. Two-five. Ah! Two-seven!" He pushed at the heavy metal door but it didn't budge.

"Hello!" he shouted. "I have a parcel for you!" He held the satchel up to the shop's window and banged on the glass.

The door swung open and Booger stepped into the shop. Hoof stopped at the door and peered in at a long counter, one end of which was covered with colorful bolts of cloth.

"Get in here already!" called an unoiled hinge of a voice. "You're letting the heat out." Hoof's nose wrinkled in protest of the swamp-like atmosphere. "Hey Donkie Otie!" called the voice. "If you're not coming in, will you at least close the Gorme-blasted door!"

Another creature thinks I look like Donkie Otie? Hoof clopped into the shop and leaned on the door until its heavy bar clunked into place. As he turned away something brushed his face.

"It's a trap!" he brayed. He drew his sword and slashed at his unseen adversary. His heart pounded as he turned to confront . . .a length of twine dangling from the door's heavy wooden bar.

171

Booger snorted. "That sneaky string ambushed you, Boss, but you got it real good!"

Hoof's eye tracked the cord up, across the ceiling, and down to a broad green-black snout that floated in a pool of murky water. It was surrounded by a flotilla of cabbages, carrots and assorted greens.

A pair of glittering black marbles glared at Hoof. "Thank you!" the snout said sarcastically. "Thank you **so** very much. Now I won't have to open the door for annoying creatures like—gee, I don't know—my customers, maybe!"

Booger knotted the ends of the cord together. "Good as new!"

He stepped to the edge of the pool and recited, "I've got a book of fine fabric samples from Captain Waite."

"So give it to me already!"

Booger took a step back and repeated, "I've got a book of fine fabric samples from Captain Waite."

"Seriously? You want to go through that rigamarole?"

"I've got a book of fine fabric samples from Captain Waite!"

"Okay, okay!" The snout sighed, then sarcastically quoted, "I am already overstocked. Not interested. Sorry."

Booger considered the response. Close enough. "These are special samples and you'll regret not looking at them."

The snout stretched open to reveal a set of fist-sized molars. A cabbage fell into the yawning maw and the jaws snapped shut, spraying green pulp across the pool. Hoof edged away until his backside hit the counter. The snout sank back down.

"Are they duty-paid?"

Booger heaved a sigh of relief. "Yeah," he said. "All requirements have been taken care of. Got that so far? Oops! Ignore that last bit."

"Just put the package on the counter."

"Hold on," Booger said, "You have to give me something first."

"Oh yeah, right." A wake formed around the snout as it headed for the edge of the pool. "It's in a drawer under the counter . . . *gurk* . . ."

The crash of shattering glass drowned out the hiss of a crossbow bolt. Hoof drove his forehead into the back of Booger's knees moments before a second bolt buried itself in the back wall.

"Hey!" yelled Booger as he fell over Hoof. "What was that for?"

"I just saved your life!" brayed Hoof.

"What are you talking about?" Booger tried to get up.

"Unh-unh," Hoof bit down on Booger's jerkin and rolled an eye at the back wall. Booger turned, saw the bolt, and froze.

"Well this sucks," said Booger as he poked a thumb through two new holes in his jerkin. "Thanks for saving me and all, but couldn't you have done it a bit quicker?"

"If you're . . . finished bickering . . ." panted a voice from behind them, "I'm having . . . problems . . . my own here!"

Hoof and Booger gasped. A large green-black creature half-floated at the edge of the pool, a crossbow bolt buried in his neck. Inky blood oozed out of the wound, turning the water black.

"Oh Gorme!" Booger exclaimed. "What do we do?"

"I'm done for," panted the creature. "Urgent . . .take parcel . . . Chamberlain." His panting grew faster.

"To the gorilla?" exclaimed Hoof. "No way can we do that! We can't even get out of here: Some creature is trying to kill us!"

"Chamberlain," the creature insisted. "Urgent." In a hoarse whisper he added, "Tunnel under counter."

"Wait," said Booger. "Where's the envelope for Captain Waite."

"Centre Drawer. Above . . ." There was a gurgle, then silence. The creature rolled on his side, one unblinking eye staring up at the ceiling. Hoof and Booger watched in horror as the body drifted to the middle of the pool.

"Who is . . . was that?" Hoof brayed. "What was that?"

"He was a pygmy hippo," Booger replied. "Captain Waite never told me his name."

"Well, we'll deliver that parcel, Mr. Pygmy Hippo," said Hoof. "You can count on us."

A loud crash shook the door. "Yikes!" said Booger. "We've got to get out of here!"

He returned the parcel to the satchel, then reached up to tug on the center drawer. "Of course it's locked," he said bleakly, "and I don't have my picks." Another crash shook the shop.

"Hurry!" Hoof brayed. "There's no time to waste!"

Booger ran his palm along the face of the counter until he felt a bump. He pushed on it, and a wide panel swung inwards. To the right of the panel was a dark void where the floor should have been. "That's the way out," he said. "But I still need to get that envelope."

"The drawer's right up there," said Hoof. "Let me try something." He rolled onto his back, positioned his hind legs under the drawer, and kicked upwards. The bottom of the drawer split in two.

Hoof rolled away and Booger reached through the crack. He pulled out a thick envelope, then felt around inside of the drawer. "There's nothing else in there." He put the envelope in the satchel.

They both jumped at another crash from the door. Booger turned to lean over the hole and looked down. It was a straight drop into the darkness. A metal ladder was bolted to the edge of the hole.

Hoof stared over Booger's shoulder. His lip quivered. "There's no chance I can go that way. I'll hold the bad guys off while you make a break for it."

"Yeah, that's not happening," said Booger. He looked back at Hoof. What about Starr's gift? Shouldn't it be coming to the rescue?"

Hoof craned his neck to look at the star on his shoulder. "According to her poem, it's supposed to 'light the way.' I don't see how that would help us right now."

Booger peered into the hole. *Well, it's plenty dark down there!*
"Hey Boss!" he said as he scootched to the side. "Look down there!"

"Huh?" Hoof shook his head. "Look at what?" He stepped up to
the hole and peered into the darkness.

"This!" grunted Booger, shoving him over the edge.

"EE-AA-EE-oof!" screamed Hoof.

~~~

The door to the shop crashed open. Booger stretched out and grabbed
a heavy bolt mounted on the back of the panel. He backed up until he
had one foot on the ladder, closed the panel and shot the bolt home.

"You okay?" he whispered into the inky darkness.

"Yeah. No thanks to you! What were you thinking?"

"I was thinking that if you couldn't get down here, a pygmy hippo
sure couldn't. It was his escape route, right?"

"Makes sense," Hoof admitted. He stumbled across a thick pile of
mattresses that had been put under the hole. "But you could have
warned . . . Oof!" he fell off the mattresses. "And brought a light."

"You were gonna light the way, remember?" Booger protested as
he climbed down the ladder.

"I guess we don't need magic to save us," said Hoof.

"That's because I saved you!" Booger crawled forward on his
hands and knees, aiming for the sound of Hoof's voice.

"That makes us square then . . . thrall!" Hoof said, looking over his
shoulder. A small arc of white teeth suddenly gleamed in the darkness.
"Hey! I can see . . ." He turned away and saw a strip of light. "Hurry
up! We go this way!"

"Coming Boss," Booger swung his feet to the floor and stood up.
"Ouch!" He flopped back onto the mattresses.

"What now?" brayed Hoof as he turned back. "Ow!"

"This tunnel's kind of low," said Booger.

"And narrow," added Hoof.

~~~

The tunnel ended at a wall that seemed solid, except for a strip of light that shone through a crack at its base. Booger crept up behind Hoof. "If this is an escape route, there has to be a way to open that," he muttered. "Let me see if I can find a latch."

The only way for him to get the wall was to squirm between Hoof's legs. When he pushed up between the Donkey's front hooves the tunnel floor shifted, startling both of them. Hoof jumped back and the floor went back to its original position.

"Hey!" hissed Booger. "I think the latch is on the floor, but I'm not heavy enough to spring it. Come back here." Booger squatted with his back against the wall while Hoof stepped forward and planted his hooves on either side of him. There was a click and Booger tumbled backwards, closing his eyes against the sudden glare.

He rolled out of the way and Hoof stepped out into a narrow passageway. Right in front of him, a ladder poked through a round hole in the ceiling. Sunlight poured down through the opening. Similar openings could be seen in the distance, lighting the passageway.

Booger stood up. "We're inside the city wall," he said. "This setup lets reinforcements move around without being seen." He looked around admiringly. "This is really slick!"

Hoof nudged the door and it swung shut. There was a click and it became part of the wall. "So now what?"

"We find a way out and then head back to the ship."

"What? No!" Hoof protested. "We've got to take the parcel to the Chamber-whozit. Like the hippo said."

"I don't know where to find the Chamberlain," said Booger. "Plus, I have to deliver the envelope to Captain Waite."

"*After* we've delivered the parcel," Hoof insisted. "You can't ignore a sentient creature's dying request. It's just not done."

"You gave your word to a dead creature," Booger countered. "I made a promise to Captain Waite." He sighed, "Don't you think one ginormous live bear's gotta trump one dead pygmy hippo?"

"What I think is you've been hanging around Pete too much," Hoof retorted. "You're starting to sound like him."

Booger pulled the satchel over his head, took out the envelope and tucked it inside his jerkin. "We'll split up. You look for the Chamberlain while I deliver the envelope. Then I'll come find you." He adjusted the satchel's strap and hung it around Hoof's neck. "Oh-oh!"

"Now what" groaned Hoof.

"Your visa's gone. If a Guard stops you, you'll be in trouble."

"Well, I'll just have to chance it," Hoof said.

"Chance it?" said Booger thoughtfully. "Not a bad idea." He rolled up his own visa and tucked it into the tube. "If they don't look at it too closely, you might get away with it. I'll stay in the wall until I get to the wharf. But we should stick together as long as we can."

They hadn't gone more than a hundred paces when they came to a side tunnel that angled toward the center of the city. "I guess this is where we spit up," said Hoof.

Booger put a hand on Hoof's back. "You don't have to do this."

"But I do," said Hoof. "I really do."

"Well, good luck Boss!" Booger said. "Though you won't need it."

Just as well, Hoof thought gloomily. But all he said was, "Thanks, Booger. You too. Take care."

~~~

Hoof plodded into the darkness, the clatter of his hooves echoing off the stone walls. The tunnel was lit by torches mounted at very irregular intervals. At times, he kept his bearings by bumping his shoulder against the tunnel wall. In a particularly dark stretch, he stumbled sideways into an empty space. To his right was a tunnel that angled up more steeply. He considered his options and stuck with the tunnel he was on.

He didn't get far before he heard voices. When a splash of light lit up the tunnel wall ahead of him he turned and ran. In his panic he almost missed the side tunnel. His hooves skidded out from under him as he dove into it at full speed and slammed into the wall.

Gasping for breath, he struggled to his hooves. *I should go further up the tunnel!* The light reached the tunnel mouth. Too late!

Three hulking mercenaries in mismatched armor stomped by. They looked nothing like the polite, polished Guards Hoof had encountered above ground; they looked terrifying! *Please don't look this way! Please . . .* They kept going, blankly staring at the floor in front of their dusty bare feet. Hoof almost dared to exhale.

A fourth soldier appeared, with a fresh sergeant's crest attached to their helm. The helm swiveled toward Hoof's tunnel. Time stood still as he stared into the black shadows that hid the creature's eyes. He closed his own eyes and waited for the inevitable.

"Eyes front, double time," called a gruff voice. The apes broke into a shuffling run.

When Hoof opened his eyes, the sound of their passage was fading down the tunnel. *What just happened?*

~ 28 ~

The ladder ended on a battlemented walkway that ran along the top of the wall. Booger found a gap he could squeeze through and peered down. An unscalable expanse of stone stood between him and *The Dancing Sea Cow*. He swallowed his disappointment, climbed back down the ladder, and carried on.

He moved slowly, halfheartedly tapping the outer wall. Suddenly a narrow panel swung out at him! He flattened himself behind it. Hairy fingers gripped the panel's edge, almost touching his chest.

There was a shuffle of feet and the panel swung away. Booger dove to jam his fingers in the gap. He gritted his teeth against the pain and waited for the alarm to be raised; for blows to rain down on him; for the prick of a blade. None of these things happened. He raised his head and watched a chimpanzee disappear around the corner.

Booger pulled the panel open and stared into a black void. He stood blowing on his bruised fingers until the clank of approaching armor forced him to step through. The panel snicked shut behind him.

Narrow strips of light surrounded him, looking like cracks between boards. There was even a small, chest-high circle of light that could be a knot hole. He stuck a finger through the hole and pulled; nothing happened. He pushed and a small rectangular door began to open. He stepped back and the door snapped shut.

He opened the door just far enough to lean one eye out. *That's the river!* Heaving a sigh of relief, he slipped out to a narrow space between two stacks of crates. *This looks like where Jawana disappeared,* was

179

his first thought. His second thought was that the burly bald ape standing on the wharf did not look happy to see him.

Hoof stared into the darkness long after the sound of the guards had faded away. *How did that gorilla not see me?* He turned and started up the steep tunnel. *I'll take my chances in the open.*

The tunnel climbed in a tight spiral, then leveled off for the last few paces. Torchlight flickered beyond the end of the tunnel. Hoof crept forward, planting each hoof as quietly as he could.

"D'ya know where the new sarge came from?" growled a voice.

"Don't know. Don't care," a second voice wheezed, "But I'd like to send the jerk to Shadehalla. He's runnin' me ragged."

That provoked a dismissive snort. "About time you pulled some honest duty around here, Lardo."

The bickering was interrupted by a third voice snapping, "Shut your cake holes and play cards. I'm due to report for duty and I want to clean you losers out before I go."

Swell, thought Hoof, *I've come out next to a barracks.*

"In your dreams, Morty," said the second voice.

"Just stop yakking and deal," grunted Morty. There was the sound of cards being shuffled, then cut and dealt.

"Gorme, Lardo, have you been eating jellied slugs again?" said Morty, "These cards are disgusting."

"It weren't me," whined Lardo. "Gimp messed 'em up."

There was a belch, presumably from 'Gimp.' "Got to keep me strength up. There's sump'n big going down, and it be soon."

"Yeah?" said Lardo. "Whadya know as we don't?"

"I'll take three," said Gimp. After a pause he said, "The armory's got every forge fired up. We'll be movin' out any day."

"Good," said Lardo. "I need the battle pay. Whadya want, Morty?"

"I'm good," rumbled Morty. "If somewhat's goin' on, it's to do with that orange ape. He's out to make a mess, and Old Strider can't help his self but to step right in it."

"Oh yeah?" said Lardo. "The dealer takes one. On which side?"

"Who knows?" laughed Morty. "I just know what side I'm on."

"Yeah. The side as offers the most coin," laughed Gimp.

A mailed paw clamped over Hoof's muzzle, almost stopping his heart. A voice hissed "Promise to behave and you might get to draw another breath. Got it?"

Hoof tried to nod. A gap opened at his nostrils, and he drew a shaky breath. When he made no attempt to move, his nose was released, but a vicelike grip squeezed his neck, right behind his ears.

"Okay," the voice whispered. "We'll play a little game called 'you do what I say, when I say it' and maybe, just maybe, you'll get out of this without getting hurt. Nod if you understand."

Hoof nodded once before the hand on his neck slid up to his ears and he was dragged into the barracks. Chairs crashed to the floor as three gorillas sprang to their feet, fumbling for their weapons. They backed away from a filthy table covered with food scraps and the shoddy bits of plunder with which they had been wagering.

"Look what I found hiding in the tunnel," crowed Hoof's captor. "Hang me if it isn't a dirty Donkey spy!"

"Hee-ee-haaaw!" Hoof screamed. A panicked eye turned back far enough to see that his captor was the sergeant who spotted him at the end of the tunnel. *I was so stupid!* he thought before another tug on his ears made him forget everything but the pain.

"Who you spying for?" growled the Sergeant.

Hoof's ears were released as his sword belt was pulled over his head. Then his head was jerked back, forcing him to stare into the black orbs that glittered from the depths of the sergeant's helmet.

"I asked you a question, Muleface."

181

"N-n-n-no creature," Hoof stammered. "I'm not a spy."

"No?" growled the sergeant, lips pulled back to reveal stained teeth. "Then why're you skulking outside these barracks?"

"I-I-I w-was looking for some creature? And I got lost?"

"Yeah?" said the sergeant sarcastically. "And you just happened to wander into a tunnel that goes nowhere but this barracks?"

"Yes?" whimpered Hoof. "Sort of?"

"You want we should take care of him, Sarge?" asked a hulking, hard-faced ape. Hoof recognized the voice as belonging to 'Morty.' "It's been days since we 'ad us any fun."

The sergeant dragged a mailed fist over their grizzled chin. Hoof tried to edge away from them but was brought up short by a dagger appearing at his throat.

"No you don't," the sergeant snapped. "Don't move a whisker until I tell you to. Don't even breath." Hoof froze, holding his breath for what seemed like a very long time.

"Naw," the sergeant said at last. "Donkey or not, he's still Equine. I'll have to take him up to The Castle and turn him over."

"C'mon Sarge," wheezed Lardo. "Who's gonna know?" The sergeant's head swung around and Lardo shrank back.

"I'll pretend didn't hear that," snarled the sergeant. "Now hand over your belt. I need it to keep hold of this idiot if he decides to make a break for it."

The fat gorilla's jaw dropped. "Give you what?" he squawked. The sergeant extended a paw and, trembling with rage, the gorilla handed over a long thin belt. His card partners roared with laughter when he snatched at his hose to keep them from falling down.

The sergeant looped the belt around Hoof's neck, then grabbed a torch. "Let's go, spy!"

Hoof was dragged to the tunnel from which they had just emerged. He fought for breath, twisting his head to the side to take some of the strain off the belt. The sergeant marched in grim silence until they were halfway down the tunnel.

"For Gorme's sake Hoof, what were you thinking?"

"Jawana?" gasped Hoof.

Booger's eyes darted from side to side. The stacks of crates were too high to climb and there was a solid wall behind him. He turned back to the massive dockworker and put a grin on his face. "Did you know there's a door in the side of that crate? Pretty weird, huh?"

The dockworker's eyes bored into Booger.

"Well, I better get back to my boat," said Booger cheerily and strolled confidently toward the wharf.

The dockworker's meaty hands curled into fists. Booger ducked his head and ran. At the last instant he dove to the side, planning to roll by before the big, slow bald ape could react. Unfortunately, the bald ape was big and fast—a backhand caught the side of Booger's head. Waite's envelope flew out of his jerkin and slid along the wharf as Booger's world exploded into a field of stars.

Booger opened one eye to a narrow slit. The bald ape with the iron fists stood over him. He held the envelope between his thumb and index finger, tapping it against the grimy fingertips of his other hand. His coworkers were spread out behind him. Booger closed his eye, hoping to gain some time.

A boot exploded into his ribs. *"Ungh!"* Booger rolled to his elbows and knees, dizzy with pain. He emptied his stomach onto the wharf. *Gorme take me. Please!*

The boot planted itself against Booger's shoulder and shoved. Booger rolled onto his back and lay still, moaning. He kept his eyes closed until he felt the boot press down on his hand; his eyes flew open. The envelope was waved in his face. "What's this then?"

"Dunno," gasped Booger. The boot pressed harder. "I don't know! Really. The Captain paid me to get it for him." Booger's eyes drifted shut. He felt nauseous and dizzy.

"Captain? What Captain?"

"Waite. Captain Waite."

"Waite from *The Dancing Sea Cow?*"

Booger nodded. There was a muttered conference. Then the gravelly voice said, "Watch him. I'll go get to the bottom of this." Booger heard boots pound up a gangway. Then he heard nothing.

"Idiot!" hissed Jawana.

"Traitor!" brayed Hoof.

"Quiet." Jawana clamped a paw over Hoof's mouth. Her eyes darted from side to side. "I can't get you out of here if you keep on attracting attention."

"*Mmff,*" said Hoof. Jawana removed her paw. "Where are you taking me?" he demanded.

"To where even an idiot like you can find the wharf."

"No!" Hoof planted his hooves. "*Gurk,*" he choked as the belt tightened around his neck.

Jawana's eyes blazed in the torchlight. "Listen, you," she began.

"No!" Hoof interrupted. "Hear me out. Please? It's important."

The gorilla looked around. "Not here. It's too dangerous. Come on." She stretched a paw toward the back of Hoof's head.

"N-o-o-o! Not the ears! Please don't pull my ears again."

"Sorry about the ears," said Jawana, stroking them gently. "Had to put on a show."

"Yeah," said Hoof. "Well, you killed. Almost literally—I thought I was having a heart attack."

"You're tougher than that, Hoof." Jawana shifted her shoulders and got back to business. "There's an alcove up ahead where we can talk," she said briskly. "It's got to be quick though."

Jawana listened intently while Hoof filled her in on recent events. She remained silent long after he finished.

"Erm . . . Jawana?" said Hoof. "Hello?"

"I'm thinking," said Jawana. "You ought to try it sometime." After a pause she said, "A lowly sergeant like me can't walk into the Palace and demand to see the Chamberlain. And you sure can't go."

"Maybe we can both go," said Hoof. "Together?"

"What? Are you insane?" Jawana growled.

"No," Hoof replied "Well maybe, but that's beside the point. Back in the barracks, you said something about taking me 'up to the castle.' What did you mean?"

Jawana reached under her helmet and scratched her neck. "Waterstrider doesn't allow his Guards or mercenaries (who are almost all gorillas) to rough up members of the Equine races. That means Donkeys and Zebras too, not just Horses. He's afraid it might give us lesser creatures ideas that are above our station. He's not wrong . . ."

"And so?" interrupted Hoof.

"So any Equines who are suspected of crimes or did something to annoy Waterstrider end up in the dungeon to be dealt with by the Equine Inquisitor."

"Is there a way to get inside the Palace walls without ending up in the dungeons?" asked Hoof.

"Not without taking a terrible risk," Jawana replied.

"I have no choice," said Hoof soberly. "A creature died! There's a lot of strange stuff going on. I don't know what it all means, but it's got to be more important than I am." He stared at Jawana. "And speaking of strange, what's with your sergeant's getup."

Jawana ignored the question. "So, we're doing this?"

185

"Gorme, kid. I hire you to do one simple job and what happens? You make a complete mess of things!"

Booger's eyes opened. "Captain Waite?" he slurred. The Captain leaned over him, with his cap sliding all over his big round head. Wat Ho stood behind him with a very concerned expression on the mobile half of his face.

Booger's eyes closed as he murmured, "The hippo is dead."

"What?" bellowed the Captain. "How?" His head swung around. "And where's that dratted Donkey?"

Wat Ho put a paw on the Captain's shoulder. "The youngster's in a bad way, Captain," he rumbled gravely. "He can talk later."

The Captain took a few deep breaths. "Okay. Get him on board."

The dock worker scooped Booger up and gently laid him in Wat Ho's arms. "Sorry about the little misunderstanding," he said.

Little? Booger's lips twitched. He managed a feeble finger wave before his eyes rolled back in his head. Pete and Manny stood at the gangway, silently watching as their companion was brought aboard and lowered to the deck.

~ *29* ~

Hoof and Jawana stepped out of a grey tunnel and into a parklike setting. Behind them, nestled among tall, brilliantly colored trees were the stately residences of the city's elite. Before them loomed the massive bulk of the Palace. Hoof craned his neck to take it in. *Who would build such a thing?*

A moat hugged the wall that surrounded the castle grounds. Hoof stepped onto a path that ran next to it, then stopped to blink at a school of fish that sliced through the water to stare up at him.

"Look but don't touch," Jawana cautioned him. "They'll pick your bones clean before you hit the bottom."

Hoof skipped to the outside edge of the path. "That's really . . . something? What is this place, anyway?"

"During the First Equine Reign, this was the Summer Palace of the Supreme Stallion. When that line died out, the Goats took it over. But they found it too big and uncomfortable. The Cattle didn't want it either; they're farmers through-and-through.

"It was decided that the Supreme Stallion's nearest kin (if any came forward) could have the Summer Palace. An alleged 'distant cousin' won that lottery, changed his name to 'Waterstrider,' and declared himself to be a 'Lord.' The Palace, along with the surrounding land, has been handed down in the same bloodline ever since.

"Eventually, the Second Era gave way to the Equine Monarchy. The then-Lord Waterstrider expected to be made Supreme Monarch. When that didn't happen, he lost his oats! He locked himself in his chambers and never left them again. The snub didn't sit well with his heirs either. They played a big role in the Monarchy's overthrow, which is why they were allowed to keep the Palace and its lands. They still believe the 'illegitimate Regency' will end with one of them taking their rightful place as Supreme Monarch."

"Nice story," said Hoof, "but why so freakishly big?"

"Because it was built for Horses," Jawana replied. "See those gigantic turrets at the corners? Inside are spiral ramps big enough for four Horses to walk abreast. The whole Palace was built on that scale. Now shut up, you dirty Donkey spy."

"Huh?" Hoof stopped rubbernecking long enough to see they were approaching a drawbridge that ended at a guardhouse. "Oh."

They pulled up in front of a pair of suddenly-alert gorillas. "Sergeant Lotishus escorting a prisoner to the Inquisitioner," said Jawana in a deep, gruff voice that made Hoof's head snap up.

The Guards' eyes darted between Jawana and Hoof. Then one of them shrugged and yelled, "Hey, Quill-pusher. This is for you."

A long-limbed bald ape appeared at the guardhouse window, holding a quill and ink in one hand and a square of writing-cloth in the other. His eyes widened at seeing an Equine being held captive by a gorilla, but he kept his thoughts to himself. "Name?" he asked.

"Sergeant Lotishus," Jawana replied. "First Foot." For several beats, the only sounds were the scratching of the quill and the Guards grumbling at their tardy relief.

"Prisoner's name?"

"It doesn't matter," snapped Jawana. "He's not coming back."

The scribe gulped, then held out the cloth. Jawana snatched it out of his hand, jerked on Hoof's leash and turned to go.

"Wait! Your weapons . . ."

"What about them?" Jawana scowled at the scribe.

"Erm . . . They aren't allowed in The Palace?"

Oh. "Well of course!" Jawana slipped Hoof's sword off her shoulder and slapped it on the counter.

The scribe's face bore no expression as he picked up the sword, then stretched out his other hand. Jawana sighed, plucked her dagger from her side and laid it in his palm. "That's it?" he asked, peering at her from under a pair of caterpillar eyebrows.

"That's it," she snapped. She tugged Hoof's leash and stalked off through the gate. The Guards stared after them.

~~~

Hoof nodded at a small copse of evergreens. "Let's go hide over there."

Jawana ran across a yellowing lawn to duck down among the trees. Hoof kicked up a spray of turf as he galloped after her. As he caught his breath, he struggled to think things through.

"Listen, Jawana," he said at last. "Those Guards are expecting you to go back alone, right?"

"Yeah, so?" said Jawana.

"So having you clank around with me will just draw extra attention. Just wait a while and then go back. I won't go back until after the Guard changes. The replacements won't have seen me, so hopefully they won't cause a problem. We'll meet up back at the ship."

"I'm not going back to the ship," said Jawana.

"What?" Hoof blinked at her.

"As much as I hate to admit it, that stuff you were rattling on about makes sense. Things are happening that are bigger than both of us." She threw her arms around Hoof's neck. "Take care of yourself, you dumb Ass," she sniffed. "I will find you at The Capital: that's a promise! Now go." She shoved Hoof toward the lawn.

~~~

Hoof had walked halfway around the castle, seeing no way in. The sun beat down on a balcony that overlooked a garden. Its sloping roof was supported by white stone arches that threw the balcony into shadow. His eyes darted back and forth, sensing . . . *what?*

He focused on the gloom at the far end of the balcony. *Yes!* There it was again, a flash of light, like a signal from a looking glass. Or a monocle! He galloped onto a ramp that led up to the balcony.

Two guard boxes faced each other at the bottom of the ramp. Their occupants snapped awake to the sound of hooves thundering past. *"What? Hey!"* But Hoof had already cleared the ramp and was galloping along the balcony toward a distant dark shape.

"Lord Chamberlain! Lord Chamberlain!" he brayed. "I'm so glad I found you! The Captain sent me to return that . . . thing . . . you forgot on the ship. He thought you might need it."

The clatter of hooves alerted the Guards at the far end of the balcony. They got to Hoof before he reached the Chamberlain. He skidded to a stop, staring at the tips of their drawn weapons.

The silverback stepped into the sunlight and examined Hoof through his monocle. "I know this creature," he said. He dismissed the Guards with a gesture. "Return to your posts."

The Guards stared at the Chamberlain, then Hoof, then each other. "But . . . are you sure . . . I don't think . . ."

"Do you presume to question me?" Somehow, the Chamberlain ramped up the power of his voice without increasing its volume. The Guards skulked away. Hoof was tempted to follow.

The Chamberlain pulled the visa out of Hoof's tube, studied it briefly and returned it. He turned away to lean on the balcony rail. As the silence stretched on, Hoof opened his mouth to speak a half-dozen times, only to snap it shut again.

"You are nothing if not discrete," the gorilla said drily.

"Sir?" said Hoof, confused.

The gorilla continued to look out over the garden. "You do me too great an honor," he said, with an odd twist of his mouth.

"Sir?" Hoof repeated. *What's he talking about?*

"You are *Equus*," said the gorilla. "I am *pollex digitus:* a humble fingered folk. In this time and place, not even the lowliest of your kind should use an honorific when addressing one such as me."

"Sorry . . . erm. Sir?"

"Never mind." The gorilla faced Hoof. "Why are you here?"

"I'm from *The Dancing Sea Cow*," Hoof replied.

The gorilla's eyes sparked with interest. "I know of that vessel."

"Well yeah . . . .you left a package there. But then the creature who was supposed to get it met with an accident."

"Oh dear!" said the gorilla. "Nothing too serious, I hope."

"Yeah. It was kind of fatal, actually."

The gorilla stiffened. "Oh, my!" He abruptly strode past Hoof. "Come," he said. Hoof trotted after him.

~~~

The Chamberlain entered The Palace and hurried down a wide pebble-floored hallway. He stopped at a narrow corridor and looked in both directions. "This way. Quickly!"

The corridor ended at an oak door. The Gorilla opened it, glanced around and waved Hoof inside. After closing and bolting the door, he padded across the room and threw open a door on the far wall. Seeing that the adjoining room was empty, the gorilla crossed to an open window. He peered out and then, visibly relaxing, pulled it shut.

"May I?" he asked, extending a paw toward the satchel.

"Be my guest," Hoof replied.

The gorilla carried the satchel to a table. Taking out the parcel, he wedged his monocle in place and examined it from all sides. "Good," he murmured. "No sign of tampering."

He turned a sharp eye on Hoof. "Do you believe these are cloth samples?" Hoof hesitated, then shook his head.

"No Sir."

191

The gorilla sighed. "I asked you to stop doing that."

Hoof's brow furrowed. "What?"

"In this demesne, for an Equine to call me 'sir' is to debase themselves. It is simply not done. I should be addressed by my title, which is Chamberlain, or by my birth name.

"Which is?"

"Blossom," muttered the gorilla.

Hoof snorted. "I take it most creatures call you 'Chamberlain?'"

"The prudent ones do."

"Fair enough . . . Chambers," grinned Hoof.

The gorilla's lips twitched. "That sobriquet is more apropos than you know. The original function of the Chamberlain was to . . ."

This ape has got to be related to Wat Ho, thought Hoof as his mind drifted off.

". . . and that's the crux of the matter."

Oh Blartz! thought Hoof. *I've missed the important bits.* "How can I help?" he said, knowing that was a safe bet when you didn't have a clue; days of being grilled by his mother on *Behaving Like a Proper Ass: Etiquette for the Don't Know Jack* had taught him that.

"Is that a sincere offer?"

Uh-Oh, thought Hoof. *Absolute worst comeback to 'How can I help?'* He gulped and replied, "Why else would I have asked?"

The Chamberlain's face cracked into a relieved smile. "Oh, Master Chanse! There's clearly more to you than meets the eye."

Master Chanse? Hoof drew a breath, but the gorilla gave him no chance to set him straight. "I left that parcel with Captain Waite, who was to get it to our, erm, late ally. A network of cloth merchants were to deliver it to The Capital. That has, regrettably, become impossible."

"I see that," said Hoof. "And you know, it is *super* unfortunate. But at least you got your parcel back. And now . . ." He made a show of looking at the window. "Oh my! Where has the time gone? I really have to get back to the ship. Sorry to dash off like this!" he added as he trotted toward the door.

"Stop!" Hoof skidded to a halt.

The gorilla continued in a milder tone. "I'm sorry but, without my help, you won't even get out of this Palace."

"And your help comes at a price," guessed Hoof.

"I'm afraid so." He waved the package at Hoof. "It is imperative that this reach its intended recipient. But my every move is watched. You will have to deliver it."

"Yeah?" retorted Hoof. "Say I take the parcel: What's to stop me tossing it the first chance I get?"

"Not a thing," replied the Chamberlain, "except your word that you won't. Please do not treat this lightly, Master Chanse. The Realm's future may well depend on the delivery of that package."

Hoof stared into the Chamberlain's eyes. Then he nodded. "Okay," he sighed, "what do I have to do?"

"Thank you," the Chamberlain breathed. "Someday your courage will be rewarded. But until then, you must proceed in absolute secrecy." His voice sharpened. "Is that clear?"

"No! Nothing's clear!" Hoof brayed. "I have no clue what you expect me to do, so how can I know if I can do it?" He took a breath, then dropped his eyes. "Sorry," he mumbled, "I'll shut my big mouth now."

"No," the Chamberlain said. "You make a valid point." Laying the parcel on the table, he went to his writing desk and selected a thick sheet of papyrus. "Can you read?" he asked as he sharpened a quill with a folding knife from his waistcoat pocket.

"Erm . . . not as such, no," Hoof admitted.

"Unfortunately, that's typical of Equines," sighed the gorilla. "If you can't write, why bother learning to read." After dipping the quill into a golden inkwell, he began to scratch away at the papyrus.

~~~

Hoof studied his surroundings. The high-ceilinged room was sparsely but ornately furnished. In addition to the gleaming wooden table and writing desk, there was a gilded stool, a deep, well-padded chair and a tall armoire. He was amused to see that the armoire was covered with a variety of brightly painted flowers. Through the door at the end of the room, he could make out a large nest perched in a faux fir tree. *This must be Chambers' own apartment.*

The gorilla stopped writing and sucked on the end of his quill while he read what he had written. "Pah!" he said, slapping the quill down on the table and spitting out bits of feather. "You'd think I'd learn."

He folded the papyrus into a neat square, then folded a second sheet to envelop it. A search of his desk drawers yielded a firestick with which he lit a candle. He tipped a few drops of wax onto the envelope, then pressed it together to seal it. Flipping it over, he picked up the quill, inked it and began to scratch away at the envelope. "There," he said at last. "That should do."

He got to his feet and retrieved the parcel. "It is of the utmost importance that this parcel get to Regency Island, in The Capital."

"The Capital is where I'm going!" Hoof exclaimed.

"Good," said the Chamberlain as he slipped the parcel into Hoof's satchel. "That should simplify things. But it is a large city, and Regency Island is a complex piece of the puzzle. At one end of the island is the Supreme Leader's Palace. On the opposite end are the most disreputable wharves to be found in The Realm. Halfway between them is a famous commercial street. It is there that all elements, savory and unsavory alike, are able to meet and mingle. And it is to a location on that street that the parcel must be delivered."

The Gorilla hung the satchel around Hoof's neck. "All we know for certain is that the shop to which it must be delivered belongs to a very talented milliner and . . ." He held the envelope in front of Hoof's eye, ". . . that it is identified by a sign bearing this image."

Hoof squinted at an outline of a Horse's head, on which was perched a narrow-brimmed flowered hat. "Hee Haw!" he brayed. "That's too funny!"

"Hmpf," sniffed the gorilla as he slipped the envelope into the satchel. "Tell the owner you are interested in a natural straw fedora and that the sketch in your satchel shows what you have in mind. The note in the envelope will tell them what they need to know."

"Do I have to memorize code words or anything?" Hoof asked.

"I think not," the gorilla replied. "Why would you?"

"But how will I recognize the owner?" Hoof asked.

"They're a mandrill monkey. Among a great many other things, they are known for a . . . shall we say *distinctive* . . . taste in apparel."

~~~

The Chamberlain bustled over to the armoire and took out a green sash. Depressing a flower carved into the wood above the armoire's door opened a hidden drawer. He stretched onto his toes and felt around inside it. His paw emerged with a large medallion squeezed between its fingertips. At another touch, the drawer closed, vanishing seamlessly into the woodwork.

He draped the sash around Hoof's neck and pinned it in place with the medallion. "This will help you get past Milord's minions. But as soon as you are safely away, you have to throw it overboard." The gorilla gripped Hoof's jaw and twisted it until Hoof's eye looked straight into the his monocle. "It must not, under any circumstances, be seen outside this city. Is that understood?"

Unable to speak, Hoof nodded. "Good," said the Chamberlain, letting go of his jaw. "You made too much of an impression on the guards at the back to go that way. I'll escort you to a different exit."

"What about my sword?" asked Hoof. "It's at the gatehouse."

The Chamberlain shrugged. "And there it will stay. There's nothing I can do about it at this point." After a brief hesitation, he went back to the armoire and took out a small purse. "This should more than cover your losses." He slipped the purse into Hoof's satchel, which he hid behind the sash. "And if all goes as hoped, your weapon should be returned to you in due course."

Hoof was skeptical but said nothing. Learning what his Grandsire was really like had made him care far less about his sword.

The Chamberlain led him through a maze of narrow corridors built for the use of servants. Twice they ducked into side passages to avoid harried-looking creatures dashing about on their master's business.

"When you are leaving The Palace," said the Chamberlain, "stride confidently, as would an important figure attending to important matters. As indeed you are."

"Okay?" replied Hoof, doubtfully. "Erm . . . sure."

The gorilla held out a paw. "Wait behind this door," he whispered. "I'll make sure the way is clear." A few beats later he heard the Chamberlain's voice: "I don't care what you were told! I need you to get His Lordship's scepter. And I need it now!"

The door flew open. "Go! Go! Go!" exclaimed the Chamberlain.

~ 30 ~

The bump of the medallion against Hoof's chest added confidence to his stride. He passed the gatehouse staring straight ahead, head proudly erect, blissfully unaware that an ill-timed bump sent a shaft of light through the guardhouse window.

Quill-pusher blinked away the sudden flash, then raised his eyes. They widened. A dozen beats later, a slender shadow slipped through the guardhouse door.

Hoof did not stop to get his bearings until the guardhouse was far behind him. Narrow lanes wound (seemingly at random) among trees, gardens and monstrous statues of rearing Horses. *Maybe Waterstrider's ancestors wanted to be two-leggers?* He picked a direction and forged ahead. The unmarked intersections looked identical and he quickly lost any sense of direction.

"Ya lost?" Hoof ignored the brazen young chimp who peered down at him from his perch on a statue's back.

"Ya are lost, ain'tcha?"

Hoof turned and fixed the shaggy urchin with a baleful glare. "Me? Lost? Why would you say that?"

"On accounta this is the third time ya passed this statue," the chimp chortled as he dropped lightly to the path. "Where ya tryin' ta get?"

Hoof curled his upper lip. "I am returning to my vessel. Unfortunately, I left The Palace by a different way from which I entered and now seem to be a bit, erm, disoriented."

The chimp hooted with glee. "Disoriented? Yer totally goin' the wrong way! Tell ya what: for two copper bits I'll take ya to yer boat."

Hoof nodded. "Okay, you've got a deal." The chimp thrust out a grimy paw. "Nuh-uh," Hoof brayed. "Not till we get to the wharf."

The chimp shrugged. "Okay then: three bits it is!"

Hoof bit off a retort. "Fine!" he said, quietly hoping Booger would be there with his purse.

"Follow me," said the chimp. He knuckled off without a backward glance. Hoof hurried after him. After a few zigs and zags, the chimp pointed down yet another narrow lane.

"Dere's a wall down dere as separates 'Snobby Hill' from where us proper citizens live. I'll meetcha on d'udder side."

"Say what?" exclaimed Hoof.

"I'm sorta chimpanzee non grata with Palace Security. On accounta some silver goin' missin' a while back. But no sweat, I'll catch ya up past de wall." With that, he scampered off.

~~~

Hoof watched the chimp disappear before, lacking a better option, he turned down the lane. After several paces, he passed through an arch in a high stone wall.

"G-r-r-identify your-r-r-self!"

This is not good! Hoof turned to face two enormous black dogs. He gulped, then thrust out his chest to expose the Chamberlain's medallion "This is all the identification I need," he said, with a great deal less confidence than he would have liked.

One of the dogs stepped forward and sniffed at it suspiciously. "Where-r-re did you get that?"

"From the Chamberlain. He said it would give me safe passage."

"I smell the gor-r-r-illa on him," growled the dog. They sniffed again. "And a stranger-r-r."

"That's just . . ." Hoof hesitated, ". . . a friend," he finished lamely.

The second dog padded forward. "This side of the wall, no shiny bit of metal will keep you safe. You should go back."

Hoof swallowed. The wall was like a knife blade between two worlds. Behind him was the green expanse of Waterstrider's demesne. Before him was the treeless squaller of a city slum. His head swung back and forth. Until, in the distance, he saw a small brown paw beckoning him on. "Thanks for the advice," he said. "But I've got to get back to the wharf. I'm going that way."

~~~

Hoof's eyes tracked his surroundings. Narrow, rickety structures hung over the lane, shutting out most of the light. Skinny pad paws skulked in doorways, watching the Donkey with suspicious, defeated eyes. "Are you sure this is the way to the wharves?" he asked.

"Trust me, I knows where I'm goin'."

Yeah, but are you taking me to my boat?

The chimp led the way into an even narrower and darker alley. About fifty paces in, he stopped. "Nothin' personal, ya understand," he said, "but ya shoulda paid me upfront."

"What?" exclaimed Hoof. There was no reply from the chimp, who was scaling the side of a building. Hoof's heart skipped a beat when his guide flipped onto the roof and disappeared. It almost stopped entirely when he turned back the way he had come.

A bulky shape was silhouetted against what little light penetrated the lane. It raised a crossbow and took aim. Hoof turned and ran, only to discover he had been led into a blind alley. He tried to stop before he hit the wall; his hooves slid out from under him and he fell hard. A crossbow bolt passed through where his neck had been an instant earlier, bounced off the wall and stuck into the muck beside him.

He watched helplessly as the shadow bore down on him. The crossbow was reloaded, cocked and, at pointblank range, raised to fire. He squeezed his eyes shut. *This is going to hurt!* He heard a fluttering sound, a grunt, and then nothing. *Is that it? Am I dead?*

Hoof opened his eyes. His attacker was on his knees, a few paces away. The crossbow lay beside him. He watched his attacker pick it up, try to raise it, then fall face forward and lie still.

He cautiously approached the sprawling body. It was an ape: that much was clear. A filthy armband displayed an orange fist, backed by a field of bananas. But what gripped his attention was the knife sticking out of the creature's back.

~~~

Hoof went back to the mouth of the alley and cautiously looked up and down the empty lane. Seeing no threats, he stepped out of the alley and into a bucketful of cold, sudsy water.

"Hee Haw!" he brayed as he spun around. He confronted a young, emaciated chimpanzee who stood frozen in shock.

The chimpanzee lowered the bucket. "I'm s-sorry, s-s-sir!" they stammered. "I just washed the floors and . . ." they trailed off.

"And you thought you'd drown the next Donkey to pass by?"

"N-no sir! I wasn't expecting . . . This back lane is for 'dirty' creatures like us, so your kind don't have to look at us." They glanced at the muck coating Hoof's side. "Though you look like a rinse didn't do you any harm!"

Hoof looked back at his side. "Point taken," he chuckled. "The thing is, I'm lost. Could you point me towards the harbor?"

The chimpanzee looked startled. "You'll never find the harbor from back here!" They tugged on their ear, then shrugged. "You might as well come through here." They led Hoof into a building.

~~~

A shadow detached itself from the gloom opposite the alley. Quill-pusher took another look at the door through which Hoof had disappeared, then spun around and headed back towards the Palace.

The chimpanzee led Hoof down a wide corridor, opened a door at the far end and waved him through. They looked back at the muddy hoofprints Hoof had left behind and sighed.

"Erm, sorry?" Hoof mumbled.

"Never mind," The chimpanzee pointed across a narrow but clean and orderly street. "That path will take you to the market square. At the far end of the square is a road that circles the city. Going either direction will get you to the harbor gate."

Hoof heaved a sigh of relief. "Thank you!" he exclaimed. "Thank you very much . . ." When he saw he was addressing a closed door he spun in a circle, looking for attackers. The scattering of passersby seemed to be studiously avoiding him. With a nervous chuckle he trotted across the street and headed down the path.

~~~

The path entered the market square near the stage that had been used for Crumpt's rally. Hoof's eye turned toward the pygmy hippo's shop. A fist of Waterstrider's Guard milled around in front of it. When a large jackal slunk out of the shop, Hoof dove for cover. The back of his neck prickled as he skirted the back of the stage, then forced himself to casually walk toward the far exit.

As soon as he was out of the market, he broke into a gallop. The green sash billowed over his back as he burst through the harbor gate and, ignoring the startled cries of the Guards, pounded down the wharf to *The Dancing Sea Cow.* He leaped across the gangway, crossed the deck and skidded to a stop behind a stack of crates.

Exhausted and trembling with shock, he sagged to the deck. A shipmonkey peered down at him from the rigging and chittered excitedly. A shadow fell over him.

"Playing a game of 'Hide the Donkey?'" rumbled a deep voice.

"Wat Ho! Thank goodness! Is the boat ready to sail?"

"The Captain's most anxious to cast off. He's been waiting for you and Jawana and, believe me, he's one unhappy bear."

"Jawana's not coming," said Hoof.

"Alas! A stranger twist of fate than I could ever contemplate."

"Back to the poetry, are you?" sighed Hoof. "Jawana will join us in The Capital. And don't ask what she's doing or how she'll find us! I have no idea."

"Very well," rumbled Wat Ho, although he clearly didn't think things were well at all. "But t'is with a very heavy heart I'll go tell The Captain to depart."

Moments later the gangway was up and the rigging swarmed with monkeys hastening to follow the Captain's growled commands.

~~~

Waterstrider City disappeared behind a bend in the river. Hoof rolled over and got his legs under him. There was a 'clunk' when the Chamberlain's medallion hit the deck. He planted a hoof on it and stretched up until it tore off the sash. Picking it up in his lips, he went to the port rail and spat it into the river. *Well, that's that!*

He turned around and found himself staring into the Captain's cold, hard eyes. The Captain's eyes flicked to the satchel that hung around Hoof's neck, then went back to drilling a hole through Hoof's forehead. The bear's lips pulled back in a grimace that would never be mistaken for a smile.

Hoof swallowed. "Booger?" he called. "I could use some help!"

"Your thrall is indisposed," Waite growled.

"Indisposed? Why? What happened?"

Waite stared at him for several beats. "He got on the wrong side of a few dockworkers," he said at last.

Figures! thought Hoof. 'What did he do? Steal something?"

"No," Waite replied. His eyes were on the satchel. "Did you?"

"Did I what?" Hoof asked.

"Did you steal something?" growled the bear.

"No!" Hoof exclaimed. "Booger delivered your package, like you told him too. But . . . stuff happened. Bad stuff."

"I heard," said Waite.

"Well . . . the creature from the shop, the hippo, said the package had to be taken to the Chamberlain. Those were his last words."

"And did you take the package to the Chamberlain?"

"Yes," Hoof replied. "Yes, I did."

The bear nodded. "Good," he grunted. The suspicious glint returned to his eye. "What did you throw overboard?"

"The Chamberlain gave me a medallion to help get past the guards," Hoof replied. "He said to get rid of it as soon I could."

Waite nodded again, then shifted his eyes to the rigging. He barked a command and the monkeys scurried to adjust the sails.

~~~

Wat Ho was holding court beside Ol' Heritance. Pete sat across from him with a deck of cards in his paw. Manny dozed in a patch of sunlight. The dog wrinkled his nose. "You stink!" he barked.

"Good to see you too, Manny," Hoof retorted. He swept his eyes over the little group and froze in alarm. "Where's Booger?"

"I'm here, Boss," a muffled voice slurred from behind Wat Ho. "Sorry about not getting up."

Hoof stepped forward and saw Booger's bare feet poking out behind Wat Ho. He took a couple more steps and saw a torso. A sun-browned hand separated itself from the torso and waggled its fingers.

"Glad you made it back, Boss. I was worried I'd have to look for a new job." The hand flopped, palm down, onto the deck.

"Your loyalty is touching," Hoof said as he craned his neck to peer down between Wat Ho and the wagon. "Great Gorme!"

Half of Booger's face was a swollen purple mass. Part of his head had been shaved and a cloth pad covered his right ear. It was held in

203

place by a strip of cloth wound around his head. Hoof turned an eye toward Wat Ho.

"That's one tough little creature," rumbled Wat Ho admiringly. "Nothing major: a few cracked ribs, some loose teeth and some bruises. His ear got the worst of it but, with any kind of luck, he'll be able to hear out of it again. Eventually."

"Who did this?" Hoof brayed. "Why did they do this?"

"Some dockworkers mistook him for a spy," Wat Ho replied. "They didn't waste time on questions."

"That's terrible!" Hoof exclaimed. "We have to say something. Do something. Don't we?"

"It's okay Boss," Booger replied. "The thing is, we kinda were being spies, right? The mix up was just about what side we were on. It was an honest mistake."

A ship-monkey came up with a bucket tied to a rope. He pointed at Hoof with one paw, while he held his nose with the other. "From the Captain," he chittered. "He says to please use soon!" Laughing hysterically, he did a back flip before knuckling off down the deck.

"The monkey has a point," Wats Ho chuckled as he picked up the bucket. "I'll help you." After wiping down the satchel, he pulled up buckets of river water until he had rinsed most of the sweat and grime out of Hoof's coat.

That night, Hoof snuck up to Ol' Heritance and, making sure there were no witnesses, shrugged the satchel off over his head. He took another quick look around, gripped the satchel between his teeth and stuffed it as far down the side of the wagon as he could reach.

~~~

It was a relief to settle into a few days of uneventful sailing. Hoof hovered over Booger as, under Wat Ho's watchful eye, he recovered from his injuries. Manny spent his time hunting rats below deck, which the crew appreciated. They were, however, less than thrilled with Pete;

when they saw him coming, they turned their backs and hurried away with their tails held erect.

As *The Dancing Sea Cow* neared its final destination, stops to load or unload cargo became more frequent. On the last day, Manny timidly approached Captain Waite. He waited until the Captain finished roaring orders to his crew. "Please excuse me, *capitán.*"

The big bear's head moved from side to side as he looked for the source of the voice. "Please *capitán,* I am down here."

The Captain cast his eyes down. He looked a bit startled at seeing the little dog. "What?" he growled.

"The place where we land in *La Capital*. Is it at what is called the Old Waterfront?"

"No." The Captain looked into the rigging and shouted at the ship-monkeys. When he looked back down, Manny was still patiently waiting. "That be way over on Regency Island," rumbled the Captain.

~~~

It was three quarters night when *The Dancing Sea Cow* slipped into its mooring at one of the smaller islands that made up The Capital. The nighttime dockworkers hunched their shoulders against a cold, steady drizzle. In spite of the cold and damp, Hoof slept soundly, undisturbed by the muffled sounds of a port that stayed active all night long.

~ *31* ~

With dawn, the noise of the port increased a hundredfold. Hoof pushed between two crates, trying to stuff his head under a blanket. This earned him a poke in the ribs. Rolling on his side got him jabbed harder. He groaned and got up.

An errant hoof sent an object skidding across the deck. His eyes widened. *What! The! Charlie D!* He'd almost tripped over his own sword! Which looked amazing! The belt was freshly oiled and the scabbard gleamed. A strip of cloth stuck out of it.

Wat Ho and Booger did double takes when Hoof clopped up wearing his sword. "What's this?" asked Booger as he pulled the cloth out of the scabbard. "Oh. It has writing on it." He handed it to Wat Ho.

Manny and Pete completed a half circle in front of the Guardian. He squinted at the note. "Wayfarers' Rest, Upper Water Street." He shrugged. "That's all it says."

"So what does it mean?" Hoof demanded.

Wat Ho shrugged. "That there's something called 'Wayfarers' Rest' somewhere called 'Upper Water Street.'"

While they were talking, Ol' Heritance had been hooked up to a crane. A brace of gorillas cranked the wagon up off the deck. As soon as its wheels cleared the railing, they locked the crank and swung the crane around on a pivot. The crank was unlocked, and the wagon dropped to the wharf with a thump that made Booger wince.

~~~

Manny hobbled ashore to the heart-felt best wishes of the ship-monkeys. Pete went to follow, and a sullen silence descended on the vessel. He stood at the gangway for several beats. "Why me?" he groaned. He threw a heavy pouch to the nearest ship-monkey. "Figure out who belongs to what." He did not look back as he stomped ashore.

Booger and Hoof were at the rail, gawking at the massive port. Around them riverboats—often double and triple berthed—were docked stem to stern for as far as they could see. Carts dodged around masses of dockworkers. On the opposite side of the channel, oceangoing vessels towered over a flotilla of smaller craft.

"Harumph!"

Hoof and Booger almost fell over each other as they whirled around. "Captain Waite!" exclaimed Booger. He snapped to attention and offered a crisp salute.

"Stop that foolishness and collect what I owe you from Killer." Addressing Hoof, he added, "I didn't charge for your visa. Goodbye and good luck." He turned and began bellowing at his crew. Hoof and Wat Ho waited for Booger at the gangway. When he came out of the Captain's cabin, a pirate-style bandana hid his hacked-off hair. Its mottled purple and yellow matched the fading bruises that covered half his face. "Killer had lots of blue and red bandanas," Booger said, "but they clashed with my new look."

"You made the right decision," said Wat HO.

Pete and Manny had stretched out beside Ol' Heritance, soaking up the morning sun. "Are you comin', or what?" Pete called.

Booger gingerly followed Hoof across the gangway. Wat Ho kept an eye on him from behind. "So then," Wat Ho rumbled when they had all gathered around the wagon. "Shall we go looking for the mysterious 'Wayfarers' Rest?'"

Hoof spied a coquettish young Donkey prancing along the wharf. "There's a Jennet over there. I'll ask her for directions."

"Nice!" Booger approved.

~~~

During an animated conversation with Ms. Verity Glitters, Hoof learned that their destination was on the far side of the Island. Upper Water Street was given over to inns and commercial concerns. Lower Water Street was lined with residences occupied by prominent city officials, whose number included Ms. Glitter's sire. They were connected by a drawbridge over the Longbough Canal.

Using the pretext that she 'had to go home anyway' the Jennet, with much giggling and batting of her eyes, offered to serve as their guide. Hoof enthusiastically accepted.

Booger tried to pick up the towbar, but Wat Ho insisted he wasn't ready yet. He rode in the wagon while Hoof took his place. Ms. Glitter pranced chattily at Hoof's side as they zigzagged uphill to the island's center, then made a more direct descent down the other side. They turned onto Upper Water Street and headed downstream.

"This is it," Ms. Glitter announced.

"This is what?" asked Hoof. They were in front of a tall, impenetrable hedge. "It looks like we're next to a forest."

The Jennet nodded at a gap in the greenery. "Your hotel is through that gate," she said.

Hoof stepped away from the wagon. "Thank you, Mistress Glitters," he said, curling his lip politely. "You've been very hospitable."

"Call me Verity," she replied with a shy duck of her head. Her ears twisted coquettishly as she continued, "Master, erm . . .?" She peered up at him through long, dark lashes.

"Hearted," Hoof replied with a bow. "Hoof Hearted."

"Really!" she exclaimed. "How droll!" She hesitated. "Will you be in The Capital long, Master Hearted?"

"Call me Hoof, please," he replied with a jaunty head waggle. "To be honest, I don't know how long we'll be here." He exposed his teeth in a bold grin. "But I hope it will be a good while!"

"Oh!" Verity's ears turned pink as she studied her hooves. "Well," she said without looking up. "I must be going. Mother will be wondering what happened to me!" She took half a step, then stopped. "The drawbridge is just ahead. I live across it, on Lower Water. Ours is the big green stable on the water side, halfway down."

"Well," said Hoof. "I hope we meet again soon." He stepped back to the towbar. Inside the gate, a driveway cut a broad circle through the grounds of the most imposing inn and stable that Hoof had ever seen. Or would have seen if his eyes had ever left the Jennet who watched him from the gate. He sighed.

"Oh, for crying out loud," Pete exclaimed. "Walk her home already! Our young pirate has the purse; we can check in without you."

"Really?" said Hoof. "You don't mind?"

"I don't care that you go," barked Manny. "It is that you come back that is annoying."

"All right! Thanks!" Hoof sang as he galloped away.

Wat Ho watched him go. "How quickly young hearts may recover," he mused, "if new love they should discover." He turned to the others. "Shall we?"

"You two go," said Pete. "Manny and I'll watch the wagon."

"A prudent plan," allowed Wat Ho. He helped Booger down, then swept a paw toward the entrance. "After you."

~~~

The lobby towered over them. A circular bar was surrounded by widely spaced tables. Elegantly groomed Equines nibbled hay from tiny baskets that were refreshed by liveried serving apes. Most of the guests (which included a scattering of Fingered Folk) wore bandanas, of which the blue slightly outnumbered the red.

A matched pair of bald apes stood behind an ornate counter. They were young, female, and wore identical gowns and hair styles. A Rhino stood guard at each end of the counter. All eight eyes were fixed intently on the new arrivals.

Booger skidded to a stop. "Do you feel just a little out of place, here?" he asked out of the side of his mouth.

"When in doubt, bluff it out," murmured Wat Ho. He stretched to his full height and strode up to one of the desk clerks. "Hullo," he rumbled, looking down his nose at her.

She tilted back, squeaked, and stared open-mouthed for several beats. "Oh! How, erm, may I be of assistance?" she said at last.

"Hmpf," sniffed Wat Ho in the manner of one unused to being kept waiting, even for an instant. "We serve the Indomitable Donkey Master Hoof Hear . . . day Hearted. Hardy Hearted."

"Master Hoof Har-r-r-day Hardy Hearted?" parroted the clerk.

"Don't be absurd," sniffed Wat Ho.

The clerk's face turned a striking shade of pink. "Does your, erm, abominable Donkey master have a reservation?" she asked, smiling through clenched teeth.

"That's . . . ah! Master Hearted was called to The Capital on urgent business. I am to arrange accommodations on his behalf."

"You'll not be doing it here, I'm afraid," said the clerk, with an even broader smile. "We have no space available: the entire Electoral Council is staying here; it is the Tridecalunium, after all."

"The Electoral Council?" mused Wat Ho. "Interesting." Something moved behind Wat Ho's eyes as they drilled into the clerk. "Surely there must be something you can do for us," he purred. His gaze flicked to a tag at her shoulder, then returned to her eyes as he murmured, "Morna!"

Morna swallowed twice, then whispered, "Well, there's, erm . . . No!" She shook her head as if to clear it. "No. It's impossible."

"Is anything really impossible?" smiled Wat Ho.

The clerk's face reflected her internal debate. "The Royal Suite is unoccupied . . . "No!" She drew herself up. "It can't be done!"

"If it's unoccupied, no creature will question us using it," reasoned Wat Ho. "Is that not so?"

"But it's reserved for the Supreme Leader and his guests," Morna plaintively replied. "But . . ." She lowered her voice and tipped forward on her toes, "he won't be using it. He hates, hates, hates the Electoral Council and won't come anywhere near them."

"The Giraffe hates the Electoral Council?" said Wat Ho.

"What? No. I don't know! He can't use it anyway, unless his appointment is confirmed by the Council."

"Is there some doubt that he will be confirmed?"

"The *real* Supreme Leader thinks so! Oh!" She clapped a hand to her mouth. "What am I saying? Talking politics is forbidden!"

Wat Ho gently eased her hand away from her mouth. "You said nothing," he assured her. "Picture us as guests of the 'real' Supreme Leader. You may make the suite available to us."

Morna's eyes glazed over. "Guests of the Supreme Leader," she parroted as she sleepwalked away.

"What's wrong with her?" whispered Booger.

"Nothing a generous gratuity won't set right," murmured Wat Ho.

"What? Oh." Booger dug a silver coin out of Hoof's purse and offered it to Wat Ho. "That should do it."

Wat Ho drew back. "You know I can't handle money."

Morna returned carrying a large gilt key. "Welcome to Wayfarers' Rest," she intoned. "You have been to the suite before, I assume."

"Of course," lied Wat Ho. "Some time ago. Is it still accessed . . ."

"Via the private courtyard and elevator, yes. I regret there will be a short wait for the elevator operator. Had we known you were coming one would have been on standby but . . ."

"No problem, Morna," smiled Wat Ho, relieving her of the key.

He bent down to look into the clerk's eyes. "Master Hearted will be arriving later," he rumbled. "There will be no need to bother him with any pesky recordkeeping."

She blinked. "Recordkeeping?" Her pale features reflected another internal struggle. Booger slipped out a second small coin. "Not . . . necessary," she choked out at last.

Booger slid the coins across the counter. As he and Wat Ho strode to the exit, Morna's eyes settled on the coins. Her gaze sharpened as she swept them into the bodice of her dress.

~~~

Wat Ho and Booger interrupted a pitched battle between Pete and Manny on one side and a pair of liveried chimpanzees on the other. "What is going on here?" boomed Wat Ho in a voice that froze the combatants in place.

"It's about time you got back!" complained Pete. "These apes are trying to steal our wagon."

The older of the chimpanzees protested, "We are not stealing anything: We are hotel valets. Look!" He pointed to the Hotel's logo on his vest. Below that was a badge that identified him as 'Jerome, Senior Valet.' "It's our job to take care of our guests' vehicles."

"Yeah?" said Pete. "Just try and touch our wagon again and I'll 'take care' of you."

Wat Ho spoke over Pete's outburst, "I apologize, Jerome," he said with a quick squint at the name tag. And, erm . . ."

"Rycliff, Excellency!" said the younger valet, dipping into a bow.

"Rycliff," said Wat Ho. "This wagon belongs a guest of the Supreme Leader. These wretches," he continued with a head tilt at Pete and Manny, "are under orders to never let it of their sight."

At the mention of the Supreme Leader both chimpanzees stood upright and clapped their fists to their chests. "The fault is entirely ours," they chorused. "We will resign our jobs in disgrace."

"That is a tempting offer," allowed Wat Ho, "but it would be more helpful if you brought the wagon around to the Royal Elevator."

The chimpanzees exhaled. "Yes, Excellency! Right away!" they exclaimed, bobbing up and down in a series of bows. "Your Excellency is more generous than our worthless carcasses deserve!"

They picked up the tow bar and struggled down a cobbled lane that ran around the side of the hotel. Upon reaching an ornate iron gate, they stopped and looked up at Wat Ho expectantly.

"Ah!" He inserted the gilt key in the lock and pulled the gate open. After waving the chimps through, he followed them into a high-walled garden. "Please leave the wagon by the elevator."

Booger had discretely fingered a couple of copper bits out of his purse. He offered them to the chimps when they finished making a show of pushing and pulling the wagon into position.

"Really Sir, we can't . . ." Jerome protested.

"Gratuities are frowned upon," said his companion.

They hurried away, leaving Booger staring at the palm of his hand, from which both coins had disappeared.

Hoof was bending Verity's ears with tales of his recent adventures when he felt a bump against his chest. He let out a dismayed bray. "Granny's garters! I forgot I was wearing Donkie Otie's sword." He looked around wildly. "Will that get me into trouble?"

"Of course not, you silly," Verity assured him. "You're Equine. We can do pretty much whatever we want in this city." She ducked her head to inspect the weapon. "Goodness! Is that really the Great Donkie Otie's sword?" She shivered. "How frightfully exciting! You must tell me all about him!"

Hoof felt a bit put out that his companion seemed more interested in his dubious ancestor than in him. "Yeah," he tersely replied, "it was his. But this sword got me out of some tough scrapes too, you know? Like the time I faced down a mad, foaming-at-the-muzzle pad paw on a bridge! The creature was all set to attack me with a dagger!"

Verity stared at him. "Really? How terrifying! I've never heard of a pad paw using a weapon before."

"Yeah, well. This creature lost a paw, so he wore a dagger attached to the stump."

"Oh my!" said Verity, resuming her amble down the street. "Like your friend. What's his name? Manny?"

Hoof stared after her. "Yeah," he admitted as he hurried to catch up. "Exactly like Manny."

Verity stopped again and narrowed her eyes. "Oh goodness me!" she exclaimed. "It was Manny, wasn't it?"

"Uh huh," said Hoof. "But he's one mean little dog!"

Verity burst out laughing and, after a few beats, Hoof joined in. She leaned in and nuzzled his neck. "You make me laugh," she said. "I like that in a Jack."

Not what I was going for, but I'll take it. "So, how much further is it to your place?"

"Not far," she replied. "It's the green stable just . . . Oh Fitz, Glitz and Blitz," she exclaimed. "That's Pappa! I think he's seen us . . . You've got to get out of here!"

"Really? Well it's been nice . . ."

"Just go! I know where to find you. Now go! Go! Go!"

214

~ *32* ~

Hoof was mentally replaying his less-than-ideal parting from Ms. Verity Glitters when the Wayfarers' Rest hedge shout-whispered, *"Hola, Señor* Hoof! I am requiring assistance!"
He shot a sidelong glance at the chatty foliage and hurried on.

"Wait! *Eh! Burro estúpido.* Stop! Stop!"

Even the bushes are insulting me? He confronted the hostile hedge. "Who's there?" he demanded. "Why are you bothering me?"

"It is I: Manuel Isareali Sobad."

"Manny?" Hoof swung his head back and forth. "Where are you?"

"I am under the big wall of trees."

"You're hiding in the hedge? Why?"

"I do not hide! I am to stop you from going to the inn."

"Wait, what? Why am I not going to the inn?"

"You will go, *Señor.* But by a different way."

"Okay?" Hoof drew out the word. "So, shall we? Go?"

"I would like to, *Señor* Hoof. But I am a little bit stuck!"

"And you are struck in the hedge why?"

"Because the big, sneaky rat, he tricked me!"

Hoof aimed an eye under the hedge. Two bulbous eyes glared back at him. Manny twisted and kicked, but he was trapped by branches that had wrapped themselves around him.

"Hee Haw!" guffawed Hoof. After he stopped laughing, he stretched a leg into the hedge and stepped on the branch that kept Manny airborne.

215

Manny squirmed free and burst out of the hedge. He glared at the Donkey. "Was not funny!" he barked.

"No, of course not" Hoof agreed. His breath escaped in an explosive snort. "Except it totally was!"

Manny turned his back on Hoof and limped along the hedge. "Please walk this way," he barked.

"If you insist!" Hoof lifted one front hoof in the air and hobbled after the Chihuahua.

~~~

"Okay *Señor Burro,*" Manny growled as they rounded the inn. "Follow me and pretend to not be a creature of no importance." He led the way into the Royal Courtyard. Hoof was relieved to see Booger's wagon. But the jowly gorilla lounging against it was a mystery.

"Hola, Señor operador de ascensors," Manny called. "My Most Exalted Master, The Indomitable Donkey Hoof Hardy Hearted wishes to ascend to the suite."

The Gorilla jumped up and bowed. *"Hola Señor* Sobad," he replied. "I am at your Master's service!"

Manny turned back to Hoof. "Your Excellency," he lisped, dipping into an awkward bow, "may your unworthy servant ascend with you to your suite." The rage in his eyes belied his groveling tone.

After a brief hesitation, Hoof decided to play along. "What*ever,"* he whined. "I need this *interminable* morning to be over!" With a toss of his head, he clopped into the cage and turned around. Manny crept in beside him.

The gorilla bowed even lower as he closed the cage door. "Beggin' your pardon, *Señor* Sobad," he whispered, "but His Excellency may want to turn around, lest his tail get tangled in the works."

Hoof glared down his nose at the gorilla. His theatrics were wasted; the gorilla kept his eyes pointed down. When a few beats had passed, Manny hissed, "If His Gracious Excellency moved his illustrious *trasero de burro*, we could get up to his suite."

Hoof swung around and the cage began a smooth, silent ascent. Manny stood beside Hoof, his trembling body facing straight ahead. "Never will we speak of what happened," he barked. *Comprendido?*"

"Oh? What happened?" asked Hoof innocently.

~~~

The elevator stopped at a brightly lit landing. "Boss!" cried Booger as he rushed to open the gate. "Oh, sorry! I meant to say 'Welcome, Your Excellentness!'" He bowed. "Your humble servant anxiously awaited the arrival of your right high . . . erm . . . muckityness!"

Hoof's knees locked as he gaped at the massive, gilded entrance hall. "Jumping Jonah's jodhpurs," he breathed. "Who's paying for this? Wait: I'm paying for this!" He aimed an accusing eye at Booger. "What am I paying for this?"

Booger straightened up and, barely suppressing a fit of giggles intoned, "I am humbly pleased to announce that Your Most Glorious Good Graciousness is paying zilch."

Hoof's eyes shifted from his thrall, who had clearly lost his mind, to the smugly smiling face of the Guardian.

Wat Ho clasped his paws together and blinked at Hoof with suspiciously innocent wide eyes. "Your Graciousness is enjoying the 'kindness of strangers.' Or, I should say, of one stranger in particular."

"Really?" Hoof took a few steps forward as he tried to take it all in. "Wow! The Chamberlain set all this up?"

Wat Ho's head rocked back and forth. "Not the Chamberlain," he chuckled. "The Supreme Leader himself!"

Hoof froze, then backed into the elevator. "The Supreme Leader?" he brayed. "I have never met the Supreme Leader! Nobody in my family has ever met the Supreme Leader! None of us has ever *wanted* to meet the Supreme Leader!"

"Exactly," rumbled Wat Ho calmly. "No stranger is more perfect than one you have never met."

Booger touched Hoof's shoulder. "Come along, Excellentness," he said. "We must tidy you up before you meet your fellow dignitaries."

Hoof stared at him blankly. "What dignitaries?"

"Well," said Wat Ho, "I believe we'll start with your friends on the Electoral Council."

"I have no 'friends' on the Electoral Council!"

"That's something we'll soon set right," said Wat Ho. "They're all dying to meet the special guest of the Supreme Leader."

"But . . . but . . . but . . ." Hoof let himself be led across the foyer and into the Royal Suite. After navigating an opulent living space he found himself in an Equine-sized bathing area, where he came face-to-face with Pete, sporting a bar of soap and an evil grin.

A knee-level chuckle drew Hoof's eyes toward the floor. Manny sat looking up at him with every sharp tooth on display. "Now this: this will be funny!" he laughed.

~~~

"I feel ridiculous!" Hoof grumbled to Pete, who sat on his back, threading gold ribbon through his short, bristly mane.

"That is natural, *Señor,*" barked Manny. "Because you are ridiculous. But you are now ridiculous in the way of the *clase superior.*"

Hoof had been pushed into a scalding bath and scrubbed, buffed, trimmed and perfumed to within an inch of his life. What was left of the afternoon was spent having his hooves polished, gold beads braided into his tail and his fetlocks wrapped in jangling bracelets. As a final indignity, his ears had been painfully stuffed through the openings of a tiny decorative helm.

"To fit in with Nobs," said Booger, "you gotta look like a Nob."

"Well, you've done a good job," said Hoof, "because a knob is exactly what I feel like!"

"Your Good Graciousness is welcome," grinned Booger.

"Thrilled to serve your Indomitable Excellentness," simpered Pete.

"One final touch," rumbled Wat Ho. He picked up a black bandana by its diagonal corners and tied the resulting triangle around Hoof's neck. "You are in mourning. Which is why you are not wearing the color of your preferred Supreme Leader."

"And who is that, exactly?" asked Hoof.

"That depends on who's asking," Wat Ho replied.

~~~

Sack O'Stuff was put to work. In addition to Hoof's baubles and bangles, it spit out livery for Booger: puffy orange breeches with matching cloth shoes; tight yellow stockings; a frilly white blouse and a purple vest covered in tiny, embroidered feathers. A flat cap, in bright orange to match his breeches, hid his cropped hair.

"You look like a big gawky bird," chortled Pete. He stopped laughing when Wat Ho handed him a short vest and cap identical to Booger's. He was, to his relief, spared the rest of the outfit.

Wat Ho donned a purple robe; it seemed advisable to cover up the ravages his body had recently suffered. In sympathy with their Master's 'state of mourning' the entire group put on black bandanas.

"Who am I mourning, anyway?" asked Hoof.

After a moment's thought Wat Ho said. "It must be the untimely passing of your great, great, great, great uncle, Bellringer Hardy III, of the NorthReach Hardy Herd."

"Really? I've never heard of them."

"Neither has any creature else."

"Close, were we?" said Hoof.

"Not at all, but the old Jack produced no foals. Given the lack of legitimate heirs, you hope to acquire his title."

Not wanting to overtax the operator, Wat Ho rode down in the elevator first, then sent it back to collect the others. Hoof left his sword behind—the belt and scabbard didn't match his posh new look. Manny, however, refused to be separated from his weapon.

When they reached the courtyard, Manny stepped aside and bowed to Hoof. "Please to excuse me, *Su Excelencia,*" he barked. "There are matters to which I must give my urgent attention." He bobbed his head at Wat Ho and Pete. *"Buenas tardes, Señores.* I hope to return by the morning." He spun around and hurried down the cobbled drive.

~~~

The sunset candle was being lit when Wat Ho, acting as Hoof's bodyguard, led the way into the Inn. Every eye in the lobby blinked at the sight of the massive creature, then slid down to Hoof, who strode behind him. Booger and Pete brought up the rear. A hush fell over the lobby, soon to be broken by whispers from all sides.

"Way to be inconspicuous, folks!" Jawana's bell-like voice rang across the lobby.

"Hee . . . *mmph!*" Wat Ho choked off the Donkey's delighted greeting with a giant paw.

"Who presumes to address the Indomitable Donkey Hoof Hardy Hearted, Heir Presumptive to Bellringer Hardy III, the late Patriarch of the NorthReach Hardy Herd?" Wat Ho rumbled.

"Mmph!" Hoof feebly struggled. "I . . . can't . . . breathe!"

"Remember who you are supposed to be!" Wat Ho hissed. "High ranking Equines are not friendly with gorillas. Is that clear?"

The Donkey desperately jerked his head up and down until Wat Ho released him. Jawana hardly missed a beat before she dipped into a curtsy that almost hid her smirk. "I beg forgiveness, Lord High Hardy-Har-Har, upon whom my eyes are not fit to gaze."

"Arise, lowly creature," Hoof replied. He paused, distracted by Jawana's hotel livery, which included a frilly maid's bonnet that perched resentfully on her round head. "Yes, erm . . . we are moved to briefly tolerate your unworthy presence," he intoned at last.

Jawana's eyes flashed as she muttered, "There is a line it would be unwise to cross, no matter how noble you pretend to be."

Wat Ho cleared his throat. "His Indomitableness has business stemming from Lord Bellringer's untimely passing. He must act very quickly to make sure the Bellringer title passes to him. As is, of course, only his due."

Jawana trained her eyes on the floor as she processed this information. "To offer condolences would be far above my station. But should His Equine Lordliness dine in his suite tonight, I would be honored to deliver an evening meal to lighten his grief."

"His Indomitableness graciously accords you the honor of serving him," rumbled Wat Ho gravely. "He will dine in the Royal Suite, where he is a guest of the Supreme Leader."

Jawana stuck a finger in her ear. "Sorry? It almost sounded like you said something about the Supreme Leader."

"Yeah," said Hoof. "Kindness of strangers and all that."

"Quite," smiled Wat Ho. "His Hooved Graciousness will expect you when the sunset candle is at its third mark."

"I am honored," said Johanna as she dipped into a deep curtsy. Out of the corner of her mouth she added, "I look forward to hearing more on a certain subject."

Wat Ho responded with a lopsided grin. Jawana turned on her talons and hurried into the depths of the hotel.

Click, click . . . click. Click, click . . . click. Manny's nails beat an uneven rhythm on the dark waterfront street. Dusk had fallen before he even reached Regency Island. Now the moon was overhead and he was still no closer to finding the elusive Kloue van Wraak. He had lost count of how many taverns he had entered, only to be met with sealed lips and suspicious sidelong glances.

The little dog stopped in front of yet another faded door. He let a small band of chattering ship-monkeys pour out onto the street, then slipped inside before the door closed. He crossed to a table that stood near the bar. It was a nice surprise that, for once, he did not have to dance around puddles of stale, reeking beer. He leaped onto a bench that faced the entrance. His bulbous eyes swept the room.

The small tavern was lit by a blazing fireplace that took up most of one wall. It had a deep wooden mantle on which a huge leopard-spotted cat was stretched out. The cat's head hung over the edge of the mantle, staring at Manny with wide inquisitive eyes. Manny stared into those eyes, transfixed. He didn't even notice the tavern's other patrons quickly drain their mugs and hurry out the door.

A sound from behind him broke the spell and Manny spun around. The silver-haired bald ape who tended bar had backed into the drinks cabinet, his face distorted by terror: His eyes were fixed on a point beyond Manny's table. Manny turned back and let out a strangled yip as he came face-to-fang with an enormous green snake. The sheath retracted from his blade as he began to raise it above the table.

"Don't." The snake's voice was the rustle of dry leaves. "We'd both be s-s-s-sorry. S-s-steel gives-s-s me indiges-s-s-stion."

Manny stopped his blade from clearing the edge of the table. "I-I-I didn't know snakes could be sentient," he stammered at last.

The snake drew up and tilted their head from side to side, as if inspecting a particularly tasty morsel. "There's-s lot-s you don't know, fool," they hissed. "S-s-starting with not to dis-s-sturb creatures-s who are bes-s-st left alone."

"S-s-sorry?" said Manny. He shook his head. "I am sorry, but I don't understand what you say: I caused no disturbance."

"You've been looking for s-s-someone. Making a great deal of needless-s-s nois-s-se."

"Looking for . . . Oh! Are you from *El Capitán* van Wraak?"

The snake's laughter was a spine-chilling hiss. "You will hear from the Captain only when . . . and if . . . the Captain chooses. Go back to where you came from, while you s-still can!"

"I cannot!" Manny barked. "The *pueblo* from where I came was destroyed. Its citizens were stolen away. They will live as slaves in a place their captors called 'Coshon Aerie.'"

The snake jerked back, flitting its tongue in and out its mouth as the cat leaped down from the mantle. In a flash, the cat was on Manny's table, mashing the dog's cheek against the cold, hard wood.

"You dare speak that name?" the cat snarled. "In my presence?"

"¡Ey!" barked Manny, struggling to get free. *"Who are you?"*

"Be careful who you s-seek," laughed the snake. "You never know when they might find you!"

~ *33* ~

A middle-aged donkey stormed into Wayfarers' Rest. The rhino guards stood up straighter as the Concierge (a rapier-thin bald ape) glided over to the new arrival. "Councilor Glitters!" he simpered. "What a pleasant—and unexpected—surprise!"

"Out of my way, fool! I'm looking for some creature." The Donkey pushed past the Concierge.

Two long strides put the Concierge back in the Donkey's path. "Were the Councilor to tell me what he seeks I might be of assistance."

"I'm looking for the ruffian who accosted my child. He bragged about being a descendant of that vile Donkie Otie creature!"

The Concierge wrung his hands. "That's awful! But why are you looking for him here?"

"Because he checked in here today!"

The Concierge frowned. "That seems unlikely, Councilor! We've been fully booked for weeks. But I will check with the front desk."

~~~

Hoof was sampling a basket of hay when he heard his Grandsire's name. Grinning broadly, he swung around . . . and froze. "Oh Gorme! That's Verity's father. He doesn't look happy, does he?"

"Living up to the family reputation, were you?" said Pete.

"No!" brayed Hoof, loudly enough to raise a few eyebrows, including his own. He ducked in behind Wat Ho's bulk. "No," he whispered. "I was just walking her home. She saw her father and panicked. The next thing I knew she was chasing me away."

The Concierge stalked up to the front desk, smiling and nodding benignly until a guest moved out of earshot.

"Counsellor Glitters is in a state!" he hissed. "He claims you checked in an uncouth Jack without proper vetting. Is that true?"

Morna looked shocked. "No! The only creature that checked in was The Indomitable High Donkey, erm, something or other. I forget."

"Indeed? Show me the register."

Morna lowered her eyes. "He didn't actually register, as such," she admitted. "His thralls took care of the details."

"But they did, of course, present his credentials?"

"Not exactly, Sir," she said, keeping her eyes fixed on the desktop. Suddenly, she leaned forward and whispered, "They are tight with the Supreme Leader: He's letting them use the Royal Suite."

The Concierge drew back in surprise. "The Royal Suite! Really!" He shot a sharp look at the second clerk. "Rona, is this true?"

Rona stared straight ahead, keeping her face expressionless. "I couldn't say, Sir," she replied.

"Look!" Morna made a subtle jabbing motion with her finger. "Do you see the scar-faced giant in the purple robe?"

The Concierge followed the track of her finger. "That would be hard to miss," he replied.

"That's who checked in, along with the youngster. The over-dressed Donkey must be the Abominable Toff himself."

The Concierge's expert eye swept over Hoof and his entourage, appraising his grooming, bodyguard and attendants' livery. It paused for a moment on Booger's face. "I will speak to them," he announced. He scooped a dollop of ointment from a countertop container. "But I will be back to discuss your disregard for proper procedures."

Pete was the first to see the tall stick-creature oozing toward them, massaging his hands like a wizard gloating over an especially nasty spell. "Scary creature!" he announced. "Coming this way!"

"Valued guests!" the Concierge enthused as he drew nearer. "I'm sorry I missed your arrival." His amiable tone was belied by the suspicious squint of his eye.

Wat Ho stepped forward to intercept him. "Quite alright," he rumbled. "The manner of our arrival was, erm, unorthodox."

"Indeed," the Concierge dryly agreed. "But as soon as you or your Master step over to the registration desk, we'll address the deficiencies in your documentation."

Wat Ho wrapped a paw around a bony elbow and drew the Concierge aside. "May I confide in you?"

The Concierge stared up at Wat Ho's scarred face. Not since early childhood had he craned his neck to face another creature. It was uncomfortable. And irritating. "If you must!" he snapped.

Wat Ho's glanced at the Concierge's name tag and forced a smile that, on his damaged face, was more likely to inspire terror than trust. "Mr. Longfellow, you will hear me out."

The Concierge stopped trying to pull free. "I'm listening."

Wat Ho studied Longfellow's face. "No doubt you are familiar with the NorthReach Hardy Herd?"

Longfellow shook his head. "Never heard of them."

"Oh well!" Wat Ho sighed. "In spite of its wealth, it remains a rather obscure branch of the Hardy clan.

Longfellow brightened: nothing piqued his interest more readily than money. "Ah yes," he sighed. "The Hardies: fine, fine Folk."

"Sadly, tragedy has struck the NorthReach." Wat Ho toyed with his black bandana as he continued, "Our Master mourns his beloved great, great, great, great uncle, Bellringer Hardy III."

Longfellow touched his fingertips together. "My condolences for your Master's loss," he murmured.

"Thank you," said Wat Ho. "Sadly, Bellringer died under suspicious circumstances. Then, when our Master was revealed to be the Heir Presumptive, he was attacked! Clearly, other creatures are working to create their own (illegitimate of course) path to the Title. Until the Title is settled, prudence calls for our Master to remain incognito. A careless entry on a passenger list or, say . . . a hotel register? Well, that could spell disaster."

The significant pause did not escape Longfellow. "I can see that," he replied. "But how is all this linked to our Supreme Leader."

"Bellringer was a loyal supporter of the Orange One," said Wat Ho. "Often, when the Supreme Leader needed to 'get away from it all' he would make a clandestine visit to Bellringer's estate. On one such occasion our Master, who was then a young foal, was visiting. It amused the Supreme Leader to feed His Young Graciousness bits of banana—a fruit he still adores!"

Wat Ho chuckled at the amusing image this brought to mind. "Several days ago," he continued, "they met by chance at an upriver hotel and reconnected over dinner. Upon learning of my Master's plight, the Supreme Leader insisted on making the Royal Suite available to him. And to his humble entourage, of course," he hastened to add. "His Supremeness would join us if the whole, ahem, 'Electoral Council' thing weren't in the way."

Longfellow nodded. "Yes. I see. How long will we enjoy your Master's presence? And how shall we address him?"

"My Master can't use his title until the Supreme Leader is Installed and announces the bestowment. It is an irksome formality that will, alas, delay things for several days. In the meantime, using my Master's current status and name (The Indomitable Donkey Hoof Hardy Hearted) would attract unwanted, probably dangerous attention. Prudence demands it be shortened."

"To?" asked Longfellow.

"Hoof . . . erm . . . Hearted," Wat Ho replied.

"Hoof Hearted?" blurted Longfellow, louder than intended. A pair of Goats veered off course to give them a wider berth.

Wat Ho beamed down at him. "Can we count on your discretion?"

"Oh, certainly," Longfellow replied. "Now, if you'll excuse me?"

He scuttled off to rejoin Councilor Glitters. Wat Ho watched them engage in a brief conversation, during which several furtive glances were aimed in Hoof's direction. The Councilor's eyes widened, his head bobbed repeatedly. He rushed out the door while Longfellow crept back to his lair.

Wat Ho turned back to Hoof and bowed. "Would his Indomitableness care for a stroll before dinner?" he asked.

"I don't know," grumped Hoof. "Would he?" But he set off with the others. With every step he took, the jewelry wrapped around his fetlocks jangled annoyingly.

Manny stopped struggling. "I surrender," he panted. "You have me at your mercy."

"Yes," a soft voice purred in his ear. "I do. As I have since you set a paw down on my waterfront. Now be a good little doggy and go back to whatever lair you crawled out of!"

Although Manny felt the pressure on his neck ease, he didn't move. His lungs filled with air. Again. And again. A few drops of blood trickled into his ear; at least one claw had penetrated his skin. Carefully, he raised his head and sat back on the bench. He studied the large, spotted cat as she sat calmly washing her paw. Her lips quirked in a small, self-satisfied smile.

"You are *El Capitán* Kloue van Wraak," Manny whispered.

The cat's only reaction was to glance at the snake, who surged up above Manny's head. "Why are you s-s-still here?" he hissed.

Manny did not flinch. *"Por favor,* I ask only for a moment of your time; just enough to hear my story. If you agree to help me, my gratitude will have no limit. If you refuse, then please kill me. Better my miserable life ends than to live with my shame."

The cat glared at Manny from under a heavy furred brow. Ignoring both the twitching of her tail and the snake hovering over his head, he met her eyes and waited for whatever was to come.

The cat's expression became thoughtful. "Your accent is from the southern realms. Yet you are here. And somehow know my name. Tell me how that came to be."

"I heard of you only a few days ago. From a new acquaintance. He said you might choose to help me."

"Who is this 'acquaintance' who dares to violate my privacy? And worse still, presumes to speak on my behalf!"

"I am sure he meant no disrespect," Manny replied. "He is a wise old Goat. His name, if I recall correctly, was *Señor* Sol Goode."

Van Wraak stood up. "You will come to my ship," she said. "You will start at the beginning and I will hear you out. But know this: if I am not satisfied, you will not leave my ship alive." The cat sprang to the floor and padded toward the exit. Manny scrambled after her. The snake was nowhere to be seen.

~~~

Van Wraak scampered up a wooden ramp and disappeared through a narrow gap in a ship's rail. Manny stared up at the looming black hull. It absorbed the sputtering gaslight from the pier, dissolving into deeper blackness within a few paces of the gangplank.

A pair of golden orbs appeared at the top of the ramp and fixed him with an unblinking stare. After a few beats, Manny set aside his doubts and climbed toward the eyes. They winked out before he reached the top.

He stopped at the rail. Light from a pair of lanterns washed dully across the ship's plank decking. His eyes adjusted to the dim light, and he made out some detail. Suddenly, a large orange paw appeared out of the shadows. "I'll take the blade," rumbled a deep voice.

"La Diosa me preserve!" Manny gasped as he leaped back. A paw slipped; he felt himself fall. The paw wrapped around his back, lifted him up and dropped him onto the deck.

A spotted golden shape stepped out of the shadows, chuckling softly. "I feared we had lost you there."

Manny held his blade out in front of him. "Be at ease," said Van Wraak. "All weapons brought aboard this ship are kept locked up until they are needed. It helps limit the foolishness my crew may get up to. Better that they save their energy for fighting our enemies than use it up on each other."

Manny stared up at a large orange shape. "You look just like . . ."

"Don't say it," interrupted the orangutan.

"Ah, *sí, sí!*" Manny hurried to agree, "As my eyes adjust, I can now see you are much better looking."

"And smarter," the orangutan added.

Manny let his weapon fall to the deck. The orangutan inspected it admiringly before locking it inside a sturdy cabinet.

"Don't worry," murmured Van Wraak. "If I let you go, your little knee-tickler will leave with you."

The sunset candle was nearing its third mark when Hoof and his 'entourage' returned to the Royal Suite. Hoof stepped off the elevator and brayed, "Get this helm off me! It pinches my ears."

"Will do, your Excellentness!" Booger gripped the helm while Hoof backed away, pulling out of it.

"Hey, what's this?" Pete discovered an enormous bunch of bananas in the sitting room. He brought the attached note over to Wat Ho who read: "To H. Hearted, with my best wishes. Wyatt Longfellow."

"Why would a creature give me bananas?" asked Hoof.

"That's a good question," replied Wat Ho as he helped himself to several of the ripe yellow fruit. Pete grabbed a couple as well.

Hoof went to stare out at the courtyard. Booger joined him. "You want the rest of the bling off too?"

"Please!" Hoof replied. "The racket is driving me nuts!"

"Don't you mean bananas?" laughed Booger.

~~~

"Someone's coming!" Hoof brayed. A gorilla pushed a trolley across the courtyard. Several bottles and covered plates threatened to become airborne as the trolley jounced over the cobbles.

The gorilla stopped in front of the elevator-ape. "Dinner for the Royal guests," she announced.

The ape eyed her suspiciously. "Who are you? I ain't never seen you before."

"I'm Wynotta Lukesea," Jawana replied. "Just started today. They needed extra staff for the Tridecalunium."

"Let's see what you got," the ape said as he reached for a lid. Before he touched it, his wrist was locked in an iron grip.

"Nuh uh," smiled Jawana/Wynotta. "That's not for you."

The ape could not budge his paw. "All right! Let go already!" Jawana let go and the ape pulled back, massaging his wrist. "I was curious, is all," he muttered. "There was no call to break my wrist."

"Our guest is particular about his food not being touched," said Jawana as she pushed the trolley onto the elevator.

Jawana stepped off the elevator and, with a hard shove, sent the trolley rolling toward the corner. "All right," she said, slapping her palms together. "We've got some things to get through."

"Yeah. Like dinner," said Hoof. "What did you bring?"

"What? Why would I bring you dinner?"

"Because you said you would?" said Pete.

"To lighten our grief," added Booger.

"You creatures eat too much!" she snapped. Then she glanced over at Wat Ho and blanched. "Or not! Wat Ho, you've lost a lot of weight! And you're going grey?"

"It's more white than grey," said Hoof out of the corner of his mouth, "and he gets cranky if you mention it."

Booger went to the trolley and began removing lids. They hid the remains of meals that had already been eaten. The third plate contained a couple of gravy-covered potatoes that looked untouched. He picked one up and took a bite.

"You brought us garbage?" brayed Hoof.

"What did you want?" Jawana retorted. "It's not like I really work here or anything."

"It's okay," said Booger around a mouthful of potato. "I ate this way for years."

Hoof clopped over to the banana bunch, bit one off, and began to chew. He spat it out. "That's disgusting!"

Booger licked the gravy off his fingers, picked up a banana and peeled it. "Try this," he said.

Hoof snapped up the peel, chewed noisily and swallowed. "Say, that is a lot better!" he said. Booger shrugged, then ate the banana.

"Focus, children! "Jawana pounded on a tabletop until she had the group's attention. "You know the Installation is in three days, right?" She shot a glance around the room. "Where's the dog?"

"He claimed he had things to do," Pete replied. "He hopes to be back by morning."

"Now what's he up to?" said Jawana, then shook her head. "Never mind. The Installation . . ."

". . . is in three days," Pete helpfully offered.

"Correct," said Jawana. "We hope so, anyway. A mob is on its way here. They claim they're coming to celebrate the Installation. But really, Crumpt expects them to keep it from happening. But they've broken no laws—yet—so we can't stop them."

"We hope. We can," Pete said mockingly. "Who's this 'we?'"

Jawana hesitated. "Let's say a group of 'like-minded' creatures dedicated to preserving the Constitution of The Realm"

"So," said Pete flatly, "this whole time, you've been a spy."

"I served in the security forces," Jawana admitted. "But after the current leader was 'selected,' I reconsidered my career choice. I went to Rock Bottom and ran an Inn. Full stop."

"Until now," said Pete.

"Until now," Jawana agreed. "Do you have a problem with that?"

"I don't!" said Hoof, Wat Ho and Booger, almost simultaneously.

All eyes turned toward Pete. "I guess not," he mumbled.

"The mob isn't the only sand in the salad," said Jawana. "Lord Waterstrider has armed a bunch of mercenaries and moved them out. Where they're going and why is any creature's guess."

"But you were pretending to be one of them," Hoof protested. "You must have learned something."

Three pairs of eyes flicked to Hoof, then back to Jawana. She shrugged. "The troops had no clue. Neither, as far as I could tell, did the officers. But if they are coming here, Waterstrider's got a good reason to keep it quiet: Leading armed troops into The Capital is an automatic death sentence."

"Why is that?" asked Booger.

"Long ago, blood was spilled by rival factions. After that The Capital Guard was put in charge of all security within The Capital's borders. They've done a great job but, lately, they've had a lot of restrictions put on them by Crumpt and his 'special constables.' I doubt if The Guard could cope with a full-blown riot. Throw in an army, even one as badly trained and undisciplined as Waterstrider's, and the Guard won't stand a chance."

Pete slowly clapped his paws together. "That's a fascinating story," he drawled. "But what's it got to do with us?"

"You still have time to get out of the city before trouble starts. You should leave now, if not sooner."

"I can't do that," said Hoof. "There's a job I've got to do first. But the rest of you should go."

"No way, boss!" said Booger, "I'm sticking with you!"

"I'm going to be here at least until Manny gets back," grumbled Pete. "Drat my luck."

"Excellent!" beamed Wat Ho. "Things are unfolding very nicely."

"Say what?" bleated the others.

"What," he obligingly replied.

"I better get back," said Jawana. She got up and banged the lids back on the plates she had brought up. When she got to the elevator she turned back and stared at Wat Ho.

Wat Ho returned her stare, then closed his eyes. "Good night, Jawana," he sighed. "I'm fine. Really!"

Jawana shrugged, then rang for the elevator-ape.

~ *34* ~

Manny told his story, starting with the attack on his village. Then he told it again. He was pressed for details on Jawana Finder and Captain Waite.

"Did Captain Waite know the gorilla?"

"Maybe? She seemed to frighten him, a little."

"How long were you at Waterstrider City?"

"Only one day."

"Who went ashore?"

"Right away, *la gorila* went away and never came back. *El capitán* went ashore with the young bald ape and *El burro*. *El capitán* came back right away. The young bald ape returned much later and was beaten by dock workers. Why, I do not know. *El burro* galloped back just before the boat sailed. He was very dirty and smelly."

Van Wraak studied Manny. "You will be our guest a little longer," she said at last. "Some things must be verified."

She turned to the orangutan who dozed at the cabin door. "Matroos!" she snapped. "Take our guest below."

The orangutan carried Manny down a ladder to a small, dark room. He left; came back with a bowl of water and a blanket; left again. Manny heard the snick of a bolt, then only the rubbing of the ship against the wharf.

Hoof cast a red-rimmed eye around the suite, then edged toward the elevator, moving as quietly as a hooved animal could.

235

"Where we going, Boss?" Booger chirped in his ear.

"Leaping lizards!" Hoof brayed. "Don't sneak up on me like that!"

"Sorry, Odoriferous Excellence," grinned Booger. He eyed Hoof's sword belt, unkempt mane and tangled snarl of a tail. "Did Your Good Graciousness get up on the wrong side of his tiara this morning?"

"I've got to make a delivery," Hoof sighed. "I thought that, with you being an invalid and all, I would do it on my own. But that's not going to happen, is it?"

"Wow! And to think some creatures call you 'slow!'"

Hoof pondered that statement as they rode down in the elevator.

The elevator-ape's eyes widened before quickly turning away. It dawned on Booger that their scruffiness might raise questions. "Is Your Good Gollyness ready for the, erm, costume party?" he ventured.

"Costume party? Where?" Hoof looked around the garden.

Boogers rolled his eyes at the elevator ape. "That is where you are going, Oh Supreme Obliviousness."

"What?" Then Hoof caught on and brayed, "Oh! What fun!"

The elevator-ape bowed deeper. "Does His Excellence require transport?" he asked his feet.

"No," Hoof replied, before he realized that Ol'Heritance was nowhere to be seen. "What? Oh, Zork! Where is the wagon?"

"I will get a valet." The ape scampered out through the gate.

~~~

Rycliff swept into a deep bow. "His Lordliness requires transport?"

"His Lordliness requires access to his wagon!" Hoof snapped. "Preferably right now!"

Rycliff straightened up. "Of course, Your Greatness. If you would be so kind as to accompany me."

They met Jerome, who led them to a large warehouse. He unlocked the door and bowed them inside, where Ol'Heritance towered over an array of carriages, chariots and litters.

"It's nice how it stands out, isn't it," Booger said. There was pride and confusion in his voice as he added, "Why are we here?"

"Remember the satchel you delivered to the hippo?" Hoof murmured. "I hid it." He nosed the side of the wagon. "There."

"What? Why? Oh, never mind!" Booger hopped into the wagon. After some grunting and thumping he emerged with a battered bag. "You want this thing?" he asked doubtfully.

"Yeah," said Hoof. Noting the valets' carefully expressionless faces, he added, "It's a prop for the costume party. Obviously." He headed for the door.

Jerome ducked his head as Hoof passed, then addressed Booger. "It appears His Imperiousness will not be using his vehicle. May I arrange other transportation?"

"I don't even know where we're going," said Booger as he shouldered the bag and followed Hoof outside.

"Regency Island, of course!" Hoof haughtily announced.

"Of course," said Jerome. "May I suggest the launch."

"'Launch' as in boat?" asked Booger.

"Yes, sir." The chimp bowed to Hoof and added, "If Your Graciousness would accompany me to the marina?"

~~~

The marina spread out behind a high dike that protected Wayfarers' Rest from the annual spring floods. It was crowded with boats of every shape, size and color.

"Because the Capital is all islands," Jerome explained, "boats are the best way to get around. We are privileged to keep the former Royal Launch available for the Supreme Leader and their guests." He extended a finger, "It's that one."

A huge launch was berthed at a stone wharf, far from any other vessel. It was so covered in gilt it was a wonder it didn't sink.

Booger's jaw hit his chest. "Oh. My. Gorme. Are you serious?"

"Quite serious, sir," Jerome replied. "The building behind it is the crew's barracks. They're ready to cast off at a moment's notice."

Hoof was startled by a sudden thought. "That vessel is all wrong!" he brayed. "We've made a great effort to look like members of . . ." he wrinkled his nose, ". . . the middle class. We require the sort of transport such creatures would use."

"As His Indomitableness wishes!" Jerome replied. To Rycliff he said, "Go flag down a water taxi. Have it pull up at the East Landing." Rycliff bowed and turned to go.

"Wait!" Booger called. "No creature can know who my master is. This morning, he's an ordinary young Jack."

The chimpanzees exchanged glances. "Of course," Jerome murmured. "We understand."

While Hoof stared vacantly at nothing, Booger watched Rycliff knuckle along the waterfront. He passed the Royal Launch and disappeared from sight. "Where's he off to?" Booger asked.

"So many guests are using our marina that taxis can't get near it. We are using the overflow facility, which is, unfortunately, some distance upstream." He turned to Hoof. "Does His Excellency wish me to call for a litter?"

"Would not the lesser classes, erm, walk?" asked Hoof.

"The deductive powers of His Illustrious Greatness continue to astound," Jerome replied.

~~~

As they passed the Royal Launch, Booger stopped and stared. "Perhaps his High Old Lordliness should inspect the vessel," he said wistfully, "to see if it is suitable for his Impermeable use some other time."

"Hmph," snorted Hoof dismissively. Then his brow cleared, and he said, "I just had a marvelous thought! Why don't I inspect the Royal Launch? I might find it useful some other time."

"Your brilliance overshadows us lesser mortals!" muttered Booger as he followed Hoof onto the launch. It was huge: ten rowing stations ran down each side, separated by cork-covered deck. Everything above the deck was silver or gold or highly polished wood.

"Oy!" A muscular bald ape burst out of the barracks, pulling a white sailor cap onto his shaved head. Two equally imposing creatures emerged behind him. "What're you lot doing there?"

Jerome intercepted them before they reached the launch. "Hold," he said, grabbing the leader's arm. He was dragged several paces before they stopped. "That's a guest of the Supreme Banana, that is!"

The old chimp was met by a skeptical eye. "Are you pulling my leg?" growled the bald ape.

Jerome's eyes travelled from the bald ape's bicep to a muscular thigh, then returned. "I'm pretty sure this is an arm," he replied, giving it a squeeze. "But never mind about that." He aimed a discreet digit at Hoof. "That's a young Toff who is acting below his station; it's all part of some childish game. But the Donkey's staying in the Royal Suite. Rumor has it he was Deity-fostered by the Big Orange One himself. I'm inclined to believe it."

By the time Hoof disembarked, the assembled oars-creatures had formed two opposing ranks with their raised oars crossed between them. A well-groomed chimpanzee waved him ashore with a sweep of her tricorn hat. "Well done," Hoof brayed. "Word of your competence shall reach the, erm, appropriate ear."

~~~

Rycliff was stretched out on the dock, keeping a slender boat from leaving. Which the boat's occupant (a shaggy baboon) was protesting vigorously. The sound of Hoof clopping onto the dock ended their dispute. The baboon turned away and glowered at the dock.

Jerome's feet entered the baboon's field of vision and their eyes flicked up, then down. "Was after tellin' this one I don' haul Donks.

Boat's too skinny-tippy." They glanced in Hoof's direction. "That one'd for sure end up in the swim. An' a gator got 'im, it's me the Law'd be worryin.'"

Jerome snorted. "When's the last time an alligator's been spotted in the delta?"

The baboon's ears disappeared between their shoulders. "Who's to say they don' come out at night?"

Booger dug out a silver coin and held it up between his thumb and forefinger. "My Master is going to Regency Island," he said. "Any delay will turn this coin to copper."

The baboon's eyes glinted greedily. "So, what're youse waitin' for?" Booger and Rycliff held the boat while Hoof stepped in and lay down. Once Hoof had settled in, Booger squeezed into the bow and Rycliff pushed them away from the dock.

~~~

"That's Regency Island?" Booger asked doubtfully as they neared an algae-covered pier. The end of the pier had sunk down and disappeared below the water.

"Yup." The baboon aimed for the sunken end of the pier.

"Wait! Where are you taking us!" cried Booger.

"Only place low 'nuff for the Donk to get out," the baboon replied. It was the most words they'd uttered since casting off. The baboon grounded the boat on the submerged portion of the pier and jammed the tip of an oar against a stone. "Youse get out 'ere!"

"What? Why?" asked Booger.

"Only place low 'nuff . . ."

Booger cut the baboon off. ". . . for the 'Donk' to get out." He scanned the waterfront; the other piers stood high above the water. "Okay, I get it."

The pier emerged from the water a few paces from where the boat was grounded. Where the water ended, a mass of algae began.

240

"What's that green stuff?" Hoof asked.

"Low tide," the baboon unhelpfully replied.

"I guess this is it, then," said Booger, tossing the promised coin to the baboon. He lowered a leg into knee-deep water. As soon as he put his weight on it, his boot went one way and his body went the other. He fell hard, drenching the baboon. The baboon bared their teeth.

"Slippy there," muttered the baboon.

"Is it?" spluttered Booger. "Is it really! Thanks for pointing that out." He got back into the boat, took off his boots, and hung them around his neck. He stepped out again, gripping the rocks with his toes. "Okay Boss," he said. "Your turn."

Hoof stood up and carefully stepped out of the boat. Snail shells crunched under his hooves as his legs slid apart. Then his hooves found gaps in the stones and he stood splay-legged but upright.

The lightened boat floated free and began to drift on the outgoing tide. "When youse wanna ride back?" called the baboon.

"Let me think," Hoof brayed. "How about never!" The baboon shrugged, then paddled away upriver.

~~~

Booger held onto Hoof's belt as they picked their way over the algae-coated rocks. By the time they stepped onto dry stone, a pack of hard-eyed dogs were on the pier, blocking their path. The leader, a torn-eared cur, curled back his lips to expose a set of blackened fangs.

"You failed to pay the mooring fee," growled the dog. "That's very disappointin' that is."

Hoof gulped. "Wh-wh-what mooring fee?" he stammered.

"The one we're gonna take out of your arrogant Equine hide." His followers obligingly guffawed at his wit.

Suddenly Hoof's fear was replaced by rage. *"EEE AW!"* he bugled as he pulled his sword from its scabbard.

241

The pack split up, preparing to encircle Hoof and Booger. A high-pitched yelp stopped them in their tracks. The dogs swung toward the top of the pier, where three large jackals stood shoulder to shoulder. They wore golden medallions that gleamed in the sunlight.

"I know you, Crosius," barked their leader. "I suggest you give some thought to what you do next."

"Meddling busybodies," growled the pack leader. "It's gettin' so a dog can't make a dishonest living no more." He slunk away, his pack trailing after him.

Hoof sheathed his sword. Under the jackals' watchful eyes, he and Booger reached the end of the pier and stepped onto the wharf.

"Hey, Donkey!" the jackal leader called. "On these docks, Equines don't get the respect you're used to. Stick to where you belong; next time, we won't be around to bail you out of trouble."

~~~

"Where are we going, Boss?" Booger asked.

Hoof shrugged. "I don't know," he admitted.

Booger laughed. "Are you kidding me? We came all this way and you don't know where you're going?"

"All I know is I have to take the satchel to a particular hatmaker, but . . ." Hoof looked at Booger and froze. "Oh no!" he brayed. "The satchel! It's sopping wet!"

"Oops!" said Booger. He slipped the satchel off his shoulder and tipped it over. A stream of greenish water poured out. He peered inside, then looked up to stare at Hoof.

"Seriously? You kept the parcel you insisted on delivering to that Chamberlain?" He took another look. "And what's with the purse?"

"Oh yeah," said Hoof. "That. I forgot all about it. But isn't there anything else?" he added anxiously .

"Just a squishy white blob." Booger reached into the satchel, then made a face. "Ew! That's pretty gross!"

"Oh Zork," Hoof moaned. "Show it to me." Booger scooped up a lump of pulp and held it out to Hoof. A bit of red wax fell to the wharf. "That was a picture," Hoof moaned. "I was supposed to show it to the hatmaker to prove who I was."

Booger squeezed the lump flat and squinted at the result. "That might be a Horse's nose," he said, pointing at a smudge.

"Yeah, that's a big help!" Hoof snapped. He looked up met the cold stare of the dog pack leader. "Let's get moving!"

~~~

They turned up the first alley that led away from the waterfront. A hundred paces later, they passed through a stone wall and smoke-blackened stone was replaced by the trim, whitewashed stables and apartments of The Capital's merchants and tradescreatures.

Booger struggled into his wet boots and they carried on up the arrow-straight street. As they got farther from the waterfront, the streets got busier and shops started to outnumber residences. At the highest point of the island was a broad, shop-lined boulevard.

Booger and Hoof joined a crowd of creatures whose progress was blocked by a steady stream of vehicles. Then a shrill whistle blew, the traffic stopped and the mob surged forward. As Booger stepped onto the boulevard, the whistle blew again and the traffic resumed its mad rush. He leaped back as an iron-wheeled truck roared by, missing him by a fingerbreadth.

"What in the name of the Goddess was that?" Booger cried. As the vehicle disappeared down the street, a dense cloud of black smoke marked its passing.

"Look! There's another one," brayed Hoof as a second vehicle roared by, pulled along by . . . nothing! "Oh my Gorme! It's on fire!"

A dry chuckle came from behind them. They turned to face a smiling chimpanzee who was waiting to cross the street.

"I'm sorry," he said. "I couldn't help but overhear." He flapped a paw at some drifting smoke. "Those are locomotors. They're the latest invention to come out of the Academy of Alchemical Research. Coal is magically transformed into energy that pulls the locomotor along. But the magic only works if the coal is set on fire."

He pointed out a slender orangutan, dressed in a yellow vest and cap, who perched on a platform in the middle of the intersection. "That's a traffic warden," he continued. "They signal when it's time to start or stop crossing the street." The orangutan raised a whistle to their lips and gave it a sharp blast. The traffic ground to a stop.

"Not yet!" gasped the chimp, grabbing Hoof's tail to stop him from stepping in front of a locomotor that roared through the intersection.

"Those things are dangerous!" Hoof brayed.

"Once they get going, they're hard to stop," said the chimp. "There's talk of giving them their own roads, away from other traffic."

The chimp hurried on his way but Hoof did not follow. "I think it's safer to stay on this side," he said. He pushed his way through the crowd that was crossing the street, then stopped to get his bearings.

"Okay," said Hoof. "We have to find a hatmaker."

"No problem," Booger replied. "I can see three of them from here."

Hoof turned in a circle. "None of their signs have Horses on them," he replied. "Keep looking."

~~~

The storefronts were separated from the busy street by an even busier boardwalk. Hoof and Booger darted through a steady stream of bald apes, chimpanzees and baboons. Often, they jumped out of the path of orangutans or gorillas who swaggered down the middle of the boardwalk. Occasionally, a jackal slunk by with their shoulder hugging the storefront walls.

The avenue dropped down a hill toward open water. The crowds had thinned to a trickle. "We're running out of street," said Booger.

"Yeah," Hoof agreed. Then he stopped dead and stared at a large white sign that hung over the boardwalk about seventy paces away. Most of the sign was taken up by a line drawing of a Horse's head. The black and white image made the Horse's colorful straw hat stand out. Tucked into the hatband was a spray of red and blue flowers.

A creature was leaving the shop. A blue purse hung from the shoulder of their red dress. The dress and a matching hat framed a shaggy bearded face; it was dominated by a vivid red and blue nose that perfectly matched the dress and purse. The creature locked the shop door and dropped the key into their purse.

Hoof broke into a trot. "Hey wait! I need to talk to you!"

The creature's eyes were black beads peering through a thicket of dark hair. They glared at the approaching Donkey. "I'm closed for lunch. Come back later." The creature turned to walk away.

"You're a mandrill monkey, aren't you?" asked Hoof.

The creature stopped. "What if I am?"

"I've been sent by the Lord Chamberlain of Waterstrider City."

The mandrill eyed Hoof suspiciously. "Lord Chamberlain? Waterstrider City? Who . . . or what . . . the Charlie D are they?"

"He's a fussy old gorilla," said Hoof, "named 'Blossom.'"

The mandrill let out a bark of laughter. "He admitted to that?"

"Yes, Sir . . . erm . . . Ma'am . . . erm . . ." Hoof shook his head. "Yes," he said. "But he prefers to be called Chamberlain."

The mandrill's eyes flicked between Hoof and Booger. "I'd better let you in." They unlocked the door and waved Hoof into the shop. Booger followed. The mandrill looked up and down the street. There were few passersby, and none showed any interest in them; they ducked into the shop and locked the door behind them.

After what seemed like a long time, Hoof broke the silence. "I'm Hoof, erm, Hearted and my thrall here is Wynaugh Tayka Chanse. We call him Booger." When this got no reaction, he babbled on. "I'm pleased to meet you, erm . . . What do we call you?"

"Do you have anything at all to identify yourselves?" said the monkey. "Something to show me, perhaps?"

"Well, I'm supposed to ask you about your fedoras—the ones made of natural straw. The Chamberlain drew a picture of what it should look like."

"Well?" said the mandrill.

"Well what?"

"Well, show me the picture," snapped the mandrill.

"That's the thing," said Booger. "It fell into the harbor and got wrecked." He reached into the valise and pulled out the soggy lump of pulp. "You can almost see what used to be a Horse's nose right here," he added, pointing at a smudge.

"It looked like your sign," said Hoof. "Only smaller, of course."

"Of course," the mandrill replied.

"Oh, wait!" Hoof exclaimed. "There is another piece of papyrus folded inside that one. Maybe it's still okay."

Looking doubtful, the mandrill took the soggy mass. They flattened it out on a felt work surface then, using the hem of their dress as a blotter, pressed out as much water as they could. They used a narrow blade to painstakingly lift away what had been an envelope flap. Two more folds were eased back to expose a barely legible note. The mandrill studied it, then straightened up. Their puzzled eyes travelled between Hoof and Booger.

"You have something else for me?" they asked.

"There's this." Booger pulled the parcel out of the valise.

The mandrill took a quick step forward. "What are you doing with that? Do you have any idea what it is?"

"Not a clue to either question," said Booger. "A big bear called Captain Waite paid me to deliver it to a pygmy hippo in Waterstrider

City. But the hippo got killed. With his dying breath, he begged us to take the parcel to the Chamberlain." He turned a puzzled eye on Hoof. "Which, until today, is what I thought happened."

"It was," Hoof agreed. "But then the Chamberlain pretty well forced me to bring it to you."

Booger handed the parcel to the mandrill. They turned it over in their paws. "Who else knows about this?"

Hoof shrugged. "As far as I know, there's just the three of us and the Chamberlain."

The mandril shook their head. "I was afraid this was lost forever. He raised his eyes to Hoof. "I can't thank you enough for bringing it to me. May I at least offer you a small token of my gratitude?"

Hoof shook his head. "No reward is needed. I was just doing what had to be done."

"Excuse me!" said Booger. "There is one thing you could do for *me*, Ma'am. Sir?"

The mandrill smiled. "Just call me The Hatter."

"Okay . . . The Hatter? Hatter? How does that work? Never mind. While we were talking, something kind of caught my eye."

When he trailed Hoof out of the shop, Booger was proudly pulling a purple fedora over what was left of his hair. Moments later, The Hatter slipped out the back door. The colorful dress and accessories were gone, replaced by a rugged camo rucksack.

~ 35 ~

Manny's eyes drifted shut and he slept a rare, blessedly dreamless sleep. When the door opened again, light flooded the room. He squinted against the glare.

"It's your lucky day!" The orangutan's eyes and teeth flashed in the light of his lantern. "The Captain decided not to eat you. But mind your tongue; she's been known to change her mind."

The orangutan stretched out a paw. After a moment's hesitation, Manny let himself be scooped up. As they crossed the deck, he saw that the sun had dipped below the horizon. *Another day lost.*

Van Wraak sat on her table, washing her face with a paw. "Ah, Matroos," she said. "Put *Señor* Sobad on the chair. Then wait outside."

She waited until the door closed before addressing Manny. "I distrust curiosity; it is an often fatal weakness I do not permit in myself or in my crew. So why do I let you interest me so?"

Many looked up and tried to hold her eyes. "It is because *mi causa es noble*. And you a *criatura* of honor."

Hissing laughter shook the cat's frame. "You may be half right," she purred, "but not more." No trace of humor remained as she continued, "You made me much inconvenience, little dog. And you promise to make much more. But you spoke the truth, so far as you knew it. So today at least, you will not die." She raised her voice. "Matroos!"

The orangutan appeared in the doorway. "Captain?"

"*Señor* Sobad is leaving us. Return his weapon when he goes."

"*Por favor no!*" Manny barked. "You must help me!"

248

The cat's eyes turned to ice. "You go too far, little dog! It is I who decides who I help. And when."

She drew a breath. When she spoke again, it was in a kinder tone. "If I choose to see you again, you will be found. Now go."

~~~

Manny trailed the orangutan to the weapons locker. The ape retrieved Manny's dagger, turned it over in his paws, admiring it. "This blade, it is bewitched, yes?"

"This I do believe, *sí.* " It was a gift from a *criatura* who is very strong in magic."

Holding the dagger by the sides of its blade, the orangutan extended it, cuff first, toward Manny. The weapon snicked into place. *"Gracias, Señor* Matroos. That is your name, is it not?"

The orangutan chuckled. "All of us are 'Matroos.' It is the word for 'sailor' in The Captain's tongue."

The boulevard terminated at a row of water taxis. "Why couldn't the baboon have brought us here?" Hoof wondered.

Booger shrugged. "Who knows? Not a paid-up member of the water taxi guild?" he guessed. "Or maybe he was in league with that pack of dogs." They hired the first taxi in line and were dropped off within sight of Wayfarers' Rest.

Pete greeted them as they left the elevator. "You stink!"

"Nice to see you too," Hoof replied.

"Pete's not wrong," rumbled Wat Ho. "You're a disgrace to the NorthReach lineage." He jabbed a finger towards the bathing room. "Get in there. Now!"

Booger snatched an apple out of a silver bowl and headed for the servants' bathing facilities. Hoof inhaled a basket of fresh green hay before plunging into the Stallion-sized gold tub that had been installed generations ago.

~~~

Pete was combing snags out of Hoof's tail when there was a sharp rap at the door. It opened a crack and the Concierge oozed through. He stalked to the middle of the room and cleared his throat.

"I have a missive for His Indomitableness Hoof Hardy Hearted, Heir Presumptive to Bellringer Hardy III of the NorthReach Hardy Herd from the . . ." he inhaled . . . "Honorable Councilor Everson Shane Glitters. Will his Indomitableness hear this message?"

"I'm right here and I'm not deaf so I don't really have much choice, do I?" Hoof replied.

Longfellow made a sour face but carried on. "His Indomitableness is cordially invited to dine at Greenstaves Manor this evening."

"Ahem!" Wat Ho cleared his throat. "We were given to believe that Councilor Glitters bears some animosity towards my Master."

"A regrettable misunderstanding!" Longfellow replied. "His Honor harbors nothing but goodwill toward the Bellringer Heir and aspires to an amicable and mutually beneficial relationship."

For his part, Hoof was looking forward to an amicable evening in the company of one Verity Glitters. "His Indomitableness accepts!"

"Very good, Your Graciousness," Longfellow replied. "A litter will collect you at the second candlemark after sunset." He bowed, clicked his heels, and slipped out through a crack in the door.

~~~

Hoof nervously stepped into his first-ever litter. The gate slammed behind his tail. Eight bearers lifted it off the ground and swept out of the Royal Suite's garden. Hoof locked his knees and gritted his teeth against a powerful wave of motion sickness.

The ride ended without incident. The litter swung open and Hoof gratefully escaped onto the Greenstaves Manor walk. The Councilor, his mate and Verity Glitters were there to greet him. Their finest jewelry was on display. Behind each of them stood an apron-garbed

Chimpanzee. One of them, an elderly male, plucked self-consciously at a decorative frill.

Mrs. Glitters touched her forehead to the ground and held it there. The Councilor merely dropped his chin to his chest. "Welcome your Graciousness!" The Councilor spoke in the cultured tone of a practiced politician. "You do our humble stable a great honor."

"Quite. Quite." Hoof replied, with what he hoped was a condescending smile. He was aware of the dashing figure he cut, with golden greaves extending from his knees to his fetlocks and baubles decorating his mane and tail. He turned his benevolent gaze on Verity Glitters. It was met with a stony glare. *Huh? I guess she has to act aloof in front of her parents.*

Oh, Zorg! The Glitters were waiting to be released from their bows. "Please," Hoof said graciously, "put yourselves at ease."

The Glitters straightened up. The dam's eyes shone with suppressed excitement while the Councilor's displayed a quickly hidden flash of irritation.

"Shall we go in?" said Mrs. Glitters. "Verity, will you please escort our honored guest?"

Two chimpanzees opened the manor's double doors. The elderly male straightened his back and, with great dignity, led the procession inside. Councilor and Mrs. Glitters walked side-by-side toward the entrance, while Verity stiffly took her position beside Hoof.

"It's great to see you!" said Hoof, bumping Verity's shoulder.

The Jennet jerked away and, in stony silence, stepped toward the manor. Hoof stared after her. After two paces she stopped with her head facing straight ahead. Hoof stepped up beside her. "What's wrong?" he whispered. "You liked me okay yesterday!"

"Yesterday," she hissed. "you pretended to be some creature else. Some creature who seemed interesting." She tossed her head at her parents as she continued, "But you're just like them, only worse."

251

Hoof shook his head in bewilderment as they stepped forward. They clopped into a sitting room which was dominated by a black Stallion who stood in front of the windows. The Horse passed an indifferent eye over Hoof and settled on their host. "Ah, Glitters," he said. "I was remarking on the quality of your cider."

The Councilor beamed. "Thank you, Lord Waterstrider. The apples come from our own orchard. It's not much, but it's been in our family for generations. We're rather proud of it."

"Really? I can't imagine why," smirked Waterstrider.

The Councilor inhaled shakily and turned toward Hoof. "So then, Bellwether . . ." he said, then paused and added, "May I call you that?"

Hoof swiveled his ears. "If you wish," he replied. "Though, to be honest, I prefer Bellringer. On account of it being my name?"

"Bellringer? Of course. And is the succession settled?"

"Well, there are no other contenders for the Bellringer title," Hoof replied. "So it's as settled as it's going to get."

Their conversation was cut short by a tall, striking Mare being led into the room. Her tail, mane and lower legs were dark, almost black. The rest of her was the color of liquid gold.

"Good," whickered Waterstrider in his odd, nasal voice. "Anastasia has finally graced us with her presence."

Mrs. Glitters cleared her throat. "Well," she said cheerily, "now that we're all here, let's move to the dining hall. Chef has outdone herself this evening."

Hoof's hopes for the evening where dashed when Mrs. Glitters deftly parked him next to the new arrival. Verity and Waterstrider were placed on the opposite side of the wide table while Councilor and Mrs. Glitters took the head and foot.

~~~

Fingered servants marched into the room to stand behind the diners. Each of them held a plate piled high with shredded carrot and apple salad. The Councilor mumbled a prayer of thanks to Gorme, after which Mrs. Glitters nudged a silver bell. The servants stepped forward, setting the salads down in front of the diners. An additional server circled the table with a jug of fermented cider.

The steady chomping of Equine jaws was interrupted only by the ringing of the bell. The salad plates were replaced by deep bowls of cold potato soup. Fresh corn was followed by oatmeal soaked in cream. Just when Hoof decided he couldn't possibly eat another bite, a sugary baked apple was set in front of him. The cider was replaced by strong, sweet ale. Hoof found room for both. His head swam from the unaccustomed alcohol and, before the bell rang for the last time, he had become decidedly unsteady on his hooves.

~~~

Mrs. Glitters stepped away from the table. "It is time for the ladies to withdraw," she announced.

The Mare whickered her disagreement. Speaking with a thick accent she said, "I thank you for the nourishment. It was mostly adequate. But I desire not female gossip. My need is to be here."

"Come, Verity," said Mrs. Glitters. Her voice was thick with disapproval as she added, "We'll leave them to it." Verity glared at Hoof before trailing her mother out of the room.

The servants set a hookah pipe in front of each diner. Waterstrider closed his lips around his mouthpiece while a servant held a flame to the herb-filled bowl. The Stallion blew out a cloud of smoke. Some of it drifted up Hoof's nose and he sneezed violently. A servant hurried to open the windows. Another lit pipes for Glitters, then Anastasia.

"The Electoral Council has ruled," said Glitters through a cloud of smoke. "The objections of honorable, right-minded Folk were ignored. That senile old Giraffe will be Installed."

Waterstrider blew another cloud of smoke at Hoof. "Changing leaders right now must concern you too, erm . . ."

"Bellringer," Glitters helpfully interjected.

"Erm, yes," said Waterstrider.

The servant lit Hoof's hookah. He drew on the mouthpiece and broke out in a fit of coughing. "Jolly good stuff," he wheezed. "but that will do, thank you." As he blinked the tears out of his eyes, he realized that Waterstrider was staring down at him. "Erm, yes?" Hoof said, dazedly echoing the Stallion's words. Between the alcohol and the smoke, his head was swimming.

"His High . . . *(Harumph!)* Glitters was cut off by Waterstrider loudly clearing his throat. "Sorry," he mumbled. "I *meant* to say His *Grace* is suggesting that you must find the timing rather inconvenient. Who knows how long a new Supreme Leader might delay your inheritance? Or the old fool may bestow it on some creature else entirely." He drew on his hookah. "New broom and all that," he continued through a cloud of smoke.

"Oh," said Hoof, resisting an urge to giggle. "No other creature will assume the Bellringer title! That's for sure!"

The others exchanged glances. "You seem very confident of that," said Glitters. "Would that have anything to do with your 'clandestine' journey to Regency Island?"

How does he know about that? Hoof pushed back at the fog swirling through his brain. "Well, Glitters," he said with an arrogance he didn't feel, "there are times when one may choose not to advertise what one is doing."

"Or who one supports," said Anastasia. "Your funeral drape is most convenient, *nichte?"*

Hoof felt a tingling in his shoulder. It spread out and, as it flowed through him, the spinning of the room slowed. "I see no trace of red or blue in here," he observed. "Your loyalties, like mine, will be shown by your actions."

"By what actions did you became the Supreme Leader's guest?" asked Glitters.

"It was nothing I did personally," Hoof improvised. "The Bellringers have supported the 'right' side for as long as . . . well, as long as the NorthReach Hardy Herd has existed."

"So you stand with those who desire the Realm's leadership to stay in the right paws?" asked Anastasia.

Paws? "I will do what's right," said Hoof.

"Hmpf," said Waterstrider. "We must be vigilant. Even my City recently suffered a 'disruption' staged by a gorilla terrorist. They went so far as to plant a forged visa in the tawdry shop of a traitor." He snorted. "The idiots in charge of my security were set to chase after a nonexistent Donkey with the ridiculous name of . . ."

"I was there!" brayed Hoof, desperately cutting off the Horse's potentially disastrous revelation. "At Waterstrider City, I mean. Maybe even when that stuff happened. Only I didn't leave my ship; some bad creatures are out to get me, so I keep a low profile."

Waterstrider twitched in irritation at the interruption. "For a creature that claims to keep a low profile, you travel with most unusual companions," he whinnied. "Especially the giant bear. I have never seen his like before."

"In my country, there are myths of giant black and white bears," Anastasia said. "From long ago. I was always thinking they were not real: stories for children, *hein?"*

"Oh, Wat Ho's real," said Hoof. "And very powerful!"

"He can be relied on?" asked Glitters.

"Totally," Hoof replied. "He'd, like, give his life for me."

A look passed between Waterstrider and Glitters. "Are you aware that a crowd will be gathering tomorrow?" asked Glitters.

"I heard that large groups of citizens are descending on the city, yes," said Hoof. "Some call them a 'troublesome rabble.' Others say they're 'well-wishers' coming to celebrate the Installation. I don't know who's right."

"Oh, they are a rabble," said Waterstrider. "But a useful one. The crowd will provide cover for our mercenaries. When the Capitol Guard is overrun, the Giraffe and his flunkies will flee like the cowards they are. Crumpt will 'reluctantly' give in to the crowd's demand that he be reinstalled as leader. Out of an unselfish desire to prevent further bloodshed, of course." The Horse whinnied with shrill mocking laughter.

"Where do I fit into all this?" asked Hoof.

"When the moment arrives, creatures of substance must stand with our Leader. It will add legitimacy to the proceedings."

"Yes, I see," said Hoof. "Well, you can count on me. Now, if you'll excuse me, I'd like to go back to the inn. I want to make sure I'm ready for the big day."

"Of course," said Glitters. "I'll call for the litter."

"Thank you but no," Hoof replied. "I'd rather walk. Truthfully, I need to clear my head. Your cider and ale were too delicious to refuse and I'm paying the price."

Hoof felt the sharp eyes of the Horses on him as he staggered out of the dining room. He bumped his shoulders into both sides of the entrance hallway before he made it to the door, almost crushing the servant who rushed to open it for him.

"Are you sure you don't want the litter?" asked Glitters, who had followed him to the door.

"No, no. I'll be fine. Jusht fine," slurred Hoof as he stepped outside. The door clicked shut behind him and he heaved a sigh of relief.

"Idiot!" hissed a voice from the bushes.

"Wh-wh-what?" stammered Hoof.

"You're such a naive fool!"

"Verity?" brayed Hoof.

"Shh!" hissed the Jennet. "They'll hear you." She stuck her face out of the bushes far enough to give Hoof a contemptuous glare. "I bet you think they're going to reinstall your precious Crumpt, don't you?"

"Aren't they?"

"Of course not! Waterstrider's out to reclaim the Equine Throne. As soon as the Giraffe is out of the way, he'll betray Crumpt and every creature foolish enough to stand with him. Waterstrider's mercenaries will be all over the city, waiting to take over the Capital."

"Verity!"

Neither Hoof nor the Jennet had seen Glitters skulk around the side of the manor and come up behind them. "Run!" Verity screamed.

Hoof turned just in time to have a noose drop over his head. The rope was pulled tight by one of the bearers who had carried Hoof from the Inn. The remaining bearers moved to surround him.

"One of you take the young . . . *traitor* . . . to her stall," Glitters snarled. "I'll deal with her later. The rest of you, follow me."

Hoof was dragged behind the Manor and shoved into a windowless stone outbuilding. Hobbles were placed on his legs and pulled tight. He fell heavily to the stone floor. A filthy rag was stuffed into his mouth. The golden greaves were torn from his legs. "You won't be needing these anymore," a voice rasped in his ear.

The door was pulled shut and a heavy bolt shot into place. Hoof lay in utter darkness, struggling to breath.

~ *36* ~

The tide had pulled the gangplank to a near-vertical drop. *"Que la Diosa me preserve!"* Manny whispered as he tumbled down the ramp. He rolled to his feet and raised his dagger in salute to Matroos. The amiable orangutan waved back.

He had no idea where he was. The air smelled of salt and fish. *El océano,* he decided. He located the moon and hobbled toward it.

After skirting a row of ramshackle buildings, he squeezed under a fence to a long stone wharf that ran west to east. The black stone ate up the moonlight, becoming one long shadow. Crumbling piers stretched into the channel like the teeth of a broken comb. Many of them were lined with vessels.

The stench of rotting vegetation made Manny sneeze. He hurried past its source: a pier that was sinking into the channel. *If I am in the 'One Great Realm,' this must be its smelly backside!* At the sunken pier he caught a familiar scent. *¡El Burro!* The trail was old and led inland. Manny kept going east.

~~~

The wharf ended at a solid wooden fence. The moon was high over his shoulders, casting his shadow on the whitewashed boards. A broken board let him squeeze through to a large, fenced marina. It faced a bay which was closed off from the channel by a stone breakwater. A single entrance allowed boats in or out.

A half-dozen barges were tied up out of sight of any vessels passing in the channel. None had any identifying markings. As Manny approached, the sheath of his dagger retracted. He stared at the naked blade. *¿Qué es esto?*

Muted voices drifted from the barges. A laugh was cut short by a muffled curse. Then there was only the soft creak of many shifting bodies. Manny hunkered down to listen and watch.

The silence was shattered by the crash of marching boots. Manny relived his worst nightmare as grizzled mercenaries poured off the barges and out through the marina gate. Two apes remained. They locked the gate and began to patrol the inside of the fence. Manny ran for the far side of the marina, hoping to reach it without being seen.

The guards reached the corner and turned. One of them saw a glint of light off of Manny's weapon. "Hey! What's that?"

Their companion kept going. "What's what?"

"Straight ahead. There's something . . ." The guard drew their weapon. "You there! Identify yourself!"

The second guard snorted. "You got spooked by a big old rat!"

"That's no rat! They've got a knife!"

Manny kept going, hoping he had enough of a head start to make it to the fence and would find a way through when he got there. The guards quickly closed the gap. A sword crashed onto the stone wharf, showering Manny with sparks. *¡Ay caramba! That was too close!* He put on an extra burst of speed and dove for a hole at the bottom of fence. Halfway through, he stuck fast.

"Aha! I've got you, you little . . ." A paw wrapped itself around Manny and jerked him out of the fence—to the other side!

The chill of the stone floor seeped into Hoof's bones. At the slightest movement, the hobbles bit painfully into his legs. *This is where I'm going to die,* he thought.

He closed his eyes and focused on breathing through the gag. Until a voice whispered, "Idiot! Do something: Call on my gift!" Hoof's eyes flew open. The star on his shoulder glowed with a clear blue light. "Hurry!" urged the voice.

Starr? Hoof shook his head, banging his cheek against the stone floor. *If I do that, what will be lost? You, maybe? I can't risk it!*

"If you do nothing, there will be war. Innocents will die! The Realm will suffer under another despot king!"

A rueful laugh was stifled by Hoof's gag. *Yeah, sure: Like I'd make a difference!*

"You have to try!" Starr's voice insisted.

Who knew you were such a nag! Hoof shot back. *Ouch! How did you do that?*

"Listen to me or I'll do it again!"

Okay already! What do I do?

"It's done," Starr replied as a thunderclap rattled the door. "Goodbye, Hoof!" The blue light died away.

The door flew open, digging into Hoof's back. A creature stood in the opening, their tall, gangly body outlined by the stars. The creature wobbled, then fell through the door, landing across Hoof's shoulders and neck. Grunting with the effort, they righted themself, dragged a heavy object inside, then pushed the door closed.

The terrified Donkey listened to several rasping breaths before a familiar voice rumbled, "Okay, then. How about some light."

A glowlamp sprang to life. Hoof blinked at the brightness. *"Unh! Unh! Unh!"* he wheezed, his white-rimmed eyes fixed on Wat Ho.

The Guardian dropped to his knees and pulled the gag out of Hoof's mouth. Now that Hoof was able to speak, he was speechless. Wat Ho's fur was a dull patchy grey and his skin hung in loose folds from his frame.

"By the love of the Goddess!" said Hoof at last. "If you hadn't spoken, I wouldn't have recognized you! How is this possible?"

Wat Ho squeezed his trembling paws together. "I got dragged hard through the ether. It was more than this old body could handle."

"Untie me," said Hoof. "I'll go get help!"

Wat Ho fumbled with Hoof's hobbles. As soon as the Donkey was freed, he leaped to his hooves. And fell down. C-c-cold," he stammered. "And dizzy."

The Guardian held out a glass vial. It rattled against Hoof's teeth, but he managed to swallow most of its contents. Warmth coursed through his body. "Okay, I'm going for help."

"No!" Wat Ho's voice was firmer, sounding more like his old self. "There's no time for that. We've got to get you ready." He began pulling things out of Sack O'Stuff.

"What's all this?" Hoof asked, gaping at the shiny objects piling up at his hooves.

"Well, let's see," Wat Ho replied. "Chanfron, criniere, peytral, flanchard, croupiere. Just the basics, really."

"You're not helping!" said Hoof.

"It's armor. Good enough, hopefully, to keep you alive."

"Keep me . . . say what! Why do I need to be kept alive?"

"Well, you can't save The Realm if you're dead!" Wat Ho selected a set of metal rings that nested one inside the other. "We'll start with the criniere." He slipped it over the speechless Donkey's head.

"Now the chanfron." A mask covered Hoof's face from the end of his nose to the tips of his ears. His terrified eyes peered from under two ridges that would protect them from anything but a direct thrust.

Wat Ho slipped a finger under the innermost ring of the criniere, pulled it up Hoof's neck and attached it to the chanfron. The rings slid apart, covering Hoof's neck. "As I said," Wat Ho wheezed, "this is the best there is: light weight, flexible and strong. You'll be able move around like it wasn't there."

Hoof swung his head back and forth. The criniere's rings slid smoothly over each other.

~~~

Taking frequent stops to rest, Wat Ho armored Hoof's chest, back, flanks, legs and hind quarters. Finally, he affixed a sharp blade to the side of the mask. It pivoted into striking position when Hoof lowered his head and out of the way when his head was raised.

"Doesn't have the personality of Donkie Otie's sword, but it's a bit more practical, I think," said Wat Ho "And we're . . . done." He slumped against the wall. His breath came in ragged gasps.

"I feel like . . ." Hoof shook his head. "My voice sounds funny," he said. "All echoey or something." Wat Ho was silent.

"Wat Ho?" Hoof brayed. He lowered his head toward The Guardian, who feebly batted it aside.

"Don't do that! You'll stab some creature to death if you're not careful!" Wat Ho's head fell forward and he slid down the wall.

"That's it!" brayed Hoof. "I'm going to get help."

"No!" Wat Ho managed a hoarse whisper. "No. This body is dying. Of old age!" He opened his eyes. "I am first of our kind to experience it: a fascinating phenomenon that's best when avoided."

"You can't die!" Hoof brayed. "For starters, I have no idea what in Gorme's Most Secret Name I'm supposed to do!"

"Find The Hatter," Wat Ho whispered. He waved a paw in a feeble salute. "Goodbye, Hoof. It's been . . . interesting." A beat later his eyes flew open. "Oh my love!" he cried. "I'm so, so sorry!"

Hoof stared helplessly as his friend's eyes drifted shut.

Manny was staring up the nose of a drunken baboon. The baboon's head flopped around as they tried to focus their bloodshot eyes. "What are you, then?" they muttered. "Are you good to eat?"

Manny slashed out with his dagger. The baboon shrieked and Manny was falling. He hit the ground hard and rolled. "I am not getting eaten," he wheezed as he wobbled into a three-legged run.

The enraged baboon roared after him. Manny darted between two buildings and turned onto a cobbled street. He looked back over his shoulder—and felt the street give way beneath his paws.

He splashed down in an underground stream, hit the bottom and kicked for the surface. The first thing he saw was the baboon swaying above a sewer access hole. The second was an armed gorilla holding up a lamp to see what had caused the splash. He sucked in a breath and ducked underwater, letting the stream carry him away.

When he resurfaced, gasping for air, it was to utter darkness. A few kicks of his back legs carried him to a walkway that ran along the edge of the stream. When he scrabbled onto it, his dagger started to glow, providing just enough light to show where he was going. Hoping to avoid any more armed apes, he headed downstream.

~~~

Regency Island was honeycombed with tunnels that merged and crossed at all angles. Every hundred paces or so, a ladder led to a covered hole that accessed the street above. These did Manny no good. He hurried on, determined to find a way out.

The light in his blade winked out. Moments later, he heard voices and a small band of mercenaries came out of a side tunnel. The light of their lantern showed mismatched armor that bore no symbols of allegiance. One of them wore a painted-on sergeant's chevron.

The group stopped while the sergeant consulted a map. "If I never see that creepy old monster again, it will be too soon!" a mercenary muttered. "He scares the hair off my knuckles."

"There be stories that say that wretch is old as time itself!" said another. "He looks decrepit enough for it be true. Smells like it too!"

263

"Silence!" hissed the sergeant. "No creature can know we're here." He snorted. "Until tomorrow. Then they'll know right enough!" His chuckle made Manny's hair stand on end. "Tomorrow," gloated the sergeant, "we'll all go to sleep rich. Right lads?"

"Right!" the platoon echoed in a ragged chorus.

"For the love of Warre, will you lot be quiet!" growled the sergeant. "Here, hold this," he snapped as he thrust the lantern at a skinny young gorilla. He held the map up to his eyes and traced a route on it with a dirty finger. "Okay. We go that way."

He took back the lantern and they all strode down the tunnel, away from Manny. They seemed anxious to put distance between themselves and wherever they had just been. When the sound of the apes' footsteps had faded away, the glow returned to Manny's blade.

When he passed the tunnel from which the gorillas had emerged, he resisted an urge to turn into it. *That way stinks of evil!* But as he moved on his stump prickled, then got hot. The burning sensation got worse with each step. He turned around. The burning stopped. *La Diosa commands!* thought Manny as he retraced his steps. He stared into the tunnel vacated by the mercenaries. A light shone in the distance and he headed toward it.

As he neared the tunnel's end he crept forward on his stomach; froze; then desperately backed away. He panted in the darkness as he struggled to get his mind around what he had just seen: The tunnel had ended at what looked like a throne room—in which the throne was made of the bleached bones of sentient creatures!

The throne was occupied by a creature so bent and shriveled Manny couldn't even identify its species. Both the throne and the creature radiated evil. Manny felt compelled to creep forward for another look. The walls of the cavern were covered with scenes of hooved creatures being torn apart by pad paws. An alter stood against one wall. Black stains ran down the alter; they looked like dried blood.

Manny shifted his eyes to the malignant stick-figure that drooped across the throne. Its torso was partly enclosed in armor of an ancient style. Bony arms emerged from the armor to dangle at its sides. Its head wobbled jerkily on the end of a wrinkled, scrawny neck.

A chant began, so loud and deep that Manny felt the vibrations in his bones. A giant emerged from behind the alter, covered from head to toe in a cowled black robe. The priest, if that's what it was, carried a glass container to which a flexible tube was attached. The tube ended with a hollow needle.

The black-robed creature crossed the throne room, followed by two more giants, one robed in red and the other in white. Their voices joined in a guttural chant that made Manny's skin crawl. The black-robed creature reached the throne and the chanting stopped.

"You're taking too long," wheezed the stick-figure.

The black-robed creature dropped to its knees. "This spirit is strong, Excellency. It resisted being made ready for you."

"Oh, just get on with it!"

The priest's forehead touched the floor. "As My Lord wills!"

"Hurry, you fool! Time is something I don't have!"

The priest put the glass container on a stand, then fumbled with thick, clumsy fingers to get a grip on the needle. He succeeded at last and jabbed the needle into the old creature's arm. The creature writhed and shrieked in pain.

"Sorry, My Lord." The second attempt was better. The priest opened a nozzle and something began to flow into the thin, shriveled arm. The stick-figure drew an ecstatic breath and its skin began to lose its sickly grey pallor.

Manny felt a sense of Wat Ho's presence. *"¡Por la gracia de la Diosa! That is what was stolen by the ice creature!"* He charged forward, leaped onto the throne and sprang at the glass container. His blade blazed a fiery red as he slashed out with all his strength. The bottom of the container fell away and its contents flowed out. Before they hit the floor they shape-shifted into an owl. The bird's back and wings where black, its breast snow-white. It circled the throne room, then flew down the tunnel.

The creature on the throne let out an enraged shriek that faded to a bubbling hiss. Its body blistered and puckered then, with a sound not unlike a sigh, disappeared. All that remained inside the armor was a small pile of ashes. The ashes stirred and a tiny white bird emerged. Twittering urgently, it fluttered off in pursuit of the owl.

Manny stared wonderingly at the scene until it disappeared behind an agonizing blaze of light. Then he saw and heard nothing.

Hoof stood over Wat Ho's body. Tears fell on the unconscious Guardian. "You can't be dead!" he brayed. "You just can't!"

A fierce shriek was heard from outside, followed by the thump of something hitting the building. Hoof's head swung around in time to see a black and white owl force its way through a gap that had appeared at the edge of the door. A wingtip brushed Hoof's ear and, for a moment, his mind was touched by a profound, ancient wisdom.

Wat Ho drew a rattling breath. The owl stretched, narrowed, and flowed into his open mouth. Wat Ho took another breath. Then another. "Oh my beloved," he rumbled, "It is you who found me!"

"Of course I did," spoke a gentle, alto voice, "and not a moment too soon: What a mess you've made of us!"

Wat Ho choked out a laugh. "I don't do well on my own."

"Like every male of every species," taunted the new voice. "Let's see if we can clean ourselves up a bit."

Hoof stared in amazement while the Guardian's hair was restored to its original midnight black and crisp white. Their body filled out, although not to its original imposing size. The scar on their cheek faded and disappeared. A breath later, a small white bird fluttered in and landed on their shoulder.

"Oh darling, look!" exclaimed the new voice.

"Hello, my precious little one!" Wat Ho rumbled. The little bird snuggled up to the Guardian's neck and cheeped contentedly.

"What just happened here?" asked Hoof.

"We have been made whole," rumbled Wat Ho.

"So you're not dying, then?"

"Not at the moment, no."

Hoof heaved a sigh of relief. "Thank the Goddess! Now you can come with me." When the Guardian did not respond, Hoof fixed them with a steely-eyed stare. "You are coming with me, right?"

"No." The reply was not in Wat Ho's deep bass voice.

"Excuse me!" Hoof brayed. "Who are you anyway?"

The Guardian gently stroked the bird with one finger. "There's no time to explain," said the new voice. "We must get this little one home. And we have done all that we can do here. It's up to you now."

"Go find The Hatter," rumbled Wat Ho.

"I can't do this on my own!" Hoof wailed.

"You'll never be on your own," said the Guardian. Then there was a thunderclap, and they were gone.

~ 37 ~

Hoof crept through the shadows beside the Glitter's manor and peered around the corner. The street was empty. *Time to go!* He picked up his hooves and ran into an even darker shadow that floundered out of the bushes.

"Oof!"

"What the . . ."

"Boss?"

"Booger?"

They untangled themselves and stood up. Booger's dark cloak and soot-blackened face made him look like a cut-out silhouette. The effect was spoiled by the white circles of his staring eyes. "Wow! That's some getup!" he exclaimed. He shook his head. "But where've you been, Boss? I looked everywhere for you."

"Never mind where I was," said Hoof. "What matters is that I have to get back to Regency Island. Right now!"

~~~

"Glitters is a traitor," Hoof panted. "He's in league with Waterstrider and they're gonna start a war. We have to warn The Hatter." He took a breath before adding, "Oh, and Wat Ho's gone."

Booger stopped running. "What do you mean Wat Ho's gone?"

Hoof pulled up. "He went back to where he came from, I think. He was dying. Until an owl flew into his mouth and somehow fixed him. Then he started talking in two different voices. Until a baby bird showed up and they had to take it home. It was strange."

"You think?" Booger shook his head. "And you look like the Avenging Donkey of the Overlord because?"

"Wat Ho put all this on me. It's supposed to keep me alive."

"Keep you alive? Why? Sorry, wrong question. From what?"

"From whatever's trying to destroy the realm, I guess."

"You're going to save the Realm!" Booger exclaimed.

"Seriously? I don't even know how I'll get to Regency Island, never mind save it!" Hoof's breath came in panicked gasps.

"Boss!" Booger gave Hoof's chanfron a slap. "Boss! Deep breaths, okay. Take slow deep breaths. We'll think of something."

The eyes staring out from the chanfron were still ringed with white, but Hoof's breathing slowed. "You're doing great, Boss," said Booger encouragingly. "Now let's see. . ." He scratched his head. "Hey! How about the Royal Launch? The old chimp said you could use it any time. And this is as good a time as any, right?"

Hoof was already galloping down the street. "Right!"

~~~

"Ready?" Booger asked.

Hoof drew himself up straight. "Okay. Let's do this!" he brayed.

Booger tugged on a rope dangling beside the barracks door and a bell jangled inside. He alternated between ringing the bell and pounding on the door until it flew open.

"What in the name of . . ." The bald ape's mouth fell open.

"I am here on behalf of The Supreme Leader!" Hoof's voice echoed from inside his chanfron. "The Realm is in great danger! Take us to Regency Island at once!"

The bald ape didn't move. He didn't even blink. Booger prodded him in the chest. "That's where you come in."

"Sir! Yes Sir!" barked the bald ape. Then he blinked. "What?"

"You. Take us. Rowing." Booger spoke slowly and clearly, miming the actions as he went. "On the Launch. Go rouse the crew."

The oars-creature's eyes flicked from Booger's commando gear to Hoof's gleaming armor. His jaw set and he ran into the barracks. "Outa the sack, you lot!" he bellowed. "We got us an emergency."

Manny painfully opened one eye. It faced a horrific image of pad paws tearing apart a helpless bovine. He opened the other eye and saw the three priests standing in a huddle. Their cowls were thrown back, exposing crudely hewn faces that looked like their creator hadn't bothered to finish them. He closed his eyes.

The shuffle of sandaled feet drew near, then stopped. Manny's eye opened on the hem of a dirty red robe. Red-robe stared down at Manny's dagger, then bent to grab the blade. The throne room filled with the stench of burning flesh. The giant fled screaming to the back of the cavern. A few ashes drifted to the floor. Manny shut his eyes on the pain that sliced through his skull.

More shuffling was followed by the rustle of fabric. Then silence. *What now?* Manny opened his eyes. The priests knelt in front of him. A thick purple tongue slid over Black-robe's lips. Seeing Manny's eyes on him, he pressed his forehead to the floor.

"Who are you, Lord?" whispered Black-robe. "What are you?"

Manny resisted the blackness that threatened to engulf him and spoke as firmly as he could. "Enough! Sit up and look upon me!"

Black-robe reluctantly rose to his knees. His eyes skittered around; settled on Manny; flitted away without meeting his eyes.

"Who dared attack my, erm, sacred body?" Manny demanded.

Red-robe's whimpering went up an octave as White-robe pointed a clawed finger and said, "It was that one, Lord." Sounding almost hopeful, he added, "Shall that one's life be forfeit?"

"*That one* has been punished for violating my sacred weapon," Manny replied. "It is enough. For now." He eyed each of the priests in turn. "What do you want from me?"

They exchanged looks. "You destroyed Our-Lord-Who-Created-Us," Black-robe replied. "We have known no other Master."

"Now you are free," said Manny.

"We don't know how to be free!" wailed White-robe

"We don't even know what it means," Red-robe added.

"It means you can do what you want," Manny sighed.

The priests put their heads together, then turned and pressed their foreheads to the floor. "What we want is to serve you, Great Lord!"

The chimpanzee barked out a rapid cadence. Hoof and Booger marveled at the speed with which the islands slipped by. Booger's eyes settled on a muscular back that glistened in the torchlight. The sight was vaguely unsettling.

Regency Island drew closer at an alarming rate, and Hoof braced for a collision. "Back oars!" shrieked the chimpanzee. The oars-creatures dug their blades into the water and the launch almost came to a stop. A flurry of commands followed and the vessel was tied up and the gangway was in place.

The chimpanzee stood before them with her tricorn tucked under her arm. "Does His Excellency require an escort?" she asked.

"Erm. No." Hoof replied. "You may go back to your barracks."

The chimpanzee bowed. "Very good, Your Lordliness."

The Hatter's shop was locked and dark. Booger pounded on the door to no avail. He looked up at the second floor. His eyes tracked a ledge that ran below the darkened windows. "Aha! That's what I need!" He tore off his boots, then scaled a downspout.

A few beats later he was on his toes, working his way along the narrow ledge. His calves were burning by the time he lowered his heels onto a windowsill. The window flew open and a blade was pressed against his stomach.

"Tell me why I shouldn't gut you here and now!"

"Please don't!" Booger resisted what would have been a fatal urge to pull away from the blade. "My Master needs to see you right away. He says there's going to be a war!"

Booger was yanked through the window. He crashed to the floor. When he got to his feet, the blade was at his throat.

"Turn around and, very slowly, start walking."

Booger slid his feet along the floor, feeling for obstacles. He stopped when his fingers encountered a wooden surface.

"Open the door." Booger pulled the door open.

"The stairs are on the left."

Booger felt his way down to the shop. Light bleeding through the windows lessened the darkness.

"When I open the door," growled The Hatter, "take the Donkey straight through to the back room. Don't try anything foolish."

The Hatter opened the door and Hoof clopped in. His armor seemed to glow in the near-darkness. Booger rested a hand on the cool metal covering his back. "Keep going straight," he murmured as he guided Hoof through a blacker rectangle in the back wall.

The shop door was closed and bolted. Then the door to the back room closed, plunging them into utter darkness. A firestick scraped; the mandrill held it up and stared at Hoof. "That's quite the outfit!"

"I could say the same," Hoof replied.

"This old thing? I've had it forever! Ouch!" The smell of burning hair filled the storeroom.

A lantern was lit. The Mandrill sucked on a finger as they eyed their visitors. "So. What's this about a war?" Their eyes passed between Hoof and Booger. "Or are we just playing 'dress up?'"

The Hatter listened intently to everything Hoof had to say. They interrupted from time to time to ask pertinent questions. By the time Hoof finished, dawn was breaking.

272

The priests moved in a slow procession, walking beside the underground stream. Black-robe lit the way. Red-robe and White-robe followed, supporting a small, makeshift litter. On the litter sat Manny, trying to look god-like while ducking overhead obstacles. The tunnel curved, revealing a light in the distance.

Manny's heart beat faster. "What is that light?" he asked. "Is it another room? Maybe it is *los gorilas!*"

"It is the door, Master," replied Black-robe.

"The door? The door to where?"

"To the World, Master" replied Black-robe.

"*¡Oh, gracias a la Diosa!*" Manny breathed.

The stream flowed out through a heavy grate. Manny's heart sank. "No!" he barked. "Even I cannot fit through that!"

Their rough-hewn faces took on a look of confusion. "Does Our Lord desire the door to be opened?"

"You can do that? *¡Sí! ¡Buena gracia, Sí!*"

The priests set Manny on the tunnel floor. Keeping well back from the opening, Red-robe and White-robe lifted the grate free and set it aside. Then they stepped away, staring at Manny.

"What are you waiting for?" Manny barked. "Let's go."

Black-robe turned to Manny and bowed. "Surely Our Lord sees that the great fireball is in the sky."

"What? Oh, you mean the sun. And so?"

"We go out only at dark, Great Lord. The fireball will burn us."

Manny curled his lip. "We go now. You will not burn."

Black-robe's eyes lifted hopefully, "Our Lord will protect us?"

"*Eh . . . si.* I will protect you. Yes."

The three priests bowed, then Red-robe and White-robe picked up the litter. Black-robe waved them on. Shooting the black-robed priest a dirty look, the litter-bearers stepped into the fresh air. They cringed at the first rays of sunlight but, thankfully, did not go up in flames. Manny exhaled. A few beats later, Black-robe followed.

"Wait," Manny said. "We need to close the grate. Can you make it so *los gorilas* can't get out?"

"Yes, Master!" the priests chanted.

Manny watched White-robe slot the grate in place, then grip the sides of the metal rim surrounding it. The muscles in his arms and back bulged as the rim slowly, grudgingly, began to bend.

"Enough!" said Black-robe. White-robe leaned against the grate, panting. A tug on the grate confirmed that it wouldn't budge.

If one such as that struck me, how am I even alive? The priests gathered around Manny, waiting for instructions. "What are your names?" he asked.

The trio looked at each other blankly. "Names, My Lord?" said Black-robe. "Never have we had names. We are insignificant tools, to be used and discarded as our master wills."

"You are *criaturas,* not objects!" Manny exclaimed. "And you will have names." After a few moments' thought, he said "You are Hablador, Quemado and Musculoso," as he pointed to Black, Red and White robes in order.

They dropped down and planted their foreheads on the ground. "Oh Great Lord!" they blubbered. "You do us a great honor!"

"I am no 'lord,'" Manny barked. "I am Manuel Isareali Sobad." Three blank faces lifted up. He sighed. "Or you can call me Manny."

Down went their heads. "Lord Manny!" they cried. "You honor us by sharing your wondrous name."

"Enough! We must go warn others of the *gorila* soldiers." He looked up at their crudely chiseled faces. "Keep your cowls up. Your skin has not before been exposed to the sun."

"Lord Manny honors us with his concern," they chanted as they pulled their cowls over their heads.

"Wait here!" The Hatter picked up the parcel and hurried out of the room. They returned wearing a flowing red dress. A black, broadbrimmed hat was paired with a sleek shoulder bag. Booger was caught in a double take. "What?" said The Hatter. "You disapprove?"

"N-no!" Booger stammered. "Creatures should feel free to wear whatever they like."

"This outfit comforts me," said The Hatter. They raised a paw to their hat and pulled out a stiletto that served as a hatpin. "I like having places to hide weapons," they added as they lifted the hem of the dress to reveal a slender blade. "And when I dress like this, other creatures may not take me seriously. Depending on what I am up to, that can be a very good thing—for me. Not so much for them." They stepped up to a mirror and adjusted the hat. "Plus I look amazing!"

They clapped their paws together and briskly strode toward the door. "Let's go, gentle creatures! We've got a city to save!"

The sun cleared the horizon as Hoof, Booger and The Hatter crested Regency Island and skirted a desolate, barren hill. Hoof found his eyes reluctantly drawn to the brooding mound.

"That's Big Axe Hill," said The Hatter. "In days of yore, creatures who the Equine Kings deemed to be troublesome were brought up there to be executed. Let me show you something," they added as they scampered up the hill.

Hoof and Booger exchanged puzzled looks, then followed. When they joined him at the peak, The Hatter pointed towards a grassy area that was visible between two high granite walls. "See that green down there? That's ViceRegal Square. During the Equine Monarchy, it was called Coronation Square. The King and his Court would watch executions from the comfort of the Royal Galleries.

"Now the Square is used to Install the Supreme Leader," said The Hatter as they dashed down the hill. Hoof and Booger ran to catch up.

~~~

They passed through a stone wall and the atmosphere changed. The Palaces of Government were widely spaced on a gentle slope that looked over the Bay. In the heat of summer, they enjoyed a cooling sea breeze. In winter, the temperature was moderated by the ocean.

"Is that where we're going," Hoof excitedly asked.

"Not exactly," chuckled The Hatter. They bypassed the ornate palaces and plunged into a warren of narrow winding streets. In spite of the early hour, they were clogged with low-level bureaucrats. "This is where the real work gets done," said The Hatter.

They rapped on Hoof's shoulder to get his attention, then ducked into an alley. Hoof and Booger followed them into an even narrower walkway bounded by brick walls. It ended at a tiny courtyard from which the only other exit was a wooden door.

The Hatter used the hilt of a dagger to tap out a coded message on the door. A small panel opened and a pair of deep-set eyes squinted out. They examined The Hatter at length, then swiveled left to glance at Booger. Finally, they focused on Hoof. And froze there.

"We're here to see W," The Hatter announced.

"There's no W here," said a voice from behind the door.

"Whichever way we went, wicked whirling west winds would wantonly whip weary, wretched, woeful widows who whimpered, wept, wailed wildly—*whatever*—while wayward waves washed wholly wasted withers."

"That's a lot of Ws," admitted the doorkeeper. "Doesn't make much sense though."

"Neither does what we've got to tell him. But he needs to hear it."

The door opened and The Hatter raced into an empty corridor. By the time Hoof and Booger caught up, they had reached another door. The Hatter raised the dagger and resumed their tapping.

The Hatter, Hoof and Booger were shown into a drab room. The door was closed and barred behind them. "What's going on?" Hoof brayed. "Are we prisoners?"

"Relax," The Hatter replied. "Almost every creature brought into this place leaves under their own power . . . eventually."

~~~

The door opened and a wizened Billy Goat trotted in. A straw fedora sat on his head. Its brim had unraveled and hung down beside his face. He waggled his head, caught the dangling straw between his teeth and chewed. His wise old eyes benignly surveyed the room.

"Hey, I know you!" Hoof exclaimed.

"Hey, that's one of my hats!" said The Hatter. Then they registered Hoof's words and aimed a suspicious eye at him. "You know W?"

"No. Or at least that wasn't the name."

"Sol Goode," Booger said. "The name was Sol Goode."

The Goat squinted at Booger. "Ah!" he said, "A MORON rally in the hinterlands, I believe. Observer, not participant." His eyes rolled to Hoof. "As to the knight in shining armor, I'm at a loss."

Hoof's attempt to puff out his chest was defeated by his armor. "My name is Hoof," he huffed. "Hoof Hearted."

Sol threw back his head and laughed, making his hat fall off. The Hatter picked it up, repaired the brim and stuffed it back on the Goat's head. The Goat blinked tears of laughter out of his eyes. "Hoof Hearted," he chuckled. "Not Hoof Hardy Hearted? Or should I say The Fourth (it is the fourth, isn't it?) Indomitable Bellringer Hardy of the NorthReach Hardy Herd?"

"No! Yes. No!" gasped Hoof . "How do you know about that?"

277

The Goat stretched his tongue sideways, feeling for his hat brim. *"Hmpf!"* he snorted, shooting a disapproving look at The Hatter. His good humor returned as he continued, "One function of my humble little organization is to keep tabs on dignitaries—real or imagined—who grace our fair city with their presence."

The Hatter watched Hoof through narrowed eyes. "I knew you were a bearer of tales," they said, "but had no idea how, erm, 'far-fetched' some of them were."

"Hold on," Hoof protested. "The 'Bellringer' thing is all Wat Ho's fault. They made that up."

"Ah, of course: the Guardian!" the Goat exclaimed. "I am disappointed that they did not accompany you."

"They're gone," said Hoof.

"Gone? Gone where?"

"Back wherever they came from, I guess."

"Really? That is surprising news. And distressing. If you would be so kind as to share the whole story, I would be most grateful."

~ 38 ~

Every creature Manny approached took one look at his giant companions and fled. Finally, a blind beggar pointed towards ViceRegal Square where, he said, the Supreme Leader's Installation would be held.

They reached the square, only to find the way in blocked by a massive iron gate. It featured the old Royal Crest and looked almost as solid as the granite walls on each side of it.

"But we need to go that way," Manny barked in frustration.

"As you wish, Master!" Musculoso stepped forward and tore the gate from its hinges.

"Not as I expected," said Manny, "but okay." He rode through the opening on Hablador's shoulder. "Can you put it back?"

Musculoso drove the gate into a crack between the paving stones. It promptly crashed to the ground. "Sorry Master," he mumbled shamefacedly.

They entered a grassy square that was surrounded on three sides by towering granite buildings. Crushed stone walkways radiated out from a central obelisk and sunclock. The perimeter of the Square was lined with benches designed for the discomfort of all species.

A large troop of gorillas had spread out over the grassy expanse. Many of them were building a wall out of sandbags. Others were engaged in weapons practice.

"*¡Hola!*" shouted Manny. "I must speak to *la criatura* in charge!" His thin voice carried to the nearest gorillas, one of whom looked up,

279

saw Manny's giant companions, and froze. His sparring partner gleefully delivered a two-handed whack with the flat of his blade before realizing there was an issue. Weapons practice staggered to a stop. Then, with a roar, the gorillas raised their weapons and charged.

~~~

Jawana was trying to meet an impossible deadline when she heard a commotion break out behind her. She swung around, then froze in shock. *Trolls in ViceRegal Square! In broad daylight*!

She was filled with both pride and dread at seeing several Guards rush forward to surround the vile creatures: pride at their courage; dread at how badly they were overmatched. They had charged into the fray armed with practice swords! She ran forward and elbowed her way to the inside of the circle.

"*¡Hola, Señorita Jawana!*"

"Sobad?" Jawana recoiled in shock. "How did you manage to get captured by a pack of stinking trolls?"

"*¿Qué?*" Manny's eyes widened. "Trolls? I knew not!" He looked at the ring of weapons that pointed at his nervous acolytes. "Wait! Since I have been with them, these creatures have harmed nothing. They obey me as if I were a God!"

Jawana's snorted, "Yeah, right. Did your delusion of divinity start when one of those monsters dropped you on your head?"

Hablador raised a fist that resembled a block of wood. "You dare to mock Lord Manny of the Flaming Sword?"

Jawana raised a placating paw. "I meant no offence. If 'Lord Manny' vouches for your good behavior you may leave this city in peace. As long as you leave. As in now."

"We do as Lord Manny commands," Hablador impassively replied, "and no creature else."

"I don't have time for this," Jawana groaned. "Fine! But Sobad, if you don't keep these monsters under control, blood will be shed."

"One of my *compañeros* is hurt very badly. All we ask is for Wat Ho to repair him. Have you seen our friends?"

"I haven't seen any of them since . . . Gorme, was that two days ago? But we have a medic in that tent over there," she said, pointing. "She's no Wat Ho, thank the stars! But if she's willing to treat that . . . whatever you're calling the troll . . . she has the skill to do it. Now I have work to do." She raised her voice. "Alright, troops! The party's over. Back to work."

But *"Señorita* Jawana," Manny called. "I have things to tell . . ." But Jawana had already hurried away.

~~~

Quemado lay flat on the turf while a soft-eyed gibbon examined his badly burned hand. "I've never seen a burn like this before," she said. "What happened?"

"I was justly punished for trying to steal Lord Manny's weapon. Chop off the offending hand; I do not deserve to be repaired."

The Gibbon's eyes went to Manny. "And is that the sort of thing 'Lord Manny' approves of?" she asked through gritted teeth.

"No! Lord Manny is good and kind!" Quemado protested. " Our old master, the Lord-Who-Created-Us was not." The giant's blocky teeth were exposed in a rueful smile. "The last of us to get hurt was fed to the werecats."

"Werecats?" Manny exclaimed. "Only now do you speak of werecats? Are they also in the tunnels?"

"No Master! The werecats were sent to Coshon Aerie. They were part of the trade made for the immortal soul of the Guardian."

The medic stared at Quemado. "Werecats? Immortal souls? What manner of creature was your old master, anyway?"

Quemado gulped. "Our old master was the God-Demon you call Warre," he replied.

"Warre? As in . . ." the gibbon's eyes flicked to Manny who looked as stunned as she felt, ". . . *the* Warre who supposedly created pad paws and starts wars?"

Quemado nodded. "Yes. But Lord Manny killed Warre so we could serve him instead. All hail Lord Manny!"

"Quemado!" Manny barked. "You have to stop saying that!"

"O-kay!" The medic dragged out the word as she wrapped a bandage around Quemado's hand. "This is so far above my pay grade I'm getting a nosebleed!" She closed her medical kit and scrambled to her feet. "You'll have to go talk with the 'Big Boss.'"

Manny felt his bowels clench. "You mean the Supreme Leader?"

"I mean Uncle Lucius. He commands the Capital Guard."

~~~

The Commander, a large gibbon whose black coat was shot through with grey, had just squeezed Manny's oversized entourage into his Command Center when a paunchy orangutan flounced in.

"Lucius," he lisped, "you must put a stop this . . . this *obscene* attempt to Install a *fake* Supreme Leader. It's . . ."

A puff of air ruffled the orangutan's hair. The ape spun around to find the room filled with floor-to-ceiling troll. Hablador bared a mouthful of teeth, silencing the blustering orangutan.

"Oh, well played!" The Commander murmured under his breath. "Councilor Tictalc," he said, loud enough to get the orangutan's attention. His icy smile did not dull the edge on his voice as he went on, "It is not my place to Install a Supreme Leader nor to prevent one from being Installed. My job is to provide security. And, to the best of my ability, that is what I will do. Now, if there was nothing else . . ."

A skinny bald ape rushed in, followed by two Guards. "Ah, Boric," said The Commander, "please show the Councilor out."

Tictalc glared at The Commander, then at the Guards, who casually rested their paws on their swords. "Well!" he huffed. "This is *so* not over!" He sucked in an outraged breath, stuck out his flabby chin and stormed out of the Command Centre.

The guards cast nervous glances at the trolls, then turned to follow.

"You two hold up!" called the Commander.

The Guards turned back and came to attention. "Sir?"

"Two things: First, send someone to seal the gate to the Square. I don't want any creature else wandering in before we're ready."

"Yes, Sir!" the Guards said in unison. They shifted from foot to foot until one of them ventured, "Was there something else, Sir?"

"Yes," The gibbon grinned mirthlessly, "if any other dung-eating creature interrupts me before lunch, at least one of you had better have fallen on your sword. Do I make myself clear?"

The Guards gulped. "Sir, yes sir!" they barked.

"Good!" purred The Commander. "Dismissed!"

~~~

The Commander directed a skeptical look at Manny. "I love my niece dearly," he said, "but she is a flighty young thing. She somehow got it into her head that you're a demon slayer. And not just any demon—she was prattling on about the God-Demon Warre."

"Your niece is a most excellent *médica,*" said Manny.

Please don't waste our time by wandering off-topic."

"*¿Qué?*" Manny bristled. "The topic is what?"

"Do you claim to have killed the Demon Warre?"

"I make no claims! I know only that a creature turned to dust before my eyes. What the *médica* was told about this God-Demon, I too was hearing for the first time." He turned to the red-robed troll. "Quemado, explain what you said to the one who healed you."

Quemado turned terrified eyes on Hablador and held up a beseeching hand. The black-robed priest swallowed. "If Lord Manny permits, I will speak." The words came slowly, as if each were weighed before its release. "In the long ago, the Creator Goddess went away for a time. Left alone, her jealous helpmate Warre turned the pad paws loose among her Hooved creations, then gorged on their life force.

"The Creator Goddess returned and was enraged. Warre was cast into a sort of exile. Then she created the fingered folk to forever serve and protect her Hooved creatures. With the pad paws, who did only what they were made to do, she made a sort of peace." Hablador's voice grew bitter, "We are the last product of Warre's jealous rage: monstrous, fingered giants who are hated by all Gorme's creations."

"You are giants," said Manny, "but not monsters. Not really."

Hablador blinked several times. "Lord Manny is too kind. For we were created to sow fear and hatred among Gorme's creatures. We did as we were commanded. Even so, Warre's power weakened. There has been peace, of a sort, for a long time. Warre resorted to the torture and murder of sentient beings to feed his hungers. The sacrifices sickened even us. But then . . ." The troll fell silent.

The Commander's eyes bored into the giant. "Then what?"

Hablador gulped. "For the first time in many generations, Warre sensed an Immortal, a Guardian, on our world. Warre's minions were made to sow the seeds of a new war, more terrible than any before. Old grievances among the Folk were revived. All in preparation for when Warre obtained the Guardian's immortal essence.

"In the dead of night, Warre attacked. But somehow . . . by dark magic I think . . . the Immortal withstood the attack. Drained of power and on the brink of death, Warre struck a bargain with Coshon Aerie: half of the Evil Dominion in exchange for the Immortal's essence. An Iceborg was sent to harvest it."

A chill ran down Manny's spine. "I was there when the ice creature came," he barked. He lowered his head. "I failed to defeat it."

The trolls stared. He lifted his blade. "Then I was given this."

Hablador nodded. "But for the Burning God-blade's magic, Warre would be Immortal. And by devouring the thousands of souls destroyed by the war that will start today, Warre would have become powerful enough to rule the world! But Lord Manny freed the Immortal's essence. Warre was destroyed."

The trolls laid their foreheads on the floor. "All hail Lord Manny of the Flaming Sword!" they chanted. "May he reign forever!"

"That is most embarrassing," muttered Manny.

The Commander pulled at the fur on his chin. "So, if I may set aside for the moment the 'divinity' of small dogs, the key point is that Warre is no more. So, won't all those 'seeds of war' wither and die? Let us get through today without bloodshed?"

Hablador shook his head. "No. Warre used only what was already in creatures' hearts. Envy and distrust were easily turned into hatred and bloodlust. Those things won't go away."

The Commander grimaced. "So it all has to go ahead."

The period of silence that followed was broken by Manny. "I am sorry," he said, "but I have more news that is bad."

"Of course you do," sighed The Commander. "Let me have it."

"Below the city, the tunnels and sewers are full of armed *soldados: gorilas,* most of them. When the time comes, they will climb out of the sewer access holes and attack from all sides."

"How many soldiers?" asked The Commander.

"Many large riverboats full."

Musculoso stirred. "If Lord Manny wills, I will go out and close the sewer holes."

Manny shook his head. "There are too many . . ." He paused, then let out a yip. "In the square are bags of sand. If they can be piled on the access holes, *los gorilas* will be trapped."

"That could work," the grim-faced gibbon acknowledged. "But I don't have enough guards for that. Or sandbags. Or time."

The trolls conferred. Hablador nodded at The Commander. "If Lord Manny permits and guides us, we will do this thing."

The Commander slapped his paws together. "I accept your offer. Gratefully!" He rang a bell and the skinny bald ape hurried in.

"We have three new recruits," The Commander announced. He pointed his chin at Manny and added, "and a new platoon leader. Round up as many canvas sacks as can be found and have them taken to the closest beach. They'll be making sandbags."

A jittery Guard led the way. Musculoso and Quemado pulled a cart loaded with woven sacks. Manny rode on Hablador's shoulder. He had been given a chevron armband, which he proudly wore around his neck. "So," said Manny. "the Demon-God was nourished by violence and gore. And you?"

"Me, Master?"

"Yes. What nourishes you?"

"Rutabagas, mostly; carrots are alright; even potatoes if there is nothing else. But not beets."

"Never beets," Quemado chimed in. "The nasty things bleed all over everything!"

~ *39* ~

Pete rolled out of his nest to learn he had been abandoned. Where did every creature go? He stuffed a banana into his face and went the window. *All I ever wanted was be left in peace. Now I get my wish and I hate it! It's that dog's fault!*

He flexed his fingers and was pleased at how well they had healed. *I should work on my 'special' card shuffle!* But his paw settled on the oversize deck that had been with Starr Knightly's magical gifts. He tore the box open and drew out a card. It looked like Hoof. No it *was* Hoof! In golden armor! *Too funny!*

He squatted down and laid the card on the floor. The next card showed Booger wearing a short white robe and sandals with wings on them. A trick of the light made his yellow hair seem to flow behind him. *Okay, this is weird.* The card went below Hoof's.

The third card showed Manny with a chevron at his throat. His dagger glowed red. *Impressive! Maybe the little warrior will get his wish.* The card went beside Hoof's. It was followed by an image of Wat Ho. As soon as the card was laid down, it tore down the middle and half of it disappeared. *This just got way past weird!*

Pete drew his own image. It wore a jester's outfit and juggled several balls. *Should I be insulted?* He laid it beside Manny's.

He drew Jawana next, in silver armor with a gold band around her forehead, then a black gibbon wearing an ornate white helm. He put the gibbon below Jawana but they switched places. *Huh! Maybe I should just throw cards on the floor and see where they want to go.*

He drew three giants, dressed in black, red and white robes. They made a triangle around Manny. *Is Manny in danger?*

A knock-kneed Giraffe slid across the floor to stop above the gibbon. Their neck strained under the weight of a heavy crown. *The new Supreme Leader?* An orangutan fell to the floor and slunk up behind the Giraffe. *That's Crumpt! This is so cool!* A blade appeared in the Crumpt's paw. The Jawana card slipped in between Crumpt and the Giraffe. Her card was slashed and something like blood oozed from the cut. *Not cool! Not cool at all!*

A flurry of cards flew out of the box. All bore the images of warriors. A few wore white helms; they surrounded the Giraffe. Most of the cards were black-helmed mercenaries. They scattered across the floor. The three giants pushed most of the black-helmed mercenaries into a pile. They climbed onto the pile and stayed there.

More cards escaped the box. A large spotted cat wearing a naval tricorn was surrounded by an assortment of creatures wearing white sailor caps. They spread out and tracked down any mercenaries that had not been trapped by the giants.

Pete scattered the remaining cards on the floor: A black stallion surrounded by bodyguards; a waist-coated gorilla; a skittish young Jennet; a large monkey in a broadbrimmed hat and red dress; a venerable Goat chewing the brim of a straw hat; a jackal with red eyes.

Pete didn't notice the jackal slinking toward the Giraffe until Manny moved, catching his eye. The dog limped over to the jackal, who raised a paw and . . . "No!" Pete shrieked. He flung the box aside. "None of this is real! It's just a stupid game.*" What if it's not? What if these things already happened? No! Please let them be in the future!* As he ran for the elevator the jester began to move.

Hoof and Booger followed The Hatter through a maze of corridors. *If we get separated, I'll be lost forever,* Hoof fretted.

"I have to make a short detour," The Hatter announced as they zagged to the right. They ducked into an armory where The Hatter selected a brass cuirass and held it up to their chest.

"Does this go with red? Oh well; needs must!"

They pushed their bag to the back of a shelf before strapping on the cuirass. Then they belted on a sword. "Good to go!"

"Don't you want a helm?" asked Hoof.

The mandrill tapped their hat. "Tough as anything from I could get from the armory!"

Booger balanced a pair of sandals in his palm. "I left my boots behind. Would it be okay if I borrowed these?"

The Hatter blinked. "Those are . . ." They hesitated for a moment, then chuckled. "Why not? Go for it!"

~~~

The Hatter set a brisk pace as they dodged across a busy street and entered a narrow, unnamed passageway. A few dozen long strides carried them to a broad thoroughfare.

"The Guard Commander is at ViceRegal Square, setting up security for the Installation," panted The Hatter. "He'll have gotten an outline of what's going on, but he'll want the details from you."

Hoof was too dazed to ask how word could have beaten them to The Commander. His mental fog lasted until he bumped into The Hatter, who had stopped and drawn his sword. Tree giants plodded toward them, pulling a cart piled high with sandbags.

"By the Grace of Gorme, what are those?" Hoof brayed.

"Dirty, stinking trolls," The Hatter replied through clenched teeth. "Putrefying pawns of Warre. Disgusting cave scum. Take your pick."

"Over here, *por favor*. This one is next!" yapped a shrill voice.

"I know that annoying, yappy voice," said Hoof.

"Me too!" said Booger. He dashed after the trolls as they turned into a side street. Hoof and The Hatter looked at each other, then followed. The three of them skidded to a stop and watched the trolls pile sandbags on a sewer access cover. The Hatter was startled to see a little dog hobbling around the giants' feet.

"Hey you! Get away from those monsters! Are you insane?"

Hoof snorted. "Yeah, he pretty much is," he replied.

The dog turned in their direction. *"Señor* Booger! *Buenos días!"*

Booger stood frozen, unable to take his eyes off the giants.

Hoof stepped forward. "Hello, Manny," he brayed.

"¿Señor burro estúpido? ¡Ay caramba! Did you trip and fall into a pit full of armor?"

"Yeah, it's good to see you too, Manny," Hoof replied.

But Manny had turned his bulbous eyes on The Hatter. "Who is this creature who insults my servants?"

The Hatter's mouth was a grim line. "If those monsters serve you," they growled, "you must be . . ."

Hoof stepped between The Hatter and Manny. "Hold up," he said, blocking the mandrill with his shoulder. "I know this dog. He's very annoying, but he's not evil." The Hatter reluctantly lowered his sword, flicking his eyes between Manny and the trolls.

Two of the giants leaned against the cart while the third, wearing a grungy robe that may once have been black, turned to Manny. "This one is finished," they rumbled in a voice that made Hoof's armor vibrate. "Where would Lord Manny have us go next?"

Manny shot a smug look at Hoof. *"Busy, busy!"* he said. "No time for chatter-chitter. We are saving your city from *los soldados gorilas!"* He hobbled back to the trolls.

The Hatter heard footsteps behind him. He whirled around, gripping his sword in both paws. The newcomer, a veteran Sergeant of the Guard, raised his palms defensively. "Easy now. I'm on your side."

The Hatter sheathed his sword and jabbed a thumb at the street behind him. "What? Who?" He got no farther.

The sergeant looked down the side street. "Don't ask," he replied. His eyes bounced off The Hatter's outfit to Booger, then froze on Hoof. "Don't ask questions," murmured the sergeant. "Ever!"

He was still muttering to himself when he strode away.

~~~

Voices leaked out of the Guard Command Post. The Hatter motioned for Hoof and Booger to wait as he peered around the half-open door. The Commander was behind his desk, squeezing its edge in a grip that threatened to snap it off. His eyes skewered a portly Guard the way a snake might stare down a mouse.

"Why am I just hearing about this now?" said the Commander, speaking with an icy calm.

"I'm right sorry," the Guard replied. He sounded almost defiant as he added, "but I was after gettin' here quick's I could!" A beat passed before he added a grudging, "Sir."

The Commander's lips pulled back in an unpleasant grimace. "And how long for you to take my reply back?" he demanded.

"Oh Sweet Gorme, Sir!" Desperation crept into the Guard's voice as he went on, "I like as killed meself gettin' here. Sure, I couldna make it back again."

"From now on, it's going to be a little more time on the exercise yard and a lot less time in the dining hall," growled The Commander.

"I'll do my best, Sir,"

"That wasn't a suggestion, *Private*. That was an order!"

The Guard's eyes widened. "Sir, yes sir!" He slipped off his chevrons and laid them on the edge of the desk.

"Dismissed!" The Commander sounded more defeated than angry.

"Thank you, Sir!" The Guard spun around and marched out, almost hitting The Hatter with the door when he burst through it.

Before The Hatter could stop him, Booger rushed into the Command Centre. "I can carry messages for you, Sir!" he exclaimed. "I can run as fast as anything!"

The Commander leaped up. "Who the Charlie D are you?"

Hoof clopped in and The Commander's jaw dropped. He was still staring at the armor-clad Donkey when The Hatter slipped in and closed the door. "Hello Lucius. Good to see you again."

The Commander tore his eyes away from Hoof. "I might have known," he growled. He ran his eyes over the mandrill's garb. "At least you look halfway normal. For you."

The Hatter dipped into an ironic curtsy, then met The Commander's eye. "We just left W. He thinks you need to hear what the Donkey has to say."

The Commander cut his eyes back to Hoof. "Does the Donkey have a name?"

"That's a long story," replied The Hatter. "But first things first: your little problem with communications?"

The Commander stared. "You were eavesdropping?"

The Hatter shrugged. "It's what I do. But what's important is that the young bald ape here," he nodded at Booger, "is as fast as he says he is. And very, erm, shall we say 'resourceful?'"

The Commander stepped around his desk to stand in front of Booger. He took in the dark clothing and the remaining black that clung to his face. "And is he reliable?"

"At least as much as me," replied The Hatter.

The Commander guffawed. "Some recommendation that is!" He turned his eyes back to Booger. "Do you have a name, son?" he asked. Or is that another 'long story?'"

"Yes. No. Yes!" Booger stammered. The Commander waited for him to go on. "I mean yes, I have a name. No, it's not a long story."

After a few beats, the Commander growled, "Are you going end the suspense any time soon?"

"What? Oh. Sorry. It's Boo . . . call me Chanse, Sir."

"Very well. Do you know The Capital well, Chanse?"

"I've only been here a couple days, Sir. But I learn fast."

The Commander didn't try to hide his disappointment. "But at least you can read?"

Booger's face fell. "No Sir. I learned my numbers, though!"

The Hatter cleared their throat. "It's a lot easier to ensure a dispatch is kept secret if the courier can't read it."

The Commander grunted. "That's a point, I suppose." He mulled things over for a few beats, then went back to his desk. The chevron caught his eye. "Put this on," he said, tossing it to Booger.

Grinning broadly, Booger slid the armband up his arm. It slid right down again. "It's kind of big," he observed, glumly.

"Here, let me help." The Hatter pulled a pin from somewhere in their wardrobe and expertly pinned the armband in place.

The Commander picked up a tablet and scratched out a message. Taking Booger by the arm, he pulled him to the farthest corner of the room. Booger's head bobbed up and down as he absorbed the Commander's instructions, then he snapped off a sharp salute.

"You can count on me, Sir!"

"It's not like I have a choice," muttered The Commander. He handed him the tablet, along with a token that confirmed he was from the Command Centre. Booger sprinted out the door.

The Commander waved at a table. "Now, then," he said to Hoof. "We can make ourselves comfortable while you tell me about yourself, including why you're wearing a king's ransom's worth of armor."

~~~

The Commander paced back and forth, firing questions. Occasionally he stopped to stare out a window that looked out over the Square.

Hoof's stomach grew painfully aware he had eaten and drunk nothing since the previous evening and far too much of that had involved alcohol. His eye kept drifting to a bowl of apples he could see beyond The Commander. This became so distracting that the old gibbon turned around to see what was going on behind him.

He cut his eyes back to Hoof. "Have you eaten?"

"Not since yesterday!" Hoof blurted. "I won't starve to death, but only because I'm going to die of thirst first."

"That won't do," The Commander declared. "Soldiers march on their stomachs!" He reached for an apple and tossed it across the table.

Hoof glumly watched the apple bounce off his chanfron and roll across the floor. "New to armor, are you?" chuckled The Commander as he reached for his bell. "I'll get someone to help you."

"I could do with a bit of breakfast myself," The Hatter mumbled around a mouthful of apple.

Booger raced across the Square, filled with a delightful sense of weightlessness. He bore down on some Guards who were trying to prop an ornate gate up across the exit. Without missing a step, he launched himself into the air and cleared the obstacle. The stunned Guards heard him giggle to himself as he disappeared into the distance.

He crested the island and picked up even more speed as he headed downhill towards the waterfront. But before long he was forced to dodge around irate, protesting citizens. He stepped off the boardwalk, finding it faster to weave through the vehicles on the street.

He sped past a yellow-vested orangutan who blew several shrill blasts on a whistle, then shouted, "Hey you! Get off the street!"

"Sorry! Can't stop," Booger called as he dodged a locomotor that barreled down the cross street. "Got an urgent message to deliver!"

A surprisingly short time later, he reached the Old Waterfront. After a moment's hesitation, he turned west. He sped past a familiar, half-submerged pier; Crosius and his pack of scruffy dogs barely registered he was coming before he was gone. But he saw no ships matching the one he had been instructed to find.

Chafing at the delay, he zigged and zagged through a cluster of rundown buildings that kept him from rejoining the waterfront. Finally he reached a wharf that looked as dilapidated as the one he had left.

Ah! There you are! He pulled up at a narrow gangplank, breathless but exhilarated. He waved at the white-capped orangutan who was watching him from the rail.

"Permission to board?" he called, holding up The Commander's token. "I have an urgent message for Captain Kloue van Wraak."

~~~

The large spotted cat stared right through Booger, her tail twitching irritably as she mulled things over. Suddenly she leaped off the table and, without a word or backward glance, padded to the door.

"Wait!" Booger called after her. "Do you have a message from me to take back?"

The cat peered back over her shoulder. Her strange hissing laughter made Booger shudder. "Tell Lucius that the price just doubled," she said. Then she was gone.

~~~

The street ran parallel to the waterfront. A high wooden fence stood between Booger and the water. On the landward side, an unbroken wall of rundown warehouses frustrated any attempt to turn inland.

A pause in the keening of the gulls was filled with the sound of approaching hooves. Booger skidded to a halt as a gate swung open, blocking his path. The clopping of hooves was joined by the sound of marching boots. Booger stepped forward and squinted through a crack in the gate. He pulled away, blinked, then looked again.

Four bald apes marched side-by side through the opening. Their fists were wrapped around poles from which long banners, emblazoned with a scarlet dragon rampant on a green field, hung down almost to the ground. The standard bearers were followed by four silverbacks whose uniforms were weighed down by glittering regalia befitting their rank and inflated egos.

Upon clearing the gate, the eight creatures pivoted through a ninety-degree turn: a complex maneuver involving much barking of commands and stomping of feet. The formation moved away. A heavyset silverback followed, dressed in a red waistcoat that was partly hidden behind a wide sash. Booger gasped in recognition even before the tall black stallion danced through the open gate.

"Waterstrider!" he breathed. "What's he up to?" Waterstrider was joined by a handsome golden mare Booger did not recognize. Eight members of Waterstrider's personal guard brought up the rear. The gate began to creak shut and Booger stepped forward. Which is as far as he got before a powerful hand closed over his mouth.

"Got an eyeful did you, you filthy little spy!" a voice growled in his ear. "Too bad you won't have a tongue to blab about what you saw."

~ *40* ~

The hatter slipped off to the armory and exchanged their distinctive garb for a plain mail shirt. Ensuring no prying eyes were watching, they retrieved their bag and ducked through a low door that was hidden in a corner of the armory. Their feet found the edge of a spiral staircase and they descended through the dark, going round and round in tight, disorienting circles.

Upon stumbling to the end of the staircase, The Hatter struck a firestick; the flickering light revealed a low, dank cave that enclosed a pool of oily water. They lit several candles that were scattered around the cave. Then they knelt and pulled a parcel from their bag.

Tearing off the parcel's waterproof wrapping exposed a narrow metal box, the inside of which was packed with wool. Setting the wool aside, they took out a small, eight-sided token. After a few deep breaths, they forced a nonchalant grin onto their face and flipped the token into the center of the pool.

Inside the expanding ripples, the surface took on a green glow that reflected on the walls of the cave. A shadow spread out from the center, resolving itself into a scarred, cat-like face. The deep-set eyes scrutinized The Hatter, then the mouth began to move. A beat passed before their words echoed through the cave.

"You have something that belongs to me," growled the voice. "If you have the wits of a flea, you will give it back. Now!"

"I know nothing of the intellect of fleas," grinned The Hatter, "but I do know about this." They drew a crystal statuette out of the box.

297

When they extended it over the pool, it fractured the candlelight; scores of tiny rainbows skittered across every cave surface.

The Hatter let it slip from their fingers then smoothly snatched it back before it hit the water. "Oops!" they chuckled. "I shouldn't eat butter before playing with your toys!"

"Be careful, fool!" the creature roared. "Damage so much as one facet of the Sacred *Conundra* and I will hunt you down, tear you open and eat your still-beating heart!"

"Really?" The Hatter replied, raising a quizzical eyebrow. All trace of humor left their face as they continued, "Well, here's *my* proposal: Raise so much as a finger against this Realm and I *guarantee* your 'sacred *Conundra*' will be ground into dust."

The Hatter waited several beats for the message to be received and digested. Then they added, "Or grant us three moons' peace and, at the end, it will be returned to you intact."

The feline eyes narrowed, then the mouth began to move. "I meant your Realm no harm," purred the voice. It grew cold and hard as it continued, "Until now! Know this, fool: If the Conundra is not in my paws in three moons you will be the first of many to die!" The image disappeared and the luminous green slime faded to an oily black.

The Hatter heaved a sigh of relief, then carefully packed the statuette back into its box. "How glibly you lie, cat!" they murmured. "Gorme grant that we gained time enough."

When Hoof had no more information to offer, the Commander summoned his senior officers. Hoof hid in the corner behind a second heaping bowl of oats. He was licking the bottom clean when a Guard ran into the command center.

"Commander," the Guard panted. "There's a mob outside the Square. It doesn't look like they're here for a family outing. And the Needle's shadow is at the Mark. The ceremony has to start!"

The Commander got up and looked out into the square. "Any sign of my young messenger?" he asked.

"No Sir. None so far."

The Commander looked grim. "What about the hopeful leader-to-be? What's his status?"

"In the waiting room, Sir, bent over a window and listening to the crowd. He seemed calm enough." The Guard shrugged, then added, "The Orange Ape showed too, with a bunch of his 'hangers-on.' We put them in a different room from the Giraffe, of course."

"Thank you, private," The Commander replied. "You may return to your post." The Guard saluted and bowed out of the room.

A dappled stallion curled a disapproving lip. "Lucius, you tolerate too much informality from the troops. It borders on disrespect."

"Your concern is noted, Captain." The Commander slapped his palms together. "You are all dismissed; go out and do your duty."

Hoof watched the officers line up and, in reverse order of rank, file out of the room. They stared back at him with undisguised suspicion. The Commander remained seated, lost in his own thoughts.

"Excuse me, Sir," Hoof brayed at last.

The Commander started. "What? Oh. You're still here."

"Sorry, Sir," said Hoof. "It's just, erm . . . my mask thingy?"

"Ah! Allow me," The Commander slipped the chanfron over Hoof's face, tucked his ears behind their guards and clipped on the criniere. A tug ensured it was securely attached before he clipped the dagger into its slot. He patted Hoof's shoulder. "Good to go!"

The Commander retrieved a tall hat box from a locker. "Now it's my turn," he glumly announced a he leaned back and removed the lid. A tall red plume snapped out, barely missing his eye. "The Hatter's handiwork," he grumbled as he lifted out a helm that was attached to the ridiculously large feather. He slipped it on over his round head. "It makes me look like a real prat!"

"Not at all, Sir!" Hoof lied. "Most, erm, impressive."

The Gibbon shot him a cynical look as he buckled on his sword. He squared his shoulders and started for the door.

"Excuse me, Sir!" Hoof brayed. He awkwardly stumbled to attention. "I'm ready to serve, Sir! What can I do?"

"I have no clue," sighed The Commander. He ran his eyes over Hoof's gleaming armor. "Perhaps you can run up and down the ramparts. The sun bouncing of that armor might blind the enemy."

"Sir, yes sir!" brayed Hoof as he tried to click his back hooves together. But The Commander had already strode out of the room. By the time Hoof trotted out after him, the hallway was empty. He clopped down a stairway, pushed through a sprung door and found himself on the Square. The door slammed behind him, sealing him outside.

"Excuse me," he said, accosting the first Guard he encountered. "Can you point me at the nearest rampart?"

The Guard's eyes widened as they took in Hoof's armor. His arm spasmed as he fought the urge to salute. He settled for flopping it up and down. "Rampart? Don't know of any ramparts hereabouts." He pointed across the Square. "There's a wall of sandbags over there."

"Thank you, private!" Hoof brayed as he galloped off.

~~~

One end of the Square was dominated by a deep stage that stood higher than a Horse's head and stretched fifty paces corner to corner. It was accessed via an arched opening through the wall behind it.

Two balconies faced each other across the stage. They were filling with the well-fed and slightly tipsy 'cream' of The Capital's society. A sprinkling of fingered folk bobbed in a sea of Equine arrogance. Bejeweled baubles sparkled on perfectly coiffed manes and tails. To the right of the stage, red rubies gleamed on a background of gold and diamonds. On the left, the deep blue of sapphire was favored.

A wall of sandbags curved around the front of the stage. It was low enough that it wouldn't block the masses' view of the proceedings but (hopefully) high enough to slow down any troublemakers intent on creating a disruption. Beyond the wall, a row of Guards stood with their backs to the stage.

A bronze bell began to toll, almost drowning out the dull rumble of a mob of creatures stampeding across the square! Hoof broke into a gallop, desperate to reach the sandbags before the mob. Two strides from the wall, he realized there were no steps leading onto it!

"Oh Snorg!" he brayed as he launched himself into the air. His front hooves clipped the top of the wall and he did a faceplant on a burlap sandbag. His momentum kept his backside going; it lifted in the air, threatening to flip him onto his back. He teetered on his chin until his back hoofs dropped down—on the wall! He staggered to his feet. *I did it! Now what?*

Booger's arms were painfully stretched behind him and bound around a ship's mast. His shoulders ached from the strain and a knob protruding from the base of the mast dug painfully into his back. Any attempt to ease one source of discomfort made the other worse.

The mast was on an elegant vessel that had anchored between the marina and its breakwater. A heated debate had raged among Booger's captors as they rowed him to the vessel. It continued as he was dragged across the deck and lashed to the mast. By which time he had learned that the vessel's small but unhappy crew had been forced to sail, with no stops to rest, all the way from Waterstrider City.

To add to their grievances, they had barely dropped anchor before being ordered to row the party to shore. Five crossings in the ship's launch followed, all to ensure the arrogant Stallion would get to 'watch all the excitement as it unfolded.' Continuing Booger's streak of bad luck, the exhausted sailors opted to see the Great Lord off, rather than head back to the ship for some well-deserved shuteye!

Booger banged the back of his head against the mast. *Idiot!* (thump) *Idiot!* (thump) *Idiot!* (thump) This did not provide the pleasant distraction he had hoped for. He stopped banging his head and listened. Somewhere in the distance, a bell began to toll.

The tolling of the bell continued as the Electors made a stately procession onto the stage. Tasseled caps balanced above impassive faces. Red tassels went to the right, alternating with blue tassels going left.

A row of luxurious benches extended the length of the back wall. The first Electors reached the farthest benches and stopped. The rest filled in behind them. When all of the Electors were in place, the bell fell silent. An expectant hush fell over the Square.

When Alddon Crumpt danced through the archway; the crowd went mad! The orangutan cavorted about, waving to his admirers. He wore a gold vest that he 'modelled' for the crowd.

The Commander strode up to Crumpt and gripped his elbow. The orangutan sulkily allowed himself to be led to a closed-off area at one side of the platform. By the time he got there, a score of his staunch supporters were already inside, eager to fawn over him.

A dozen trumpeters filed onto the stage. They formed two rows, faced each other and blared out the opening bars of a regal march. A dappled head ducked under the arch and preceded a long, skinny neck onto the stage. This was followed by a bony chest and rickety legs. Josephus Archibald Bidet, *genus Giraffa,* began his stiff-legged march toward Installation as Supreme Leader of the One True Realm.

The lead trumpeter cut his eyes to the Giraffe and signaled for his fellow musicians to lower the tempo. 'Regal' gave way to 'stately' gave way to 'funereal.' Then (to the relief of many) the music was drowned out by boos and catcalls from the mob. Lumps of vegetation sailed over the sandbags to plop wetly onto the stage.

While all eyes were on Bidet, a shadow slipped out of the archway and edged to a position behind Crumpt's enclosure. It froze there while the Giraffe continued his stiff-legged shuffle across the platform. Crumpt leaned over his barricade and waved a tiny paw at Bidet, calling out to get his attention.

When the Giraffe cut an eye in his direction, Crumpt beckoned furiously for him to come over. "I have a message for you!" he shouted. Bidet changed direction to shuffle towards the orangutan's enclosure. The crowd noise fell to a dull grumble, overlaid by a few sharp curses as a group of burly creatures bullied their way up to the sandbag barricade. A weak cheer was heard from the 'blue' balcony; the 'red' balcony began to stir confusedly.

Crumpt was taller than most creatures, but Bidet towered over him. The orangutan leaned back, craning his neck. Then he beckoned for Bidet to lower his head. "This is for you alone," he said.

When Bidet lowered his ear to the orangutan's mouth, everything happened at once: A knife appeared in Crumpt's paw; he struck at Bidet's throat; a streak of white placed itself in the blade's path; time slowed down.

Hoof had a horrifyingly close view of the action. "Jawana!" he brayed as the blade found a gap beside her breastplate and slipped into her chest. "Oh Snorg! No!"

"Psst!" Booger cocked an eye toward the side of the boat. A bright blue and red face grinned through the railing. "Don't you have a message to deliver?"

Booger rested the back of his head against the mast. "Did it already," he tiredly muttered. "Was headed back with the reply when I got tied up."

"Where are your nautical friends?"

Booger listened to the snoring coming from below decks. "They're all asleep, by the sounds of it."

The Hatter slipped over the railing and crossed the deck. They wore only a belt and sheath, from which they pulled a slender blade. "Do you swim?" they asked as they sliced through the ropes binding Booger to the mast.

Booger's hands fell to his sides. "Like a stone," he replied.

The Hatter went to the rail; stepped over it and balanced on his toes. "Come on. I'll tow you to shore." Booger nervously went to stand in front of The Hatter, who took a grip on his jerkin. "This would be easier if we weren't weighed down by waterlogged clothes."

Booger's face turned white and he shook his head. "No!" he said. "No way, no how! You'll just have to leave me here."

The Hatter shrugged. "Fair enough," they said. "As you once said, a creature should feel free to wear what they want." He hooked an arm under Booger's chin and, pulling him over the rail, slipped backwards into the water.

At the deepest corner of the 'red' balcony, a pretty young Jennet was pinned in place by the glare of a bald ape. The gold chain that surrounded her neck clattered against the railing as she trembled with rage and disgust. Which suddenly turned to shock and horror.

"Hoof! Behind you! Look out!"

"Verity?" Hoof spun toward the voice. A massive blow that would have broken his neck glanced off his shoulder, knocking him off balance. As he stumbled forward, his razor-sharp blade punched into the chest of his would-be assassin. The creature, a full-sized grizzly, gurgled weakly, then tumbled off the wall, crushing a gorilla that was trying to climb up behind them.

Hoof swayed dizzily, looking down at the carnage he had created. *I killed that creature!* His stomach heaved. *I shouldn't have eaten that second batch of oats.* He saw motion out of the corner of his eye and swung his head to the side. Blood sprayed from the tip of his blade, persuading the creatures nearest to him to fall back.

A silverback gorilla had climbed onto the far end of the wall. A couple of Guards fought him from below. *They don't have a chance!* Hoof lowered his head and charged. To his relief, the gorilla saw him at the last moment and dove back into the crowd. Hoof spun around, looking for another target.

The cart had been filled up with sandbags and emptied three times. Not even a rat would crawl out of the sewers anywhere near ViceRegal Square. Manny was certain of that. He also knew that, as tired as he was, the trolls had to be more exhausted.

"You have done well," he said. "It is time to rest."

The trolls bowed half-heartedly. "Lord Manny is gracious to think of the welfare of his humble servants," Hablador mumbled.

Manny scratched an ear. *"Es posible* you will cause alarm among the citizens. It will be best if you find somewhere to hide."

"This is not new for us," Quemado replied. "Always we hide. Never are we seen if we do not want to be."

Realmente? thought Manny. *It must be like hiding a Cow under a basket!* But he chose to say nothing.

"We will go to the river," said Hablador, "where there is marshland and forest. We will wash ourselves and our robes. We will eat the roots of lilies. We will sleep. We will not be seen."

"How will I find you?" asked Manny.

Hablador scratched their head, releasing a small landslide of sand. They looked at the small mound that had formed at their feet. "Go to the river where the sand was. We will know. We will come."

"Es bueno," Manny barked.

Something moved farther down the street and he turned to look at it. By the time he turned back, the trolls had disappeared. After spinning around twice and seeing no sign of them, he decided to follow the creature he had glimpsed. Almost immediately, he picked up a distasteful scent he knew all too well. Snorting in disgust, he hurried on until he heard crowd noises. *The ceremony, it has started!*

Eora Wurest-Gnitemere padded up the steps of a building that backed onto the Square. The jackal's head swung back and forth, as if making sure she was not being watched. Then she slipped through an open door.

¿Qué? Doors like that should not be open. Something here is not right. Manny followed the jackal's trail. More doors were propped open, as if a path had been prepared for her. He caught up to her at an archway through which angry crowd noises were pulsing. His sheath silently peeled away from his blade.

Booger was on his hands and knees coughing up half the river. The Hatter was unsympathetic. "All that cloth weighed us down."

"Sorry," said Booger. He rolled onto his back. "Next time I get kidnapped and tied to a post, I'll make sure it's on dry land."

The Hatter extended a paw and pulled Booger to his feet. "What happened to you anyway?"

Booger shrugged. "I was on my way back when my way got blocked by Waterstrider and his top brass. Oh, and that Chamberlain was with him too. The one who sent you the package?"

"Really? Why would Waterstrider want to sneak in the back way like that? And where did he go?"

Booger thought about it. "Well he wasn't exactly sneaking: He was surrounded by banners and guards and whatnot! But there's no way he'll show his nose at the Installation until he knows things have gone his way. Still, the sailors complained about breaking their backs to get here, just so he could 'watch all the excitement.'" The young bald ape pounded his thigh in frustration. "So where . . ."

"Big Axe Hill!" they both exclaimed at the same time. The Hatter slapped Booger between the shoulder blades. "For a skinny half-grown bald ape, you can be pretty smart sometimes!"

Wurest-Gnitemere's red eyes took in the scene unfolding before her. Crumpt was struggling with a gorilla but had lost his knife. *Bungling idiot!* The jackal's eyes narrowed. *It's that imposter of an innkeeper. And she's bleeding!* The jackal's lips pulled back in an evil smile. *Maybe the fat old ape isn't completely useless after all.*

She shifted her attention to the front of the platform. *The Guard should have been overwhelmed by now!* She stared at the golden Donkey who galloped over the sandbags, beating back armed fighters who had been planted in the crowd. *That will have to be dealt with later! But first things first.*

Her belly hugged the stone platform as she crept toward the Giraffe. When she was within a couple of paces, she gathered her legs under her and prepared to spring.

Manny ran forward, barking a shrill warning. Just before he reached the jackal, she sprang. But instead of leaping forward, she twisted in the air and brought a paw down on Manny's back. "Now you will die!" she snarled through bared teeth.

Something dropped from the balcony and landed on the jackal's back. Sharp teeth locked on her ear and she yowled in rage. She leaped to her feet and spun around, trying to reach the new threat.

Manny leaped up and chopped at the jackal's back leg. His blade sliced through a tendon. The jackal rolled away, dislodging the creature on her back. But by the time she got to her paws, The Commander was there with his sword drawn. Hissing with rage, the jackal fled, leaving a trail of blood behind her.

Manny's savior groaned feebly and raised both paws to cover their face. Manny stared. "*Señor* Pete? Is it you?"

"Of course it's me, you dumb dog! Who else is stupid enough to keep pulling your tail out of the fire."

A disturbance rippled through the crowd, like a wind blowing in from the back of the Square. As the ripple moved forward, creatures flooded toward the exit. The fleeing crowd stranded dozens of rough-looking characters who were either tied up or held at knifepoint.

Their assailants were a mixture of creatures, linked only in that they wore white sailor caps. The exception was a large spotted cat who wore a gold-trimmed tricorn on her head and a purely decorative cutlass strapped to her side.

Members of the Capital Guard took custody of the prisoners while teams of medics removed the casualties. After which the cat stood on her hind legs and saluted.

"All hail Supreme Leader Bidet," she yowled. She dropped to all four paws. "Let's go, crew!" she sang as she trotted toward the exit.

A few heartbeats later, Captain Kloue van Wraak and her *matrose* had vacated the Square; Crumpt had disappeared during the excitement, leaving his entourage to their fate; The Commander had escorted Pete and Manny off the stage; the medics knelt over Jawana, struggling to staunch the blood flowing from her shoulder. Oblivious to everything happening around him, Hoof stood on the wall of sandbags, staring up into the adoring eyes of Verity Glitters.

Jawana was eased onto a stretcher. Tears flowed down the soft-eyed medic's face as she kept a cloth pressed tightly over the gorilla's wound. Bidet stretched down to whisper into Jawana's ear, then stepped aside and urged the bearers and medics to do their best. The

Giraffe's wide eyes blinked a few times as he looked out over the rubbish-littered grassy square.

By the time he turned back, the stretcher had disappeared through the arched opening at the back of the stage. The Electors were either huddling behind or hiding under their benches.

"Gentle creatures!" The Giraffe spoke calmly and matter-of-factly. "Haven't you a duty to perform?"

Angry shouting drifted across the marina bay. The Hatter gripped Booger's elbow. "Time to go!" they snapped.

"No argument from me," Booger replied.

The Hatter set a fast pace as they navigated a snarl of twisted streets, catching Booger by surprise when they ducked down a blind alley. Booger skidded to a stop, then doubled back just in time to see The Hatter enter a long-abandoned warehouse.

Booger caught up with the Hatter at a dusty locker that leaned against the back wall of the warehouse. The Hatter jerked the locker open to reveal several sets of clothing hanging on wooden hangers. They selected one and hurried over to the slightly better light of a grime-covered window.

"Perfect!" they crowed. "Hold this." They thrust the hanger at Booger, who struggled against the unexpected weight of a full military dress uniform.

"I always keep a few extra outfits handy," The Hatter explained as items were pulled off the hanger and onto themself.

"Where are we going?" Booger asked as they left the warehouse

"To make sure that today's little drama, amusing as it was, doesn't result in the creation of any martyrs."

"Well, thanks a bunch for clearing that up!"

A handsome young Goat cautiously approached ViceRegal Square. "What do you think?" called a voice from behind him.

The Goat turned back to where his mate and kid were watching. "I don't know what to think," he replied. "Except for the creatures on the stage, the Square seems to be empty."

"Well," said his mate, "we promised our son an Installation, so an Installation is what he's going to get. Come along, Junior!" she bleated over her shoulder as she strode briskly onto the Square.

Other creatures had hung back watching. When nothing alarming happened to the young Goat family, they began to follow them onto the Square; at first they came in twos and threes, then in larger numbers. They all *oohed* and *ahhed* at a Golden Donkey who seemed to be stuck on the sandbags but they kept a prudent distance away as they spread out across the Square.

~~~

The two Electors at the center of the stage got shakily to their feet. The blue-tasseled Elector was a small trim Mare who had unsuccessfully tried to hide the sprinkling of grey whiskers on her chin. A red tassel was proudly worn by a tidily groomed Barbary ape.

The Mare watched disdainfully as the Barbary ape made themself as tall as they could and cleared their throat. "Josephus Archibald Bidet," they squeaked, "do you promise to faithfully uphold the laws and traditions of the One True Realm, on the honor of your ancestors and in the name of your Folk, for the welfare of our citizens and their descendants, for so long as you may rule?"

Bidet seemed to consider this question for quite some time before saying, "I so promise."

The Mare whickered. "Josephus Archibald Bidet," she neighed, "do you promise to defend the One True Realm, to keep safe its borders and to protect its citizens from every peril, with all your strength and with the strength of your Folk, for so long as you rule?"

The Giraffe suppressed a wry grin as he looked at his arthritic knees. "To the best of my ability," he said, "I so promise."

The Mare seemed unimpressed with this reply but held her tongue. She and the Barbary ape turned towards each other and nodded. Then they turned their backs on each other and, looking down the row of Electors, intoned together: "Does any Elector object to the Installation of Josephus Archibald Bidet as Regent and Leader of the One True Realm? Speak now, or ever after hold your peace!"

There was much sideways twitching of heads, but no creature spoke. After an appropriate pause, the Mare and the Barbary macaque chanted, "Will the Electors rise and swear allegiance to the newly Installed Regent and Leader of the One True Realm!

The Electors struggled to their feet. When they were all upright a whistle sounded and, more or less simultaneously, they mumbled "We promise to faithfully obey and serve Josephus Archibald Bidet, Regent and Leader of the One True Realm. We so promise on behalf our ourselves, all our Folk, and our descendants."

The bronze bell began to toll, signaling the end of the ritual. A spontaneous cheer erupted from the spectators.

The Eleventh Illustrious Stallion Waterstrider squinted down at the Square. He was amused to be reviving a practice of his alleged ancestors: the public execution of a 'traitor' against the Equine Monarchy. True, he would be watching from Big Axe Hill rather than the other way round. But there would soon be ample opportunities to remedy that; he did, after all, have so many deserving enemies.

Doubt intruded on the Stallion's reverie; things were taking too long. "What's happening?" he neighed. "My army should have taken The Capital long ago! Why isn't that idiot of a Giraffe dead yet?"

"Lord Waterstrider!" The Stallion's head whipped around to goggle at the trim figure marching up the hillside. They wore a

311

beautifully tailored uniform, covered in gold braid. A proud plume thrust up from the gleaming helm that the creature carried under their arm. Black button eyes stared shrewdly from a bright blue and red face.

The Hatter feigned a respectful bow. "Your Grace!" they murmured as they moved to Waterstrider's side, then turned to peer at the Square below. "What an excellent location for watching the proceedings! And it's well away from the riffraff."

They turned a sharp eye toward the Stallion. "It's good to keep some distance, isn't it? In the unlikely event that some creatures got it into their heads to cause trouble."

"Trouble!" neighed the Horse in his high, nasal voice. He tossed his head. "Is there trouble?"

The Hatter shrugged. "A few minor issues, which have been dealt with. Be that as it may, Your Grace, you should slip away the same way you came." After a pause, they grimly added, "We'd all prefer you to avoid complications that could, erm, 'bite you in the neck?'"

A waistcoated silverback hurried up to stand between The Hatter and the agitated Stallion. "Thank you for this opportunity," he said quietly. "The situation will made clear to His Grace." He extended a paw; The Hatter shook it, then spun around and marched down the hill.

A bell tolled, announcing the Installation of a new Supreme Leader. Loud cheers wafted up the hill. Waterstrider reared up and bugled with rage. Briefly, he resembled the Stallions he claimed as ancestors. Then he dropped down and blubbered like a newborn Colt.

The Chamberlain slipped a lead over the Stallion's head. "Come along, Your Grace," he said. "It's over now. Let's go home."

~ *41* ~

The Capital shrugged off the turmoil of the Installation: deals were made; pardons granted; mercenaries ransomed and sent on their way. A mountain of sand was returned to its rightful place beside the river. And Josephus Archibald Bidet settled in as Supreme Leader of the One True Realm.

Silence cloaked the antechamber to the Octagonal Office, disturbed only by Hoof's restless pacing. He paused to glare at Pete, who was rifling a deck of cards. "How can you be so relaxed?"

Pete shrugged. "It wasn't me that pretended to be a Lord High Muckity Muck."

A slim, yellow-haired bald ape laid a hand on Hoof's neck. "Don't let Pete get to you, Boss. He's just jerking your bridle."

"Thanks, Booger!"

"Erm, Boss? Could you call me 'Wyona' from now on?"

"What?" Hoof studied his thrall. He seldom noticed the cloth that bald apes wrapped themselves up in, but something had changed. Jerkin and breeches had been replaced by what looked like a spring meadow. A matching hat, courtesy of The Hatter, was pinned to yellow hair that had become a mass of swirls and bends.

"Wyona? That sounds . . ." He paused, then blurted, "Say, do you know you look kind of like a female?"

Wyona's lower lip trembled. "Kind of?"

"Oh Zork!" Hoof groaned. "Now your eyes are leaking!"

"She is a female, you dumb Ass!" Jawana snapped. "She has always been a female!"

Wyona blurted, "I didn't lie! It's just that life for young female orphans is so dangerous I never corrected creatures who thought I was male." Her shoulders slumped. "But I did deceive you, I guess. If you don't want me as your thrall any more, I . . . I understand."

Hoof blinked at her. "Your eyes aren't going to leak like, *all the time,* are they?"

Wyona swiped at her face and tried to laugh. "No!"

"Then of course you're my thrall. It's a lifelong job, remember?"

~~~

The door opened and a harried-looking Secretary beckoned. Jawana pushed herself out of a deep chair. Her right arm was immobilized so she used her teeth to straighten her armband, on which shiny new Captain's bars glinted.

"Okay," she breathed, beating back an attack of nerves. She glanced down at Manny. "After you, Sergeant Sobad!"

Manny proudly led the way into the world's most famous office. The five of them fanned out inside the door. The Secretary cleared their throat and announced, "They are here, your Supremacy!"

Bidet pulled his head in from the window. "Only place I can stand up straight," he grumbled. "Ah! The heroes of the hour!" he exclaimed as he shuffled to the center of the office "Well, not this hour. And I'm sure the excitement lasted more than an hour . . ." He fell silent.

"Sir," brayed Hoof nervously. "If this is about me pretending to be royalty, I can explain!"

"Hm?" said Bidet, climbing out of whatever mental hole he had fallen into. "Oh yes! That reminds me." He swung around to confront the Secretary. "George?"

"It's Jorge, Sir."

"Hm? What did I say?"

"Never mind, Sir."

The Secretary unrolled a scroll and read, "For service to Our Benevolent Autocracy and stalwart defense of the One True Realm, Josephus Archibald Bidet bestows upon Hoof (full stop) Hearted the Honorable Title (newly created) of Lord Bellringer, along with an allotment of arable land (to be identified at a later date.) Said title and land are to be enjoyed in perpetuity by the titleholder and their heirs. Yada, yada, yada." He rolled his eyes. "His yadas not mine."

"Hm, yes," said Bidet. "I can't make you Bellringer the Fourth," he chuckled. "Have to kill you three times first and all that, heh, heh. Messy business, killing creatures."

"Delighted not to be killed by you, Sir!" said Hoof. "But, but . . . land? What land?"

"We'll slice off one of the better bits from Waterstrider's Estate," Bidet replied. "I hear he's been a very naughty Horse indeed."

The Giraffe nodded vaguely until one eye landed on Manny. "I've seen you before, haven't I? Oh yes! You were with . . ." His head swung around, bumping a chandelier and sending several crystal teardrops tumbling. "Where are the tall chaps in the funny outfits?"

"My *gigantes* servants chose to stay away, *Excelencia*. They thought they would break something."

"Really?" said Bidet as he crushed a crystal under his hoof. "How odd!" He turned to his Secretary. "Why did I care about them?"

The Secretary held up three tablets. "Because your Good Graciousness generously granted them citizenship." He thrust the tablets at Jawana. "Please accept these on their behalf."

Bidet continued to stare at Manny. "There was something else. Don't tell me . . . it will come to me. Oh yes! Something about a permanent commission in The Guard." He beamed proudly. "How about that! I got it first time!"

"Gracias, Excelencia," Manny barked. "Your offer is most generous. It is with great sadness that I must refuse. I have other pressing duties to which I must attend."

"So," said Bidet, looking puzzled. "That would be no, then?"

Pete stepped forward. "And before you say anything else, your Indomitable Sirness, I'm with *Señor* Sobad. Where he goes, I go!"

"Good to know," Bidet replied. He cranked his head down to mumble in his Secretary's ear, "Who's the monkey?" When the Secretary responded with a puzzled shrug, Bidet straightened up and flashed his even white teeth in a benign grin. "Well, that's that then."

A *harumph* erupted from a corner of the office. Bidet jumped, almost punching a stubby horn through the ceiling. He swung his head toward the corner. "Lucius? What are you doing here?"

The black gibbon pushed out of an overstuffed chair and went to stand beside Bidet. "I am here, Josephus, because I knew you were going to mess this up."

He beckoned to Jawana. "Captain Seekhehr, please approach." Jawana handed the trolls' tablets to Wyona and hurried forward.

"Commander," she snapped briskly as she came to attention. Her bandaged arm waggled in its sling. "Not on top of the saluting thing right now, Sir! I hope you understand."

The Commander chuckled. "I'll overlook it this time."

He turned toward the Secretary, who stood behind him, clutching a red velvet box. The Commander removed a ribbon from which hung a golden medallion. "Captain Johana Seekhehr, in recognition of exemplary service and courage in the face of great adversity, I award you the highest military honor we have to bestow: *The Star of the Immortal Hero of the Realm."*

Jawana's shocked gasp was drowned out by the small audience erupting into heartfelt clapping, whistling and hoof stomping.

"I-I-I don't know what to say!" Jawana managed, at last.

Bidet nodded thoughtfully. "I find that if I don't know what I am saying, it is best not to say anything."

"And yet you say it anyway!" snapped The Commander. He hung the medal around Jawana's neck and stepped back. They stared at each other until he elbowed the Supreme Leader's knee.

"Ouch! What . . . oh, yes." Bidet cleared his throat. "Sadly, Lucius has decided to retire. I tried to talk him out of it, but he is adamant. When we discussed replacements, one name kept rising to the top of the list." He blinked down at the perplexed gorilla.

"Who . . ." Her face blanched. "No. You can't be serious!"

"Perfectly serious, Johana," smiled The Commander. "There's no creature in whom I have greater confidence."

Jawana flung her head from side to side. Then she straightened up and drew a breath. "I'm sorry!" she said. "I am flattered, but I can't accept. I really can't." After a pause, she added, "There's this little inn out in the hinterland. It's not much, but I've become attached to it. I miss it terribly. That's my life now."

"So," said Bidet slowly. "Another no then." He glanced down at The Commander. "I've got to work on my powers of persuasion."

"You think?" the gibbon growled in response.

"Pardon me, Supremacy," the Secretary murmured in a discrete attempt to get his attention.

"What?" the Giraffe grumped. "Can't hear a word you're muttering, Georgie. Speak up, will you?"

"Your Excellency is overdue for a meeting with the leader of the Northern Realm!"

"Good glory, Georgie! There's no need to shout! I'm not deaf, you know." A hopeful look crept across his long, narrow face. "Do you suppose I'd be missed if I didn't show up? Don't bother answering: I know what you're going to say."

He cast a resigned smile around the assembled group. "Would you good folk care to join me? I could use a little civilized backup."

~~~

The party left the Palace and crossed a lawn, creeping toward the tall wrought iron and glass edifice that was the Royal Conservatory. Two Guards walked in front of the Supreme Leader and two more fell in behind him. The lead Guards kept glancing back to make sure they weren't leaving the geriatric Giraffe behind.

They pushed through the glass doors and skirted a mound of discarded wooden signs that forbade creatures from snacking on the Supreme Bananas. Images of monkeys with their eyes replaced by crosses hinted at the penalty for ignoring that rule. Pete shivered.

The Secretary noticed his discomfort. "The previous Supremo was very fond of his banana plantation. Which is now being dug up." He choked off a chuckle and glanced around guiltily, as if afraid of being overheard. "Being replaced by acacia trees!"

An open space stood at the center of the Garden. It was filled by a tall Moose whose neck strained under an enormous rack of antlers. The antlers were decorated with the crudely drawn red leaf that most Southerners took to symbolize some sacred Northern tree or other.

Bidet pulled up eye-to-eye with the Moose. "Well, you're a lot bigger than I expected!" he said.

"*Honk!* I'm up here!" Bidet's eyes rolled up to face the unblinking glare of a Northern Goose. Their flat, webbed feet danced on the moose's head. *Splat!* The goose froze, then hopped forward and peered back between their feet. "Uh, sorry about that Bob! *Honk! Honk!*"

Bob rolled his eyes at Bidet. "Quite all right Sir," he said good naturedly. "Stuff happens!"

The goose turned back to Bidet. "I take it you're the new head honcho down here?" he demanded.

"I am the new Supreme Leader yes. But you can call me Joe."

"Pleased to meet you, Joe. I'm Justus Contrefait, political genius and duly elected leader of The Great Northern Realm. Or, as our original inhabitants used to call it, *'Aneasi Weitofrieze.'*"

"Used to call it? What changed?" Bidet politely asked.

"Don't know, don't care. I expect they all just froze."

An owl dropped out of a tree, causing the goose to flutter up in panic. "Holy Hopscotch," he honked as he settled back down. "Will you stop doing that! It made me . . ."

"Quite all right, Sir," Bob interrupted. "It can be a pleasant splash of warmth on a cold day."

The owl hooted in the goose's ear, who nodded. "Oh, right," he said. "I misquoted myself. What I really said is that I greatly value the heritage and shared wisdom of the First Creatures who bravely led the way and made the great wide North habitable for us. Who could have guessed that those commemorative 'thank you' blankets we gave them were full of plague dust?"

Bidet waited a few moments before asking, "So, Justus . . . may I call you Justus?"

"I'm thinking of calling myself 'The Great Northern Light,'" said the goose as he reached around and preened his feathers.

"I'm thinking of calling you a . . ."

"Press conference," interrupted the Secretary.

"What?" said Bidet.

"I suggest we proceed directly to your joint press conference. The National Guild of Town Criers has been waiting for a while now. You know how testy that lot gets if you leave them on their own too long."

~~~

Josephus Bidet towered over a thigh-high lectern in the Royal Palace's East Garden. Justus Contrefait perched on top of a second lectern. A cold wind blew from the northwest, ruffling the goose's feathers.

Gathered in front of them was a small group of shivering Town Criers, mostly from nearby villages.

A snow leopard raised a paw. "I have a question for . . ." she hesitated. "First Citizen Contrefait? Mr. Contrefait? What do I call you?"

Contrefait hopped from foot to foot. "Perhaps you could call me 'The Great Northern Light?'"

"Or not. In any case, it has been reported that you have promised every citizen of your realm a clutch of golden eggs."

"Ah yes, my top Election Promise, *Honk! Honk!* I'm very proud of that. I'm a goose, you see? And I'm promising golden eggs? It's like a fairy tale! Pure genius if I do say so myself. *Honk!"*

"My actual question," persisted the snow leopard, "is 'when and how will you deliver on your promise?' Especially since you're sort of 'gender-challenged' as regards that particular deliverable."

A ripple of laughter ran through the Town Criers. Contrefait indignantly fluffed up his feathers. "Okay, technically that's two questions! And why in the world would I want to do any of that?"

"Because you promised you would?"

"Honk! Honk! I made it abundantly clear that this was an election promise. As in every four years, potential leaders wander around promising stuff. Then the citizens vote on which creature made the wildest, most impractical promises. I won by a landslide! *Honk! Honk!"*

"So you have no intention of honoring your promises."

"I'm sorry. Was that a question?"

The snow leopard shook her head. A shaggy brown dog tentatively raised a paw. "I have a question for the goose."

"Yes, my canine friend?" said the goose.

"Every winter, untold thousands of you creatures flock down to our southern territories. And frankly, you make a terrible mess!"

"Yes. I'm glad you asked that. That's a good question."

"But I haven't asked the question yet!"

"No? I misunderstood. I thought maybe it was a new fad. *Honk! Honk!* Like, to phrase questions in the form of an answer. *Hm.* Could be an interesting parlor game. Needs work though. *Honk!*"

"If I may?" barked the dog. "Every year, you and your fellow creatures turn much of our fine realm into a smelly, disgusting mess. What do you propose to do about it?"

"Ah yes. *Honk!* Now that is a good question. In the form of a question. As the duly elected leader, I take responsibility. The buck stops here! *Honk!* And I have never been one to prevent a buck from stopping. Especially here. Thank you for your question."

"You're welcome. Now, are you going to answer it?"

"What? I gave you a full and detailed response. About responsibility. And bucks. And stopping. Are there any other questions?

"Yes!" shouted the dog. "When in Gorme's name are you lot going to stop messing up our realm?"

"Stop it? Why in the world would we do that?"

The press conference deteriorated from there. Hoof turned away and spied an elegant brown nose peeking out from behind a bush.

"Verity?" he said, stepping forward. The Jennet timidly stepped out from behind the bush, hanging her head in embarrassment.

"Why were you hiding behind a bush?"

"I heard you had an audience with *'el Supremo.'*" She peeked up from behind her brows. "I hoped I'd get to see you."

"I repeat, 'Why were you hiding behind a bush?'"

"Because you must hate me! After all the horrible things I said, and what my father did . . ."

"Hate you!" Hoof brayed. "You saved my life! How could I hate you? In fact I kind of . . ." he trailed off.

Verity looked up and met Hoof's eyes. "Yes?"

This time it was Hoof who lowered his head. ". . . really like you?"

Verity giggled. "That's great, because I really like you too."

Hoof's ears drooped. "Well, not for long!"

Verity looked hurt. "How can you say that?"

"Well, you liked me when I was a nobody; then you hated me when you thought I was a High Muckity-muck; then you found out I really was a nobody and liked me again."

"Hoof, whatever else you are, you're not a nobody!"

"That's true," Hoof sadly replied, "because Bidet turned me back into a Muckity-muck; as of now, I really am Lord Bellringer."

Verity's eyes widened. "Well," she said thoughtfully. "Whatever honors he gave you, you earned. I'm okay with that."

Hoof huffed out a sigh of relief. "Want to go for a stroll?"

~~~

It was a rare sunny day, and Hoof and Verity made the most of it as they ambled along the waterfront. "What I don't understand," said Hoof, "is how you knew it was me up on those sandbags."

"Oh Hoof! Of course I knew it was you! Right from the moment you did that faceplant on the wall."

"Well, that's a bit unkind!" Hoof exclaimed. Then he was struck by an alarming thought, "Your father's still going to hate me!"

"Not when he finds out that you really are Lord Bellringer!"

"Oh. There's that I guess," said Hoof, sounding relieved. "How's he making out, after . . ."

"Like a bandit, as always! He was at the front of the line of bureaucrats swearing loyalty to the new Leader. He might even keep his word this time. 'At least Giraffes have hooves!'" She shuddered. "Those were his words, not mine."

The end

A note of appreciation

If you got this far you either read the entire book or cheated and skipped to the end. Hopefully the former is true—or will be.

Either way, the author is grateful to you for your interest in his work. If you read it, please take the time to leave a rating or brief review on Amazon. There are many thousands of books out there and readers like you are in the best position to guide others with similar tastes to books they may really want to read.

So please, let your voice be heard!

www.ingramcontent.com/pod-product-compliance
Lightning Source LLC
Chambersburg PA
CBHW070627260626
47161CB00007B/2613